PRAISE F

A Love Like

"Sometimes you read a book and you just know that no other writer in the world could possibly have written it—that this story was destined to be told in just this way, at just this moment. Riss M. Neilson's *A Love Like the Sun* is one of those books. It's funny, heartfelt, and fresh, with dreamy prose and vibrant characters. Nielson has crafted something extraordinary in Laniah and Issac's story: a raw, vulnerable, breath-stealing love you can feel as you read. Perfect for fans of Abby Jimenez, Kennedy Ryan, and Carley Fortune (aka me)."

—Emily Henry, #1 *New York Times* bestselling author of *Happy Place*

"Dazzling, tender, and romantic, *A Love Like the Sun* is a beautiful story about taking risks, being brave, and letting the people who know us best love us fully. I adored this friends-to-lovers romance!"

—Carley Fortune, #1 *New York Times* bestselling author of *This Summer Will Be Different*

"Sexy, heartwarming, and soulfully human, Riss M. Neilson's stunning adult debut is an homage to home, family, love, and the fears that hold us back from our destiny."

—Shirlene Obuobi, author of *On Rotation*

"Riss M. Neilson paints a poetic, sexy, and intimate portrait of falling in love in *A Love Like the Sun*. I absolutely devoured the best friends-to-lovers dynamic between Laniah and Issac, and cheered (yes, out loud!) when they finally gave in to their inevitable fall. Neilson's prose is as warm and effortless as the love story that unfolded, and just as compelling. A stunning read."

—Jessica Joyce, *USA Today* bestselling author of *You, With a View*

"*A Love Like the Sun* is a beautifully crafted and achingly tender story that offers a fresh take on the well-loved friends-to-lovers trope. Laniah and Isaac's chemistry is undeniable, and I so enjoyed witnessing them find their way to each other. A must-read!"

—Kristina Forest, author of *The Partner Plot*

"*A Love Like the Sun* filled me with warmth and shined as brightly as the star itself. A truly remarkable, achingly tender, and deliciously sexy romance that will stick with me for years to come. This childhood friends-to-lovers novel brims with the giddiness of a first love and the enduring glow of true love. Neilson's adult debut is a romantically powerful force to be reckoned with, and I loved every page."   —Mazey Eddings, author of *The Plus One*

"Riss M. Neilson masterfully crafts the fears and fireworks of best-friends-to-lovers romance while showcasing culture, curls, and sizzling chemistry. And yes, Isaac brings that star power, but Ni is otherworldly—for these two, it was only ever a matter of time."

—Taj McCoy, author of *Zora Books Her Happy Ever After*
and *Savvy Sheldon Feels Good as Hell*

A
Love
Like
The
Sun

RISS M. NEILSON

Berkley Romance
New York

BERKLEY ROMANCE
Published by Berkley
An imprint of Penguin Random House LLC
penguinrandomhouse.com

Library of Congress Cataloging-in-Publication Data

Names: Neilson, Riss M., author.
Title: A love like the sun / Riss M. Neilson.
Description: First edition. | New York: Berkley Romance, 2024.
Identifiers: LCCN 2023042082 (print) | LCCN 2023042083 (ebook) |
ISBN 9780593640494 (trade paperback) | ISBN 9780593640500 (ebook)
Subjects: LCGFT: Romance fiction. | Novels.
Classification: LCC PS3614.E44326 L68 2024 (print) |
LCC PS3614.E44326 (ebook) | DDC 813/.6—dc23/eng/20231101
LC record available at https://lccn.loc.gov/2023042082
LC ebook record available at https://lccn.loc.gov/2023042083

First Edition: June 2024

Printed in the United States of America
1st Printing

Book design by Daniel Brount

For anyone who has ever felt hard to love,
to those afraid to ask for what they need,
and for myself.
It's not easy being brave, but I believe in us.

A LOVE LIKE THE SUN

WHAT I REMEMBER

Eleven years ago. Eagle sticker.

Sun starting to cut across the sky, the smell of an early rain still in the air, my father on the front steps of our house, fine-tuning his guitar. When I opened the downstairs door, he beamed at the sight of me, as if my existence meant he was unable to contain his happiness. I threw my arms around his shoulders, hugged him close, inhaled the scent of tobacco on his warm skin.

"The only thing that'd wake you up this early on a Sunday is a boy," he said.

I rolled my eyes. "You know Issac's not a boy the way you're saying he's a boy, Dad."

"How am I saying it?" he asked, just as my best friend came out of his house across the street and our eyes locked from a distance. When Issac Jordan smiled with his whole face, my father hummed, "I'm waiting for an answer, sweetie," which earned him a wide-eyed look from me and a whisper begging him to drop it. My face was already flushed when he teased, "Because the boy who's not a boy is heading over here? Fine, but may I ask where you two are heading this morning?"

The corners of my lips twitched; I raised a single brow.

"You're right," he said. "Spare me the details that might save me from your mother's scrutiny over your whereabouts later. But remember to walk with courage and . . ."

"Trust our instincts," I finished with a smile.

He tugged on my long braid, and when Issac made it to my porch to collect me he called out, "Take care of each other."

At Issac's quick "Always," my satisfied father began strumming his guitar. It was the last time I heard him play that particular song, one he'd sing to my mother with a goofy look on his face, and the first time I heard him struggle to breathe through a melody. We didn't know that afternoon he'd receive news from his doctor that would forever change the path of our family. Right then, I was still mostly carefree, not exactly trusting my instincts but convincing myself I was about to walk with courage.

And as soon as we were out of my father's eyeline, Issac and I hit the pavement running. We normally weren't in the business of stealing bikes, but Benjamin Cooper was Issac's personal bully, tormenting him by throwing rocks at his head on the way home from school, laughing at Issac's "used clothing," and most recently slashing the tires on both of our "cheap bikes" so we were "doomed to walk like peasants," while he rode beside us on his fancy Aventon Soltera for the rest of the year.

That's when Issac agreed to my suggestion of stealing it.

We snuck into Benjamin's yard before his family got up for church, and I hopped on the pegs of his bike with a rush in my chest, but Issac was shaky, the bike wobbling as he rode us away, and I worried whether agitating his bully was the right move. A few streets over, in a neighborhood full of beautiful houses, we hid the bike behind someone's rosebush.

Issac glanced at it longingly and finally spoke. "Maybe instead of leaving it here, we should use it to travel the world."

A smile stretched my face, relieved. "Do you think we can make it across the country?"

Issac examined the tires, then nodded. "We'd have to pack a lot of the food we find in your pantry. Maybe shower in random water fountains at parks along the way."

"How long do you think it would take for our parents to notice we were gone?"

"We'd leave notes not to worry yours," Issac said. "But I doubt Howard and Alice would notice me missing. Not with the new kids they just took in last month, anyway."

I stopped myself from insisting he was wrong about his foster parents, then considered apologizing, but watched as Issac bent down to rip an eagle sticker off the bike instead. He had just started making collages by gluing random things to notebook pages, so when he pocketed the sticker I figured it was for that.

"How long do you think it'll take *him* to notice it's missing?" I asked.

"He'll probably send out a search party for his precious bike by noon," said Issac.

"Do you think he'll cry?"

"Definitely."

"Is it bad that I'd pay to see it?"

"If I had money, so would I." He grabbed my hand and pulled me toward the street. Said, "You make me feel brave, Laniah."

I glanced down at our linked hands, my heart warm at his

words. Issac always said things raw and outright, while I struggled to express myself. But I loved that he seemed content with me bumping my shoulder against his in response while we walked back home.

We were always braver together.

1

—

THE WAY IT
SHOULDN'T BE DONE

F MY CALCULATIONS ARE CORRECT, I'LL BE ALONE IN THE SHOP for at least ten minutes before my mom comes back from the bakery, which is plenty of time to take a sexy picture. I sit in a chair at the break table in the back room and slide my pants down. Not all the way, just enough to expose my soft belly and the black panties creased between my hips and thighs. I take a few shots and stare at them, positive that they're sexy enough to entice someone and leave them wanting for more. The someone is a guy I've been on five really good dates with but have only slipped some tongue before we said good night. His patience with me not wanting to rush sex is attractive, but this morning he asked if I'd *send him a little something*, and I've been distracted all day thinking of taking risks. I pick one, take a breath, hit Send.

Darius looks at the picture immediately but doesn't answer back with the same energy. My heart races in my chest while I wait. And wait.

Read. Read two minutes ago.

The bubbles finally pop up. Darius is typing. He stops. Starts again. And then . . .

"Laniah Leigh Thompson, why in the world are your pants at your knees?"

I startle, drop my phone onto the table, and scramble to my feet. I'm twenty-five years old and the tone of my mother's voice can still strike fear in my heart. "I . . . uh."

She takes a step forward, a paper bag and cup tray in her hands, dark penciled-in eyebrows low on her face. "Were you taking a . . . a nude photograph?"

The back of my neck burns while I pull up my pants and button them. A heartbeat. Two. "I was . . . checking for swelling, actually," I say.

"Swelling?" she repeats.

"Mm-hmm. Yeah. Just thinking of my doctor's appointment in a couple of days."

I've been having headaches, and I think it's from elevated blood pressure, so this seems like a believable lie. Still, we stare at each other for the longest thirty seconds of my life—her top lip curling a little, suspicion in her eyes, a small smile on my face, convincing enough I hope. So much for Seven Stars Bakery being lunchtime-rush busy. She finally sighs and places the cups on the table. I hurry to snatch my phone and pocket it, even though she's not wearing her bifocals to see anything that might be waiting on my screen.

"You swear I was born yesterday," she says. "I just hope you're not being stupid, but whatever."

Whatever has been her general mood lately, and I briefly wonder how she would have reacted to me sending dirty texts if things were different. My mom and dad were always openly flirtatious, which was awarded with many eyerolls from me as a kid. But my dad died nine years ago, and I sometimes wonder if her playfulness died with him.

She takes a cookie out of the bag, her coffee from the tray, then leaves me. I know better than to stay in the back, she'll think I'm looking at my phone, and though I'm tempted to do just that, I grab my cup of tea and follow her. As soon as I'm in the front of the shop with its half-empty shelves, I feel the same *whatever* mood my mom does. We opened Wildly Green three years ago, giddy to have a storefront for the natural body butters and hair oils Mom had been mixing in our kitchen since I was a little girl. We'd had big plans, but reality struck, and instead of building our dream, we've pulled in serious debt.

Only a week ago this place was teeming with the smell of coconut and fresh flowers, there was art on the walls and a neon sign that blinked HELLO, GORGEOUS in bright green letters. But we've been packing for a few days to close its doors—plants in boxes and all the cardboard at our feet—and we haven't even played music over the Bluetooth speaker to do it. The once colorful space has been leached of life. Most days, I prefer coming after working my second job at the hotel, when my mom's not here, so we don't have to pack in misery together.

My phone dings in my pocket and I bite back a smile, anticipating sweet words that Darius seems to have a knack for, but I begin clearing off the conditioner shelf as a distraction.

"You can check your messages, you know," Mom says from behind me. She's sitting on the floor, looking through old paperwork to see what we should keep, and I can hear the curiosity hiding in her voice. This is a trick. If I look at my phone now, she'll know I'm anxious because a response to a nude is on it. But if I *don't* look at my phone, she'll know I was avoiding it because she's here. It's a lose-lose. So I do what any reasonable, anxious, and sweaty person would do: put the products in my hands down and pull out my phone.

Except it's not a message. It's a thumbs-down reaction on my picture.

My stomach sinks slowly while my brain rushes to make sense of what I'm seeing. Did Darius just react to my sexy picture with a thumbs-down? He had to have hit that by accident. He definitely did. But then he texts, Wow. I waited all day long, and this is what you have to show me? I'm starting to think you're playing games.

The jump from confusion to disappointment is immediate.

"You good, baby?" Mom says, cutting through the noise in my head.

I turn to face her and hope she can't see my annoyance. "I'm fine, Mom. It's nothing."

She nods. "Well, come help me with these papers, then."

While I'm sorting through receipts on the rug, my mind is working overtime. Darius is the first guy I've gone on more than a few dates with since a long relationship in college. It's hard explaining that I'm mainly looking for companionship with the potential for more—in a sea of people on dating apps asking for sex or something serious straightaway. My best friend, Issac, calls me a hermit crab because I avoid social media, limiting my dating pool even further, but I was just bragging to him about how I met Darius the old-fashioned way: while buying samosas at Kabob and Curry downtown. Darius told me to cut him in line because I was in a rush to get back to work. On the way out, I wrote my number on a napkin and handed it to him.

As if reading my mind, Mom asks, "Have you told Issac we're closing the shop yet?"

The question makes my throat thick. Before I can respond, my phone vibrates on the floor beside us and my eyes dart down to another message from Darius. The preview on my lock screen reveals a picture of his . . . *Oh.* My face burns hot. I hurry to tuck my phone under my leg and look at my mom, praying she didn't see the photo I just saw. But she's busy squinting at a utility bill. I laugh a little, selfishly relieved.

"You really should start wearing your glasses, Mom."

She sulks and picks up another piece of paper, hating the reminder that her eyesight has changed in her midfifties. I sometimes tell her Dad would've thought she looked cute in glasses, and she'll temporarily soften to them, but I'll get sad inside that he's not here to tell her himself, then days later she'll be walking around without them. "Don't ignore my question," she says.

"I haven't talked to Issac about it yet," I say, "but I will."

"Tell him before I do," she orders. "I'm not going to keep lying to that boy."

"Yes, ma'am."

———————

TWO HOURS LATER, I SAY BYE TO MOM AND HAUL ANOTHER BOX TO my car. The early-June weather is perfect in Providence: high seventies with a breeze wafting through the treetops and sending a fresh scent of green and coffee and baked goods toward me while I walk. When I first found the space for Wildly Green, Mom was ecstatic. It's in the heart of the city, between all the diverse neighborhoods that make up much of our clientele. The building sits on semi-busy Broadway Street, right beside shops we already loved. There's Seven Stars Bakery and Julian's for lunch and Schasteâ for tea and crepes. Columbus Theatre was renovated and recently reopened and has breathtaking old architecture inside. On the next street, there's Heartleaf, a co-op bookstore with a beautiful shop cat named Penny, who I adore. Workers are always waving at me through glass windows, and there are at least four other pets that need petting each day.

I glance up at the Wildly Green sign, and a pit grows in my belly, a sad ache.

Inside the safety of my little Honda, crammed full of boxes, away from Mom, I open the text thread with Darius to find a picture of him in boxers with a visible outline of his asset, which is tame compared to the video he sent doing unspeakable things to himself (mainly because he doesn't deserve the mention). Not only would Mom be traumatized if she were wearing her bifocals, but she'd be downright pissed at Darius's audacity.

This is how it's done, he wrote below the video. What might have had me clenching my thighs under better circumstances only leaves a sour taste in my mouth.

I take my time reacting to each of his messages with a thumbs-down, then silence our text thread before starting my car and recording a voice note for Issac.

"Remind me again why I still like men. Because some members of your kind make me wonder if decency among the general population actually exists. And don't even say you told me Darius was *a dud in waiting*. I'm not in the mood, big head."

I'm halfway home before I get a response from him. A single emoji. (:

2

HOW TO SWING
A LOUISVILLE SLUGGER

M Y MOM WOULD SAY THESE BOXES ARE HEAVIER THAN ONE
person can carry, but that never stopped her from trudg-
ing ones like this up the stairs to our third-floor apartment when
my dad was at work. I was tiny back then, but I'd drag a plastic
shopping bag up behind her because I *really* wanted to help. That
was two decades ago, but the memories have been bleeding
through like watercolor and weighing on me. She's getting older,
and I won't allow her to do the heavy lifting now that we'll be
selling our natural products from home again.

My arms ache when I slide the last box out of the car and it
slips from my grasp, hitting the ground with a shattered-glass
thud. I stare at it for several seconds, wishing for the ability to re-
wind time, hoping that the fragile pieces inside will be miraculously intact.

But the box is still on the ground, and now I have an audience.

Wilma Murphy from across the street walks over, cane in one
hand, cup of coffee in the other. She stops a few feet in front of me,

takes a slurpy sip, then says, "You know, it'd be smarter if you pulled into the driveway and unloaded the boxes at the back door."

I'm annoyed she's probably right, but I won't give her the satisfaction of seeing me shaken. "Is that so?" I say. "I'll remember for next time."

She narrows her eyes, surely sensing the sarcasm in my tone. "So, you're really closing the store? Does this mean your mother will be cleaning rooms with you for the rest of her life?"

Fun fact about my neighborhood in Providence: Silver Lake has fewer than nine thousand residents, which means there's a decent chance the boy you have a crush on two blocks over could've already hooked up with your cousin. What it means for me: Wilma Murphy's grandmother used to babysit *my* mother in the same house Wilma still lives in across the street. Even more interesting: Wilma's sister, Bridget Murphy, is a permanent resident of the hotel where I work and just so happens to be one of my favorite people in the world. And it might've been a nice thing, working in a space with one sister and living on the same street as the other, but Bridget and Wilma haven't spoken in decades. The reason is still unknown to me, but I believe it when my mom says Wilma was always petty or judgmental because the longer I live in this apartment, the clearer it becomes that this seventy-one-year-old woman can often be both at once, so I'm certain she must've done something incredibly spiteful to her younger sister.

"Maybe," I say, "but at least we'll have good company with your sister living there."

Wilma's top lip curls at the mention of Bridget. "Guess you aren't the businesswoman you thought you were," she says, before pointing to the lawn with her cane, a sour look on her face. "You should get someone to mow the lawn." With that, she turns away, whistling a song while walking toward her house with its perfectly mowed lawn.

Once I'm inside, I take one look at the shattered jars of sugar scrub and sink against the front door, still feeling the sting of Wilma's words below my breastbone. When we opened the shop, my mom was able to quit housekeeping to focus on creating products, something she started when she was a teenager who was sick of being sent to the salon every Saturday for relaxers. She never knew she'd find joy in making hair products, but six-year-old me was already dreamy while I listened to her sing and whip shea butter till it was smooth, waiting for the chance to mix something too. All I hoped for was to be as cool as her when I grew up, for her to look at me the way I looked at her, and I finally felt that when we first opened our shop.

I glance up at the wall to stare at the picture of us hugging in front of Wildly Green on grand-opening day, remembering that she couldn't keep tears out of her eyes. "I can't believe this is real," she said. Then with a shaky voice: "If only your dad could see us now."

My gaze flicks to another picture, of the three of us, which is in the same worn wooden frame I've had since high school. Dad with a handlebar mustache I'd poke fun at, me on his back with small six-year-old fingers pulling at his blond hair, Mom in stilettos with beautiful brown legs, tiptoeing to place a kiss on his cheek. He was staring straight into the camera, and it feels like he's staring right through me now, knowing that the business degree I was so proud of, the one I flashed in front of Mom's face, insisting we were ready to transition from a stable kitchen business to a store, didn't mean I'd have smart solutions to save it.

I pull my phone from my pocket. Nothing else from Issac. He's been in Cali for two years, and I still struggle with him living across the country. That he's too far for weekly movie nights. I hardly remember the last time we browsed a bookstore together. And I can't bring myself to tell him about Wildly Green over the phone. If I'm being honest with myself, I haven't wanted to tell him at all.

But right now, I need my best friend.

My finger hovers over the Call button, debating because he's probably on a photo shoot for a clothing line or making new art on video . . . or maybe he's on a romantic getaway with Melinda. My stomach squeezes at the thought. It might be my imagination, but it seems like ever since they started *casually* dating months ago the texts have become less frequent, our phone calls shorter, and he hasn't flown back home in half a year. And I can't help but wonder how casual the dating truly is, if something is changing between him and me because of them.

You're the worst friend in the world, I type to him instead. Hoping it'll elicit a *Don't be a brat* or *There goes my brat* or even *Tell me what's bothering you, brat*, but he reads the message and doesn't respond.

I sigh and click out of the conversation. Right underneath is Darius's now muted thread. I should probably block him, but the petty part of me wants him to sweat it out. I scroll through the photos, a little amused. Has he been home all day buck naked or are these recycled dick pics?

You want me to come over? he texts, like he knew I was in here lurking.

Hell no:), I reply, my stomach tight at the feeling of being caught.

But then the doorbell rings and startles me to my feet.

Last week, Darius dropped me off after our date and kissed me on my front porch. Before this afternoon the memory had made me feel good, but now I'm quietly creeping to peek out the blinds and make sure it's not him. And I might've been able to if my landlord had come and cut the overgrown bush outside my window to give me a better view of the door like he was supposed to last month.

I swallow, call out, "Who is it?"

But no one answers. When the doorbell rings again, a shiver shoots up my spine. I blow out a breath and pick up the Louisville Slugger from beside the door. My dad taught me to swing a bat *just in case*. I reach for the lock, then the handle, carefully twisting and letting it creak open. But I don't swing because the man standing before me has deep brown skin and even deeper eyes, which bore into mine like they're searching my soul.

Issac pulls his gaze away to glance at the scene in front of him—me gripping the Slugger, ready to swing—and a smile breaks across his face, dimples deep, visible even under facial hair.

"Hi, Ni," he says, voice warm, the sun growing dim behind him. "You have a bad day?"

After a sharp inhale, I squeal, the bat clattering to the floor, and jump right into his arms. He stumbles back, laughing, but catches us like he always does. Since he has thirteen inches on me, I'm able to bury my face right in the center of his chest. He bends low to drop a kiss on my head, and the tension releases from us both: a shared breath. We stay that way awhile, wrapped in each other, connected limbs and familiar affection. But then he clears his throat and steps back to give us inches of physical space I'm not used to.

He swallows hard, then rubs the bridge of his nose like he does when he's nervous or even disappointed, but I can't get a read on why he's doing it now. My mind begins to worry over the imperceptible distance between us, something I was hoping I wouldn't feel in person, while my body needs another one of his hugs after six months without my best friend, and the disappointing days I've had since last seeing him. But I stop my limbs from doing awkward things to get closer to him again and pick up the bat instead.

"What are you doing here?" I ask. "Why didn't you tell me you were flying in?"

"I love surprising you," he says, like it's the most obvious answer in the world. "And I came to be a better best friend. Sorry it took me so long."

3

HOW TO NOT BE
A WASTE OF TIME

SSAC TELLS ME TO TOSS MY PHONE OUT THE WINDOW AFTER DAR-
ius sends another nude. "This guy needs some damn lessons on
being a gentleman."

I raise an eyebrow, laugh a little. "What kind of lessons do you
have to offer?"

We're both sitting on the living room floor, having drinks and
hand mixing raw shea butter for a product I'm hoping to launch.
Mixing certain butters by hand is key, but my wrist gets sore and
my skin is dry from overwashing at the hotel, so sometimes I'll
cheat and break out the electric mixer. I'm happy Issac is here to
help. He puts down the bowl and presses his back against the bottom of the couch.

"If it's the first time sending risky photos, you have to go slow.
Just a pic in bed with only boxers on or whatever." He pretends
like he's laid out, lifts his hand like he's taking a pic. "You send
that. See if you get anything back."

"And then what?"

"If they make a move or seem interested, you ease it out until you get to the real dirty stuff," he says. "But listen, since you didn't respond to the first one, which was already a red flag, he absolutely should not be messaging you with more."

I pick up my phone, glance at a picture again. "I mean, it's not half-bad-looking. Maybe he thinks I won't be able to resist."

Issac laughs, but there's a look I can't describe in his eyes when they meet mine. "Maybe you shouldn't resist? Could be worth a shot."

I nudge him with my elbow. "Anyway, it's not just about the unsolicited dick pics."

"Well, what else did he do?" he asks, some trepidation and protectiveness in his tone.

Issac and I have always talked about intimate things that we probably shouldn't share. Still, it's a little weird to tell him, "I sent Darius something first, actually . . ."

His eyes go wide before he tilts his head. "And then what happened?"

Heat works its way up my neck. "He gave me . . . a thumbs-down reaction," I say.

"A what?"

I'm already embarrassed, and now Issac wants me to explain. "You know . . ."

"No, I mean . . . what the hell?" He pushes the bowl out from in front of him and leans forward. With him this close, all I smell is sandalwood. It's not his usual cedar scent, and I briefly wonder when he switched to something a little sweeter.

"Guess the picture I sent him wasn't sexy enough."

Even though I tried for a lighthearted tone, Issac doesn't crack a smile. His eyes darken to match the shade of his skin as he stares at me. He opens his mouth like he wants to ask something but then shakes his head and forces out a breath. After a few seconds, he pours us a shot of rum and says, "To meeting better lovers."

We raise our glasses. "Actually, I'll be happily single for a while," I say.

Issac narrows his eyes. "You've already been single for a long while. Is that what you want?"

"Pretty positive," I say, and he shrugs before the shot makes our faces sour. But it hits me while my chest is still burning. "Wait, what about Melinda? Isn't she your *better lover?*"

Confusion contorts his features, and he says, "We're not dating anymore."

Now I'm the confused one. "Weren't you just with her last week?" When I went on my last date with Darius, Issac said he was having lunch with Melinda.

"That was . . . sharing a meal with a friend," Issac says, surprising me. "It was fading for a while, but we decided to officially call it quits over that fine lunch, actually. Sorry, I thought I told you."

I cut my eyes at him, a tiny seed of betrayal growing in my belly. How long would he have gone without sharing this with me? I'm sure the internet was first to find out.

"Did she break it off with you?" I ask. "Is that why you look gutted over my mention of her?"

Issac shifts uncomfortably. "It was a mutual decision," he says. "But gutted? Is that what I look like?"

Melinda and Issac weren't in a relationship, they *were dating,* but he spent so much time with her I thought I'd have to prepare to be the best man at his wedding. Because Issac has big feelings on love, and he shared them with the world. Before reaching this level of fame, he already had a substantial social media presence by being a mixed-media artist who'd create on video, but after he started talking about his dating life, his platform skyrocketed. Turns out, people love watching a beautiful shirtless man use his hands to make sculptures while listening to music, but they love it even more when he tells them he's not into wasting a woman's time. That he hardly makes it past a few dates before realizing the compatibility just isn't there and, politely, being up front about it. The best part is that Issac believes firmly in soulmates. Everyone has one, his is out there somewhere, so why would he string along someone else's other half?

Does this mean he doesn't have sex? Of course he does. But those *agreed-upon* situations are discussion for another day.

Issac's revelation made people worship him. If only all men were this honest; get someone like Issac; if you date me you'll realize I'm your soulmate, they'd comment on videos of him creating collages adorned in fresh flowers with a crown of them on his head.

Brands from all over the world realized *his* potential to help sell *them*, and he met Melinda on a photo shoot while they were modeling jeans. One date turned into twelve, and it was easy to assume he might've found his soulmate. I've never met her, but weeks ago he said he wanted me to, and I took that as more evidence to prove she was different. I guess *different* doesn't always mean soulmate. Unless there's more to the story.

I frown. "Sorry for assuming. It's just . . . Melinda's the first girl you've seemed serious about in as long as I've known you. I thought you were in love."

"What about Bianca from back in the day? I might've loved her."

"The one Mom hated from high school?" I give him my best skeptical face. "You went to Providence Place mall to share a plate from China Wok with her like twice."

"We watched a movie the second time." Issac laughs. "But Vanessa really did hate her, didn't she? Guess that was my sign that it wouldn't last."

"When does anything last with you? One date wonder."

"At least I'm not out here with a busted radar like you. Picking mediocre men who turn out to be less than, and that's when you actually give anyone the time of day."

"You must have a busted radar too. Didn't you think Melinda could be *the one*?"

Issac reaches for an open jar on the coffee table and brings it to his face. "This is a winner," he says. But then his eyes dart around the room. "Wait, why do you have all of this product here? Why's it not at Wildly Green?"

My stomach clenches. I grit my teeth. "We're renovating," I tell him, which feels like only half a lie. Then, quickly: "But don't change the subject. Did you or did you not think Melinda might be it?"

He seems to accept my answer about the shop before he says, "She's beautiful and smart, doesn't mind my bad jokes. For a while there I thought . . . this could be special. But never *the one*. And she knew I wasn't it for her either. We were only keeping each other because we enjoyed spending time together. That isn't enough."

I lean forward, chew my lip. "But what if she finds someone

else and you realize too late that you should've given it a real chance? Maybe a soulmate connection isn't something you just feel, maybe it's something you have to be committed to building."

A curious expression crosses his face as he watches me. "Do you believe that?"

I open my mouth to answer, but no words come out. I don't know what to believe about love and relationships anymore. Not after I thought my parents were soulmates, then death ripped my father from my mother so cruelly.

After a few seconds, Issac sighs and looks away. "I tried to see something that wasn't there. I really did."

Not for the first time, I wonder if the death of his parents has affected his view on relationships too. His mom and dad died in a car accident when he was twelve.

"I believe you," I tell him, and his shoulders sag in relief. If this news *has* already come out on the internet, I'm sure people are circulating their own theories and he's been bombarded with questions about Melinda, so I take the jar he's holding and say, "Does your hair need love?"

"Please," he answers with a smile.

But when I sit on the couch, expecting him to scoot so he's on the floor beneath me, he awkwardly sits still for a few seconds. "We can go to the kitchen," I offer, wondering if in the six months since I've last seen him we've transitioned to stool sitting instead. But then he kisses his teeth like I'm being ridiculous and moves into position. Because of his hesitation, my body is aware that he's between my legs like it hasn't quite been before.

Growing up together on Mercy Street meant my mom would see him day in and day out without *proper hair care*, and though she'd grow frustrated that his foster parents never took him to the barbershop, he'd shrug it off: always sunshine energy on the outside. Vanessa Thompson wasn't buying it. We went to school with a lot of Black and brown kids, many of whom loved to brag about their fresh haircuts from barbers on Broad Street. So, she took it upon herself to give him a fade with the clippers one day, and started the routine of Issac coming over before school for help with his hair, working her magic through each of his hair phases, until she started asking me to do it instead. While I conditioned his hair back then, we'd share pastelitos from Johnny's chimi truck and talk about our crushes. I'd follow up his soothing song-voice and sing to him completely off-key, and he'd read me comic books while I did my best to make him look as good as my mom did.

I run my fingers through his hair now. It's denser than mine, thick in the middle, the curls are pencil-sized ringlets, and it's gorgeous. He has the sides faded and the top is long enough to braid if he wanted me to. If I could braid better, maybe he would. I dampen his hair with a spray bottle and work some cream through it. He tells me it smells *so damn good*, quirks his eyebrows, and starts listing off ingredients that might be in it.

Then, finally: "You know what, don't tell me. I trust you."

I smile and tug his hair a bit. "You better. Now, pay up."

He pulls out his phone, knowing exactly what I want. Issac may be a model now, an *influencer*, he may do commercials and campaigns for Nike, but before this he was just a boy with passion and an eye for beauty. He's sickening, I like to joke. One of those humans who is both good-looking and good at too many things. God made him and said, *Let me add extra*. But even though he's *Hollywood* now, he hasn't gone a day without making some type of art. And I love when he gives me little insights into whatever he dreams up.

"First," he says, then leans his head against my thigh. The feeling gives me unexpected goose bumps after he's seemed distant and momentarily distracts me from the way he lifts his phone to take a picture of us. I snap into the moment, insisting I look hideous. He argues that hideous and me don't belong in the same sentence.

"Sure. Sure," I say. "You better not post that."

"Zero social media," he says. "I got it, hermit."

He swipes through pictures, then stops on a video that he shows me. "It's not a project," he says. "But I'm hoping it can be." The video is of a botanical garden three times the size of the gorgeous one we have in Roger Williams Park. This one has exotic plants and tall trees with lush green canopies.

"Some big names put together a new art exhibition they're calling *Year of the Lotus* for the end of summer," he explains. "They want to rotate between art and fashion exhibits each year, and they're hoping the event will eventually become something like the West Coast's version of the Met Gala. They already asked if I wanted to showcase *Secret Sun*."

Excitement shoots through me. *Secret Sun* is a code name for the project he's been working on privately since high school. I pinch his neck. "You finished it?"

He swats my hand away playfully. "Almost," he says, and I can hear his joy in that one word.

I'm excited I'll finally get to see it.

"But I've heard the team hit a snag with location and might cancel the exhibition. My plan is to pitch the botanical garden, and myself. I'll suggest an artist or two from Providence to be part of the show, ask if I can help with last-minute designs for the space, and maybe they'll even let me be one of the hosts that night." My fingers go still in his hair. He realizes immediately, tilts his head back to look up at me. "What happened?"

Issac is so good at what he does, and Lord knows the camera loves him, but he still wants art to be at the center of it all. I've been bugging him for a while to speak to his team about finding more chances to show his art on a larger scale, but he's been worried because he'll have to dial back on other work. His face and openness online may make him (and them) the most money, but that doesn't mean his heart is fulfilled.

I wrap my arms around his head and squeeze. "I'm so proud of you."

He tells me I'm suffocating him, and when I loosen my grip, I expect him to joke about liking it, but instead he runs his fingers through his hair and tries to stand, laughs when his knees crack, mumbling about old age creeping up, even though he's only turning twenty-six.

"Speak for yourself," I say. "Because I'm young and thriving."

"No truer words have ever been spoken," he says. "Living your dream. You and Vanessa looking like goddesses at the face of it. I'm proud of you too, Ni."

The guilt of not telling him what's going on wrenches my gut again, so I deflect with: "Are you trying to make me feel good after Darius came through with the thumbs-down?"

"I forgot all about him. But clearly you didn't. Did the pics leave you wanting for more?"

"Oh, shut up."

"The only thing that'll make me shut up is some food." He holds out a hand, then pulls me to my feet too. "Let's order chicken parmigiana."

"That's all we eat when you're home."

"There's nothing like home chicken parm in Cali," he says, then eyes me suspiciously. "Why? How many times have you had it since the last time I was here? Don't tell me you brought your boy Darius to our spot."

He's faking jealousy and the normalcy of it feels nice. "Not even once," I say, seriously disgusted by the thought. "And I'm not saying I don't want it."

"Well, dial the number already then, big head."

"My hands are tired from all that work I just did on you, but I'm the one with the big head?"

He rolls his eyes in response and passes me my phone.

I won't tell him that I never feel right ordering chicken parm without him.

4

GIRL NEXT DOOR MEETS
MOST GORGEOUS MAN ALIVE

THE FRONT LAWN IS FRESHLY MOWED BY THE TIME I WAKE UP. Without me having to ask, Issac watered my plants and cut down the bush in front of my window with a hedge trimmer he found in the shed. He asks me to call out of my shift at the hotel, insisting he'll pay me to spend time with him and knowing I'll refuse to take his money, even though I'm so broke I should. But I call out anyway, greedy for more of him too, with the condition that we'd have to drop off baskets to customers who couldn't pick their orders up at Wildly Green. He remembered the days we'd do drop-offs for Mom when we were young, then he helped me pack up the products pretty.

By noon, we have only one basket left in the back seat of my car, but we take a break and stop at a local music store first. Just outside, there's a group of men laughing with their whole bodies. Issac stares at them, a soft smile spreading. I picture his father, who Issac has described as someone that would debate with his boys on the block about basketball games before his mother called her husband home.

He turns and holds the door open for me, says simply, "I wish you could've met my dad," and I feel a rush at being let into his mind, that he doesn't feel the need to explain why he said it in this moment and that I'd already thought the same.

I reach for his wrist, give it a reassuring squeeze. "Sometimes it feels like I did. Especially when you sing Aretha Franklin and make a squinty face."

"Like this?" Issac asks, and makes a series of outlandish faces.

"The last one," I say. "You look just like him when you squint that way."

"Guess I'll have to sing Aretha more often," Issac says. "My old man was handsome."

I roll my eyes. If Issac was any more handsome than he is, someone might lock him away in a museum and the only way I'd see him is through shiny glass.

Once we're inside the store, he carefully browses the old CDs before we sit on the floor with stereo headphones to listen to samples like we did back when we couldn't afford to buy anything. We fail to notice the store getting busier, and we're only halfway through Tyler, The Creator's *Igor* record when a teenager rolls her finger across the vinyls on display in the rock section, eyes growing wide upon spotting us. I nudge Issac because his glasses are sliding off his face, the bucket hat he borrowed from me is tipped, and his curls are showing.

"I think your disguise has failed you, sir."

He looks up, but before he can even blink, the teen whips out her phone and starts to record. "It's Issac Jordan, everyone," she squeals. "My husband."

"Uh . . . ," Issac says, clearly horrified by the last declaration.

I'm stunned silent, but Issac gives her a forced smile, waves at the camera, and says "Good to meet you," his voice like butter.

"He spoke to me," the girl says, takes one last look at us, and disappears down an aisle.

With her out of sight, I'm quick to get up off the rug. "Where did she go?"

Issac laughs. "Maybe you frightened her with that look on your face." He dusts off his pants when he stands. "Or maybe she went to go get the crew."

The crew? Something flickers across my chest right before we're ambushed, suddenly surrounded by teenagers in a frenzy of asking Issac for hugs and pictures with them. For a moment, I remember how silly I acted with my friends at my first concert, and I didn't even get to meet the band, but then one of the girls looks at me—acknowledges my existence—and I shrink back. She has thick lip gloss on, hair down to her waist, says to Issac, "Are you dating again already? Why haven't you posted about it?"

"Is this why you couldn't commit to Melinda?" another says.

"You chose this plain girl over Ms. Melinda Martinez?" one chimes in.

"She's not that plain," calls someone at the back. "Her curly hair is nice."

"Hold up," Issac starts, hands in the air, but they drown him out.

"Plain, but in that sort of gorgeous girl-next-door kind of way," the one with the glossed lips says, pointing her phone camera straight at me. "What's your name? Are you Hispanic?"

"Wait. Isn't she his childhood best friend?" one of them cuts in. "She's a mixed chick."

"Oh, yup. She'd be a biracial baddie if she got her eyebrows microbladed. Maybe a BBL," Lip Gloss decides.

They're talking so fast, Issac can't even get a word in, and even though I'm used to people wondering out loud what my race is, I'm done with this entire conversation.

"You're on your own," I tell him, before hurrying away and leaving him in the wake of madness that being what the magazines call *Most Beautiful Human of the Year* has created.

MY INSTAGRAM PAGE IS SIX PICTURES OF FALLEN LEAVES AND FLOWERS and random pieces of poetry. I'm sitting on the hood of my car, scrolling my feed and wondering if Issac is trying to convince the girls to delete the videos. What will people think of me if they post them with captions like plain, comparing me to Melinda the model, who is the opposite of plain?

Issac surprises me when he raps his knuckle against one of my windows. I didn't see him coming.

"You left me back there." He frowns. "Are you ever gonna be okay with the fact that this is my life now?"

My stomach sinks. "I am okay with it. I'm happy for you, so happy. But it's your life."

"And you've always been a part of it." The words are said softly, but they still feel sharp enough to sting. I watch him pull something from his pocket. "Anyway, I got you this. Tried to get you Shida Anala's new record, but the girls noticed me looking and snatched up the last one."

"It's pretty," I say, taking the sunflower key chain from him. The fact that he thought of getting my favorite singer's album makes me feel worse for leaving him in the store.

"A token of forgiveness for attracting that attention with your face?" I tease, hoping it breaks the tension.

"Something like that," he says. "Did it work?"

"Only if you forgive me for being a hermit." I pout.

"There's nothing to forgive," he tells me. "Sometimes, I just can't understand how you're brave enough to climb a mountain but not brave enough to post a picture of you doing it."

"It's been a while since I've climbed a mountain. In fact, I'm completely out of shape," I joke, but Issac just narrows his eyes. "And it's . . . different. I don't like to be the center of attention the way you like it."

"I know," he concedes. Then, with a cheeky grin: "Let's go make that last delivery, because I'm sure Katrina can't wait to see my face, and I do like attention. No matter the kind."

"I'm sure she's so excited." I laugh.

He met my friend Katrina the last time he was here, and he seemed to enjoy that she wasn't exactly starstruck.

"Great," he says, "and I'm controlling the Bluetooth on the way. No more of your sad music today."

"Hozier's music is not sad; it just has soul," I say.

"Yeah, yeah."

IF THERE'S ONE THING TO KNOW ABOUT KATRINA ASHLEY, IT'S THAT she's notoriously known to leave you waiting outside her door. The day before her thirtieth birthday, she called me over after a bad breakup but took twenty minutes to let me inside because she'd decided to get in the bath to shave her legs before I arrived. We're waiting on her steps when Issac's manager calls him.

"I'm good, Bernie," he says as soon as he answers it. "Yeah. I'm laying low."

I shoot him a look, fighting off my laughter. He's not a good liar. He probably gives his manager headaches. I bet Bernie won't even be surprised if the teens upload a video.

"Nah, I don't want you tagging along," Issac tells him. "Three days is all I need. Uh-huh. Yeah, my best friend will protect me." He wiggles his eyebrows at me. "She knows jujitsu."

I snort, and he jabs a finger into my side before walking across the lawn to finish his conversation in private. Finally, the door opens. Katrina answers in her bathrobe with a toothbrush in hand. She takes the bag from me with her left, struggles to hand me some money with her right, mumbling about my bad timing. Katrina's been a customer since the shop opened because she lives two streets from it, but over the past year we've fallen into a friendship. I ask if she has work today and she shakes her head.

"I desperately needed a personal day."

"And clearly you're taking one," I say, reaching to poke one of the rollers in her hair.

Katrina's career issues are different from mine. She has *too much* success at her job but not enough respect and credit for it. Her eyes go wide when she finally notices Issac on her lawn, but she's only surprised he's here for ten seconds before: "Do you want to do nasty things with him?"

I'm taken aback by her randomness, though I shouldn't be by now. "Excuse me?"

She points a finger at me. "Correct answer. That was a test. We don't need you falling for him and ruining your friendship. Especially now that he's not dating and is emotional."

"Do I really have to explain platonic love again, Kat?" I ask, annoyed by how often Issac and I have had to defend our friendship because people have seen romance where there wasn't.

But then Katrina says, "Until you tell me he's like a brother," and heat curls in my cheeks. We're close, but *brother* feels like something else.

I ignore her and shift to glance at him. He's still on the phone but waves a hand and smiles at Katrina.

"He's certainly sexy," she purrs. "Too bad he's commitment averse."

I turn toward her, ask, "You really think he's sad?"

"Oh, hell yeah," she says. "Who wouldn't be if Melinda Martinez cut them off?"

This surprises me. Issac said it was mutual, but is the internet saying something different?

"Anyway, he better start dating again soon," Katrina tells me. "His image is being tarnished. Some outlets are saying he preached dating with purpose, then proceeded to waste Melinda's time; others are wondering if she found him hard to love. They have photos of him looking sad on the streets."

Issac . . . hard to love? A feeling stirs inside of me. A protectiveness of him. He hasn't mentioned anything about his image, but haven't I noticed that he's more pensive? Is he sad?

"So, have any celeb gossip for me?" Katrina asks, snapping me from my thoughts.

I push down the worry for Issac and roll my eyes. "Bye, Kat."

She grumbles something about me being stingy and other things I choose to ignore. Before I turn away, she says, "I feel like you must be hiding bad prom sex because of regret. Or even a first kiss back when you were kids. Something."

There was that one time we almost kissed when we were thirteen and curious. It would've been the first time for us both, but after leaning in, we agreed it was the grossest thing we've *almost* experienced. That was the end of that. Besides, relationships are messy, and one thing that's never felt messy is our friendship.

"We've never done anything. Ever," I tell her.

"That's what scares me. Until you try it, how will you ever know you're strictly platonic? And believe me, Laniah, you don't want to try it now that he's a *sad* superstar."

I laugh at her persistence but humor her with, "Don't worry, my heart is safe."

"Fine," she says, blows me some kisses and shuts the door.

On the walk over to Issac, I do a quick Google search and stare at the first headline I find:

Issac Jordan, heartbroken over Melinda Martinez and finally ready for a relationship, but is he even relationship material?

5

CAR CONFESSIONAL

WHEN WE GET IN THE CAR, ISSAC APOLOGIZES FOR BEING too busy to talk to Katrina. "Seems like the more magazine covers I get booked for, the more bodyguards Bernie wants to hire," he explains. "And he thinks I want him in my face twenty-four/seven. Happily forgoing freedom."

"I like that he's protective. Wouldn't want an obsessed fan to decide it's time to wear your skin," I joke, though the ridiculous thought hasn't been far from my mind. Issac's been desired since we went through puberty, when his voice deepened and he grew to be a damn near giant, but how does one prepare for their best friend to reach this level of desirability? "Maybe we could set Bernie up on the couch?"

Issac scrunches his nose before I start to drive. "Trying to imagine Bernie on the couch is like trying to imagine *you* making content for YouTube."

"So never a couch for Bernie. Got it." I only know Bernie

from stories I'm told and quick hellos over FaceTime. He's been Issac's manager for a year, but he already seems like a better fit compared to Issac's old manager, who hardly picked up his calls. Bernie even helps with financial advising, since Issac went from having very little money to having too much of it.

When I turn left, Issac taps the dashboard. "We were so close to the shop. Why are we passing by? It's been a while since I've been inside, and I'd love to see Vanessa and Lex."

The guilt sits in my esophagus. It suffocates the air in my small car. I can't keep it from him any longer. "They're not there because there is no shop," I admit.

"Wait, what?"

Seconds pass, and when I don't answer, he makes a motion with his hand for me to pull the car over.

Once we're parked, he tilts his head at me, demanding attention with his eyes. "What do you mean?"

I grip the steering wheel, say, "Well, it still exists, but not for much longer."

Issac's face falls. The pit in my stomach grows. He smooths down the hair on his chin before he speaks. "All the boxes . . ."

"We're trying to clear stuff out. Going to give the key back to the owner soon."

"But why?"

"You know why," I whisper.

"I want you to say it out loud," he says, voice soft as it is firm.

I sigh because I know he won't let it go. "First-year blues and then . . ."

"And then?" he asks. "And then second-year profit. That's what you told me."

"And now it's the third, Issac, and the profit has poofed. We're in serious debt. Had to lay off our help months ago. Lex is basically helping us for free now."

Lex Chen was the designated product delivery driver when Wildly Green was a kitchen business. More important, he's my only other close friend in the world, and lately it feels like I've been taking advantage of that friendship by keeping him from earning money elsewhere.

"Is this why you've been working all those extra shifts at the hotel?"

One side of my mouth lifts. "You didn't think I was cleaning rooms for fun, did you?"

The look on his face takes my smile clean off. "And Vanessa?" he asks quietly.

I feel the embarrassment coil in my chest, getting tighter and tighter with each breath. I glance out the window, then back at him. "She just got hired back at the hotel too."

He takes his bottom lip in his mouth, then rubs his face. "So, you've been having money issues and didn't think to tell me? You've been lying to me?"

I think of how many times I've practiced this answer and say, "You would've tried to fix it and—"

"I'm going to help," he cuts in. "Then *you're* going to fix it. How much do you need?"

"That's exactly why we didn't want to tell you yet. A loan from you isn't the solution."

"Who said it was a loan? Watch your words."

"And you watch your tone."

His eyes are on fire, but I can match him. We stare at each other until his flame dulls, and when he frowns, my own fire goes out too. "If money can't help, then what will?"

"It's complicated," I tell him. "There are so many natural-product businesses out there right now. I've had meetings with investors. We even considered signing with a big company, but on top of the fact that we'd lose power over our product line, we aren't the commercial pretty picture they want us to be. Lex is running our social media accounts and our website, but they haven't brought in much action. I tried to find solutions for sustainable profit, but it's just . . . I couldn't. And we've accepted it. We knew it could come to this."

"But the business . . . you love it with all your heart."

At the sound of tears in his voice, my eyes begin to burn. "I do," I say, trying for another smile, "and we will still have it. Right in the kitchen, like we've done before."

"But remember when I posted that thing about my hair growth months ago and landed you some sales?" he says. "Maybe I can do more of that and . . ."

I bite back a laugh because he's serious, and it's cute and maddening too. "You actively promoting our products might bring in sales, but I doubt that kind of promotion alone can sustain us long-term. And Mom . . . she's not loving it the way she used to. I can't be selfish. I shouldn't have pushed for a store in the first place."

Issac doesn't reply, and I can feel his disappointment cloud the car.

"We will be fine," I insist, then lean toward him and sing "I Want You Back" by the Jackson 5.

He groans, but I can see the corners of his mouth tugging up. I sing and sing, my horrible vocals eventually drawing out his smile.

"You're sickening," he says, but takes both of my hands in his. For how little he's touched me since he's been here, the action surprises me. "I'll never forget slaving at Burger King after high school, trying to figure out how to get my art—me—seen. You didn't understand why back then, but you researched hashtags, came up with PowerPoints of ideas you'd found on Google; you encouraged me at each step."

The memory makes me smile. Issac laughed at my color-coordinated flash cards back then. I didn't know how much they meant to him.

"I can't make any promises that I'll accept you and Vanessa being miserable at the hotel," he says.

"You have to," I tell him. "I'll need your help carrying the boxes while you're here."

"But what if . . ." He lets go of my hands. And then: "What if I have an idea that doesn't involve throwing money at you but could potentially sustain profit?"

"What do you have in mind?" I ask, skeptical yet curious about what wild solution he's come up with during this conversation when I've spent months racking my brain for one.

"I can't say right now. You'd just have to trust me. Can you do that, Ni?" he asks.

His eyes are hopeful, certain. But it takes more than trust to believe there's anything he could do when we've already put the CLOSED sign on the door. Still, I can't help the small seed growing inside of me, a wish that he's thought of something solid. I blow out a breath.

"Alright. I'll trust you," I say. "And I'm hungry again. Would you like to help with that too?"

He shifts away, gives me the side-eye. After a few seconds, he says, "Can't stand that we know the way to each other's heart."

I think he's finished, but when I start to drive again, he adds,

"I wish I would've brought the pen. You'll need to be brave for my plan."

I laugh and wonder if, after a few drinks with me tonight, he'll break down and grieve the shop too. Because whatever he's dreaming up must be absurd to bring up the pen.

WHAT I REMEMBER

A span of years. The pen.

An ordinary white ballpoint pen with black ink and JOYJEWELS engraved across the length. Given to my father, Dennis Thompson, and hundreds of other employees by factory owners who showed their appreciation for a solid production year in pens instead of pay raises. But Dennis believed in transferring energy into objects; he did it with his guitar each day, and so he gathered his nerves, every fiber of his imposter syndrome, and channeled it into the pen. It was in his pocket when he pitched himself and landed an assistant manager position.

The pen was lost and found four times after that, the logo half worn, out of ink from normal use but prized all the same. When my mother needed fibroids the size of tennis balls removed from her uterus, the thought of getting put to sleep for surgery and never waking up terrified her, so my father got down on his knees in front of her tear-stricken face and pulled the pen from his pocket. Issac and I, both thirteen, watched from our waiting room chairs as he told her, "Put all of your fear into this pen." She refused at first, though didn't call him silly, only argued the doctors wouldn't let her have it in the surgical room. But my father convinced a nurse to let my mother keep the pen up until the moment she was put to sleep. Vanessa Thompson, nervous as she still was, gripped it to her chest as she walked through the double doors and into surgery.

While my mother was grief-stricken three years later, unable to even glance at my father's things, I took the pen from his drawer. During his wake, while everyone else had beautiful words to say about him, I felt I needed to hold the pen close just to stand next to his casket in silence.

Nearly four years ago, I drove Issac 185 miles in my beat-up Honda to his first brand-official photo shoot in New York. When we arrived, he said, "Screw the shoot, let's go eat pizza instead."

I was confused—we were just dreamy over the possibility of this job changing his life.

But then he asked, "What if this path takes me from you?"

Which is when I thought of my then boyfriend Noel, who'd recently proposed to me after I caught him cheating with a girl from our college classes, whose reason was that he was never sure how I felt about him and was jealous of the deeper connection I seemed to have with Issac. Noel, who said he'd wait for me to open up to him if I could forgive him for his mistake. But in the car with my best friend that day, I felt the same fear I did the night Noel got down on one knee. I could understand why he needed more attention, needed words that were hard for me to form, but what if that path—forgiveness and marriage to someone who never gave me butterflies but provided companionship—took me from Issac somehow? My throat was thick. I squeezed Issac's shoulder, promised us both, "Nothing will keep us apart."

There was no future for me that meant a lesser connection with Issac. I handed him my dad's pen, which I still kept close, and said, "This is yours until I need it again. Now go in there and be brave."

I haven't held the pen since.

6

THE PROBLEM WITH TRUTHS

SUNLIGHT COMES THROUGH THE OPEN BLINDS AND FILLS MY room with morning glow. Issac isn't here, but there's breakfast on my bed. He always wakes up before me, and I get lucky when he cooks. I stretch my legs, trying to blink away sleep, but lately it's been getting harder, even after a full night's rest. I make a mental note to mention it at my doctor's appointment tomorrow, then stare at the tray of food in Issac's place. Who needs a man when you've got a best friend who makes lemon sugar crepes and blesses the bacon, even though he doesn't eat it? Katrina would have jokes about all of this. I imagine her narrowed eyes if I told her that Issac and I share the bed without so much as cuddling. She'd never believe that it's only good conversation and laughter before sleep.

I smile and sit up to grab the note beside the plate.

Promise to eat and drink the orange juice before you do anything else. If you touch your phone before your food,

*I'll know. Had to catch an early flight, but I swear I'll come
back soon.*

—*Issac*

The sadness hits me in the chest before it radiates everywhere
else. I knew spending three days with him was too good to be
true, but one day feels cheap. And he didn't even wake me to say
he was leaving. I reach for my phone but there's a sticky note cov-
ering the screen. *Eat first. You promised.* I roll my eyes, take a sip
of orange juice, smash my crepes in the sugar. He knows I'll be
angrier without food in my system, and he's right.

But when I notice my phone lighting up with repeated notifications, I snatch it from my nightstand and rip off the sticky note.
Issac's slick self put it on vibrate.

My lock screen is a mess of messages I can't explain. *Ding.
Ding. Ding.*

Old friends texting me. Hi, Laniah. What's up, girl? Omg, is the
news true?

With a piece of bacon halfway in my mouth, I scroll through
fourteen messages from Katrina that range from Freaking out to
Girl to I. Am. Not. Happy. There's one from Lex that says, Answer
your damn phone or I'm heading over, and my insides twist, thinking the teens at the music store must've posted something. But
why is everyone so worked up over a dumb video?

Right as I think it, Issac's voice reverberates through my mind.
You'd just have to trust me, and I let the bacon fall back on the plate
while mentally preparing for my search on social media. But there
was no way to prepare for the three thousand follow requests
waiting for me. Am I dreaming? What the hell did Issac do? As

I'm staring, the number of requests goes up. And up. I steady myself before checking my DMs. There are dozens of them from family, former colleagues, even a message from someone I matched with on a dating app and forgot to block.

And then there's the one. The one from Issac.

I'm barely breathing when I click on the message. Except it's not a message, it's a notification for a tagged picture posted to his page at 11:58 last night. I was asleep by then, but the photo is of us. He knows I don't want to be on social media, yet here we are. Issac between my bare legs because I had shorts on, me on the couch while I did his hair the night before, a hint of a smile on my face while he leaned his head on my thigh.

My temperature is already rising before my eyes flick to the caption. A side smile emoji sits beside the words: It's always been her. There is no one like my baby.

A choked gasp escapes me. I read it again. And again. *My baby?*

I'm hot. Prickly. Skin scorching. But more noticeable is the flicker in my chest, the strange tug on my heart while rereading the words. Was this . . . his plan?

I scroll the caption, ready to read It's a joke, she's just my best friend, but find instead: And she makes the best products my hair has ever known. I'm blessed to call her mine.

Out of his nineteen million followers, over one million of them have already liked the picture. There are seven thousand comments, but I see only two before the dizziness comes.

Where've you been hiding her? I need me one.

DROP HER BUSINESS PAGE.

Resting on my chest is a brick, restricting my air supply, forcing me to take shallow breaths. Five. Four. Three. The world slowly stops spinning, but then my phone rings.

It's Mom. "You need to get down to the shop," she says. "Right now."

SEVERAL CUSTOMERS ARE STANDING OUTSIDE OF WILDLY GREEN when I arrive. Are they waiting for me? Mom is smiling at someone with a camera, and white dots cross my vision while imagining paparazzi have come for me. Have they? I pull my car around the side of the building and use that entrance. From the back room, I creep to check through the storefront windows and watch Mom talk to them. Part of me wants to chicken out, go home and take shots of Patrón and hide under the covers, but I can't leave her with these people. Just as I make a move to go out there and rescue her, she comes in and locks the door, but the customers stay, press their fingers against the glass of our store window, and look inside. I shrink toward the shadows, waving at her to follow. Once we're in the back, she leans her hip against our break table. She looks good today in her button-down and black slacks, her salt-and-pepper hair tied up in a topknot. She is the definition of *prim and proper* with a side of attitude.

"You better start talking," she says, crossing her arms over her chest.

I open my mouth, close it. Open again. "You're looking nice today, Mom."

She ignores me. "Are you . . . is Issac?" Even Mom can't wrap her mind around it.

"No. We're the same as we've always been. Just friends."

Mom's shoulders slump. "Okay. Here I thought something crazy happened and you told the damn internet before you told me. I'd kill you both."

"Oh, ohh . . . You should still kill him," I say, taking out my phone and giving him another call. Voice mail. "I'm going to. I know that. And so does he, apparently."

"So, what is all this?" Mom asks. "Your aunties were calling me at midnight about it."

"Issac thinks this . . . thing he has done is going to save the shop somehow," I say.

Mom raises a perfectly sculpted eyebrow. "You asked him to do this?"

"Of course not. Seriously, Mom? I'm panicking inside."

Her facial expression changes from confusion to . . . amusement? She smiles just a little, and I squint at her, suspicious. "I can understand the panic," she starts. "But, baby, he was right. All those customers out there . . . they want product."

I blink at her. "Do they want product, or do they want to interrogate me?"

"Both, I think."

"And did you tell them we're closing up shop?"

"I told them we were redecorating," she says. "And to come back in an hour." I gasp, horrified that she already thought to run with this and that someone else is making decisions without me, but she shrugs. "What? The opportunity is here. I see no reason not to use it."

I try to process what she's saying, but my mind keeps flashing back to Issac's post, him calling me his *baby*. "But Issac and I are *not* together," I whisper.

She points toward the front. "What they don't know won't hurt them, but it *will* help us."

I can hear the relief in her tone, can see the hope in her eyes, and realize Issac has truly tricked people into thinking we're together and my mother is considering it a win for Wildly Green. Is it? There's no denying the attention that a day of being *his* has caused, but does that really mean a long-term solution? Are star power and social media truly that powerful? And how do I know exactly what Issac's playing at, how far he's planned without me, if I can't get him on the damn phone?

Oh. He must know how much I want to throttle him right now.

But something shifts inside of me while staring at my mom's eager expression, and I wonder if she's right to be hopeful. I want to be hopeful about saving the shop too, but I can't help feeling cautious over her excitement. Images of us during our first year, when money was rolling in and we'd dance in the shop after getting a product *perfectly right*, flood my mind. She hasn't wanted to dance like that in a long time, and I find myself afraid of failing her again.

"What if this plan of his doesn't work the way you want it to? What if it doesn't work for *me*? I don't want to disappoint you," I say, honest, vulnerable.

"You could never," she replies, and I want to tell her we both know that isn't true, but she squeezes my shoulder just as the shop bell rings up front. She doesn't look fazed by the sound. She holds eye contact, and I need to hear her speak again. For her to tell me she's not going to count on this when I don't even know what we're counting on yet. And then she does: "Emotionally, you can deal with this situation however you'd like. But if we can sell what's still in stock today, I think it'll put us in a good place regardless of how long this lasts."

"Thanks to Issac and Laniah's inevitable love affair, I have no doubt that we'll sell what we have in stock," Lex says, standing in the doorway, his faux-fur pom-pom key chain in hand, the key to the shop dangling from it.

At the sight of his face, sharp angles and soft eyes, I finally feel some relief trickle in. Lex Chen is our calming balance. Me sometimes too realistic, Mom overly hopeful, Lex a little bit of both and not easily swayed one way or the other. I've missed seeing him here. And I'm so tempted to tell him the truth about what Issac did, especially after he used the words *inevitable* and *love affair* in the same sentence, but my dear mother shoots me a look that makes me think silence is the best course of action for now.

"Vanessa here told me it's all hands on deck today," Lex explains. "And I have two with freshly manicured fingers, but they're still ready to get to work when the both of you are."

I huff out a breath, worried about what I'll be agreeing to by opening the shop, annoyed that Issac's ignoring my calls, nervous for the crowd and the questions they may have and the answers I won't. Still, I recall Lex's words about having no doubts, and a smile tugs at my mouth. When Mom sees it, she skips out of the room right behind Lex, both overly excited and screaming happy things as they get ready to open the store.

I stay in the back for a few seconds, almost composed, nearly calm—until I hear the music kick on from the shop speakers and picture Mom swaying to it.

You really should've talked this through with me first, I text Issac.

7

THE PLAN

BY NIGHTFALL, I'M SEETHING. I'VE SPENT THE WHOLE DAY AVOIDING phone calls while Issac spent the day avoiding mine. I do answer my mom, who sent me home an hour after we opened the shop because people wouldn't stop harassing me with questions, even when she hit them with: "You look like you could use some oil for that dry scalp. Let's focus on that." We've sold more products in one day than we have in six months, she tells me, then I hear her and Lex giggling in the background while they count the money in the cash register.

I'm three Netflix episodes into the fourth season of *Stranger Things* and have no idea what happened in any of them, when Issac finally calls. There is no second ring. I practically dive for my phone on the couch.

But the fire and anger leave; my words come out so soft.

"Issac," I say, "Issac, where have you been?"

"Hi, Laniah." His voice is softer than mine. "My sweet Ni."

"Don't you dare."

"I had to do it."

"You should've told me."

"You said you trusted me."

I shift on the couch, cross my legs, rip some strings off of a pillow. "I did, but why would I ever think *this* was your plan? And you decided it without me. Then ran away before we could talk it through. Now everyone thinks we're together and . . . Issac, what does this mean for us?"

"What do you want it to mean?"

His question confuses me, but before I can ask him to clarify he clears his throat. "I feel justified for being a coward. You scare me, sometimes. All that fire inside of you, those deadly pinches."

I laugh even though I shouldn't.

"But I didn't run away. I'm still here, for now."

My back straightens, I look around the room. "What?"

"I'm out front," he says. "Let's talk about this in person."

I move to peek through the blinds and rest my forehead against the wall near the window when I notice Issac's rental car. We both breathe into the phone. I don't hang up until I open my front door and find him sitting on my porch. His long legs are stretched, feet hitting the bottom steps, he's not smiling when he turns his head to look at me. "My sweet Ni."

"Oh, hush," I say, and sit down beside him.

It's still humid out. Summer is setting in and making most nights in Rhode Island feel like a sauna. Issac and I listen to the bugs tick in the bushes and see Wilma part her curtains to spy on us.

"When we spent last summer stoop sitting, she watched us every night," Issac says, "but we didn't care. You were so proud to finally have a porch to sit on, and I was so proud to sit anywhere near you. We were dreaming up my growing career, the shop was still blossoming. We played spades and music, grew flowers for your box windows, and hung these plants on the porch that were just babies back then. But you never talk about sitting out here anymore."

I wrap my arms around my knees and swallow. "I don't sit out here much."

He tilts his head, examines me. "Because I haven't been around?"

"You're so full of yourself."

"No, I know you. I know us. Just like you should know that I won't be able to concentrate on anything, nothing at all, if you're back here unhappy without me. I thought you were happy. You never said you weren't."

"And you think deciding something about my life without me will make me happy?"

He's quiet for a moment. Then: "I hope you'll forgive me for the way I went about it, but if you let the world think we're together for a while, I won't have to find out you had to move to a cheaper place without a porch in a few months. Call it selfish, but I don't regret it one bit."

"It is selfish," I say. "And have you considered how this will affect your reputation? What does Bernie think? You just stopped dating Melinda. Katrina said the media is calling you a . . . a sad boy. What will they say about you now?"

Issac doesn't look offended. "What if I said that doing this with you will actually help my reputation? That maybe it'll get me out of the tabloids and the media will take me more seriously as an artist if I'm actually in a committed relationship?" he asks. "If I said part of this was for me, would that make you want to keep this going?"

"Maybe," I answer honestly.

"And if I said you helped me launch my dreams, now let me help keep yours steady?"

"I'd say you don't owe me anything. They were just silly flash cards, Issac."

"You and Vanessa, Dennis . . ." Issac trails off. "It wasn't just flash cards, Laniah."

Hearing my father's name from his mouth makes my heart squeeze. "We love you," I say. "You're our family. My family."

Issac looks down into my face. "Am I like a brother?"

Katrina's words snap into my mind, and suddenly I'm wondering if he could've overheard her while he was on the phone with Bernie yesterday. There's no sign on his face. He just looks curious.

"Something more than a friend. Family," I repeat.

He responds with a smile, then bumps me with his shoulder. "Listen, if you really don't want this, I'll give a statement, clean it up the best I can. Maybe say it was a prank or my account got hacked. I think the attention will fizzle out fast. I'll go on some dates and give them something else to focus on." He releases a breath, his eyes dancing in the dark, hopeful. "But I do think this could work. Get you noticed by my fans, maybe even brands I work with, let people know those products and the people behind them are magic. And hey, if you need to talk to someone about everything you're feeling along the way, my therapist is a virtual-meeting pro."

"Your . . . therapist?" I repeat, surprised by his serious tone. "Since when?"

He inhales. I see the guilt cross his face. Another thing he hasn't told me. "Just six months or so," he says.

I shift away, shoulders slumping, stomach twisting, but then . . .

"I was having a hard time, missing home, and . . . other things. My mind was full of them. So Bernie urged me to go. Said after my childhood, and with my career taking off so fast, it'd be good. And it has been," Issac says. The admission makes me realize he doesn't have to tell me everything, and he especially didn't have to tell me this. "All I'm saying is, if you need one, I'm sure she'd be happy to help."

"So just . . . fake date?" I ask quietly. The question sounds ludicrous out loud, but hadn't I already felt the relief at the shop? The hope that within his temporary plan I could figure out how to sustain us? Hadn't I been fantasizing about selling out the stock in my house before he called?

He wiggles his brows at me. "It'll be just like those romance novels you like to read."

He says it as if I hadn't caught him reading one off my shelf last summer. I laugh. But thoughts shoot across my mind at rapid speed. Maybe I could afford to stay in my apartment. Maybe Mom doesn't have to clean hotel rooms. But will my whole life be exposed to the internet? Will people hate me? Will they love Issac more or less? Will pretending to be with him be hard to come back from? I can't lose what we have.

But there's something else, sitting just beneath the surface, making my heart stutter. A selfish need to keep him close. A voice whispering that pretending to be in a relationship with him might bridge the growing distance between us. Then I wouldn't have to find out important things six months after the fact.

"Or maybe . . . ," Issac says, examining my face, "that's what you're really afraid of. You're desperate to save the shop, I know it. So why are you hesitating? Do you think you'll fall for me like the heroine does the hero in your favorite books?"

His directness has made me stumble over my words many times, but this question causes a bodily reaction that involves twitching and frighteningly rapid heartbeats. I chew my lip, shake my head like he's had a ludicrous thought.

"Of course not," I say.

"So, then, we're doing this?"

"We're doing it," I agree, because he's not going to elicit a different response with that challenging look on his face.

"Good." He smiles.

"Great," I say. Then when reality hits: "What exactly are we doing? And how are we doing it? I think we need rules."

Issac's laughter bubbles between us. "Rules? Like children? Why?"

"Issac! This is serious. You're my best friend."

"And you're mine."

The words wrap around that nagging worry that distance is changing things, but something is still different about our closeness. I can feel it. Still, I scoot to put some more space between us for the conversation that needs to be had. "What would your team expect? Of you having a . . . you know."

He raises his brows, taunting me with them. "A girlfriend? Okay, well, I guess they'd want you to attend some of my events, photo shoots. The big ones at least."

"Aren't they all big? I can't travel all the time because of Wildly Green."

"Just two or three times," Issac says, in a steady, calming voice. "Maybe you can spend a weekend with me walking the Cali streets? Eating at restaurants? We can relax on the beach."

My breathing slows. "That sounds normal for us."

"Exactly. There will be more cameras, but it's just you and me, Ni."

"And you'd make a point to come here more?"

"Of course. Help you at the shop. And we can do all the things we always do. This doesn't have to be a big deal. Bookshops and hitting up the arcade. Just like we've always done."

My eyes grow heavy. That familiar fatigue I've been struggling with lately is catching up to me, but I don't want the conversation to end, and there's still other things I need to know. The most important things. The hardest to ask. I hug myself and am thankful for the darkness so he can't see the flush on my face. "Just like always, except, will there be kissing?"

Issac doesn't answer for a while, and it makes me want to qualify my question, but then his eyes meet mine and he holds a steady stare. "There are other ways of being affectionate in public, other things we can do besides kissing if you don't think we should." His words promptly send a series of intimate images through my mind: ones of him and me doing things we've never done before, and I have trouble swallowing. "I respect you so much, Ni. We can be as physical as you're comfortable with."

He always knows what to say. Whether it was back in high school when boys would make fun of my *bushy hair* . . . or if I'd slip and say I missed my dad, even though he didn't have either of his parents to care for him. Part of me wants to ask him what *he* would be comfortable with, but another part of me doesn't want to know.

"No kissing on the lips," I say.

He smiles just a little. "There will be no kissing on the lips."

"And I don't want to personally post on social media."

"You can be your same hermit self online. I'll probably hire someone to help Lex with your business accounts though. And you'll have to be okay with me posting pictures of us, talking to the media, all of it. Don't come for my neck every time you see something new. And stop calling yourself hideous."

"You're so bossy," I tell him, sulking a little. "And what about a timeline?"

"A few months? Something flexible and loose?"

"No." I shake my head, needing to be sure we're doing this right. "Something solid so it doesn't get messy. How about until the end of summer?"

"We do love our summers," he agrees.

"We do." I smile. "This all sounds . . ."

"Horrifying?" he asks.

"But maybe worth it?" I say.

"It will be," he promises.

"When we end things, what if they call you a sad boy, for real?" *Call you hard to love*, I think, but decide not to say. "What if you resent me?"

He looks startled by the last question and ignores the others. "Resent you? Never in a million years. You could take every last cent of my money, run my name through the mud, if it meant you'd be okay. Resenting you is impossible. I just hope you won't resent me. Social media. The secrets. We couldn't tell anyone. If it leaked, that would definitely put some heat on my career. But I still wouldn't resent you. This won't feel like work for us. We both can continue to do what we love and be around each other a little more too. Does that sound so bad?"

I lie back on the cold planks of the porch and stare up at the stars. There's a feeling skittering across my chest, something like a warning about what we're agreeing to do, but then he lies down beside me and it eases a little. "I just really want to be careful. For our friendship."

"Understood . . . and me too," he says. "I trust the way we love each other, but do you need us to define exactly what *messy* means?"

"I don't think so," I say, because I can't bring myself to ask if *other things* means he'll be placing his hand on the small of my back and whispering in my ear and trailing his fingers up my spine in public. Maybe I do need Dad's pen back for this.

"So where do I sign? We can make a contract on a food menu inside," he jokes.

"We can sign in sauce from the chicken parm," I say.

"Deal." He sticks out his pinkie; I lock mine with his. "Be prepared for things to be even more intense after I speak to the press about you tomorrow."

Tomorrow. I don't know if all the hours in a month can get me ready for our plan to start tomorrow.

"And I hate to say this right now, but I do have to leave for Cali."

My stomach sinks. I pull my hand away, and he tucks his bottom lip between his teeth.

"Bernie is bugging me to get back now that I announced this. He also wants me to meet with a new designer from London for a potential endorsement opportunity. I spent the day hiding out from you in a small coffee shop and studying Bernie's notes for it. My flight leaves in a few hours." At the look on my face, he apologizes. "But won't it help to have some breathing room before things blow up?"

How can I tell him that if I needed breathing room, I'd be

happy just sitting six feet away from him in silence for a while? I can't. Not when it might be him who needs some breathing room from me.

"I'll miss you," I tell him instead.

He sits up and squeezes my knee. My body recognizes the contact.

"And I miss you already. But not for long. We have a contract now. You'll see me soon."

"Doesn't it make you feel bad that I need a contract to spend time with you?"

"So we're just going to forget that I flew out here to surprise you?"

"That half counts after the stunt you pulled today."

He shakes his head and stands to leave, the stars shining in the sky around him. "Get inside, big head. You'll need the rest."

Since Issac is *not* the boss of me, after he leaves, I pick up my phone and check his post again instead. This time, looking at the picture brings a different wave of feelings. I'm not panicked or angry, but I'm still very aware of my heart beating in my chest. Because Issac, with his head touching my bare thigh and that smile on his face, *does* look like my boyfriend. And apparently, I look like his *baby*. Each time I read the words, I feel more flustered than the last. I've never heard him talk about a woman this way. But he's saying it about me, and even if it's pretend, I can't control the flutters spreading through my stomach.

They don't fade—even after I pry my eyes away from the picture and head inside.

8

THE PART OF ME THAT MIGHT WANT TO KNOW

THE KNOCK COMES JUST AS I SLIP INTO A T-SHIRT FOR BED. I open the door for Issac, smile up at him. "Delayed flight or did you forget something?"

He doesn't speak. His eyes crawl the length of my legs, lingering at the flesh exposed below the hem of my shirt before traveling to my face. My breathing turns sharp, sure that the hungry look in his eyes isn't normal. This isn't how he's supposed to look at *me*. He takes a step, then another, until he's close enough to brush a strand of fallen hair from my shoulder, giving him a view of my neck. When he lowers his head and places a soft kiss on my skin there, a stunned sound escapes my lips.

"I forgot to do this," he whispers, the words giving way to small waves of pleasure as his mouth moves against me. "Forgot to show you what it can feel like if there's kissing involved in our plan."

"Issac," I breathe out, my brain winning the battle over my body, "we can't."

"Why not?" he asks, leading those kisses up, up, up, before catching the lobe of my ear with his teeth.

A moan slips when he tugs softly, my back bends. "Because . . ."

He pulls away to tilt my chin, runs his thumb down my bottom lip, watches as I shiver. "Tell me you don't want me. That there's not a part of you that's always wanted to know what it would be like."

"I . . . But we . . ." He's too far now, my body begs for him to come closer. And then he does. The kiss isn't soft and sweet, it's urgent: tongue and sucking and biting lips. His hands roam my backside, fingers grazing right below my ass, pulling me in until I can feel him hard against my stomach. He groans into my mouth when I arch into him, needing the friction. And then he leads me backward through the door, slams it shut behind him, and cups both of my ass cheeks before lifting me off the ground. My legs wrap around his waist, I'm wet and warm between them, anxious for him to take me right here.

But we're moving, kissing and moaning while making our way to my room, and then I'm on the bed, squeezing my breasts through my shirt and Issac's watching with heavy breaths while sliding his pants down and . . .

I wake gasping for air. Somewhere behind the frantic thumping of my heart is the sound of my alarm. I clutch at my shirt, searching for him in the room. But Issac isn't here. He left last night. He wouldn't say what he said to me. Hasn't kissed me, not even once.

Dust particles float near my window when I kick the covers off, but I'm still trying to catch my breath, so I lie there, ignoring the insistence of my alarm and feeling delirious.

Did I really just have a dream of Issac doing ungodly things to me?

When my chest stops heaving and the denial fades, it leaves room for blame. This is because of the plan. It's already putting toxic fantasies in my head. Actually, Katrina started this. She's the one who planted the seed, and then Issac watered it and gave it sunlight, and now my subconscious mind is imagining what his tongue feels like. And discounting my ridiculous decision to say yes to Issac's idea, am I really to blame for my hormonal delusions? Wouldn't it be normal for my body to begin feeling things it shouldn't feel once he starts touching me like he's my boyfriend? The dream was just my taunting brain and a bodily reaction driven by three different hormones that I have little control over. Because if I'm being honest . . . when Issac called me his *baby*, when he did all of that without asking me, some traitorous part of me might have liked it just a little bit.

But it's downright maddening when I've worked hard over the years to lock away any attraction that may have existed when I was younger. When I didn't know what I know now. That Issac is my very most favorite person in the world, and I won't mess our relationship up over some damn desires. Not even now that I've potentially unleashed those untapped urges and surviving the summer of being Issac Jordan's girlfriend while wondering what his hands would feel like on my ass might be nearly impossible.

Right now, he's sleeping peacefully across the country while I'm trying not to hyperventilate, and I'm tempted to wake him, tell him to have Bernie do damage control over his post and for us to forget about our arrangement.

Or . . . I can grit my teeth and silence any urges that may come because I am a grown woman, and eight weeks go by in a flash when you're adulting. Soon, Issac and I will go back to being platonic in every way and I'll remember freaking out and laugh like I was silly.

I finally silence my alarm and pick up the ibuprofen on my nightstand to ward off an impending headache for the day ahead. If I don't get out of bed now, I won't be on time for my doctor's appointment, which will make me late for my four-hour shift at the hotel. Mom and Lex will be at the shop unpacking boxes and trying to make it more presentable again, but I won't be able to help them until the afternoon. A fact that makes me more relieved than anxious. I'm not sure I'm ready to face customers yet, or to have a possible showdown with paparazzi.

――――――――

ONE MIGHT THINK THAT AFTER HAVING A SEX DREAM ABOUT SOME-one who needs to be in the friend zone, the brain would naturally fail to store it like it does 80 percent of all dreams. But *my* brain flashes to the finest of details while in an extremely inappropriate setting. Take for instance the way Issac unbuckled his belt while staring into my eyes. Such a minute detail that has no business being the culprit of the warmth between my thighs while I'm at the doctor's office.

I smooth over the hospital gown I'm wearing, tempted to reach underneath and touch myself right before a knock comes on the door. Guilt laden, I clear my throat. "Come in."

Dr. Rotondo greets me with his signature smile. Mom came with me to his office once and said he's got a slick smile, the charming kind that can make a girl forget her own needs. He is handsome. In his early forties. With startling blue eyes and a

clean-shaven head that fits him right. We exchange quick pleasantries before it's straight to joking about the tan line he got from
wearing sunglasses on the beach. He asks me if he looks goofy.

"Only a little," I tease, thankful for the distraction from my
dream. "Just a tad."

He says he's satisfied with my answer. We laugh. But then he
asks what brought me into the office, and even though he's charming, when I remind him about the headaches and fatigue I've been
feeling he acts like it's the first time. I've talked to him over the
phone twice.

When he asks if I'm under stress, I smile and say, "Show me
an adult who isn't."

"Fair enough," he says. "But I am wondering if they're tension
headaches."

I've already considered stress a possibility with problems at the
shop, but there's still a nagging feeling in the pit of my stomach.
Something feels different with my body. "Yeah, it could be," I tell
him. "But what about my blood pressure? It's been pretty high
lately."

Dr. Rotondo looks at my chart again, and says, "Not higher
than it usually runs."

"But I'm taking my meds," I say, struggling to keep frustration
from my voice. When I was eighteen, I went to the emergency
room for bronchitis and left with a hypertension diagnosis. The
doctors also found a small amount of protein in my urine, but it
was just above normal limits and they weren't concerned about it.
Everything's seemed steady until recently.

My doctor sits on the stool and moves closer to me. "Honestly,"
he says, "high blood pressure doesn't cause headaches unless it's
at a life-threatening level, and I promise you're nowhere near that.

Maybe you're just nervous to be here today. Sometimes when people are nervous, it temporarily elevates their blood pressure. We see it frequently in our office, actually." A pause, and then: "Are you nervous to be here for some reason?"

I've been my doctor's patient for five years. We joke, talk about his family and mine, but I can't deny my sweaty palms or how quickly my heart jumps when he walks into the room or the way it's racing now at his proximity. Maybe my mom's right. He's good-looking, possibly a little flirty, and it could be the charm about him . . . or maybe it's just *me*. Heart failure took my dad from me, and knowing heart disease can be genetic, that I've had high blood pressure for a while now, always sits at the back of my mind.

"I am a little nervous," I admit.

"There's a term for it," Dr. Rotondo says. "We call it white coat syndrome, and maybe you feel it when you're around me."

I chew the tip of my tongue, avoiding his eyes as he continues.

"What if I told you there's nothing wrong with you? Will that make you feel better?"

Part of me wants to agree so that he doesn't think I'm paranoid or needy, but if I don't ask this next question, I'll be stressing about it for weeks. Until I finally give in and call him anyway. I take a breath, say, "I know you told me that the protein in my urine wasn't a big deal before but . . . do you think it has anything to do with what's going on with me now?"

A fleeting look of confusion flashes across his face, causing me to wonder if he remembers saying that to me or if he didn't remember I had proteinuria at all. I wouldn't blame him for forgetting, he is human, but I feel better when he opens his laptop, taps on a few keys, then gives me a reassuring glance.

"I doubt it has anything to do with that, Laniah. I'm guessing this is just stress. Anxiety. But we could get you some new lab work and adjust your blood pressure medication to see if that helps." I'm instantly relieved I didn't have to ask for blood work myself. I thank my doctor, and he touches the stethoscope around his neck. "Of course," he says, "but before we mess around with your meds, you should take your blood pressure every day for the next few weeks, write it down, and call me with the results."

"Will it be okay being high for that long?"

There's an award out there somewhere for the slick smile stretching his face, but his tone is gentle when he says, "It'll be just fine. And after we get the results back, we can talk about possibly putting you on something for your anxiety. I know you haven't wanted to take anything for it in the past, but you worry a lot."

"I probably worry enough for this whole office," I say with a laugh. "But I wanted to try to manage the anxiety on my own through meditation. Exercise. I should get on that."

He drops the smile, and suddenly I wonder if I said something wrong.

"Even a small dose of Prozac can do the trick and fix all of this for you," he says. "Think about it."

An uneasiness settles in my stomach, though I'm not sure the exact reason why. I shift and the exam paper under my butt crinkles. "I will," I tell him.

"It's always a pleasure seeing you, Laniah," he says.

9

NOT THAT DIFFERENT

BRIDGET IS SEVENTY, WITH BOUNCY BROWN HAIR AND NATU-rally pink cheeks. She wears pearls around her neck and sends her clothes out to the dry cleaner's, and she owns thirty pairs of slacks. As soon as I told her about my blood pressure, she pointed to the automatic machine in her room for me to take it again.

"How about this one?" she asks while holding an outfit on a hanger.

"You wore pink a lot last week," I tell her.

What I don't tell her is Wilma was wearing a pink shirt when I saw her watering her lawn this morning and they already look alike as it is.

"Oh, that's right. Maybe green? I really like the way it brings out your skin tone."

She's the queen of compliments. "I think it'd suit you too, B."

I'm happy to be able to hide in her room until the end of my shift. My coworkers pulled out their phones this morning, asking, "This your man? Damn, girl. Isn't he worth millions? Why are you working here?" But regardless, it always feels nice when the rooms on my list are taken care of and I can come hang with Bridget until someone needs me. Out on the floor, I ache to be in the shop, pouring oils and crinkling up flowers to add to glass jars instead of changing bedsheets and picking up wet rags from the carpet. But Bridget tells me to sit on her couch when my feet hurt and she can tell I'm not feeling good without me saying it.

My blood pressure is higher than it was earlier: 155/98, and I've been awake only a few hours. I write the numbers down in my Notes app, and Bridget turns around to frown at me.

"Not surprised your doctor thinks it's stress," Bridget randomly groans. "If you're a woman, it's always stress to a doctor who can't see past it. My doctor has a vagina like everyone else in her office. You should go there. Bet you'd get better care from someone who probably worries enough to wipe front to back."

I laugh. "Pretty sure most men wipe front to back too, Bridget."

"You would think that," she says like she's had an ill experience that proved otherwise.

"I've been with my doctor for years. And he does seem to care," I say, then realize I'm not entirely sure if that felt true during our visit this morning. "But I'll certainly keep that in mind." I point to the mint-green outfit Bridget laid out on the bed. "That one is going to be perfect for today."

"You think he'll be watching from wherever he is?" she asks about her ex-husband, who is *not* her late husband. He's very much still alive but left her twenty-seven years ago for another woman while they were traveling through Costa Rica. Bridget has made a tradition of *mourning* their marriage.

"He'll think you're a hottie," I say.

She's heading out soon to lay flowers on the plot she bought for said ex, whose body is doing what living bodies do in a different country. The words *It was a marriage while it lasted* are written across his black slate tombstone. I think the most cathartic part is that her eldest son goes with her once a month, and he too speaks at his father's *grave* with a champagne flute in his hand to toast with his mother. This is the same son I see visiting Wilma's house sometimes, though to avoid causing tension I've never asked if Bridget knows he does. But after my ridiculous dream, I'm more curious about the reason two people would abandon a lifelong relationship, and I can't help myself from asking, "So, do you think you'll ever talk to your sister again?"

"Who?"

"Bridget!"

She laughs, then shrugs one shoulder. "Possibly when we're on our deathbeds. Though I should make her a tombstone too. I'm sure we'll both hold on for eternity so that one of us doesn't die before the other." Her mouth curves into something like a smile. "You're desperate to know what happened between the two of us, aren't you?"

"Definitely yes."

She nods, then: "Help me with these buttons, and I'll tell you a very boring story."

The story goes: Once upon a time, a woman named Penelope raised her two granddaughters. She made sure they were properly dressed, that they could cook but also build a desk without the help of a man. When she died, she left more insurance money than two twentysomethings knew what to do with and the house she spent so many years loving them in. The younger of the two,

Bridget, didn't linger in her grief, didn't care when a lawyer mentioned selling her grandmother's house, was ready to *live*. So
Bridget left her older sister, Wilma, who decided not to sell the
house, and traveled the world with her lover, later turned shitty
husband, David. All the while, Wilma expressed her hurt by berating Bridget over *reckless* decisions, and the two stopped talking
after arguing on the phone (Bridget was sipping a fine mojito on a
beach in a foreign country; Wilma had just caught a splinter in her
big toe from the old hardwood floor in their grandmother's
passed-down house). When David left his wife and the two kids
they made while traveling, Bridget decided to come back to Rhode
Island, where she started an insurance company with the money
that remained. The two sisters never got in contact, even after
Wilma was severely injured in an accident that meant she'd walk
with a cane forever. Because somehow it was easier to feed the
distance and let it grow than face the fact that they should've
fought harder to stick together.

There's a flurry of feeling in my chest when Bridget finishes,
my voice is waterlogged when I thank her for telling me. Suddenly, a different part of their relationship has been revealed and
I'm not sure how to feel just yet. Especially about Wilma. A
thought hits to drag Bridget back to my street, force them to
speak, but my mom would tell me to mind my business. Except, it
also makes me think of Issac and I briefly wonder if I should tell
him I'm worried that our physical distance might be causing an
emotional one too.

While I'm adjusting Bridget's shirt, she pokes my chest with
her pointer finger.

"Ouch," I say. "When's the last time you clipped those sharp
claws?"

She ignores my question. "You're worried about ancient history between me and my dear sister, but you didn't tell me about your beautiful fiancé, Issac Jordan," she says.

I should've expected it from Bridget, who uses social media more than me and knows all the gossip in this hotel. But my stomach jumps at the word *fiancé*. "We are not engaged. One hundred percent not my fiancé." For all the nonanswers I've given people since yesterday, it feels good to be sure of something I can say.

"That's too bad." Bridget smiles. "*He's* the hottie, and you'd look beautiful in a gown. You could even wear my grandmother's diamond earrings for something blue."

I laugh, fix her shirt collar, feeling touched. "That's really sweet, Bridget."

"My question is, does he know how hard you work here?" She straightens out her pants and looks at herself in the mirror. "I love seeing you, but a man with money . . . letting you work two jobs the way you do? He sounds like David, and who would want a David?"

"And you sound like my coworkers," I say, catching her eyes in the mirror and fighting the urge to defend Issac, who is definitely not *a David*. I wish I could tell her he made it all up just to make sure my future involves doing something I love. And if Issac knew we are usually working short-staffed, and how exhausted I really am, he'd never want me to work another shift here in my life. But I shake my head.

"That's old-fashioned, Bridget. I can make my own money. I want to make my own money. You did it. Without David and did it well."

"You make your own money too," she says. "But it seems like

he's supportive of your business. Why wouldn't he offer to help you with it? What are partners for if not to help?"

Oh. There's a smile on her face and it has me wondering if she has a feeling that Issac did what he did on purpose. She's a smart woman, very perceptive, and she might just be trying to get juice out of me. I keep my mouth shut and start fastening her bracelets.

"Fine," she says, "keep the story to yourself, even though I told you my sordid past. But at the very least tell me you brought more of your mother's lotion. It smells like heaven, and Lord knows I need to smell something other than the literal shit I smell walking in the hall because the man in room 1010 keeps clogging the toilet."

My gum gets lodged in my throat when I laugh. Bridget taps my back, but I've already swallowed it. Moments like this remind me she and Wilma have more in common than even I'd like to admit.

"I'll get some for you when I leave here," I say, "and you're foul sometimes."

"At least I don't smell foul," Bridget says.

10

WHAT *I* SMELL LIKE

GOOD MORNING FOR ME, AFTERNOON FOR YOU, ISSAC TEXTS. You're officially my girl, and I might've made a photo dump of us for my socials. Hope business is booming. I'll call after my shoot. Bye babe lol <3

The message makes my chest hot. I'm not parked across the street from the shop anymore. Suddenly, I'm home and Issac's standing in my doorway saying he forgot to show me how good kissing can feel. I blink the fantasy away and berate myself. What would my best friend think if he knew I was on the other end wondering if his lips feel better in real life than they seemed to feel in my dream? I send a wide-eyed emoji back before sliding my phone in my pocket and glancing out the window. Is that . . . Pete's car in front of the shop? If Broadway wasn't busy, I'd have panicked and practically dove across it to get to Mom. Neither of us prepared for the landlord to stop by the shop, and I can't imagine the reckless things coming out of her mouth.

I'm anticipating customers when I throw the door open, but

there's not one. Instead, Mom turns to give me a small wave, Lex is nowhere in sight, and Pete doesn't smile when he sees me. Worse than that: the wrinkles on his forehead are unusually severe when he frowns.

"Neither of you thought to tell me you decided to stay open?" he asks.

Relieved there's still time for damage control, I open my mouth to respond, but Mom beats me to it. "We would have called you had we had the time yesterday, Peter. But you're here to hear the news now, aren't you?"

At the insulted look on his face, I rush to cut in. "This was a last-minute decision due to an influx in customers and some potential for investors. We were—"

He shakes his head. "Don't bother with details. The only thing I need is the rent you can't pay, which is why you said you'd be out the first week of the month. And well, it's the first week of the month and you're still here."

"Peter, can you—"

"Listen, Vanessa," Pete says, "I'd appreciate you calling me Pete like I've asked you to." A quick laugh almost escapes my throat. Mom insists on using his full name. Sometimes I wonder if it's her way of flirting with him like a teenager, but I can't imagine she'd admit it. "And I'm supposed to list the space for rent today, but I can't if you're trying to squat. Is that what you're trying to do? Just tell me now."

Mom lets out a long breath, but I give her a warning nudge. "No, no," I say. "We appreciate renting from you. We know we owe you money; we're going to get it for you. Fast."

"With interest," Mom adds, then punctuated and with pursed lips, "Peter."

I grit my teeth but agree. "Can you give us the rest of the month?"

When he starts to protest, I hold a finger up. "Three weeks. Just three weeks to pay you and make sure we're solid enough to sign another lease."

Pete mumbles under his breath, glances around the shop. "For an influx of customers, it sure seems dead in here, but if you're sure."

Dread coils in my stomach over the possibility that people don't care as much as Issac thought they would. He might be in magazines as the sexiest man alive, but who am I to them?

"We'll see you in three weeks," Vanessa Thompson says to Peter Scott, and with a smooth smile and an impressive bat of her lashes, extends her hand for him to shake.

Pete's not the friendliest man, but every time she smiles at him, he gets this goofy look on his face. I think he secretly enjoys her calling him Peter. "Alright, three weeks," he says, then shakes on it.

As soon as he's out the door, Mom explains how she and Lex opened the shop at 11:00 a.m. but have only had two customers. Both pretended like they were looking around but were really looking for me, then they left. Somehow, the thought that the focus was on *only* me makes the whole situation worse. Lex comes out of the back room after a damn nap, and I wonder how the hell we're going to pay him next week as promised.

He strides through the shop with a smile on his face. "The deliciousness that is you and Issac posted on his page was the perfect thing to wake up to," he says, and my worry balloons to new heights. The post is probably littered with insulting comments about me, about Issac not choosing Melinda. Did we do this for no reason? But before Lex can shove his phone in my face, the bell on the door jingles and four customers walk in.

"Issac was sent from the heavens," Mom says, doing a little happy dance.

And it's not a trickle after that, it's one after another, groups of teenage girls, and before we know it the store is full of people. Most are buying more products than necessary, but who are we to tell them they shouldn't?

Hours later, Lex cashes out another customer and I lean over the counter to whisper, "What did Issac say to get all of them here so quickly?"

"With a man that fine, anything he says can draw a crowd," Lex says. "But the caption under the pics he posted said you smell like baked peaches and pineapples, and I'm pretty sure everyone here wants to smell *and taste* like you too."

My face must be redder than Mom's lipstick. I open my mouth to say something, but Lex slaps the counter and points. My eyes dart to the door.

"Let me send the damn paparazzi away," he says. "I'm not going to let media-attention-seeking whores ruin your relationship for me."

For me. He saunters away to deal with them and I laugh. When he finds out none of this is real, he might just throw a bottle of conditioner at my head. I turn to watch Mom open test jars for customers while swinging her hips to the old-school music playing. She even gets some of them dancing too. She's so fun; she radiates and glows. I wonder if people who came in just to be nosy have forgotten all about me by now.

When they do ask if I'm really with Issac, the most I do is nod my head before directing them to a product they probably weren't considering picking up. It's fine. Better than fine. It's the most business we've had in years, and I'm starting to get excited. Especially after Issac calls as promised to happily soak in the good news before our busy day pulls us apart again.

I'm by the leave-in conditioner section when a teenager with beautiful 4c hair comes up to me. "I love your curls," I tell her, admiring the high puff on her head.

Her braces flash when she smiles. "I wish I could wear it out, but it's so flat and dry."

I smile, say, "I think I can help with that."

We spend the next few minutes discussing her hair routine. I tell her that curly hair doesn't have to be shampooed or trimmed as often as straight hair, and ask her if I can touch it to feel the texture. "I know how it is when people touch my hair, so if you're not comfortable it's okay."

She seems to appreciate that we have shared a similar experience, bends a little so I can touch it.

After deciding what products might work best, I hand her a leave-in conditioner. "Start with this. It's lighter than the curl creams you use, so it should help you get some bounce. I love it because it's not sticky and doesn't cause dandruff. Your hair isn't dry, it just needs to breathe."

She reaches up to touch her curls again, as if testing for the dryness while she examines the bottle. "But how will I know if my hair likes it?"

"You can return it if it's not for you," I offer, but I can still see the hesitation on her face. "What's your name?"

"Destiny," she says, the braces blinking in her mouth again. "But most people call me Des."

"Well, Des, how about I test it on you right now?"

Her posture changes, her eyes brighten. "You'd do that?"

"I would," I say.

Des sits in a chair near the sink at the back of the shop and tells me about school and a girl she used to have a crush on. Says, "My braces are coming off soon. I'll miss changing the colors."

While we talk, I do my best not to get water on her, but we both laugh when I do. She asks if I've ever wanted to be a licensed hairdresser, and I tell her no. Not the kind that does blowouts anyway. When I begin diffusing her hair dry, people in the shop start to notice and walk over to peek, some stay and watch.

Destiny's curls look more defined than they already did. When I'm done, she takes a hand mirror from me excitedly but doesn't turn it over to see right away. "No wonder Issac loves you," she says instead. "I was going to tell you how lucky you are. He's so nice. And he's really cute too." She looks shy when she says it, and it makes me smile. "But so are you. I'm happy he finally has his match. I hope I'll meet mine someday."

For a moment, I'm speechless. I want love for her, but something squeezes my stomach considering a real *match* for myself. I push the thought away and the guilt down with it for the lie she'll never know about, then tilt my head to tell her, "You will, Destiny." I reach out to touch her beautiful hair. "And that person, they're going to love you for everything you are."

She smiles the cutest silver smile and takes a breath before looking in the mirror. "Oh my God." She laughs, fluffs her hair, shakes her head. "How did you do that?"

"It wasn't me; it was my mother's magical recipe." I put the leave-in and the oil I used in a bag and slide it onto the counter in front of her. "Just don't tell her I gave you this."

She stands to give me a hug, and my heart blooms the way it

used to when I would watch Mom do Issac's hair and help other people in the neighborhood.

———————

THE SHELVES ARE HALF BARE AS PROOF THAT WE HAD AN UNBELIEV-able day. We pay Lex for the workweek up front. He claps and says, "Gonna buy me and my man a full rack of ribs tonight."

Sometimes Lex feels bad that his cardiologist boyfriend pays for everything. I smile knowing that won't be the case tonight. "Tell Shane we said hello."

Lex winks at me. "Thanks for smelling like peaches, babe."

With my neck burning, he blows us both kisses and he's out the door.

"What was he talking about?" Mom asks, arriving with takeout.

I tell her it was nothing but pull on a lock of hair, wondering if the fruit smell from this morning's conditioner is still lingering there.

While we eat behind the counter, there's a strange energy buzzing between us, like if we talk too much about our success today it'll somehow evaporate. So I text Katrina and we make plans to see each other tomorrow.

Can't wait to hear the juicy details of the relationship I warned you not to have, she says.

My mom puts down her fork to wipe at her tired eyes. "I feel bad, baby," she admits. "I don't want you and Issac to feel obligated to do this for me."

After swallowing a big mouthful of lo mein, I pull her into a half hug and say, "It's for us. For you, me, Lex, and even for Issac. I want the shop to stay open with all my heart. Don't worry."

She might be crying into my shirt. She's been a crier my whole life, and I'm pretty sure she passed the habit on. But I say nothing about it. We hug awhile, the smell of food surrounding us, the strange energy gone.

When she pulls back, she touches my cheek. "Good, because I'm really, really happy." I want to tell her I am too, but I'm already thinking of how to use this attention to sustain our happiness. "Oh, and we'll need to make more pineapple shea body butter for tomorrow," she says. "It flew off the shelves. I swear two women were about to fight over the last one."

A warmth pools in my belly. I try to concentrate on the way Mom smiles while she talks so I don't think of all the things Issac will tell the world this summer.

When it's time to lock up, she asks me to wipe the counter one more time, but as I reach for the paper towel, white dots float across my vision. I blink, but I'm suddenly drowning in dizziness. My mom begins calling my name, but I shut my eyes against the world shaking around me and focus on keeping my feet on the floor.

Mom rushes to my side the way she used to for my father, pulling a stool toward me and forcing me to sit. "Is it your blood pressure, baby?" she asks.

At the strained sound of my mother's voice, I exhale and steady myself by gripping the bottom of the seat. "My doctor said I shouldn't notice any symptoms," I tell her, willing the world back into focus. When it comes, I reach to squeeze her hand in the hopes that it'll reassure her, but I realize how clammy my skin must feel.

"What if this really is just anxiety?" I ask between deep breaths. Because while she was smiling over our success, I was stressing about making it last.

She rubs my shoulder. "I want to say there's no one who knows our bodies better than we do ourselves, and if you feel like something is off, then it probably is. But, baby, you have been worrying that pretty head of yours since you were old enough to count. You used to tell me to put on my seat belt when you were still drinking from a bottle in your car seat."

My lips curve. "So, what you're saying is I was always this annoying?"

"Yes, that, and if it's anxiety, maybe you should take the meds. They help with mine."

I nod. "After the doctor calls with my blood work results, I'll talk to him about prescribing me something."

"You do that, and in the meantime, please take it easy."

I can see the fear in her eyes and hope she's not nervous that the pressure from the shop is making me sick. I hope she's not thinking about my father, his high blood pressure, his heart failure, like I am.

"I will," I say. Then: "You know what we should do before we head out of here? Count all the money we made again today."

"You're trying to distract me, and it's working," she admits with her signature eye roll. "Speaking of money . . . don't think I didn't notice you slipping free products out the door."

I give her my most innocent look. "Just to a few kids."

"We can't make it a habit," Mom says. "Not until we're steady, okay?"

"So you're saying you didn't give out any free products today? That's always been your specialty."

"Why do you think I used *we*, Laniah? Don't get dumb with me."

We laugh, and I let the good feelings chase away the bad. Hoping Mom is doing the same.

WHAT I REMEMBER

Ten years ago. Vanessa Thompson's business card.

Printed double-sided on thick cardstock, bright green for eye-catching quality, a buy-one-get-one-free product special on the back to attract customers, gifted by my father, who wanted my mother to feel more confident dropping them all over town. Upon receiving them, she twirled around the kitchen, thinking the prospects of her small business were only going to get brighter because of this thing my father helped her do. But it was fifteen-year-old Issac and I who walked around on weekends, leaving them everywhere from local libraries to department stores, happy to get out of our houses while doing it.

We had just come through the door after dropping some at a hair salon a few streets over and ran into my parents on their way out. They were heading to my father's doctor appointment together, something that had become more frequent to align with the progression of his illness, when he spied the stack of business cards in my hand and reached for them.

"Oh," he said, excited by an idea, "let's leave some of these at the front desk with the receptionist when we get there."

But my mother, who was becoming a quieter woman in certain regards, shook her head, saying simply, "Not there."

And I remembered a visit I went to with them, how she clutched my father's arm before they called him in the room, how she didn't speak the whole time he was away from us, how as soon as she saw his face she seemed to return to herself. When they kissed hello as if they weren't apart for a short time, I felt the way their love brightened the room.

Afterward, I'd make excuses so I didn't have to go to any more visits with them.

11

A CAROUSEL TO REMEMBER

MY HEAD IS HANGING OFF THE COUCH, FEET UP ON THE WALL, looking at my cute living room upside down. Before this, I lived in a tiny run-down apartment with only one working baseboard heater, a shower I had to crouch down to use because of the slanted ceiling, and a landlord who said I shouldn't be bothered by rats barreling through the bedroom. I told myself I'd work seventy hours a week as a maid if it meant getting to stay here, but it does seem like I won't have to do that. Maybe I could even grow some veggies in the backyard for spring.

I straighten out and rest my head on the solid surface of my sofa before signing into my social media. The notifications make my heart palpitate when they pop up, persistent and red, but I go straight to Issac's page. The first picture in Issac's carousel is of us doing cartwheels onstage after he was lead in our eighth-grade school play. The other pictures are of us throughout the years: me doing his hair; giving him a piggyback ride; him tying my shoes;

us painting on an old leather couch; his arm around my waist before senior prom, even though we had other dates. The most recent one is from the day he signed his first modeling contract. He's alone in the photo, but I'm holding the camera close to his face while he's looking past it into my eyes.

The caption of the whole post taunts me as I stare at this one picture.

> Get someone who distracts you by smelling like
> peaches and pineapples all day long.

A warm feeling breaks across my chest remembering the way I hovered over him that day. I lift my shirt, do in fact smell the body butter still on my skin, swallow. He's stolen butters from me before. But I'm surprised this was the first thing that came to his mind when considering what to write. Was it only a tactic to get people to Wildly Green? Or does he think about the way I smell often? What if . . .

Woof. I refuse to go down that road. Issac's lack of romantic interest in me is proven by him knowing me so thoroughly that if he thought I was his *soulmate*, he would've definitely made a move by now. Therefore, he is not sitting around thinking about the way my skin smells.

To shake off the thoughts, I scroll through the comments and immediately feel like a masochist. There are people I've never heard of with blue checks near their names and hundreds of likes on their comments. And thousands of others with things to say.

> Y'all are cute. Couple goals.
>
> She's a whole snack.

You've finally decided to try a real relationship. Too
bad it's not with me.

Awesome <3. Dm @theclothingbambino to promote

We'll see how long this is gonna last before he's back
on the serial dating shit.

Her hair is gorgeous, but Melinda is beautiful and
deserves better.

I suck in a breath, close my eyes like it'll soothe the stinging in
my chest.

Our relationship is open to the opinions of the world, and none
of it feels fake anymore. How does Issac handle being exposed like
this? Before opening my eyes, I steady myself to scroll through his
feed. It takes a few swipes to realize I'm seeing layers of him like
a perfectly curated mood board. This newest layer is green. He's
walking away from his old-school car with its sage-green paint and
beautiful white seats. There are plants and trees and darkness in
shadows, and there is the sun and him, his energy effervescent in
the camera lens without even trying. This is how the world sees
him when he lets them but how he always looks to me.

In each of these photos, I'm nowhere to be found. *But* I could
be if I wanted to.

I scroll a little farther and there's the smallest slice of a bedroom.
My bedroom. Just the sun hitting the hardwoods and the edge of
my platform bed. Issac and I picked it out together before I moved
in. The caption: Nothing like it. My heart starts to swell before
looking at the next picture. It's of him in my kitchen, at my oak
wooden table with my huge monstera behind him. He has a spoon

in his mouth and he's eating food I'd just cooked. At my table.
With me taking the picture. Caption: Coming home for cooked
meals.

Home. I laugh, feel silly and even giddy for a moment. I've
been in his new life all along, but I didn't know it. I decide to stop
feeding my insecurities, remembering I felt similar when Issac
turned eighteen and left his foster home. My mom asked him to
live with us, but Issac preferred to come and go, spending a few
weeks at our house, then a few with friends. Mom said he might
be scared to put down roots, but it annoyed me. When he told us
he was moving in with some random guys from Craigslist, I almost panicked. Issac laughed and said he couldn't wait to have me
over, but it took him too long to actually invite me. I found out
later that while I was agonizing over losing our friendship during
classes without him at Rhode Island College, he was just adjusting
to living with roommates who left pizza boxes around for weeks
and to life after deciding not to take out loans when he knew he
didn't need to go to college to do art.

Each time I've worried that Issac might be growing too far
from me, something subtle reminds me that I'll always have a
place in his life. I blink back happy tears, proof that I'm a crier like
my mom, before clicking on his tagged photos. The first thing that
pops up is a video Lex mentioned to me earlier. Issac's walking
through the airport with Bernie and holding a green smoothie in
his hand. The reporter says something and Issac stops walking,
despite Bernie's background protests.

"What was that?" Issac asks.

"Is it true that you and Laniah Thompson are a couple?" the
reporter repeats.

Issac gives the reporter a nervous laugh. "Yeah, Laniah's my girl. We're together."

I pause the video to stare at the sloppy smile on his face. He looks . . . happy? And he told me what he said earlier, but hearing it out loud hits different. *Laniah's my girl*.

Goose bumps cut across my skin. Something stirs in my chest. I click Play again and lift one of the couch pillows to my face, shielding myself as if someone can see me smiling.

Good Lord, why am I smiling while listening to him lie?

"How long have you been together? Did you date at all or go straight to a relationship because she was already your friend?" the reporter asks.

Issac shakes his head. "The details are between me and her. But just know she's my person." He points a finger at the camera, not exactly at the reporter but at the world. "And I'll know it if you get out of line with her." Then he flashes that famous smile everyone swoons over and walks off with Bernie and his bodyguards.

Just as the video ends, Issac texts me. I'm still working but call me as soon as you wake up tomorrow, no matter how early it is for me. I want to hear about your day at the shop, and I want you to hear my voice when I say I told you so.

I sink farther into the pillows, rereading the message again and again. He's always been my person too, and that is enough to know this plan will work. It just might require me to allow myself a temporary lapse of good judgment so that I'm not beating myself up each time I wonder what his voice would sound like if he were whispering sexy things in my ear instead.

12

A RUMOR WON'T RUIN THIS DAY

S BUSY ADULTS, KATRINA AND I FIT IN TIME TOGETHER HOW-
ever we can get it. For instance, we spent the early morning
checking things off our lists: she went with me to a warehouse, I
went with her to notarize documents for her clients, we made a
decidedly quick Target run (because when are Target runs truly
quick), and we picked up breakfast from Athena's in Cranston to
eat in the car, where she interrogated me on the nature of my *new*
(she air-quoted this) relationship.

It's not fun keeping the secret from her, but telling anyone besides my mom is too great of a risk, and there's no denying Katrina
loves to gossip. Thankfully, she believed that Issac and I didn't
decide to be together until after we visited her a few days ago. In
fact, she was pleasantly pleased with herself, making the deduc-
tion that she's the reason I realized Issac wasn't *just a friend*. When
she said it, my mind jumped back to the sex dream, and I had to
shovel home fries into my mouth to stop from spilling about it and
revealing my lie. Afterward, I squeezed details from her about her

most recent interaction with her coworker, who she constantly competes with for big clients. They bicker so much, I think they have hate-to-love potential; she thinks he'd be only good in the bedroom, and even then, he probably doesn't do much to spoil his lovers, so she'll pass on any future opportunities he might present her. By the time Katrina drops me off at the shop, I'm fulfilled in the way that girl time tends to give. My walk is lighter, I'm laughing more, my pores are smaller, and we didn't even have to get facials.

Midway through another beautifully busy day at Wildly Green, my doctor calls to say I'm in the clear. My labs are looking about the same as they were last year, and I'm doing just fine.

"And the blood pressure issue?"

"Have you been keeping track of it? I think we said a few weeks, right?"

I laugh nervously and glance around like someone else can hear our conversation, but I'm alone in the back room of the shop. "Right."

"Good, so keep doing that and call the office with the results in a couple of weeks. And we'll adjust as needed. Everything will be good. Okay?"

"Okay." I breathe out, the relief finally settling in. "And about the anxiety . . ."

"Would you like me to prescribe that Prozac?"

"Yeah, I think I would."

"No problem," he says. "I'll have it sent to the pharmacy."

After the call, I walk into the main room and shoot Mom a smile. She raises her fists and gives them a happy little shake, knowing it means good news to add to our already good day. Mom and Lex have been skipping around the place like kids on a playground, and it's times like this that I think about Dad and miss things that never happened. I could almost picture him dancing with Mom to the music, chatting up the customers on the way out about how high gasoline prices are right now or playing his guitar out front thinking he'd attract people that way. He'd make my stomach hurt from laughing so hard while working the register.

"Excuse me?" someone says, breaking the spell of my daydream.

"Oh, sorry." I smile at the woman. "Ready to cash out?"

She's got a basket full of products, but hugs it to her chest. "Actually, I'm still shopping, but I was wondering if I could take a picture with you."

A small laugh breaks free. "A picture? With . . . me?"

Maybe Katrina wasn't lying earlier when she said I'll become famous by extension.

The woman nods. "Please? I watch Issac's videos every morning. He's such an inspiration. I mean, he'll be hanging string lights and giving his thoughts on the expectations partners should and shouldn't have and it's just . . . ugh. He's so real. You know? And you're . . ."

"Okay. Sure," I rush to say to save her from further explaining, and to save me from the explanation too. "How about a selfie?"

"Actually, I was hoping to get the store sign in the background."

This is good, I tell myself. More exposure for the shop. But I feel silly when Lex comes up, pokes me in the back, and injects himself in the conversation with a playful smile. "I'd be happy to take it."

The customer practically shoves her phone into his hands and rushes to get into position near the small sign we have hanging over one of our product tables. I was hoping to attract as little attention as possible, but a few people are already watching. She poses with the basket, tilts her head toward me. I wonder if she has a large following, how many people will see this picture, and I start to sweat. One might think Lex's dedication to getting the right shot is endearing considering he takes photographs on his weekend hikes with a fancy FUJIFILM X-T4 camera, but I know he just wants to stretch out this uncomfortable moment and tease me about my fake smile later.

The woman follows me back to the register, giddy as she swipes through the pictures in front of me. "How long did you say you've been dating Issac?"

The question catches me off guard. "I didn't say. And that's a personal question, so I'd rather not answer."

She lifts her head to stare at me. "Interesting," she says, scanning me from my waist to my ponytail.

What kind of manipulation is this? She was just shy and sweet two seconds ago.

"I was just wondering because there are rumors going around that Issac was dating both you and Melinda at the same time, even though he already knew who he would choose."

Lex sucks his teeth. "Everybody loves a scandal. Too bad you won't find one here. And it's not like he was in a committed relationship with Melinda. Any fans who truly love Issac would know that rumor is out of character. He's been honest on the internet since day one."

The woman's face falls and doesn't recover. "Oh, of course. I didn't mean anything by it. I'll just . . ." She points to somewhere far off in the store. "Let me get back to my shopping."

I smile at her. "It was a pleasure."

"Barely," Lex says before she's even out of earshot.

I give Lex my most thankful expression and say, "You know I absolutely hated that. People are really—"

"You know what I hate?" Lex cuts in, jet-black hair falling

over one side of his face and making him look like a model. I always tell him he should do a shoot with Issac, but he says he's much happier behind a camera than in front of one. "Liars," he deadpans. "Is there something you want to tell me?"

My stomach twists; I shake my head. He gives me a pointed look.

"I've known you and Issac for years. It's clear you're keeping secrets. How fake is this whole thing on a scale of one to ten?"

"Shh . . ." I glance around, whisper through gritted teeth. "This is not a good place or a good time for your interrogation. What did my mom tell you?"

Lex narrows his eyes. "Do you remember that time we were in front of mixed company, and you asked me about that weird guy I dated who showed me his sex doll?"

"That was an accident," I say. "It just slipped."

"Fine, but no one can hear us; your mother is putting on a show by the perfume section. And she didn't tell me a thing. I'm smart enough to read the signs on my own, and even smarter because I just got you to admit it."

"You tried to trick me with your words like that customer just did."

He leans against the counter, says, "But I was successful at it, sweetie."

I smack my lips together, sigh. "I was going to tell you . . . eventually."

"Whatever," he says, waving his fingers at me. "Just give me the details, every single one of them, before another fan pulls you in for a picture."

———

WHEN THE LAST CUSTOMER OF THE DAY LEAVES, MOM AND LEX lock up while I head to the back room to make lip balms. I'm melting wax when Issac calls, and, despite the run-in with one of his fans, who didn't end up buying a damn thing, he can hear the happiness in my voice. My health is better than I thought it was. We've made a ton of money. And mostly, I feel relieved to have Lex to talk to about this whole fake-dating scheme.

"Omph," Issac says, like the sound of me being happy hit him right in the chest. "Alright, crew"—he's talking to the people on his shoot—"the love of my life is in a good mood. I can literally hear her smiling. No work today. Everyone go for a swim out back. I just want to sit in this for a while."

I hear applause, then laughing, someone saying, "You wish. We'll be here until eight."

Can I grin any harder? "Love of your life? You're really milking this, aren't you?"

"Hell yes, I am," Issac says, and I imagine his brows piecing together, his tongue between his teeth where it usually sits when he's being funny. "Anyway, called to see if you work at the hotel this weekend."

"You asked me this morning, and I definitely told you that I do."

"Did you?" He's smiling now. "I don't remember that."

"Stop playing," I say. "What is it?"

He exhales, then, "Call off so you can be with me."

The words make my heart thrum for some reason, worse when he softens his voice and he adds, "Please?"

"I can't. I already switched shifts for the week to work in the shop. I'll get written up."

"Luckily, you don't need the hotel job anymore," he says. "What if you just quit?"

"We can't say that from a few days of good sales. I should play it safe," I tell him, though all day between customers I've been wondering how I'll even have time to work at the hotel if business keeps up this way.

"I don't like it, but I get it," he says. "If you change your mind, there's something I'd really love to bring you to . . . as my girl."

I wonder how close his crew is. If he meant for them to hear that. "I'm sorry, but even if I called out or quit the hotel, I still have to worry about the shop orders. We weren't prepared to have this many customers."

"Knew you'd say that, so I went ahead and asked Vanessa before you," he says. "She's happy to have you come out. Says she and Lex can handle the orders and stocking this weekend."

"You would," I say. "And I bet she did."

"What's that bitter tone for?"

"Nothing," I tell him, but make a mental note to have a talk with Mom. I wonder if she wants me to be seen with Issac in public to get the business more traffic. "First official outing?"

"First official one," he says, and I can hear his happiness, him grinning now. He thinks he has me decided. "And I don't think even you, hermit crab of the decade, will want to miss it."

"Well, you might not know me at all, then," I say, "because there's no place you could bring me that would outweigh my desire to crawl inside of my shell."

"You talk a lot of shit for someone who's not going to be able to resist a chance to attend an album listening party for the one and only Shida Anala. It'll be fun, Ni."

My brain freezes on the name for a moment, and then: "You're fucking with me."

"I wouldn't," Issac says. "Not about this."

13

FREDDIE FOR FRUSTRATION

THERE MUST BE MAGIC IN MOM'S SCALP OIL BECAUSE I RUBBED MY head before bed and woke up braver, spontaneous, hopefully far from silly. As soon as I clock in at the hotel, I beeline for the elevator instead of getting my assignment for the day. Bridget is already outside, walking up the hall when I reach the tenth floor. She's got a basket in her hands so big it's blocking the bottom of her face. She startles when she sees me standing in front of her.

"What are you doing back here? I was hoping you quit."

I follow her up the hall. "Are you not enjoying my company anymore?"

"Your company is most enjoyable," she says, passing me the basket to hold. It's full of cleaning products and candles, Febreze fabric spray. "Come with me on this mission."

"What's the mission?"

"If I tell you, you'll try to throw a wrench in my plans," she says.

The toilet bowl cleaner is clue enough. "Would it happen to involve the man in 1010?"

"Would you stop me if I said yes?"

"Not today," I tell her.

She glances at me with a knowing look on her face. "So, today's the day you quit, isn't it?"

"Are you a psychic? How can you tell?"

"I'm usually your last stop on the cleaning tour," she says once we reach room 1010, "you don't have your cart, and you've got this glow about you."

"I'm nervous and I'm excited," I admit, "but I'm sad too."

Bridget grabs one of my hands from where it's curled around the basket handle. "This place will be here, this work will always be available, but your business won't if you don't give it your all."

"It's not the work," I say, looking down at the rings lining her wrinkled fingers: glinting blue and green and ruby stones set upon delicate skin.

"Oh, I know, sweetheart," she says. "I'm a hard woman to shake. Don't you know David miraculously manages to dial my number from beyond the grave to beg for my forgiveness twice a year?"

Tears burn at the backs of my eyes. I laugh and hope they don't slip. "I did not know that, but I can't blame him. I'll miss you terribly."

"And I'll miss you, but you're strong, talented. You don't come back here. Not ever," she says, then shakes her head. "Well, except to visit me. Listen, when I die, I'll come back and haunt you if you leave this place and don't drop in to see me once a year."

"I'll visit more than that. Gotta make sure you don't get fickle and decide to haunt me because one day isn't enough. Maybe you can even come visit me?" It's a question I know she'll refuse with Wilma on the same street, but I selfishly wonder what it would be like if Bridget made up with her sister. Would I be able to tolerate Wilma if it meant getting to see Bridget more?

She purses her lips, but doesn't say no, just simply nods, takes the basket from me, and knocks on the door. When the man who clogs toilets opens it, I can't deny there's a sour smell wafting from his room.

"If you're going to be staying here awhile, we all need you to have this," Bridget says, holding the basket out to him with a polite smile on her face.

———————

AT NIGHT, KATRINA AND LEX COME OVER TO HELP ME PACK MY BAGS for tomorrow's trip. They tear through my closet and my drawers and pick too many outfits for the two days I'll be in Cali. It doesn't help that I'm so indecisive. I hold a jean jacket to my chest and stare at myself in my standup mirror before tossing it on my bed.

"What if everything I bring is wrong?"

"Then he can take you shopping," Lex says, wiggling his brows. "Matter of fact, maybe you should go there with an empty suitcase and come back with a packed one."

"I'm in agreement with Lex," says Katrina, pulling three dresses from the closet and handing them to me. "If you're going to date a rich boy who soaks media attention more than most B-list celebrities, better to reap all the benefits. But . . . since we already know you're not about that life, why don't you try some of these on for us?"

Lex sits on my bed and cups his hands together. "A little Laniah fashion show."

I roll my eyes, but the corners of my lips rise. "Alright, put on some music."

While we listen to hip-hop and R&B throwbacks from the early 2000s, I try on every dress in my closet. We settle on two: a really short black one because *you can never go wrong with a black dress* and a pretty hunter-green one that hugs my curves so well I wonder out loud why I've never worn it in public.

"Because you're the picture of modesty," Katrina says. "Except when you wear those tight tank tops and your titties be tittying."

I frown. "They do?"

"Without your consent or knowledge, apparently," Lex pipes in.

"Hm," I say, and tug the dress down a bit. "Feel like maybe it's doing too much for a listening party. No?"

"You can wear that one to brunch and everyone will think you're the definition of perfect," Kat tells me.

"It's giving exactly what it's supposed to give, no matter where you wear it," Lex says. "And you will wear it sometime on the trip, even if it's just to bed, or so help me I will make your working life at the shop miserable."

"And how might you do that?" I ask.

"I'll side with your mother during every single one of your petty arguments. Even when she's wrong."

Katrina's loud laugh masks my quieter one.

I run a hand along my hip and admire my shape in the mirror. "Fine. I'll bring it, but I need a few casual options just in case."

"If Issac sees you in that dress, no way he's going to want you to wear something casual," Katrina says, and she wouldn't recognize the face I make in the mirror. She doesn't know how off she is. That Issac might think I look amazing, but he doesn't see me like she thinks he does. "And you better send me and Lex pictures. I want one with every single celebrity. Sneaky videos too."

"I'll do my best," I lie, "but no promises."

Katrina opens up my underwear drawer and tosses some lace panties at me, a bright red bra I bought on sale a few months ago, and a few thongs I doubt I'll ever get used to wearing. She even pulls out a two-piece white lingerie with crotchless panties, which probably doesn't fit me anymore.

I snatch it from her. "What are you doing? Get out of that drawer."

"We don't know how long it'll be before Issac decides he's really not made for committed relationships, and is back to dating other women."

"That's fucking rude," Lex hollers out.

Katrina shrugs, smiles at me. "I'm just saying, you have to bring some sexy stuff for your man while he's still your man and not for the streets."

For my *pretend* man. It almost slips from my mouth, but then Lex whistles and starts to fiddle with my suitcase zipper. Whatever sign of amusement forms on my face makes Katrina look at me wild. I shift, avoiding her prying eyes, and shove the *sexy stuff* deep in my luggage.

"I'm confused," she says. "What was that face? Does Issac not enjoy you in some lingerie?"

"Oh, come on, Kat. We know our little lady here probably has boring sex," Lex says, trying on a pair of my sunglasses before tucking them in his pocket. He looks proud of his own joke. I cut my eyes at him. Thief. Beautiful asshole. Yesterday, he asked why I wasn't telling Katrina it was a fake relationship, then agreed that she doesn't have the track record for keeping secrets. *She loves hearing herself speak*, he said. It never seems malicious or ill-intended, but this isn't something I can trust she'd keep to herself. Still, now that we're around Lex and he knows what she doesn't, I feel a little guilty. But my justification goes like this: As soon as the shop is in the clear, I'll tell her that Issac and I broke up. She'll say she saw it coming, she won't even be surprised, *I'm a prophet*, she'll tease me for months. It'll be annoying, but at least I won't have to talk about a sex life that doesn't exist.

"What goes on in my bed is my business," I say.

"Uh-huh. I see." Katrina slowly shakes her head. "So, it *is* boring. What a damn shame. With a man that fine? Girl, you have to spice it up. I know it's been a while since you've been in a relationship, but have fun while you have the chance."

"I resent you for continuously insinuating that Issac and I won't last," I say. "But I'll humor you. How do you suggest I spice things up?"

Kat takes my vibrator out of the drawer. I'm sure it's collected dust and lint from lack of use.

"Why are you touching that?" I protest. "Do you know where it's been?"

"Unless it's been between your cheeks, then . . ."

"That's enough," Lex says, holding out a hand, "even for me."

Katrina smiles and stuffs the vibrator in my suitcase. "Bring Freddie to help. Issac will be shocked and enjoy it. Believe me, it works every time."

"Her name is Linda," I correct with a smile, but inside I'm squirming, thinking of Issac and sex and a vibrator all in the same sentence. Thinking of what someone would do with Issac and a vibrator and thinking that someone is *me* in Katrina's mind. All the thoughts make me feel like the biggest liar in the whole world.

What if Issac's friends ask him about me and our sex life? What will he say to them?

Katrina waves her hand at me. "She looks more like a Freddie; Linda is too cute of a name. Remind me to get you a new one for Christmas this year."

I look to Lex for help, but he's enjoying this interaction and knowing what's hiding under it a little too much. "You really should bring it," he says, hinting something unnecessarily at me. "Just in case you need to let out some . . . frustration."

Why did I tell him about the sex dream yesterday?

"That's a wild thought, Lex," says Katrina. "They are definitely sexing on this trip, might be boring sex but I'm sure she won't be—" She interrupts herself with a gasp, then takes my hand, giving it a supportive squeeze. "Don't tell me he can't make you cum. Is that the real reason he usually doesn't make it past the first date?"

My insides twist. Heat finds my face. Lex leans his forehead against my wall to laugh, shoulders shaking. This is going to be the longest lie of my life.

14

WARNINGS AND THINGS

SHOULD BE SLEEPING. INSTEAD, I SPEND SIX HOURS IN AN AIR-plane attempting to drown my anxious thoughts by alternating between e-books and an assortment of Drake and Taylor Swift songs. But truly, who could blame me when I'm traveling to see my best friend for the first time now that we're a couple?

My stomach is a wreck while exiting the plane. I convinced Issac to let me take an Uber to the condo he's staying at for the month so he can avoid the airport. And, if I'm honest, so that I can avoid reuniting with him in front of an audience. I've never been good at acting, I'm positive Issac got secondhand embarrassment that one time I performed in a school play, but I need to get good at it. This isn't hometown shoppers with their phones—this is celebrities, the media; this is a different level of pretending. And LAX is busy compared to T. F. Green, people push past me like I'm not even here. Someone cuts right in front of me at the baggage claim, and I shoot them a look so fierce they push their

glasses up, apologize, and move aside. But right as I grab my suitcase, my breath gets caught in my throat at the sight ahead. Issac's
height helps him stand out in a crowd, but there will always be
something else. Something that makes it easy for me to find him
in a sea of other people.

Bernie is beside him with the body of a guard and a balding
head. He blocks people from approaching Issac with an obnoxious
shoo of his hands.

And there's no warning for the way my nerves spike. They
bubble under my skin and bring pinpricks with them. My mind
takes me to a time where everything was simpler: just me and Issac, two people with big dreams and a few dollars in our pockets,
who couldn't afford plane tickets to travel across the country and
little Rhode Island was all we'd ever known. But at least we had
each other. The loneliness of reality hits me like a wave and brings
me back to the present.

Will I ever stop missing the way things were before?

He turns his face the moment I think it, just enough for his
eyes to find mine, and it takes all of two seconds for him to excuse
himself from his fans to get to me. The windows from above douse
his skin in sunlight, and his smile is lopsided like he just finished a
plate of warm chicken parm. He's excited, I deduce.

But there's something else in his eyes too. A flicker of nerves.
A thread through his voice when he says, "Hi."

I tilt my head to search his face. "You didn't listen," I say.

He scratches the back of his neck, his smile growing wider.
"You knew I wouldn't."

"If you always do whatever you want, how will I ever trust
you to do what I want?" I hear myself ask, but his smile is contagious. It's so damn obnoxious.

"That's unfair. I care about what you want. I'll listen when I think you're right," he says.

I laugh. "That'll be about never."

"You're right. Sometimes." He shrugs. "But you weren't right about this."

Then, just like that, no one is staring or taking pictures. It's just us. In a bubble where everyone and everything else fall to the background. The worry sinks under the surface, and I'm in his arms and he's wrapping his around me tight. We don't need to make a show for the public because the love we share is authentic enough.

And . . . he doesn't pull back the way he did when he surprised me on my porch.

"I'm so glad you're here," he whispers into my hair. "Thank you for coming. I know you're nervous, but I'm with you."

I breathe in the scent of him: something like the ocean and firewood, forever changing a little, but always familiar like *home*. "I think I'll be okay," I say.

"Not if we don't get you out of this crowd," Bernie's voice comes from behind.

ISSAC'S SAGE-GREEN OLDSMOBILE PULLS UP IN FRONT OF LAX, AND Bernie gets in the front seat while we slide in the back. It's a pretty ride. Reconstructed from the engine up. The night he got it he FaceTimed to show me little details, but they were lost to the darkness. He used to dream of rebuilding an old car when he was driving a hooptie with a hole in its muffler around Providence, and now he's done it. I'm sure neither of us imagined it would look this good.

"For a while there, I wondered if you'd only drive cars fresh off the lot," I say, nudging him with my elbow.

He laughs. "Not as humble as J. Cole riding a bicycle around the city with these long ole legs, but I'm also not too bougie for a used car . . . shit, I'll even take the bus again."

It's my turn to laugh, and I'm not the only one. The driver, who Issac introduced as Tom, chuckles from the front seat, and Bernie says, "Ha. I'm going to pretend I didn't hear that."

"Let's pretend you're not even in this car," Issac jokes, "sound good, Bern buddy?"

I'm guessing Issac tried to come to the airport alone but Bernie decided to join for damage control. He grumbles something from the front seat about how Issac's worse than his two kids. I watch him put his headphones on and I try to picture him with children. Does he bring the grumpy face from Issac duties home with him?

"Pure nonsense," I agree, smiling at Issac. "You're definitely too bougie for the bus."

Issac sucks his teeth. "You're gonna diss me all weekend, huh?"

"Only half the time."

The rest of the way to where Issac's staying we talk about the bumpy plane ride and joke about what he wishes he would've eaten for breakfast instead of what Bernie made him eat. It's so regular, I almost can't tell there are nerves still buzzing between us because of a situation that's hard to forget with Tom glancing at us from the rearview like *he's* wondering why we're not doing whatever Hollywood couples do in back seats with a built-in audience up front. When we pull up to the house, Bernie and Tom both stay in the car, and Issac takes my bag from the trunk, then leads us up a small path toward the house. It's white, a

vintage-style home with terra-cotta-colored stucco stairs and
black metal railings along a patio. It's bigger than the one he
stayed in when I came to visit a year ago. And this time, we aren't
going to be playing video games and eating our weight in chicken
wings while staying out of the public eye. Now, I'm going to get a
front-row seat to what Issac's life is really like.

The house is immaculate, stainless steel in the kitchen and
wood everywhere else, oversized monstera in corners, open with
white walls. If Issac wanted to settle, I could see it being somewhere like this. The last one was sleek and black and looked very
designer. It had palm trees in the kitchen, which were a little over
the top, even though they were pretty.

"I can't believe the owners let you stay here," I say.

Issac shrugs. "Bernie makes the short-term arrangements, and
it helps that I showcase the houses on my socials. Gets the owners
more interest, but don't be fooled. They cost me big."

"I bet, Mr. Showcase."

He rolls his eyes, I poke him in the ribs.

"What's it going to be? A few weeks until you get bored and
hop around to the next? Wouldn't it be easier on your pockets to
just buy something? You can have whole rooms dedicated to your
art."

He starts climbing another staircase, and I'm still trying to
catch my breath from the first. "Do you like it?" he asks, ignoring
my question.

"It suits you. The wood, the green, how open it is."

He puts down my bags between two doors upstairs and smiles.
"Sounds like it suits *you*."

I bite back a smile, but my mind wanders a little. Issac treats
his living situation the way he treats his dating life. "Aren't you

tired of not having a place to call home? I mean, at least you've graduated from the expensive hotels you were staying at. But I'm worried about you not having somewhere solid."

What's his reason for not wanting to put down roots?

He examines me as if he was the one to ask the question, then says, "I'm hoping I figure all of that out soon." He nods his head toward one of the rooms. "That there is where I sleep . . ." He trails off, then touches the door in front of us. "Didn't know if you'd want to stay in this one?"

I think it's a joke, but he looks serious. "Wait," I say, clapping my hands together and trying to play it cool, "you get to sleep in my bed and hog the covers and drool on my pillows when you're home but I have to kick it in the cold guest room when I visit? Since when?"

His laughter can shift the walls, but there go those nerves in his eyes again. For a second, I imagine he stole a peek into my mind and found out about the sexy dream I had. Now he's feeling uncomfortable to share a bed with me. It's a wild thought, but I think it no less. Anxious until he snatches my bag off the floor, says, "You know what, you're right. Please drool on my pillows and leave me cold at night."

His words should ease the tension, but I quietly follow him, hoping I didn't just impose.

The room he's staying in has a skylight in the ceiling, and the balcony puts my front porch to shame. His tripod is set up by the dresser for filming, and one of the walls is covered in collages. There are plants hanging from the ceiling, candles everywhere. But the bed is simple, an oak platform like mine with a white down comforter folded up at the bottom.

"I mean, if you're uncomfortable with me sleeping with you

now that we're a *couple*," I say, running my hand over the softest gray sheets in existence, "the other end of the bed is far enough that you can pretend like I'm not even here."

"You talk so much shit. And I missed it. I missed you, Ni."

A relieved sigh escapes me. "It's only been a week, but I missed you too, big head."

He grins. "I know that. And you're the one with a big head."

I pick up a pillow, throw it at him. He ducks the first one but not the second before escaping to the bathroom. "Why are you hiding from me?"

"I gotta pee, woman!"

While he's in there, I search the room for hidden gems. He usually has books stacked on the floor, little findings on the nightstand: bottle caps with quotes he loves, notes Mom wrote him, things he collects for collages. Today, I find a ceramic jewelry dish on the nightstand and pick up the small gold ring sitting at the center. It's antique with a green stone and very familiar. I'm pretty sure Melinda was wearing it in a picture Katrina sent me once. I wonder why he still has it and if it means something that he keeps it this close to him. Does he miss her? A tight, fleeting feeling crosses my chest at the thought, and I reach up to touch the ring I'm wearing on a chain around my neck. A memory starts to form: me and Issac, this ring, a name bracelet, but before I can be swept up in it, someone clears their throat and startles me.

"Laniah," Bernie says, simply, nothing else. A warning or an announcement of his presence? Probably both. He sees the ring in my hand and a curious look passes over his face.

I put it back in the dish and open my mouth, but then Issac comes out of the bathroom.

"What's up, Bern? Told you to take the day off," he teases. "I don't need secondhand hate from your wife. She knows it's you who won't leave my side, right?"

"My wife knows there are no days off when it comes to you." Bernie doesn't sound bitter; he sounds like a parent proved right. He holds his phone out, and Issac takes it. Tension clouds the room. There's a frown on Issac's face while he reads.

Several seconds later, he passes the phone to me.

15

ON AN EMPTY STOMACH

MAY THEY ALL GO TO HELL," LEX SAYS, AND I CAN HEAR HIM slam a rickety old cabinet at the shop. I didn't mean to call him on a bad day when he was already fighting with his boyfriend, who he claims is acting like a *know-it-all with a superiority complex*. Yet here we are.

"Don't break the cabinet," I say. "We can't afford to fix anything right now."

"Why am I madder about your situation than you are?"

The situation: Paparazzi took pictures of me leaving the hotel yesterday. There are already three articles out about me working as a maid, two of them said I looked "rough." To be fair, I had stains from spilled yogurt on my uniform, my hair was in a haphazard bun, and my eyes were red rimmed after crying in the bathroom about leaving Bridget. But "rough" was nothing compared to the questions less reputable sites raised. How will being with Issac help Laniah's life? Is Laniah with Issac because she needs the money? One that didn't do their research questioned:

Was Issac Jordan pretending he was into Melinda Martinez to hide a relationship with Laniah Thompson because he's ashamed of the way the latter lives?

Oh, the meta of it all.

Issac and Bernie are discussing the situation inside, and I was sick of hearing them say *damage control* and *It's going to be fine*, so I came out to the patio for fresh air and to be mad with Lex. Except I'm not that mad anymore. "Because I've been through every emotion," I tell him, "including feeling utterly creeped out that they were watching me, and I didn't even notice. Now I'm numb. But I am mad for *you*, even though you won't tell me what Shane did to piss you off."

"He laughed at me during game night with his friends, reexplained the rules, and was all *Got it now, babe?* It's not my fault they play Magic: The Gathering. How will I ever understand?"

"I'll never understand Magic," I say. "But I can kick Shane's ass if you want me to. One of his doctor friends will have to give him some stitches."

"Please do," Lex says. "And I swear if anyone says anything about you in the shop today, I'm going to fight them in the parking lot."

"Rip some hair out so they need to come back for our growth products."

"You're a genius." He laughs. "Anyway, I have to go help your mom with this electric mixer we bought. You know how she is with new things and anything that plugs into a socket."

When we hang up, Issac finds me standing by the edge of the patio. My curls are pulled by the wind, and he looks like he'll reach for one. But he doesn't.

"I went live on my socials to remind my followers I literally grew up poor and had to work *hard jobs* before this ever became my life," he says. "Told them it doesn't matter how much money you have in your pockets or what you do for a living, I'll love you regardless." He sighs a tired sound. "Damn, kindness is free."

I turn to look at him, trying to smile. I know what he's saying is true, but wonder if Bernie is upset about me coming here with articles about me being a gold digger attached to Issac's image. I'm not ashamed of where I worked; working as a maid brought me to Bridget and helped keep food in my stomach, but it isn't exactly what the media considers a glamorous job. The articles are one thing; I bet they're running me ragged on social media.

"Don't give me that fake smile," he says. "You don't have to pretend with me. Being stalked by paparazzi is jarring. Especially the first time. And those articles were fucked-up. I wasn't expecting that."

He looks sincere, and I realize that we're both from a different world than this one. No matter how long Issac has been under public scrutiny, there might be times where he's naive to its harshness. The numbness begins to melt, and I reach for a hug on my own. He accepts me, wraps his arms around my body, and I try not to look for differences in his embrace.

———————

ISSAC ASKS ME ONLY ONCE WHAT I'M IN THE MOOD TO EAT, AND AS soon as I say, "Umm," he tells his driver where to go. Something about the way he takes initiative causes the fantasy to materialize in my mind: him standing in my door and knowing exactly what I'd like. Suddenly, I have to keep from squirming while sitting beside him, face hot, hormones battling in my body.

Dream him and real him aren't the same man. And I need to forget dream him exists.

When we show up at a small spot instead of a restaurant with celebrity-level fine dining, I smile. "Should I be offended that you don't want to be seen with me at a place where servers refill our glasses with vintage wine and feed us grapes while fanning us? What if they call me a cheap date and a gold digger all in one breath?"

"You're annoying," Issac teases. "We can go to a fancy spot if you want. I'll ask Bernie to make a reservation. Lord knows he'd prefer I go somewhere like that anyway. But I'm sorry to tell you there won't be grape feeding. That's mostly for television, I'm afraid."

"I just don't want you to change the way you usually do things for me," I say. "If you think I can't handle it because of the articles . . ."

"Stop right there," he says. "This isn't about any of that, I just want a few hours of being with my best friend. The real me and the real you."

"Okay," I breathe out. Then: "How do you always know just what to say?"

Issac gives me a sly smirk. "Could be that I've known you most of my life, could be that I'm smooth like that. It's probably both."

I roll my eyes and shove him against the door. He pulls my hair, and I twist his beard. Tom clears his throat from the front seat, and we stop acting like children. I almost forgot we weren't alone while my heart was thrumming at the familiarity of being playful with Issac.

He gets out of the car and walks around to open my door. "This beautiful spot has the best pho in town," he says. "It might not be as good as your favorite from Four Seasons back home, but I think you'll approve of the nime chow, and I might just let you eat mine too."

My cheeks hurt from smiling. "Alright, alright. You're a pretty good best friend and, so far, an excellent fake boyfriend."

"Shh. Even the streetlights have cameras." I look up at them, and he laughs. "Just kidding . . . I think. But I am an excellent boyfriend, huh?"

"You are," I say. "Melinda must have really enjoyed those dates."

The moment my words land, Issac's face falls. I open my mouth. To say what? I don't know. But then his phone begins to vibrate. Seeing that mentioning Melinda affects him this much gives me that same uncomfortable sting I felt finding her ring on his nightstand. I make a note to avoid that topic while he stares down at his screen.

"Shit. It's Josh," he says.

The things I know about Josh: he's one of the youngest directors in Hollywood, he has an orange tabby cat he named Orange, and he has grown closer to Issac in these past few months when I've felt farther.

"I may have mentioned where we were eating earlier," Issac admits with a sheepish look on his face, "and now he's heading here to eat with us and bringing his . . . I think she's his girlfriend. He has a new *serious* relationship every other month. I can't keep track. Anyway, do you want to leave? We can find someplace else."

The hermit crab in me wants to hide behind the building, go back to Issac's place and order delivery, but now I'm hungry for pho and I think whether I'm Issac's best friend or his pretend girlfriend, it's probably time I meet other people in his life. "No, it's okay. It'll be good," I say.

Issac raises both eyebrows. "Good? You sure? I was talking all that stuff about the real you and the real me and . . . I don't want to overwhelm you already. Tomorrow might be a lot."

"It'll be good," I repeat. "But we may have to order an appe-tizer before Josh gets here because I'm about to get *hangry*. I can feel it."

"Of course." He pushes me toward the entrance of the restau-rant. "Can't have my girl out here trying to rip off my head over an empty stomach."

———————

JOSH HAS PRETTY GREEN EYES AND THAT CALIFORNIA LOOK I'VE seen on TV, as if he's rolled out of bed just to spend the entire day on a surfboard in the hot sun, tired but in that incredible kind of way. The woman holding his hand is completely opposite, in a blazer and jeans with pink heels for a pop of color and a slick ponytail.

Before Josh moves to hug Issac, he acknowledges my exis-tence.

"Oh man, Laniah, the pictures do you no justice. You're even more stunning in person."

His girlfriend looks completely unfazed by this comment, and because he doesn't sound like a creepy uncle or a slimeball, I'm flattered. "Thank you, I'm sure. Especially if you saw the pictures in those articles that went up earlier or any candid shot Issac's taken of me."

Josh tilts his head and smiles. "I don't know, I think you looked perfectly beautiful in every single picture I've seen of you on Issac's end. And even in those untoward articles."

Issac raises the siracha on the table and uses it to point at Josh. "Don't be flirting with my girl while your girl is on your arm. Don't flirt with my girl at all, please."

I smash my elbow into Issac's side, my cheeks warming. He's

so ridiculous. But Josh's girlfriend laughs and says, "I'm not mad. She's a gorgeous woman."

"Thank you," I say, smiling, "and I swear this isn't compliment because of compliment, but you're stunning."

She flips her ponytail like she knows it. "I'm Lauren. Since Josh didn't introduce me."

"She's Lauren," Josh says, and kisses her cheek. "Sorry, babe."

"I'm happy to meet you both," I tell them.

"Finally," Josh says, sitting across from us with Lauren following. "Issac has kept you hidden from the world. Then he brings you to a place like this on your first day in town."

My stomach sinks even further for two reasons. (1) *A place like this* feels like it has a certain belittling connotation. It might've been too soon to be flattered by anything Josh says. (2) My joke about Issac taking me somewhere out of the public eye might have been warranted.

Issac must see the tension on my face because he clears his throat. But Josh beats him to it. "Though, I must admit Issac has the best taste in food. And all of us would've been starving, eating from those tiny plates at Lasheá."

"He does have great taste," I agree, and though I'm still suspicious about Issac's taste in new friends, I'm feeling the need to defend him. "Besides, being somewhere quiet feels like a relief after what happened today."

Issac's eyes flick to mine, and I wonder if he's just as surprised about me admitting that to strangers as I am.

Lauren cuts in with an eager nod of the head, says, "Oh, we definitely get that. Listen, when I first started hanging with Josh, it was a shit show. I like attention, but not the kind I got." She winks at me. "If you ever need someone to vent to, I'm here. And

honestly, those articles about where you work will blow over in a
few days."

I don't clarify that I no longer work at the hotel because I refuse to look ashamed in front of rich folk. But I do decide I like
Lauren already.

––––––––

THE BOARDWALK IS BRIGHTENED BY FAIRY LIGHTS, AND THE NIGHT
air gives way to the smell of salt water when the wind blows, but
I'm feeling fatigue's greedy fingers trying to coax me to get some
sleep soon. I ignore them. Back at the restaurant, we all picked off
of one another's plates. Josh told three bad jokes in a row, Lauren
attempted to get me to eat the squid tentacles, and I softened up to
the idea that they're just normal people who happen to be in the
spotlight, same as Issac. Lauren went with me to the bathroom
like Katrina would've, she adjusted my dress straps so that my
titties were *sitting pretty*, and we took a picture in the mirror she
asked permission to post. Josh wasn't caught off guard by my
smart remarks or the banter between me and Issac, he showed me
the cutest cat pics, and he seemed genuine in his kindness to the
waitress when she gave him the wrong order, which was when I
decided to stop imagining I wouldn't mesh well with the people in
Issac's new world.

While we walk, we make comfortable conversation about the
new movie Josh is directing, Issac modeling in upcoming Fall Fashion Week, and Lauren just landing a crazy commission on the seven-
million-dollar house she sold. And it feels nice to tell them about
Wildly Green, how it's a dream to create the way Mom and I do.

A big wave crashes on the shoreline, catching my attention,
and I turn to rest against a railing. I'm happy to be here, to see the

perfectly halved moon in the sky and the dark water with its rolling waves in this place Issac might make *home* for real someday.
He pulls out his phone and takes a picture of me, says the shadows
were complimenting my face, and I don't tell him not to post it.

Josh smiles. "Issac tried to convince me the two of you were
only friends. I kept bothering him about it. How can you be that
close, for so many years, and have no romantic feelings?"

My stomach tightens. Even though I'm used to this line of
questioning, something about hearing it now, and from Issac's
friend, makes me question whether it's normal that he's never had
feelings for me. He calls me beautiful, but that doesn't mean he's
attracted to me. Would I care if he admitted he wasn't?

"Guess he was just lying to me the whole time," Josh says,
saving me from my thoughts.

But then Issac's hand finds mine. "I think I was lying to myself, but I'm happy I finally figured it out," he says.

His words make my heartbeat stutter, and something different
happens to my body when he rubs the pad of my thumb with his.
This is not the way he used to touch me, not the affection I had
been missing; it's something more. Each time his skin meets mine,
it feels like something inside of me is going to burst. I fight the
urge to pull away from him, to stop this big feeling in my chest,
but Lauren's still watching.

"Y'all are most definitely, absolutely too cute," she says just as
Josh wraps his arms around her.

But I'm too busy trying to catch my breath to say something back.

———————

AT THE HOUSE, I TAKE AN IBUPROFEN FOR THE HEADACHE SETTING
in and stare at the bottle of Prozac sitting on the sink. There's an

achy pain on the right side of my lower back (the "flank" area according to Google) and it might be my body reacting to nerves, but I haven't started the Prozac because I've been nervous it'll cause symptoms. I hear Mom's reassuring voice in my head, her telling me not to feed a vicious anxiety circle before I open the bottle for the first time.

When I go back into the bedroom, Issac's taping a clip of the menu from the restaurant we were at to the wall. He looks shy, I caught him in the act, but he doesn't say anything. Just slides into bed and grabs his notebook from the nightstand. He always writes before bed, but he never lets me see. There's soft jazz music playing from his record player, and his broad chest is bare. I avert my eyes before he notices me enjoying the view, because well . . . he can't notice that.

I shouldn't have noticed his smooth skin or the rigid lines leading to his torso.

Since when are his nipples sexy?

I climb in bed, curl up next to him, trying to see what he's writing and trying harder to ignore the smell of shea butter after he showered and how fresh my dream about him feels tonight. He shoves me away so I can't see a single word. I talk shit, begging for a peek, but I'm too tired to fight when I lay my head back on the pillow.

"Despite the online messiness, today was easy," I tell him.

He looks at me for a long while, then runs his pencil along the skin of my forearm, eliciting the sweetest shiver. And he's the one to sigh.

"It's always easy," I can hear him say before sleep finds me.

16

PEOPLE ARE MAGNETS TOO

'M DRIPPING WITH SWEAT AT SIX THIRTY IN THE MORNING. NOT THE
cute trickle-on-the-forehead kind, the shirt-soaked, in-need-of-
a-shower-before-seeing-another-soul kind of sweat. I tried to run
today. It was a horrible experience. I probably looked silly out there,
worse than silly when I had to pull out my inhaler to take several
puffs as the real runners cruised on by. But when I woke up with
nagging flank pain and a racing heart, I decided to make exercise
a consistent thing to lower my chances of developing heart disease
like my dad and help with worrying over it. Issac had already
gone to meet with his trainer, so I couldn't join him in the gym.
Hopefully my effort today counted for something. Though I'm
not sure I'll ever become a runner. I'd rather hike through a forest
with a demanding Lex, who barely breaks a sweat, than attempt
that form of exercise again.

Back at Issac's, I make us both smoothies and smile at my ac-
complishment. By the look on his face when he walks through the

door, I can tell he's pleasantly pleased. Or maybe that's shock I see. I'll take it either way.

"Since when do you wake up early?" he asks, putting his gym bag down and examining me. "Wait. Did you work out? What's going on with you today?"

"I'm changing for the better," I say, sticking out my tongue. "And now you don't have to drag me out of bed to be a cheerleader at your photo shoot."

He sighs. "Yeah, well, you might still have to rush. My shoot got moved up to nine a.m."

"That's two hours from now. Don't tell me the frown on your face is because it'll take you longer than that to make yourself pretty," I tease. But then realize Issac is seeing me drenched and gross, hair in a huge messy bun at the top of my head, probably looking like I'm close to death after attempting a mile and barely making it a half. I wrap my arms around myself, unwrap. Remind myself this is Issac and he's encountered my morning breath more than my ex-boyfriend ever had.

"You'll insult me till the end of time regardless of how I answer," he says before snatching the portable blood pressure cuff off the counter. Mom sent me with it, and I forgot to put it away. "You're recording your blood pressure again? Thought you had it under control."

I take the machine from him, attempting to jam it into the little bag it came with. Why do they make them so small? Issac comes over, pushes me aside, and uses that patience of his to put the cuff back in the bag.

"Evasive is one of your cute quirks, until it's not," he says. "Are your meds not working?"

I lean against the counter, pick up my smoothie, and take a sip. Immediately regretting my decision to add spinach. I wonder if I can dump Issac's in the sink before he tries it.

"Ni, I'm waiting."

"You're a persistent prick," I joke. "But I'm still having headaches, and my blood pressure is up and stuff."

"And stuff?"

"Yes, let me finish." Another sip makes my throat thick and grainy. I shift away so he doesn't notice me gag. How does he drink these daily? "I've been getting dizzy here and there," I say, "so my doctor told me to keep track of the readings for a few weeks and report back. Other than that, everything's looking great. I'm mostly trying the whole healthy thing to help with my anxious brain and because . . . you know, because of my dad."

Issac's eyes soften before he takes my smoothie from my hand and sips on it. His face twists, he spits in the sink. "These are the kinds of things you don't keep from me," he says. "I could help. Starting with teaching you how to make a proper smoothie. This is disgusting. Did you use garlic or something?"

I cover my mouth to hide my smile. "You're so damn overbearing, which is why I waited to tell you. You'll probably be checking my blood pressure yourself the rest of my stay."

The joke doesn't land. His face grows serious, he puts the cup down and moves toward me. "You wait to tell me too many things, Ni," he says. "I hope you break that habit, for my sake. I don't want to be kept in the dark. Please try?"

Issac's never pushed me on this before. Not even after my dad died and I found it even harder to tell him what was on my mind. He takes another step. We're only inches apart. I could reach up and touch the Adam's apple in his neck.

"I'll try," I whisper into the space between us.

He brushes a loose curl from my shoulder; my skin tingles where his fingers touched me. "Thank you."

I wonder if he can hear my heart race as he stares into my eyes.

I hope he can't tell that I'm documenting each time he avoids touching me and each time he doesn't.

I'm finally able to breathe when he backs away.

"Overbearing, huh?" he says with a smile. "Wait until I start steering you away from all that pho you've been eating. I doubt that much salt is good for your blood pressure."

I laugh. "Don't start."

"I'm going to start and finish. Just like I always do."

THE FIRST AND LAST TIME I WAS AT A SHOOT WITH ISSAC HE WAS UP-and-coming, but they treated him with so much respect I was astonished. I'd watched him ask for scraps of attention from his foster parents throughout our childhood, and all they ever did was complain about him bringing *so much junk* into their house to do his artwork. The people working the shoot we're at today treat him like he's a legend, looking for his attention at every turn. They let him set up his tripod to record clips for his followers. They pamper him, laugh too loud, and smile too much. Others seek his opinion: Is the furniture arranged right? How does the lighting work for your skin tone? It's like the shoot is his vision and everyone else is only here to make that vision come alive. But even though his artistic instincts kick in while working, even though he always fights to control his own narrative, he's so kind. He looks people in the eyes, is a well of pleasantries, remembers everyone's name, asks the stylist who's dressing him how her aging parents are doing and wants to see pictures of her dog.

Issac is a magnet made from star matter and ocean reef, plant soil and old magic. Everyone in the room pulls toward him, including me.

As soon as the shoot starts, my throat grows thicker. When he's in his element like this, zoned out and in front of a camera, that ethereal energy about him becomes magnified. There are things the world doesn't know about his life, but it doesn't matter because he wears everything he is on his skin, and it gives him the beauty of the sun.

Seeing the way his love of art translates to the work he does here makes me appreciate it for him even more. I feel the sting of tears in my eyes remembering all the nights we spent lying on my old front lawn when we were kids, dreaming of futures in different dimensions. We were thirteen and he wanted to be an actor to my math teacher, the president to my writer, an astronaut to my florist. We were fourteen and he had just found a love of watercolor and scrapbooking through our freshman art class. We were fifteen and he was dreaming of what his future home might look like with a longing in his voice because he had been living in a house that never felt like his. Without caring parents to guide and love him, a boy having to be a man early. And then there was me. Trying to hold on to the family I did have, wanting nothing more than to stay in the small apartment my mom and dad made a home. My dreams were of rooting myself forever to my old bedroom, remaining a child there, building a time machine between four walls so that life could be the way it was before my dad got sick.

But things changed, we grew up, and Issac was eighteen, waiting for Burger King checks to keep his cell phone on because maybe . . . maybe one of his videos making art on the internet would take off and he'd get paid for his content. And I was still beside him, wishing and praying and hoping that the magic I had always seen in his eyes could pour out of him, touch the earth, and give him everything he ever wanted and never stopped believing he could have. Until dreaming things for him made me start dreaming for myself again. And I realized all I had to do was tell my mom that her love had become mine too.

I'm so caught up with the memories, the tangible evidence that Issac made magic out of his life, and that I might be on my way to making magic out of mine, that when a woman with glistening skin walks in from hair and makeup, I don't even notice who it is at first.

But Issac does.

17

THE MOMENT WE MET

MELINDA." ISSAC'S VOICE IS BREATHY, SO LOW I WOULD'VE thought I was mistaken if it weren't for how he's looking at her. Who could blame him? She has perfectly square, perfectly white painted toes, and is wearing a nude silk dress that hugs her frame. A single diamond hangs around her slender neck. Issac blinks, glances at his manager, Bernie, then back to her. "Wait, you're the model I'm working with?"

She crosses her arms over her chest, pouts a little but doesn't look at him. "No one told him I was on the shoot? What's wrong with you people?"

I slowly scoot back in the chair I'm sitting in, consider just how small I can make myself.

Bernie claps his hands together. "What's the problem? You're both adults here. This is an industry. Work. Nothing more."

Issac gives him a warning look—right before Bernie pulls him to the side. I can hear bits and pieces: Issac asking why he wasn't alerted, who thought it was a good idea, something about a Christian and my name and my name again and then *Melinda agreed to this?*

The coil in my gut grows tighter. Is Issac using our fake relationship as an excuse not to work with Melinda? Does he not want to see her? The articles questioning if I'm a gold digger pop into my mind again, and I sink farther into the cushion. Did Bernie set this up to show Issac he should be with someone like Melinda instead?

"Listen, it's not a big deal. It was an honest slip of the mind," he says, no longer whispering. "Just do the shoot. We'll make sure you're both alerted next time."

Issac keeps his composure, turns, and walks over to Melinda, who isn't doing as well holding hers. He says something to her that I wish I could hear and I'm happy I can't. When Melinda no longer looks like she wants to take someone's head off, there is audible relief from the crew. But I'm conscious of every bone in my body, every breath that I exhale, every muscle I try not to move. Maybe if I'm still enough, I'll go without being noticed.

The director doesn't need to give Melinda or Issac any instructions on how to be positioned. They know what they're doing. This is how they met; this is how they found out they have chemistry. The position of their tangled bodies is so compromising, so damn sexy, that I can't look away. They are striking together, matching the other's moves with fluidity. And Issac doesn't look like an accessory next to her the way most male models do.

It looks easy for them.

Last night, Issac traced his pencil over my forearm. *It's always easy,* he whispered. Now my stomach clenches when he pulls Melinda closer to him, touches her cheek. I don't know what I'm feeling, but I don't like it at all. When Melinda runs her fingers through Issac's hair, I wonder if she smells my products on him. I wonder if she thinks it's soft. I wonder if being in a fake relationship with me is going to stop Issac from trying to commit to the relationship he should probably be in. Melinda's tall enough that she doesn't have to tiptoe to press her lips against the underside of Issac's chin. It's for a picture, but my mind says I'm interrupting a private moment of a reconciliation. Passion I've never witnessed in person before. Until Issac turns slightly and catches my eyes. His shoulders tense, and he puts the slightest distance between him and Melinda. I'm still small, still stiff, still trying to figure out why I'm feeling like this. Throughout the years, I've witnessed Issac kissing girls and holding hands while going on dates, but I'm not quite sure it's ever made my heart race.

Melinda must notice Issac's distraction because she finds me across the room. She seems perfectly poised, but the photographer says something to her twice before she hears it.

Issac tears his eyes away from me and pulls Melinda flush against him to finish the shoot.

I can't watch anymore. I need to get up, to move, to not be in this space. I don't know the whole story about what happened between them—Issac says it was casual and mutual—but I saw the look in Melinda's eyes. The hurt that I caused by being here, and I'm not the type to want to hurt another woman on purpose.

THIS IS THE FANCIEST BATHROOM I'VE EVER SEEN. THE MIRRORS ARE oversized vanities, and there are lush couches and pink chairs in the corners. I splash water on my face, feeling silly. Issac and I've been close for over a decade, and one weekend of pretending can't change that. I hear Lex's voice in my head, teasing before I left

Rhode Island, *You're going to fall for him*, but I don't want to fall for anyone, to feel like I'm being dropped into something without my control, and the last thing I want is to do is feel out of control with Issac. That's not what's happening here. This is because I've been celibate for too long. This is the body. A trick of the mind. My heart is still safe. And I'll be okay. But will Issac? What if he realizes that he does want to make it work with Melinda and now he's stuck with me for the summer?

Because fate is funny that way, the bathroom door swings open and there she is. Wide-eyed and gorgeous. We stare for a few seconds, the sink water still running. "I'm sorry, I was just . . ." I shake my head, shut off the water. Why would I apologize for using a bathroom she doesn't own? "Excuse me," I say.

She steps aside to let me through the door, and when my back is to her, she finally speaks. "You don't have to worry about me, girl."

I stop moving, but by the time I turn to ask what she means, she's already walking toward the stalls.

Issac's propped against the wall across from the bathroom when I come out. He's changed back into the clothes he came with, and his lips are set in a straight line. "I've been looking for you," he says. "Wondered if you were in there. I saw Melinda head in and . . ."

A smile starts to tease at the corners of my lips. I cock an eyebrow at him. "You thought I needed your protection? Even though I know jujitsu?"

He laughs, then nods his head for us to start walking toward the front of the building. I pretend like I don't notice him glancing back to the bathroom door, checking for Melinda.

"I know you can fight," he says. "Remember when you almost

knocked me out in ninth grade after I put that glue in your hair by accident?"

"You claim it was an accident."

"It was," he says. Then: "For real, everything alright in there?"

"Actually, no, she pushed me into the sink, and I was about to rip out those pretty-ass eyelashes she's wearing, but then she started to cry," I say. "Her mascara was running, and I just couldn't bring myself to give her a real black eye."

"Woof. Saucy." Issac clicks his tongue against the roof of his mouth. The sun is bright above us when we make it to the parking lot. "So the two of you didn't talk in there at all, then?"

"Not really," I say. "Why, would that have been weird?"

"I mean, no but . . ." He stops on the sidewalk, rubs under his eye with his thumb. "Well, maybe a little."

"I get it," I say, and find a random car to stare at. Does everyone that works here own Cadillacs? "The *could've been girlfriend* you're not over surprising you on a shoot while your *pretend girlfriend* is there. Plain weird. She's really stunning too. I mean, damn . . . how's someone that beautiful in real life?" When I finally turn back to Issac, his brows are almost touching. "What'd I say wrong?"

He shakes his head, a distant look in his eyes. "Yeah, she's a beautiful woman."

An awkward silence sets in after he says it, and I'm stricken by just how many of them we've had in the last few months. They're becoming even more frequent now that we're tied together in a lie.

Finally, Issac clears his throat. "Are you okay?"

I tilt my head to look up at him. "Why wouldn't I be?"

His bottom lip flicks out, he licks it, I track the movement.

Accidentally. "Well, I didn't know if it was weird seeing me and Melinda together like that. . . . You left so abruptly."

I blow out a breath, bite my own bottom lip because I'm annoyingly conscious of his right now. "Are you asking if I was jealous?"

"No, no." He shakes his head, smiles. "I mean . . . Why would you be jealous? That's crazy. Wait . . . *were* you jealous?"

The curiosity in his voice makes me laugh a little. But the truth is I was jealous. Because Issac and I aren't romantic, but he had always felt like *my* Issac . . . until he told me he might be able to see himself with Melinda, and the little ways things were already changing between us became more noticeable. Seeing them together today reminded me of feelings I've tried to repress. It's already enough that we live across the country and distance keeps us from being the way we once were. What if he decides to commit to a relationship with her, with anyone, and I lose him for real?

"I wasn't prepared," I tell him, so I don't have to say any of the other stuff. "I didn't know how to react as your public girlfriend, being put in that situation out of nowhere. Should I have been acting jealous? Or playing it cool? You know I'm not an actor and just . . . I'm sorry if it was embarrassing." Before he can speak, I add, "But what about you? Have you realized you're missing her more than you can handle?"

I see something shift in his eyes. He stares at me for a while, then says, "You're infuriating sometimes. And oblivious. The most oblivious human on earth."

"What?" I jerk my head back, surprised. "Why are you saying that?"

He laughs again, rubs his face with his hands, then slings his arm around my shoulder. "Never mind. Just know that you didn't do anything wrong at the shoot. What's embarrassing is Bernie putting us in that situation. Which is why we're ditching him for the rest of the day."

Issac wasn't lying, he shoots Bernie a text then shuts off his phone. I hop in the front seat, a rush of excitement running through my body like we're doing something we really shouldn't be doing.

"Is Tom going to take an Uber?" I ask when we leave his driver out on the curb.

Concern passes over Issac's face for no more than a second. "He'll go find Bernie in the building and catch a ride with him. They both need a day off. And so do I," he says.

18

THE SUN FINDING ME

SANTA MONICA PIER IS PACKED WITH PEOPLE, BUT ISSAC AND I came dressed like tourists to fit in properly. He has on a bucket hat, colorful glasses, a Surfs Up T-shirt, and orange swishy shorts. I'm wearing a jean jumper, white skippics, and a short black wig that I might take to Rhode Island. At the ticket booth, he confesses that this adventure is mostly for him. "No one ever wants to do these kinds of things with me out here," he says.

I could leave it, but I'm curious. "Not even Melinda?"

"Especially not Melinda." He laughs while we walk through the entrance, and I watch him place our tickets in his wallet. The action fills me with a small joy. Later, he'll use them in a collage to remember us cramming ourselves into seats for every kiddie ride in the park, sharing a cotton candy the size of my head, spending entirely too much time competing at the water gun race.

We play balloon darts, and after Issac loses for the seventh time, he convinces the employee to let him buy me a stuffed animal.

I hug my polar bear under my arm while we walk. "You're a cheat."

He shrugs and picks a flower from a pot on the ground, pockets it. "This is our first real fake date, can't go out like that because they made the games impossible to beat."

"But I won you something."

Issac's got a stuffed frog hanging from the top of his shirt. I flick it.

"Oh, this?" he says. "*You* cheated to get it. You weren't standing behind the white line when you threw the dart. I tried to alert the employees with my eyes, but I could tell they felt bad for you."

"Boy, shut up," I say, and pull him toward the Ferris wheel.

By a miracle, we almost make it through the whole park before someone sees through Issac's disguise. He's about to get pulled in for a picture when I propose that we run for our lives. He laughs and laces our fingers, and we take off through the crowd. Once we reach the boardwalk, we catch our breath and dip into a souvenir shop to buy palm tree key chains for Mom, a lighter with Harry Styles on it for Lex, and an oversized T-shirt with the words YOU WISH YOU COULD printed across the middle for Kat. Issac insists on buying me a hermit crab with a yellow shell and a yellow tank and has the man behind the counter fill it with artificial plants.

The sun is starting to set when we reach the beach. He pulls me through white sand, toward the water.

"Make a wish," he says, picking up several seashells. I think of Wildly Green while I blow on them, and he throws them into the water.

"Your turn for a wish," I say.

His eyes crinkle at the corners. "I already made one."

A wind blows in from the sea and my belly does a somersault

wondering if his wish had something to do with me. But why would it?

I wiggle my brows at him. "You want to go skinny dipping?"

He looks like he's considering it before we see a small crowd coming toward us. They might not have noticed Issac, but we run for the car anyway. I'm exhausted, the afternoon fatigue hitting my bones, but this is the most fun we've had in so long. I know that I miss Wildly Green, miss home, but wonder how much I'll miss him after summer ends and we're back to trying a cross-country friendship again.

I wrap a seat belt around my hermit crab tank and tell it to be safe on the drive, then climb up front with Issac. He brings the top down on his Oldsmobile as he heads for the freeway, and then we just drive. I slide out of my shoes and sit cross-legged, enjoying the smell of sea and wet sand on our skin. Issac takes videos of my feet on the dash and me in his glasses and says he loves the way the sun finds me.

"If we didn't have to go to the listening party, I'd want to do only this for the rest of the night," he says. "But I'm excited you'll get to meet Shida."

I dance in my seat, squealing at the thought that *the* Shida Anala will be recording a new song at an infamous studio, and I will be sitting right there.

"I'm not even nervous," I say. "Maybe the hermit in me has gone."

Issac laughs. "We'll see for how long."

"GET THAT SMUG LOOK OFF YOUR FACE," I SAY.

"This is just my normal face," says Issac. We've been back at the condo for two hours, and I've spent all 120 minutes of them asking him how much I'd hate myself if we ditched the listening party and stayed home to eat pizza. "There is no *we* on this one, Ni. I'm going. I'll be swaying to her music by myself. Feel free to stay here and order takeout."

I get behind him while he adjusts his outfit. "Seriously? You'd be cool with that?"

"No," he says, eyeing me from the mirror. "You're going with me. End of story."

A warmth pools in my stomach at the serious look on his face. Still, I sulk. "You're not my daddy."

He fixes the collar on his shirt, a hint of a smile crossing his lips, and if I didn't know any better I'd swear he was thinking, *But I could be.*

I turn from the mirror, wishing away my wild imagination with a deep breath. Franklin the hermit crab is on the nightstand. I poke his shell to make sure he's still alive before agonizing over what to wear. The ridiculous number of outfits Lex and Katrina helped me pack aren't even outfits anymore. They are pieces I can't put together, that won't look good enough. Issac picks the black dress up off the bed by its straps. I tell him I'll be overdressed, and he insists there's no such thing around here. "Don't be surprised if you see someone in a ball gown tonight."

"But you look so . . . regular," I say.

Issac glances down at his outfit with a frown. "Thanks, I guess."

"You know what I mean, big head." He's wearing black cargo pants with a soft-pink designer-print shirt that has an embroidered flower over the breast pocket. He's also wearing it open, revealing a slice of his dark chest and the two delicate gold chains that sit there. He throws on a jean jacket and hikes his My Hero

Academia socks up high. The outfit looks perfectly put together and completely casual all at once. It took him zero effort to get ready, just like in high school when he'd manage with what little his foster family passed down, and whatever my mom could afford to buy him. Meanwhile, he sits on the bed and watches me scramble, going in and out of the bathroom and trying on four different outfits for him. Each time he says *That looks perfect*, I groan and take it off.

The cycle repeats until he reaches to touch my side, asks, "Can you tell me what's wrong?"

Seconds pass. Then, "What if I said I'm nervous everybody will be scrutinizing me because I'm your . . . girl?" My cheeks flush at the word. Issac sucks his bottom lip. "Especially after you had someone like Melinda on your arm. And with the articles out, you know people there might be able to tell that I nickeled and dimed it to put whatever I wear together. How will you feel if they say something?" I hate how insecure I sound. It's only ever been this bad in high school when I didn't know how to make my thrifted outfits look as cool as Issac did.

But he responds by wrapping his arms around my waist, pulling me closer to where he's sitting on the bed. When he rests his forehead against my stomach, it sends an image to my brain: us like this, but my belly big and round.

I stiffen in his embrace, suddenly short of breath. Where the hell did that come from? Issac aside, I don't even know if I want kids. What's wrong with me?

"I wish you wouldn't worry," he finally says. "You're one of the best dressers I know. Nickels and dimes get you on the same level, or further than most of them, and they have stylists to help. Even Melinda has a stylist."

His words make my heart return to a nearly normal rhythm. I take a chance and look down at him. "Yeah?"

He smiles, and says, "Ni, you could look like laundry day, and I'd still think you were the baddest there."

"Now you're just being silly." I laugh and push him, thankful for the space that follows.

He's quiet for a second, and I wonder if he feels something shifting between us too. He runs his fingers over the fabric of my green dress on his bed. "This feels smooth. And it's my favorite color. Wear this one."

I can almost hear Katrina and Lex squealing. "You sure it's not too fancy?"

He stands and towers over me, giving me a great view of the defined lines of his neck. "Get your fine ass in the bathroom and put it on. We're going to be late."

19

MOONLIT AURAS AND RISKY THINGS

WE GET DROPPED OFF AT THE LISTENING PARTY A HALF hour late, which Issac says is standard, and we're more punctual than we would've been at a cookout back home, but it still feels *too* late. There are dozens of ready paparazzi who take pictures of us. Issac hugs me close and poses willingly for the onslaught. The whole time my stomach is in knots. It's worse when we walk into the loft. I wasn't expecting to see so many people. The lights are dim in the oversized open kitchen, and there's a bartender at the island in the middle serving drinks. People are standing by the windows, dancing and swaying to the music. They see Issac, but they seem to focus on me. Issac simply laces our fingers and pulls me through the crowd. I'm barely breathing, time slipping somewhere behind us, I smile, nod, shake hands; my heart races. These are Issac's people, they aren't fans, but there are a lot of them.

When we get a second to ourselves, I whisper, "Some of them won't stop staring."

Issac's quiet for a moment, but his eyes trace the length of me, lingering on my midsection before making it back to my face. He licks his lips and leans in close. "I'm convinced anything you wear will have them staring," he says, "but this dress . . . that body. Your hips."

Heat flicks across my chest. I can't believe he just said that. But he pulls back enough to meet my eyes and there's no denying the daring glint in his. He's testing me, wondering how I'll respond. For a moment I consider what would happen if I answered by kissing his lips. In the next moment, I think he might like it.

Thankfully, someone calls our names from behind and breaks the challenge brewing between us.

"You made it," Lauren says, glamorous as ever as she pushes her way through the crowd. She hugs me and points to Josh in the corner of the room. I'm happy to see familiar faces, and happier that Lauren is chatty. Better to distract me from Issac's relentless stare and that smile tugging on his mouth.

"Snatching your girl for a bit," she says before pulling me away from him.

At the bar, Lauren and I sip on margaritas while she tells me about her ex, a singer, who is currently sitting a few feet away, pretending she doesn't exist. Said ex used to hide her at home instead of bringing her to these parties, so she never got the chance to be the social butterfly she is on this side of town until Josh.

"And I'm glad you're here too," she says. Then: "Oh! You'll be with us during Fall Fashion Week, right? Issac is going to need his girl in the audience for how special this one will be for him. Maybe we can sit together."

Issac and I will be *broken up* by September, and even though we're going to tell the media that we're remaining friends, it'll be too soon for me to show my face. And hopefully I'll be buried in business at the shop by then. Besides, Issac hasn't told me how important Fall Fashion Week is to him, so maybe it's less than Lauren thinks. Or maybe it'll be special, but he doesn't think I'd want to be there because I haven't shown him otherwise.

The last thought has me decided. "Of course I'm going," I tell Lauren. Because I should try to be a part of his new life, regardless of if we're *together*. I turn my glass to lick salt off the rim, figuring that one night of old habits won't hurt my health. I feel good today, anyway. I'm not as tired, and I haven't had a headache, and I really, really need this drink right now with the group of women staring and whispering close by. I push my hair out of my face, smile, and wave. I'll feel less than only if I allow it.

Lauren snickers, noticing them shifting their focus to something else. "You'd think Issac was Barack Obama the way they're examining you. But . . . they're probably wondering what designer styled you tonight."

My face flushes as I remember the heat in Issac's words. I take another long sip. Then, "Shout-out to this thirty-dollar number for giving more."

The woman I'm talking to makes more money in one commission than I might see all year, but she still bumps her hip against mine and says, "Way to wear it, boo."

Yeah. Kat would love Lauren. I pull out my phone, shoot her and Lex a quick text in the group chat. I love y'all. The dress was a success. When I look up from my screen, I catch Issac watching me from across the room. He smiles, then shifts to continue his conversation with two people wearing stunning lavender suit jackets. I selfishly wonder when he'll come grab me so we can meet Shida Anala because I haven't forgotten for a single second that somewhere in this loft there's a studio, and in that studio songs that I'll probably cherish are being recorded. I wonder how many times Lauren got to meet Shida. I wonder how she seems unaffected by being in this space right now. I take note, hoping to keep my composure tonight too.

Lauren and I start to sway to a song while sipping our drinks, but then Issac comes up behind me like he heard my wishes through our shared mind.

He bends to put his chin in the crook of my neck, and my traitorous body aches for him to kiss me there.

"Lau," he says, quick with the nicknames, "would you mind if I steal my girl back to show her the studio?"

The words *my girl* are so smooth on his tongue, I can't pretend my pulse wasn't picking up before he got to the part about the studio. Lauren sulks and tells him he'll have to bring me back soon.

"Oh, that part is all on her," he says. "Don't come for me if she decides to kick it solely in the studio after meeting Shida. I might have to leave her there myself."

"I love how you're both talking about me like I'm not here," I say. "But he's right, Lauren, I'm worried a bodyguard might have to drag me out of there. I'm a raging fan."

She laughs and raises her glass at me. "Noted. I'll make sure no one records you getting thrown out."

"I appreciate that," I say, then turn in Issac's arms, beaming up at him while he gently rubs my lower back. "I'm ready."

———————

ISSAC LEADS ME DOWN A LONG HALLWAY INTO A DARK ROOM, through a door, and into another room. The studio is large, has a white love seat on one wall, fluffy floor pillows, and blue string lights hanging from the ceiling. I wonder if they set it up like this just for Shida and her ethereal vibes. The six other people here make my throat go dry. I grew up on the music of Kayln Connor and Kid Krews and they are in this very room, watching Shida Anala sing in the booth in front of us. They nod their heads at me and shake hands with Issac before we slip to the back to sit on the love seat. Shida Anala has a soft voice but commands attention the same way Issac commands a room. Her lyrics aren't for the weak of heart. She tears apart past lovers with her melodic words. Her newest song is about catching a case for finding out the love of her life left her for someone else but is trying to come back for just bits and pieces of what they once shared.

Everyone is in a trance listening to her. Chills climb my spine; goose bumps travel my bare thighs. I blink back tears, thankful that it's dark while she fills the space with magic.

Issac's eyes are locked on Shida when I glance up at him. Music has always been a part of our relationship. We were barely four-teen, walking home from school together, rapping Tupac's and Biggie's lyrics back and forth while sharing a big stick of Slim Jim. We were fifteen and lying on my bedroom rug listening to album after album till the songs soothed small heartbreaks. We are grown now, and when we want to say *Hi, I miss you, I'm thinking of you*, but the space between us feels too big to do it with a phone call, we'll do it with a song. I'm happy to see Shida live, it's like a dream, but I'm not sure it would feel the same way if Issac weren't sitting right beside me. After this night, I'll forgo my turn with the Bluetooth three times to thank him.

In the dark of the room, with no one watching us, with no need to pretend, I find his hand, and he doesn't hesitate to squeeze mine. We are still linked when Shida Anala takes off the headphones and gives a small, shy smile through the booth window. Everyone's hyped after that, singing the lyrics back at her through the glass as the engineer gets to work on the track to replay parts for us. She comes out of the booth and is yellow and blue energy, radiant yet calm in the chaos of excitement she just made happen, a slow-moving river with power just beneath the surface. She spies Issac first, grins, and heads toward us. He lets go of my hand and stands to hug her, wrapping her tiny frame in his. She's even more slender than Melinda, and I hate myself for wondering if he likes the way she feels in his arms compared to the way I feel.

"You made it," she says, excited, sounding surprised.

How is she shy and not shy all at once? I remember what Issac said to me about being brave and decide maybe Shida is kindred, even though I probably couldn't tell her that without her wondering why I'd think to compare us.

"Of course I did," Issac says. And because he'll always have unfiltered jokes, adds, "Don't want to be on your hit list."

Shida Anala must think it's endearing because she points at him as if to say he's right. I think they'll go on like this, and I'm happy just to sit and watch, but then he reaches a hand to help me up. "And I brought your one demand with me. Meet Laniah."

My heart is ripping through my chest when I awkwardly extend my hand to shake hers. She takes it, then uses her other hand to sandwich both of mine. Her skin is soft, and this is Shida Anala—the artist who makes me cry in the shower when she sings about healing—holding *my* hand. *She* demanded for me to be here? I feel like I'm going to faint staring into her piercing cat-shaped eyes.

"I couldn't wait to meet you," she says. "I hope we can talk about Wildly Green. My natural hair could use special attention."

I'm shaking, the already hard-to-come-by words hiding, but Shida just mentioned my shop, the dream I've built with my mom, and I won't mess up this opportunity for either of us by smiling and nodding like I always do.

"I'd be happy to find exactly what works for you," I say. "We can come up with a care plan and adjust from there."

"That sounds lovely," she says with a pleased smile. Then: "I've been told that your aura is like moonlight, and I don't know you well yet, but I can already tell Issac was right."

I smile, breathe deep, eyes burning while watching him rub the bridge of his nose.

Is he nervous? I know I am.

Because Shida Anala is exactly as I imagined, but he's the one who made my heart glow.

──────────

THE CROWD IS DENSER THAN IT WAS EARLIER, THE MUSIC LOUDER. Lauren is with Josh, and she pulls me and Issac between them. We run through four songs together, dancing silly then serious and back to match the beats. I dip Lauren, and she throws her head back and laughs. I even dance with Josh. It's all fun until the song switches and Josh steals Lauren from me. I grab Issac for a reggaeton song, thinking it'll be normal, but when he grasps my hip and turns me around so my back is to him, I shiver.

When I start moving against him, he matches me, then runs one hand up my torso while we grind. We're moving so well together that I try not to think of how much time we've spent *not* doing this. We did dance close during senior prom, but adult Issac uses the hand resting against my stomach to bring me flush against him. Adult Issac bends so his lips are inches from the shell of my ear. I can feel his breath there, my ass pressed into him, I'm on fire everywhere our body touches.

"You look so damn good," he whispers, sounding drunk off the feel of me.

I close my eyes, heart thrumming, and slide an arm up to hold the back of his neck, to keep him right here. But I wasn't prepared for the swelling, the pulsing ache between my thighs at the feel of him growing hard against me. A soft moan slips from my mouth just as the song changes.

My brain is hazy. Something else plays over the speakers. Everyone throws their hands in the air. It takes me and Issac a few seconds to pull apart and start singing the lyrics.

And for the rest of the party, I have to remember to breathe.

20

HOW IT SHOULDN'T FEEL
WITH FRIENDS

THIS TIME COMING OUT OF THE BATHROOM TO ISSAC WHILE HE'S laid out on the gray sheets of his bed feels different. I had to hype myself up just to open the door after showering. There was so much to talk about on the way back to the condo after Shida's party. I danced with rapper Kid Krews at some point, and I'm not even sure how that happened. But we didn't even talk about that. I wonder if he's thinking about us violating the messiness part of our agreement with our dance. I count to ten, breathe, begin to walk toward him. The lights are already off, but the moon from the balcony window fills the room with dim light. Issac's not reading or writing, he just watches each step I take. With dread? Desire?

For how big the bed is, and even though we both made sure to leave some distance between us, he's still too close when I climb in. He shifts his gaze to the ceiling while I try to get comfortable.

Is he regretting what we did? Am I?

I hear him exhale, then he turns toward me and slides his pointer finger down my bare arm.

"Hi, Ni," he says, cautious with his words but not so much his touch.

"Hi," I say, fighting the urge to whimper at the feel of him. To ask him not to stop touching me.

His eyes are dark, he takes his top lip into his mouth and releases it slowly before saying, "Checking in that we're still okay with all of this. Doing my best friend due diligence, I guess."

I don't know what I wanted him to say at the moment, but it wasn't those words.

"Thanks for checking in," I say. "Tonight was intense. In a way I'm not sure I prepared for. But maybe it's not possible to prepare for . . ." I trail off, glance up at the skylight, brush down the bedsheets at my sides.

"Biology?" he offers. "Chemistry?"

"Yes," I whisper, and meet his gaze again, relieved to hear out loud that he'd felt the pull too. That the desire wasn't in my imagination or one-sided.

"Because good Lord, Laniah. You in that damn dress." He groans just a little, and it's as if he did it right between my thighs. I clench them together, warmth pooling, my body begging to bend toward him.

Chemistry. That's all this is.

"I'm not sorry for wearing it," I say, smiling. "But yeah."

He glances at my mouth, my collarbone, scans my face, says, "I would never ask you to be. This was always going to be hard. We knew it would be. Maybe weird too." His words change the mood. My stomach tightens. "It is weird, right? But do you think . . . it's bad?"

He asks like it's a question, but my brain warns that it might be another test. So I say the smart thing for the both of us: "It was weird, but it doesn't change anything between us."

Issac's eyebrows piece together. His eyes flick away before he closes them. "Yeah, we're good. Always. But we probably should do our best not to cross lines like that, okay?"

Something stirs in my chest. A throb, a pang. I wonder if I said the right thing. What was he looking for? What am I running from?

"Okay," I tell him.

Silence creeps up on us for so long I swear he's lying about us being good, but then he says, "Something amazing happened tonight. I talked to the people behind *Year of the Lotus*. I think you saw me with them. They had on those dope purple outfits."

I nod my head, anxious for him to say more. He beams, the smile contagious.

"They love all of my ideas and want me fully on board. I'll have to be quick at booking the botanical garden, and dedicated with the short timeline, but . . . they believe in me, Ni."

"Of course they do," I say, wrapping my arms around him. "I'm so, so happy."

"So am I," he says, and starts playing with the fabric at the small of my back.

My mouth opens. I place a kiss on his shoulder. Delicate and soft. Still, he inhales sharply. Heat builds between our bodies. His hand dips lower, fingers nearly grazing my ass. *Squeeze it*, I want to tell him.

But then he pulls away, shifting to give us distance.

"You must've been my good luck charm this weekend," he says, breathy to match the way mine is catching. "Good night, Ni."

"Good night, Issac," I say, and turn toward the balcony to put more space between us.

But sleep evades me because he keeps unintentionally moving closer while he dreams. It always happens, but he's shirtless again and I turn around to watch his chest, his stomach, the hard lines of his torso above his boxers as he breathes. My body wants things and doesn't consult well enough with my heart about them. I hate it. Chemistry, loneliness, whatever it is, I can't want these things. Issac thinks we should do better with our boundaries, but telling myself this doesn't stop me from aching to nudge him awake and beg him to touch between my legs. I glance at him one last time before slipping out of bed and sifting through my luggage for a small black bag to take to the spare room. There's a king-sized bed waiting for me with the same soft sheets and a large bay window to let in moonlight. And it's empty, which is exactly what I need right now.

Except my mind won't leave me alone. I can't escape Issac even here. I'm already wet before I part my thighs. I trail my fingers over my breasts, pinch my nipples, walk them down my stomach. When I touch myself, I remember Issac's hand running down the curve of my hip, him pressed against my ass while we danced, how hard he was behind me. I switch on my vibrator and let it hum along my clit, but I'm too quick to get close and don't want the feeling to end. So I roll onto my stomach, place a pillow between my thighs, and grind against it. The ache builds slowly. I imagine Issac's body below mine, him gripping my waist and slowly stroking till I cum.

21

STICKY SITUATION

A KNOCK INTERRUPTS MY DREAM. I HEAR ISSAC CALLING ME from the other side of the door, asking if he can come in. I'm blinking away sleep, saying, "yes." While my mouth feels dry from drooling, he enters the room fully dressed.

"You're not going to be able to eat before your flight if you don't wake your ass up," he says.

I groan, roll right onto my vibrator. It sticks to my cheek and— *Oh God*. I hurry to push it under the pillow and pull the covers up to my neck.

Issac walks over, sits at the end of the bed. "Whatchu hiding over there, Ni?"

Blood rushes in my ears; I turn to him with a grin. "Nothing."

He lifts both brows and smiles. I wonder if he's already seen it.

"What time is it?"

"Almost noon," he tells me.

"Shit. Shit."

"Mm-hmm."

He doesn't ask why I slept in this room. I didn't mean to; the orgasm must have put me to sleep without consent. *The orgasm.* Suddenly Issac being this close makes me feel a prickling shame that starts in the center of my chest. If he knew what I did last night we'd have to reevaluate this plan. No. We'd absolutely have to stop. Maybe we should.

But then I remember our talk last night about chemistry and remind myself these feelings are normal. Maybe I'm delusional, but I release a breath. I'm only human. It's been a while since I've had sex, I was tipsy and feeling good in *that damn dress*, it doesn't matter that it was Issac. It could've been anyone. Yup. I'll just ignore the fact that I danced with other people last night and Issac's the only one who made my body ache.

He sits there searching my face for something, and I can hardly meet his gaze. Clearly there's some delusion going on because feeling chemistry is one thing but having an orgasm while thinking of him is another. Maybe after the summer ends, I should be more liberal with my body and give it what it wants. Just not with him.

"They loved you, everybody did," he finally says. "I mean, how could they not." His words help shift my focus. I'm still in shock about the way I spent my night. "Lauren's sad you're going back home. It's kind of cute."

Issac's laugh is like a balm on my anxious heart. I sit up in bed, push the vibrator farther under my pillow just in case. "Shida Anala gave me her number so we can talk through the Wildly Green product line," I say, feeling the spark from last night reignited. "Shida. Anala."

"And honestly," Issac says, smacking my thigh that's hanging out of the covers, "she's the one who's winning. Her hair is about to be blessed. Especially by Vanessa's growth oil."

"You're such a sweet talker," I say, wishing he'd smack me again. Good Lord, I need to get home or I'll . . . His phone vibrates on his lap. I look down at the caller ID, see *Melinda* on the screen. Issac's eyebrows meet in the middle. My stomach twists with ugly jealousy when he stands to leave.

"I'm going to take this but get downstairs and eat something good before your flight."

When he walks out, I throw myself back on the bed. My vibrator bounces and accidentally switches on.

Did seeing us together fuel Melinda's desire to try dating him again? Did dancing with me last night make Issac realize how much he wants *her*? Maybe I was wrong about getting between the two of them. Maybe this dating scheme will actually push them together instead. I try to feel happy, relieved even. I fail.

———————————

BERNIE OFFERS TO BRING ME TO THE AIRPORT BECAUSE ISSAC HAS A meeting with a new designer, but he's an impatient man who doesn't take any of Issac's shit. Grumbling something under his breath when Issac warns him to watch for paparazzi, Bernie takes one of my bags to the car. I like him better for it.

"I'm a grown woman," I say, standing in front of Issac. "I don't need a babysitter."

"If it's not me, it's Bernie. Period."

I cut my eyes at him, but he doesn't care. He gives me money for airport souvenirs I don't need, makes sure my phone is charged, shoves his favorite new sunglasses and one of his hoodies at me for the flight.

"Franklin, your other favorite hermit crab, will keep you company while I'm gone," I tell him.

This morning, we decided Franklin was better off here with Issac. Hermit crabs don't live very long, and I'd be worried about him on the long flight.

"Thank goodness for Franklin," Issac says, wrapping me in his arms and lifting me from the ground. For some reason, during this intimate moment, I feel the urge to ask about his conversation with Melinda, if things are truly over between them, but instead I kiss his cheek. He loosens his hold on me, and leans against the doorframe to watch me go.

AFTER ALL THE JUNK ISSAC SAYS ABOUT HOW OVERBEARING BERnie is, I'm surprised that I don't mind his company as we walk through the airport and check my bag. He's got a scratchy voice to match his serious eyes, and he isn't a small talker; he tells me he just celebrated his wife's fiftieth birthday last week, shows me pictures of his two kids, and admits he really loves working for Issac. When they first met, Bernie was getting ready to leave the industry due to lack of success, but then he found Issac and saw something special in him. It's a story I already know, but it's nice hearing about the soft spot Bernie has for my best friend.

"Issac's a pain in my ass, but we just click," he says as we walk through the crowd. "And I've been thinking of how, before all of this, we were both coming from living the broke life, you know? Maybe we connect because we can't always relate to people who got here differently, who don't appreciate success the same way and know how fragile it can be." Something stirs in my gut while he speaks, but I let him press on while we approach my gate. He stops walking, turns to me. "I know it was rough seeing that article about where you work."

I hurry to speak, to tell him I'm fine and I nearly forgot about it, but he shakes his head.

"Listen, there are worse things that can happen when you're *romantic*"—he stresses the word like he's suspicious of how true it is—"with someone like Issac Jordan. If there's anything you have in your past, anything people can find to expose, they will."

I blink up at him. "Are you trying to scare me away or something?"

"No," he says with a cautious laugh. "I'm trying to prepare you. You don't seem like someone that can handle the negative attention."

"Bold of you to assume I can't."

"Sorry if I offended you," he says, "just observations. You don't even use social media."

Oh. Now he's getting on my nerves. "I'm fine. I'll be fine."

"Well, I hope so. But my main concern is Issac. Because if his image falls, that affects my life. It might be all pretty and easy with him now, but these people? This lifestyle? It can come for you. And Issac needs to be on his game. His career is shining, he can go even further with his art. I think he has A-list celebrity potential. But he can't be distracted . . . or heartbroken."

The last one makes me want to laugh because there's no way *I* can break Issac's heart.

"Got it," I say through gritted teeth.

"Good. I'm glad you do," he says, and I wonder what I'd feel like if it was a real relationship between me and Issac. Would Bernie's words have been enough to scare me off?

For a moment, I consider texting Issac to tell him, but I hate the thought that it could put a strain on their working relationship. I understand what survival instincts are. I know what it looks like when someone has no intention of going back to where they came from. I decided to agree to a crazy scheme as a last effort to save the shop. Bernie isn't playing games with his career or Issac's—he's being protective, and I can't blame him because I'd never want to put Issac's stability in jeopardy. Especially not when his art is about to move toward center stage.

"I got Issac," I say again. "I care about his career too. You don't have to worry."

Bernie smiles but still looks weary. "Okay," he says, "it was good talking to you. By the way, Issac said you might be able to give me some stuff to help my hairline grow back in."

I laugh, but, as Lex would say, the energy between us is stiff as hair spray now. "I can try, but Issac swears I work miracles, and that's not the truth," I tell Bernie.

He rubs his head, says, "Definitely see what Issac likes about you. Pretty, quippy, loyal."

Bernie enunciates the last word, and on my walk to the gate I find myself wishing he knew that there's no one else in the world besides Mom who cares for Issac the way I do.

I'd never hurt him. I'm not even in the position to break his heart. But when a text comes through from him, it makes mine squeeze a little.

> I know we're probably not supposed to talk about our dance at Shida's party, boundaries and all, but I just wanted to say that it reminded me of dancing during prom. You wore a great dress then too. Had me singing the chorus of Brent Faiyaz's "Jackie Brown" when you walked out my door today. Have a safe flight, Ni.

My chest warms, I bite my lip to stop from smiling. **I thought of the same night**, I reply.

He loves the message, and I get on the plane, wondering if he knows I'll be spending the next six hours scrutinizing every sentence of the song.

WHAT I REMEMBER

Eight years ago. Prom tickets.

Told more than once by strict faculty that losing them meant forfeiting our spot. Nothing was said about drawing on them, Issac Jordan pointed out when I found him using orange permanent marker to design a corner of his with fallen rose petals. I asked him to do the same for me; he offered a trade: I design his, he design mine, despite him knowing his ticket would probably look like it was decorated by a preschooler.

I debated asking my mother what to draw on his ticket, but when she wasn't in bed, grieving my father silently, she was dragging herself out of it for work to keep our lights on. Neither instances were good times to talk to her, which meant trying my best and hoping Issac was expecting less.

My mother did put aside her grief to do my hair and help lace my shoes for prom. But when Issac's date, Lisa Hotchkiss, and my date, Liam Roger, came to the house for pictures, Vanessa Thompson, embarrassing as she was at times, forced the two of them to watch as she snapped pictures of me and Issac in around-the-waist prom poses.

"Dennis would have loved this," she said, and the moment the name left her mouth, I spied her eyes watering and felt my own mood shift. Issac, noticing me getting quieter, anxious to leave, pulled me to the kitchen to *talk in private*. But he didn't ask why my face had fallen, only hugged me hard before giving me the ticket he'd designed. It was bright and intricate with stars, the ocean, an oak tree. I flushed handing him his, which was stick figures of the two of us stealing a bike and lopsided music symbols with random song lyrics surrounding the edges. *Perfect*. That's what Issac called something I thought wouldn't be enough.

And that night, while Liam was busy smoking weed in the bathroom, and Lisa was in the prom photo booth with her friends, Issac asked me to dance. I told myself that it was the same position as the hundreds of times we'd hugged, but Issac smelled so good, and he touched me softer, and I swear I heard his heart pounding over the music. It made mine do the same. And soon it felt like we were meant to match that way.

But while my head was on his chest, I briefly wondered if my mother had felt this kind of alignment with my father. And when the song changed, Issac didn't move to leave me, his fingers still flitted along my dress, and I pushed him playfully, insisting he go dance with Lisa.

An hour later, I'd find the two of them kissing under the strobe lights and realize that the confusing feelings I had for him didn't have to be confusing at all. It was normal that I wanted to be close to him. That's how it should feel with friends.

22

THE IDEA THAT'LL
MAKE OR BREAK US

'VE BARELY HAD TIME TO PUT MY LUGGAGE DOWN WHEN MY DOOR-
bell goes off. One time, then three more.

When I open the door, Katrina waves her phone in the air.

"Bitch," she says, barreling through the house and almost trip-
ping over my rug.

I plop down on my couch, say, "It is I."

I'm exhausted from the flight, still trying to adjust to the time
difference, and Katrina's been a burst of energy since the first day
she entered our shop with stilettos and a crisp pantsuit on. She says
she's been like that all her life and has a hard enough time toning
it down at her consultant agency to keep the *stiff* men running the
show satisfied with her performance, so she refuses to do it with her
friends. I'd never ask her to; I just can't always match her bravado.

"What are you going crazy about?"

"You." Kat stands over me, shoves her phone in my face. "I'm
crazy about you, just like 856,000 other people in the world." She
tilts the phone to look at it again. "Scratch that—998,200 now."

My stomach leaps into my throat. I sit up straighter, grab the phone from Katrina. Shida Anala posted a carousel on her Instagram of the listening party, and in the third slide she's looking beautiful, cool, otherworldly, and I'm right beside her, looking pretty good too. We're both laughing, glowing, clearly happy in each other's company. Part of the caption for the carousel reads: Laniah is the most perfect moonstone I've ever met. We all love her already.

Me. Shida referred to me as *perfect* and a *moonstone* in the same sentence.

"Look at the next one." Katrina claps her hands excitedly.

A shiver travels my spine. I take a breath, slide right to a picture of me and Issac, his arms around my waist, his face in my neck. I'm smiling like it's the best day of my life.

"Well, shit," I finally say, sinking back in my seat and trying to slow my racing heart.

"Yeah, girl. The press have already changed their tune about you. No one cares about those stupid maid articles anymore. And in fact, there was one posted a while ago about how happy Issac seems. It was littered with praise for him. Kind of sickening if you ask me, but my girl is a good look for *him*." Katrina starts to dance in front of me. "You're a celebrity."

"Shut up. Definitely not, and you know I don't care about that," I say.

"And yet you're grinning really hard."

"My face hurts," I say. Then think of my conversation with Bernie. How does he feel about all of this? Issac needed to get out of the tabloids to be taken more seriously as an artist, and maybe being with me really can help.

"As it should," Kat says.

"Shida," I whisper. Then louder, a happy scream: "Shida Anala."

"Your wife," Katrina says, and we burst out laughing. "The love of your little life."

We stop abruptly, stare at each other in silence for a few seconds before we crack. Katrina starts singing the lyrics to Shida's summer sensation. I stand up on the couch and try to hit one of the high notes. Doing an injustice to the song, honestly. But the good feelings from the weekend double back all over again, and Kat slips out of her shoes to join me. We dance across the cushions like teenagers.

I'm happy she's here, and always herself, no matter what energy I can offer back.

———————

MORNING COMES AND MY HEAD IS POUNDING AS SOON AS I SWING my feet off the side of the bed. When Katrina left last night, I called T-Mobile to change my phone number and added extra privacy protection. Much like the first time Issac posted a picture of us, I spent hours warding off texts from people I haven't heard from in years, even prank callers that brought me back to being twelve at a sleepover. And after reading comments comparing how happy Issac looked in the pictures with me compared to how happy he looked with Melinda, I can't shake the thought that he's with her right now. Maybe they've met up somewhere in private, maybe his tongue is . . . Okay. Nope. This isn't how I'm spending my time. I down two ibuprofens with a glass of water, then get ready for a jog. I speak to my body ahead of time. Tell my legs this is a thing we do now, tell my lungs to be strong, my head to be easy on me, then I go.

This is only my third day, and I won't lie to myself and say it's getting any better. Everything burns, my vision is blurry from sweat stinging my eyes, my lungs feel like they might burst, but the one thing that helps is distraction from thinking of the shop. While I was in Cali, it sustained a steady amount of business, but what happens in two months when things between me and Issac die down completely? Will people go back to shopping for their products where they usually do? Worse than these thoughts is the fear that this will all backfire and people will hate me after the breakup. Issac said he'll do whatever he can to make sure that doesn't happen, but the truth is even he can't control the outcome, especially where social media is involved. Another truth: we might not make it until summer's end. Issac's love life shouldn't be put on hold to help my business. So Mom and I need more than just our products to set us apart. My brain runs wild, memories of each day in the shop coming at me quicker than I can handle. But I'm able to latch on to one: little Destiny with her beautiful 4c hair, sitting while we tried products to see what worked for her. It was similar to what Shida wants me to do with her soon.

An idea hits me and makes the half-mile jog back home feel easier.

THERE'S A NERVOUS TICK IN MY CHEST WHEN I WALK INTO WILDLY Green and see Lex and Mom setting up for the day. I'm only two steps into the shop when the words rush out of me. "I have an idea."

"Good to see you too, baby," Mom says, putting the last stack of dollar bills in the cash register and closing the drawer. "Nothing like coming in, saying good morning, and telling us about your weekend with Issac."

I mumble a quick hello, move to slap both hands down on the counter. "But I need you two to listen."

"Baby, we've got five minutes until the shop opens; we need to get ready."

"And we're moving like snails today," Lex says, without sparing a glance at me. "My eyes are half crusty from sleep still, and Shane made me a big fattening breakfast this morning to absolve his guilt, so I'm sugar and grease tired."

"I'm happy you two made up and I don't have to fight him because I fear I'd lose," I say, "but this is important. Eyes and ears and hearts on me. Right now."

Lex stops what he's doing and leans against the counter, giving Mom a shrug. "Don't you want to hear about what has our little celebrity here so excited? I can't say I'm not intrigued."

I roll my eyes, but his bait makes Mom close the cash register drawer. "How much money have we made since I've been gone?" I ask. She tells me more than we have in months and I clap my hands together, making a note that I need to check inventory and plan for the next wave Shida's post could send. "But the hype from me and Issac won't last long, and even though our products will speak for themselves now, we need something more sustainable. Something we can grow with. To make *us* memorable in the sea of good companies out there. And I've been thinking, it's this store."

"I'm not following, baby."

Lex plays with sunflower petals in a vase on the counter. "You have to tell us a little more. Time is ticking."

I feel like everything inside of me is buzzing with light to counteract the seconds passing by, and I hope they can catch some of it as I look around the room. "We need to make Wildly Green a whole experience."

Mom raises an eyebrow, but then: "Keep talking."

And so with three minutes to spare I rush to tell them more about Destiny, about curating a hair-care plan for Shida Anala, about so many people saying they try things that don't work for them. I run through quick scenarios of us creating hair oils and leave-in conditioners for people with them right in the store. I tell them we can let the customers browse while we're getting their custom orders ready or give them a time to come back and pick up the products. I see the idea getting lost in Mom's eyes and remind her that she'd do something similar for me and Issac when we were young, creating salves on the spot for our scrapes and burns, balms for our eczema, shampoos that wouldn't dry us out.

Lex's hums, points a finger. "Oh! Maybe if the hair products do well, we could make creams and body butters for certain skin types too."

"Yes. That's perfect," I say. "We'd have to really put our heads together on inventory, how much it would cost us for our time. If it's scalable. How much we should charge without people feeling like they can't afford it. And we'd have to do something about the shop, redesign the space. It'll be a huge effort on all of our parts, on our pockets, but I think it'll be worth it. I know it."

Mom frowns. "I think it sounds too risky, baby. We've been doing so well here. Your idea sounds lovely but like it'll eat up all the money we've made and then some. I might've made special things for you and Issac when you were kids, but I couldn't afford the time or the supplies to do that with anyone else. It wasn't even an idea on the table back then."

I grab both her hands. "I understand, but I'm afraid if we don't do something different now, things will dwindle down. And I believe in us. But a lot of those customers can easily go back to getting their products at the big retailers, where they're cheaper and easier to find. We need to give them a reason, make them feel special. The time to take risks is now. I wrote up a quick business plan before coming here, and we can talk logistics together, make spreadsheets, but Mom, we need something like this," I say. "There are soap-bar and candle-making spots across the country, but I haven't heard of something for the hair-care industry yet. I think it will help us entice investors. Offering a one-of-a-kind service to customers might make us stand out. And the best part is, creating new products is something we truly love. We'll enjoy this so much. You just have to believe in us."

A customer knocks on the door, and Mom glances at the clock on the wall. My stomach sinks as she sighs at me. But then a smile splits her face. "We'll discuss details later. But, baby, you're a genius."

"A whole genius," says Lex, then dances toward the door to flip the sign to OPEN.

Mom's eyes are shiny, and they make mine water as she reaches across the counter and squeezes my hand. "Do you really think we can do it?"

"I know we can."

She nods, and for the rest of the workday there's some extra sunlight surrounding her.

23

ARGUABLY THE MOST
GRUESOME *FINAL DESTINATION*

W E LOCK THE DOORS AROUND TWO TO EAT LUNCH AND catch our breath. Mom is beaming with pride while showing me the picture she took of the line that wrapped around the door during lunchtime rush, but it was almost too busy for three people to handle. I spent the day half distracted over imagining the store blooming to something bigger, and half successfully fielding the more intense questions about Issac and about Shida's party. For the first time, I wasn't as anxious when people asked me.

Lex comes back with our food, and we all sit on the floor with our backs pressed up against the counter to dream up what the shop experience could be like. We'll move the shelves on the left side and have a booth there. A cute stand in the center of the shop for fragrance oils, jars with fresh herbs, blocks of shea, cocoa, and mango butter. The products will sit on slatted shelves at the bottom of the booth. Toward the back of the shop, we'll open up the area near the sink, lay contact paper over the old wood to make it pretty or hire someone to come in and give us a new vanity. Lex has a picture in his phone of two cute chairs and a beautiful mirror we can hang fairy lights on. We'll have plants everywhere, ones we could pick leaves from if we need them for recipes. I'm sure customers will love being able to pick flower petals for their mixes. There will be sign-ups for the experience, and we'll limit how much we do in a given week, which will make the service more desirable.

Planning makes us high on excitement. For the rest of the day, we'll be running on dream adrenaline. But first, I have to make sure Mom's alright with what this all means for our finances so I don't drag her into something she's not mentally prepared for like I might've done the last time. I must make sure I'm clear too. I can only expect one more paycheck from the hotel to help carry me through. But Issac went to Cali with nothing. Bridget used whatever she had from her aunt's life insurance to grow a business from scratch while raising kids. We'll never know how great Wildly Green can be if we don't bet on ourselves.

"Are you ready for this?" I ask her. "You were right about the cost. We've just started breaking even again, and from my calculations we'll be taking quite a loss shutting down while remodeling the shop."

"I'm scared," she admits with a sigh. "But . . . I love Wildly Green. I want this to work. What about you, Lex? Are you ready to ride this out with us? There may be a lot of bumps."

Hearing the clarity she has brings me relief, and then Lex smiles and pulls us in for a hug, saying, "There are no two women I'd rather spend my time riding with."

We clean up our food, and Lex goes to use the bathroom. While he's in the back, Mom's phone rings. She doesn't answer the first call because she's too busy straightening things on the shelves for when we open back up, but when her phone rings again she sucks her teeth and pulls it from her pocket.

"Whoever is calling me has time to hear my mouth today."

"Maybe it's an emergency," I say.

She mumbles something under her breath before, "Oh, It's Issac."

His name rings through my body. My chest tightens at the thought of *him* calling her for an emergency.

I stop sweeping and walk over to her. We're both nervous when she picks up the phone.

"Is everything okay?" Mom asks, and when the muscles in her face relax and she laughs, I breathe better. "Mm-hmm. Yeah. Ohhh, that would be great. Thank you for . . . okay, okay. I won't, but you better come home soon for some of my chili. I saw your newest photo shoot and you're looking too slim. I don't like it. Of course, boy. I know I make the best chili out here. But keep telling me. I love to hear it." Mom giggles like a fan. I roll my eyes, and she sticks her tongue out. "Alright. I love you too, Issac."

Instead of hanging up the phone, she passes it to me. I turn away from her prying eyes.

"Hey, big head," I say, walking toward the window. "You had me worked up with worry."

There's no *Hi, hermit* back, just a soft, "You were worried? I was half sick."

"What? Why?"

"I couldn't get in touch with you. Your phone . . ."

"Shit." I shake my head like he can see me. "I changed my number last night and forgot to text you with it. I'm sorry. But why were you worried? It's only been—"

"Eighteen hours since your plane landed," he cuts in. "You sent a Laniah-style text letting me know and that was it." He laughs, but I can tell he was seriously worried. I sit on the windowsill and wait for him to say something else. "Just leaving your man out here ready to take a red-eye flight and track you down."

I snort. "You're dramatic. But you know what, maybe I should turn my phone off all day tomorrow, call your bluff. If it does get you over here, that just means more time with you."

"Mm." He's smiling; I can hear it. "So, what you're saying is you miss me already?"

"Quit it," I reply, but I'm smiling too.

Until I realize how different it feels to have a simple conversation with him now. We've shared our affections and worries before, but this feels romantic in a way it hasn't before. Or maybe it just feels romantic to me.

He lets out a deep breath. "Nah, but for real, Ni. I'm happy you're okay."

"What'd you think happened to me?"

"Thought maybe you were done with me because I'd leaped over our boundary line mentioning the Brent song," he says. Then, "Or you slipped in the shower, or you got behind one of those eighteen-wheelers with the logs. You've also been getting them headaches and what if . . . I don't know, Ni."

"Damn," I say. "The *Final Destination* worst-case scenarios, huh?"

"Movie-number-two-type gruesome. I was about to tell Franklin the crab Mommy wasn't coming home."

"Arguably the most traumatizing movie in the franchise." I laugh. "But I think Franklin would be just fine without me. So would you. Though I suppose I can keep my phone on and make sure to touch base whenever I can, if you promise to do better with yours too. I worry when you disappear for three days. You know?"

He doesn't respond for a second, then, "I'll have Bernie put your call on speaker in the middle of a shoot. How's that?"

"I doubt Bernie would enjoy it very much, but it sounds fantastic, my sweet king."

He laughs. "You've got jokes."

"Better than yours."

"I'll let you have that, babe," he says, and the endearment coming from his mouth after the weekend we spent together makes my heart soften in a scary way. But then he drops his voice to tell me, "Bernie was walking by, and I wanted to try it out in front of someone. How was it?"

"Maybe we don't do that one? Crossing more lines than the Brent song, I think."

"Really? Okay. Sweetheart?"

"Um . . . sure."

"I thought babe was a little much right there," he says. "But, Ni, I gotta run. Don't forget to text me your number or we'll have middle school–style beef."

"You don't want beef with me," I tell him. "I know jujitsu."

"You're such a punk," he says, and hangs up.

Mom was waiting until the phone call ended just to clear her throat. I'm surely blushing when I turn around, trying not to smile. She's closing the lid on a jar, and she's got those perfectly drawn eyebrows arched high.

"What is it, Mom?"

She skips straight to it. "Were you two . . . flirting?"

"Don't even . . . of course we weren't."

"Sounded a whole lot like flirting, you didn't even tell him about our plans for the shop."

Oh. I was excited thinking of talking to him about it this morning, but the conversation just now caught me off guard. "It was a quick call; I'll tell him later," I say.

She shakes her head. "I'll drop it, but don't come to me crying when you're falling in love . . ." She trails off, but butterflies are already beating their wings in my belly.

Falling in love? Crying . . . over Issac?

Suddenly an image of my mother weeping at my father's bedside breaks through and squashes any butterflies inside of me. Because falling in love with Issac might be like riding behind a rickety old 18-wheeler that's swerving and carrying cut logs, and that's absolutely not the position I want to be in.

"We're all family," she says. "Don't get caught up in this and hurt each other."

"You don't have to worry about that. And you'll never see me cry over any man."

I say it jokingly, but something curious flashes in her eyes.

She frowns. "If you say so."

24

CONVERSATIONS ARE
BETTER WITH RAMEN

MY PARENTS GOT ME HOOKED ON SIXTIES MUSIC WHEN I WAS still in diapers. Etta James, the Temptations, Ben E. King. I used to dance to "My Girl," shaking my small curly 'fro and banging spoons on pots and pans with my dad when the beat dropped. Designing the shop while listening to old albums makes me feel like that kid again. The music fills us all with rainbow light. It helps me fight the fatigue I feel working long stretches so we can make every hour count. And the days go like this: Lex and I buying the wrong screws to hang shelves, then realizing we don't know how to hang shelves even with the right screws. Mom picking a pretty lavender color that reminds me of springtime, then Lex and I doing our best to paint the walls without getting purple on the shop floors. We set up two stations: one for skincare consulting and product testing, one a mini hair salon with two beautiful yellow chairs by the sink we hired someone to revamp. We print colorful labels in the shapes of flowers for containers, and while I'm out trying to pick art for the walls, I call Issac just to help me choose between two options. He inserts his opinions about styling the curtains and other shop decor without overstepping. Lex tells Issac he can feel free to step everywhere he likes, and feeds us all with laughter.

I tell Issac to take this opportunity to open his big mouth all over the internet, so he does.

With the two weeks we've spent apart, things have settled, we haven't sent any risky songs to each other, and I'm relieved that I've stopped fantasizing about sex with my best friend. But I can feel the summer tick by, and I wonder if he can too. As a gift for our venture, he hires someone to redesign our website for online booking. And I buy Mom a beautiful book so she can do the in-store booking by hand because she's excited about it. We post a couple of announcements on our social media with pictures Lex took and graphics he designed. Mom, being old-school as she is, passes out flyers at the hotels she's worked at. Then she pays Destiny and a gang of her teen friends to hang some around the city. Bridget sends a beautiful new shop sign she had made for us as a gift. Lex helps me with our finances and even gets Shane to move new furniture with a U-Haul truck so we don't have to pay absurd delivery fees. And I don't tell any of them that I haven't been feeling well because they'd insist I not work as hard as everyone else.

But I do report my blood pressure readings to my doctor's office. I don't forget to mention the fatigue, though I can't recall if it's gotten worse since starting the Prozac. I tell the receptionist about the flank pain and how I've been having to pee more frequently, and she says my doctor will get back to me. It's the day before our grand reopening, and we've surpassed our budget—we're veering on broke again—but Mom calls the landlord to tell him to come pick up the rent, and she's so excited, laughs a little when she thinks I'm not paying attention, smiles into the phone. She nervously fixes her hair in the mirror after she hangs up.

When Pete walks in, he looks as nervous as she does; he also looks confused. His big bug eyes dart around our space. "See you've done a whole lot of work here," he says, probably wondering how we can afford it since we haven't even paid rent, and why we didn't ask him if we can replace the sink vanity with something prettier. But he smiles at Mom, his teeth showing. "It looks nice. Very nice."

Hm. Points to Mr. Grumpy Landlord for saying that, but he's staring at my mother with the sex eyes right in front of me, and something twists in my stomach.

"You know what else looks nice," I say, handing him an envelope of cash and watching the whites of his eyes widen when he opens it. "All the rent we owe and half of next month's rent. We hope you'll let us stay."

"We really love it here," Mom says, voice softer than it usually is. Yuck.

Pete taps the envelope. "Was willing to let y'all stay without the extra show of good faith, but appreciate it."

Within the next few months, I plan to pay down our credit cards and our loans, but this is the first paid debt and it feels like a weight off my soul.

He glances at the vanity again, then: "My daughters were going on about how they've been waiting for the grand reopening. I wish y'all would've told me."

I'm instantly suspicious. So is Mom. She puts a hand on her hip, asks, "Why?" in the sassy voice she reserves for DMV workers.

If Pete notices, he only smiles. "I could've helped around here."

"Is that right?" Mom nods, and points a finger at him. "Well, then, I've got just the job for you." She grabs supplies off the counter and leads Pete out the front door. I watch from the window as she makes him hang our reopening banner on the building. They laugh and linger, and I wonder what their banter is like when I'm not within earshot. Watching them makes my heart squeeze. I think of her and Dad, sweet kisses and steady heartbreak.

When Pete leaves and she comes back into the shop, she's quiet while she wipes down the windows. It feels like I should ask if she has a crush on him. I wonder if she does and if she wants me to know. But I grab some paper towels to help her, and I don't say anything about Pete at all.

I CAN'T AFFORD TO EAT OUT RIGHT NOW, BUT KATRINA OFFERED TO pay for me and Lex as a way of celebrating our big day tomorrow. We're seated at the table, waiting for Lex to arrive, when my doctor calls. I'd rather not pick it up in public, but I've been waiting to hear back all day.

"After going over your results, I think it'll be good to increase your dose of lisinopril to see if it helps lower your blood pressure. I'll send the script over to your pharmacy now. Just call the office back in a couple of weeks to let me know how you're doing with it."

"Thank you," I say. "But what about . . . my bladder stuff?"

Katrina glances up from the drink menu, and I realize I haven't mentioned it to her.

"Your bladder stuff?" my doctor asks, as confused as Katrina is. Katrina must see the frustration on my face because she shoots me a look and taps her fingers on the table. I breathe out. "I told the receptionist I've been having these weird pains in my flank area and getting up so many times at night to go to the bathroom. And I don't want to seem paranoid, but it feels like something's wrong."

"Are you?" he asks. "Are you paranoid that something is wrong with you?"

A knot forms in my stomach. I wonder if he's teasing, but the words still sting. "Um . . . no."

"I'm kidding," he says. Then: "But sometimes when we're overworried, it could cause our bodies to respond, creating a ripple effect of symptoms that are leading you to feel off."

Should I be insulted, sad? I feel embarrassed.

Has he been thinking I'm paranoid all along?

"Does that make sense?" he asks, tone the way you'd check in with a child.

Kat mouths for me to put the phone on speaker, but I ignore her. "I think so," I say.

"Great. I'll leave a lab slip at the front desk for you to get a urine sample. Sometimes UTIs can be sneaky. Are you still having headaches? Any chance you might be pregnant?"

Warmth cuts across my cheeks remembering that strange vision of me and Issac, my stomach round. "No chance for pregnancy," I say. "Yes to headaches."

"Okay. Don't worry, we'll figure this out. Like I said before, the headaches aren't connected to your blood pressure. They're probably from stress, but let the office know when you call back with a lisinopril update, and I'll see if it's wise if we order you a CT scan."

Order a scan now, some voice inside of me wants to tell him. But another voice comes, says it'll come back clear and he'll feel proven that I'm paranoid.

Kat is waiting for an explanation when I hang up the phone. I have the immediate urge to keep it to myself because something about saying the words out loud makes them feel sticky, strong enough to sink into my brain and stay. But I see the concern in her eyes, feel the comfort when she reaches for my hand across the table, and the words start spilling out. She listens quietly while I describe my last doctor's visit and the phone calls since.

"What if I'm feeling worse because I'm paying more attention to my body? Or what if I just think I'm feeling worse? Maybe he's right and I'm being paranoid."

"Or what if he's dead wrong?" Katrina asks with a frown.

Our waiter comes over before I can answer, and Katrina orders us appetizers but tells him that we're still waiting on our friend to order the main meals. I take a sip of my watermelon mojito, wishing I'd asked for extra tequila.

Kat tilts her head, says, "No, but you really trust his opinion *just* because he's a doctor? Doesn't Lex tell us all the time that Shane's witnessed great doctors do wrong things? I'm sure some of them are bad *and* wrong. It sounds like yours was insulting you. I hate to throw around the *gaslighting* word, but that too."

I want to feel relief that she noticed, something other than nerves, but I sigh and shrug. "Now, I'm going to be worried he thinks I'm a hypochondriac."

"He shouldn't because you're not." Katrina sucks her teeth. "What he said was straight-up unprofessional, and frankly, he was a dick." She pushes her drink away like she's too disgusted. "Find a new doctor, or I'll do it for you."

I think of Bridget offering the name of her own PCP. "Alright," I tell Katrina because even if my doctor's not wrong, I won't feel comfortable talking to him about anything after that call. "But let me check in with this other office before you demand my insurance cards to make the appointment yourself."

Kat doesn't laugh. "You know, you can always tell me when you're not feeling good. I can come over and we can watch *Twilight* and *Hunger Games* and all of your other favorite movies to rewatch."

Tears burn at the backs of my eyes. "I love you," I tell her.

"I love you more," she says, "And I think I need friend advice too."

She tells me how down she's been feeling at work because her supervisor puts a lot on her shoulders but hasn't approved her raise. Even though he's admitted that she's one of the best consultants he's ever had.

"It's because I'm a woman," she says, anger in her voice.

She always tells me about her ideas for gaining more clients and working with bigger corporations. I think her office would be silly to lose her. "Do what a man would and demand a raise or threaten to walk."

"You're right. If you're going to ditch your doctor, I should be ready to ditch my job."

"I can help you draft the email to your supervisor," I offer.

Her shoulders relax; she smiles. "You can make sure I don't say anything reckless."

"I got you, girl."

"What do you got?" Lex says, making the most dramatic entrance by closing up his rain-soaked umbrella and spraying droplets all over us and the table. We're happy he's here.

When the waiter brings out our appetizers, Katrina claps, Lex does a shimmy. We came to our favorite ramen spot, Ebisu in Providence, and my mouth waters at the sight of the perfectly seared gyoza in front of us.

"I'm sorry if this is strange," the waiter says, "but you're Ms. Thompson, right?"

Kat snickers and picks up her chopsticks. Lex looks downright satisfied. I shrink lower in my seat and nod.

"I'm a huge fan of Issac Jordan, so I just wanted to introduce myself. I hope the food is perfect and the service has been to your liking."

"I'm sure the food will be amazing," I say, smiling. "And the service is always perfect here. Thank you."

He gives me an awkward little wave, says, "I'll be back with your ramen soon."

When he leaves, Lex laughs. "Do you think we can get free fried ice cream? I'd love a good Japanese soda as well, but my wallet wouldn't love it."

"Yes, let's use your newfound celeb status and enjoy the perks," Katrina agrees.

"We will not be doing that," I tell them, and shove a warm gyoza in my mouth.

Lex chews on garlic chili edamame, then clears his throat. "I guess this is a good moment to tell you both that Shane finally asked me to move in with him. I already have a toothbrush there, and I leave my boxers around the house as a sign, so it's about time."

Katrina and I scream, drawing attention from other dinner guests. We reach for him over our glass plates, barely being careful because we're so happy.

25

THE THINGS WE REMEMBER

NERVES HARDLY LET ME SLEEP LAST NIGHT, EVEN WITH DRINKS in my system, but the sun is doing what it does this morning: I'm buzzing when I step onto my front porch and it beats down on my skin. It's grand reopening day and adrenaline has me heading to the shop early, but I can't neglect my morning glories. They're purple and pink trumpets that are thirsty for water, but the first thought that pops into my mind when I hear a throat clearing behind me is that they could've been thirsty a little longer.

I turn to face Wilma with the watering can in my hand and the fakest smile I can muster. "Good morning."

"That's what you're wearing to work?" she asks, gaze flicking from the New Balances on my feet to the floral T-shirt I'm wearing. "That skirt is mighty short. Are you okay?"

It's a slip dress that hits above the knees with a shirt layered on top of it. I think I look cute, but apparently, I must look like I'm going to the club. "Why wouldn't I be okay?"

"Was drinking my coffee and wondering if maybe you lost it

after reading the article in this here magazine." She bends to drop it onto the top step below my porch. "Then I come over and see what you're wearing, and yep. You've definitely lost it."

"I appreciate you caring about my mental health," I say through gritted teeth, "but I think I'm alright. Is there anything else you want to say before I head out?"

She nods to the magazine. "Well, I wanted to warn you that people like him have a world of options at their feet. Make sure he's willing to stay committed to you while you're across the country. And remember he's the one who ran away from *little* Rhode Island in the first place."

I turn the words over in my mind, then ask gently, "The way Bridget did?"

Wilma's face falls, her sadness hard to hide. "I'm not talking about my sister."

"But it hurt when she left you here and it never seemed like she wanted to come back, didn't it?" Something swells in my chest, telling me to push further. "Do you miss her? Because I can—"

But Wilma waves a hand, cutting me off. "Good luck with the shop today," she says.

I don't pick up the magazine until she's gone, and I wait until I'm in the car and parked around the corner to flip it open and find the article. It's dated two weeks back with some information about Shida Anala's upcoming album. There's a picture of me and Issac, and a warmth spreads through my stomach at the smile on his face as he stares at me. But a nagging feeling stirs there too, a whisper, maybe a warning that Issac might not be looking at me the way you'd look at a friend or someone you're *only* attracted to. I tear my eyes away from the picture and focus on the caption underneath: They are a treat to look at, but can we truly say our most

eligible bachelor has finally committed to love? It didn't work out
so well with the last one we thought he might commit to, and this
one lives all the way in little Rhode Island.

As soon as I read it, I'm reminded of the opposing opinions
and theories about Issac's love life in the media. No one knows
whether he's afraid of commitment, or if Melinda broke his heart
and he came running to me. Not even I'm sure how he truly feels
about her, because when she called him during my last hours in
Cali, he excused himself to take it, even though he didn't have
much time left to spend with me. Who's to say that it didn't work
out so well with her when second chances happen all the time?

I toss the magazine in the back seat and put my own confusing
feelings about the two of them on the back burner, but I can't tuck
away Wilma's words because part of me does wonder if Issac will
ever move back home.

———————

OUTSIDE OF WILDLY GREEN, I FIND LEX WIPING DOWN THE GLASS
door. He hugs me and tells me how *incredibly cute* I do in fact look,
then he shakes off the jitters.

"We have to be absolutely perfect. And the customers, all of
them, better be on their best behavior because the shop is so
lovely. Too pretty for me to fight them in," he says. "And there's
a surprise waiting for you inside that made it even prettier."

He opens the door, and I gasp. It was already gorgeous, filled
with greenery, but now there are dozens of extravagant bouquets
everywhere. The shop smells like a field of wildflowers.

"What is all of this? And how could we afford it?"

"We can't," Lex says. "But Issac can."

My heart races. I try to hide my smile, aware that I'm under

Lex's scrutiny when I pick up a card on the counter. *Because you would've said no when you wanted to say yes*, is all it says. I should've known this was Issac as soon as I walked in.

"You're right, the shop is way too lovely to fight in," I say to Lex, but he's already out of earshot, walking toward the back room, where Mom probably is.

He picked the perfect word to encompass the way it feels being in this space. It's organized, every section has a purpose, the lights, the vine plants in the window, the scent of white linen and cedarwood candles burning complements the smell of the flowers. The skin-care table has prewhipped butters that look good enough to eat. It feels like a haven here. At least until we open it to the public and they make a mess. It'll be the best kind of mess today though.

I spin the chair where I'll be testing products on people and admire my own hair in the mirror. It's rounder than it usually is for day-two hair. It's long but still looks like a green growing thing, reaching for the sunlight coming through the windows. I could be just another plant in the shop.

I'm still looking in the mirror when the door opens.

That strange sensation squeezes my stomach again. Butterflies spreading their wings when they should be sleeping. I bite my bottom lip and watch in the mirror as an incredibly tall, broad-shouldered man walks toward me.

"I thought the flower delivery meant you wouldn't be able to make it," I say after a beat. "But I'm happy I was wrong."

The plan is for me to fly out to California next week and celebrate the reopening with him before we attend the art exhibition he's curating, so it would've been fine. But Issac flashes me a smile in the reflection, and says, "I told you I wouldn't miss this day."

I don't turn around, too deep in my body, having so many big feelings there I don't know what to do with. He plucks a flower from one of the bouquets and comes up behind me to tuck it into my hair. Even though he'd pick flowers from the front of houses after school to hand me, this gesture is more intimate. Nothing feels as innocent as it did before he posted that first picture of us. We stare at each other in the mirror. I'll tell him I plan to steal his sunglasses and the black utility vest he's wearing when I remember how to breathe.

He bends to rest his chin on the top of my head and wraps an arm around my waist. I sigh into him.

"We look even better together in real life than we do in the pictures we took at the party," he says. "And we looked so good then."

That damn dress, I can almost hear him saying.

The tension between us thrums. What if instead of resisting it, I let myself lean into the chemistry of these stolen moments? Just because this will never be real doesn't mean I can't enjoy it for a few more weeks.

I laugh nervously, shaken by my own thoughts.

"We are kind of cute as far as humans go," I say.

But he trails his fingers down my arm absentmindedly, and goose bumps rise in their wake. The tension doesn't break, especially when he touches the ring dangling in the center of my chest.

He doesn't speak. I watch him swallow while we both examine it. The importance of this ring and this necklace lies heavy in the air. He inches his fingers to the skin below it, and I close my eyes at his continued touch. Does my body even belong to me anymore when he's this close?

This is not . . . we can't. We said we wouldn't.

"We're crossing those lines again, Issac," I warn.

"We're just friends," he whispers against my ear. I wish he'd bite it. "Fake dating friends."

It's like his voice in my dream, him saying, *Tell me you don't want me.*

I shiver, almost say that means we should stop, but then Lex clears his throat like he's got the flu.

"We've got five minutes till we open, *lovebirds,*" Mom says, a question for me in her tone.

When Issac and I pull apart, he grins, clearly amused by her comment; he's unaware that she wants to make sure we know what we're doing so we don't hurt each other. Do we?

Issac squeezes my hip before he goes, and I take one last look in the mirror, silently berating myself for having so little control over my body. But when I turn around and see him hug Lex, then take a tulip from a bouquet of them to hand to Mom, it's my heart that aches.

"You remembered," my mom says, voice heavy with tears. Because tulips were the flowers my dad would bring her every Friday when he got paid, for no reason other than he loved her and she loved tulips. Issac might not always remember to call her on her birthday, or not to call on the anniversary of my dad's death because she likes to grieve alone, but there are some things that stay with us, and for some reason, the tulips stayed with him.

I release a breath and watch Mom fuss over her outfit. He helps her fix the strands falling from her bun. My bones throb to walk over and wrap my arms around them both. But with three minutes to spare, Lex and I triple-count the cash register, make sure we have enough sampling sticks on the tables, then flip the sign on the door to OPEN. We're as ready as we're going to be.

WHAT I REMEMBER

Nine years ago. The ring, the bracelet, the tulips.

Vanessa Thompson, by accounts from outsiders glancing into the situation with her husband, might've seemed like a strong, unfazed woman. That was what she presented, even to Dennis Thompson himself, when the brain fog set in and she'd have to remind him of things, when she'd sit on the curb with him because he couldn't walk up the street without stopping to catch his breath, when he could no longer sing while strumming his guitar.

It's alright, she'd tell him. *I'm okay. I love you more than life. There's nowhere I'd rather be than at your side*, she'd say when he worried that she was falling apart on the inside. But I'd listen on late nights, watch from the darkness of the hall while she cried with the sink water running, trying not to make a sound louder than the steady stream. It wasn't always possible. One night, she couldn't help the ragged sounds coming from her throat, the quiet way she begged, "Dear God, I'm so tired. Please." And my own chest hurt with wondering whether she was asking God to save my father, for a miracle that wouldn't come, or to put an end to both of their suffering. Because Dennis Thompson was supposed to die a year ago, then six months later, then *it'll be any day now*, but he was still holding on to her hand like an anchor to this earth.

My throat was sandpaper dry when I slipped into my room and picked up my phone. It was past midnight, but Issac still answered my call. "Ni, what's wrong?"

How could I get the words out? Why did I expect him to hear my voice and know what I'd need to say?

I was ashamed, suddenly remembering he had lost both parents.

Was crying to him over one I hadn't lost yet cruel?

"Nothing, I'm sorry," I said. "It was something silly, but I didn't realize the time. I don't want Mom to hear me talking. I'll tell you tomorrow."

I hung up the phone and tried to keep my heart from splintering into pieces. Minutes later, Issac knocked on my window. Something heavy gathered in my throat as I watched him haul himself inside, and as soon as his feet hit the carpet, I let a cry escape. And then we were hugging and he was saying soothing things and rubbing my back, and he didn't care that his shirt was tear-soaked or that it was hard for me to explain why I needed him that night.

"Shh. I'm here," he said. "You can tell me, or you don't have to say anything at all."

His words broke a dam inside of me. For the first time, I let my feelings pour out, telling him I couldn't imagine a life without my father in it but hated that my mother was becoming a shell of herself. Hated that my father couldn't dance with me anymore, or that there hadn't been tulips on the kitchen table in months. That I wanted both for it to be over and to prolong it forever so that we'd never lose my father.

Issac listened and held me until the sobs left. When I pulled back, self-conscious over the tears still slipping, he was crying too. I apologized and he tilted my chin.

"It's me. Please don't do that."

The words felt tender, released the feeling of being a burden, so that when he asked if I wanted him to stay awhile I answered honestly. We lay on my bed, our limbs tangled above the covers. He smelled like mint and grass after it rains, and I was quickly lulled into sleep. When I woke alone the next morning, there was a note along with a small silver ring he always wore on his pinky. *Took your name bracelet and left a ring from my mom's jewelry box in its place.* A trade that didn't feel fair when my bracelet was a thing strung together haphazardly to pass the time. But even back then I'd realized Issac Jordan trusted me enough to wear his mom's ring. It felt like a responsibility and a promise all at once.

I put it on the necklace my dad had given me two birthdays ago, and decided I'd keep both forever.

Later I'd learn that when my mom walked into the kitchen after waking up, she found pink tulips Issac had picked from a neighbor's yard sitting on the counter for her.

26

REOPENING SURPRISES

THE DAY HAS ITS HICCUPS: COCOA BUTTER OVERFLOWING ONTO the counter, too much peppermint in products, remaking things we shouldn't have to, but hours ago, Shida Anala announced to her followers that I'm helping her, which prompted phone calls from out-of-towners asking to make appointments. We let journalists that Bernie vetted come in for interviews and to take photos of the shop. Since then, the traffic hasn't died down. There's a line of customers outside, waiting for their chance to enter now that we have a hundred-person capacity. We know a lot of them are here for Issac, but that's okay because he offers his best smile while suggesting his favorite products in the store. He seems as happy to be here as we are having him here. While Mom's at the hair-product station creating custom mixes, Lex is doing the same on skin care, and Destiny came in around 10:00 a.m. to help with the cash register. Even Bridget dropped in to organize things she doesn't have to organize and *gently* suggest some customers check out our deodorant. But my job is the best one. Four lucky customers won free slots for what we're calling "the Experience" today, and I get to be the one to put their custom mixes to the test.

I rub balm into a man's beard, but then I catch his wife's curious eye through the mirror and hand her the product to finish the job.

She smiles and asks if she's doing okay while rubbing the balm in circles. By the way her husband's shoulders fall as he leans back in the chair, I wink and tell her she's doing it just right. She giggles when he closes his eyes and mumbles something to her in Spanish. I turn away, flush creeping across my face for invading a private moment, and because I can't help but think about how long it's been since I've had a romantic partner of my own. But then my gaze lands on Mom, standing by the cash register with Pete, throwing her head back in a laugh at something he said. When did he get here? And why is he here . . . other than to flirt with my mother?

The thought leaves a sour taste in my mouth, and when my customers leave, I rush to wipe down the chair for my next appointment. But Bridget walks over, pokes me, and says, "Should you add the ability to spice up a sex life to the list of what you do here?"

I laugh. "They were really into it, weren't they?"

"A little too into it if you ask me." Bridget nods her head in Issac's direction. "But your Issac . . . He's very adorable. And he's been watching you all day."

"Really?" I chance a glance at him. My body has been aware of his presence, vibrating whenever I hear his deep voice across the room. There's a tether between us, every time I turn to look for him it feels like he's looking for me too. "So, do I have your blessing to keep seeing him?"

"Well, he's no David," she says with a wink, reminding me of how different my interaction was with her big sister this morning.

Still, I say, "Bridget, about Wilma . . ."

Her eyes narrow right before Lex comes up from behind us. "Who's David?"

"My scumbag of a late husband," Bridget says, then saunters away before I can try to convince her to have a conversation with my grumpy but obviously hurt neighbor.

Lex raises a brow, asking for the juicy details about David, and I give him a quick rundown. He laughs, then helps me organize the vanity in front of us. "Bridget is right, you know. Issac's no David. Someone will be lucky to have him, and you better figure out your feelings soon so that someone can be you."

I throw a balled-up paper towel at him, but he successfully runs from it. When I bend to pick it up, I'm met with the sight of familiar jeans that encase long legs and something else I know more than I want to about.

"Hi, Laniah," comes a voice I can't say I've missed at all. "I'm next. And I'm excited."

When I straighten up, Darius, or more importantly, thumbs-down dude, is grinning at me. He doesn't hesitate to slide into my chair while I open up Google Calendar and read the list of names for appointments. Sure enough, his initials are right here on my screen. Slick.

"It's been a bit," he says. "I missed you."

"Why are you here?" I ask.

"Because I won an appointment." He runs his fingers through his wavy hair. "Was hoping you could help with the dryness."

"I wonder how many times you entered to be a part of the free trial, but I meant . . . why would you come? We haven't spoken and—"

He cuts me off by saying, "I entered once. I'm lucky like that, and I came for hair care. What can you do for me? Other than bless me with your incredibly *stimulating* conversation?"

Was that a dig? Is he insinuating that I'm boring?

I hold eye contact through the mirror. "I think I can find someone else to help you."

He swirls in the chair until we're face-to-face. "Why did you block me?"

"Is that why you really came? That was weeks ago. Are you . . . stalking me or something? Because I have nothing to say to you."

"Stalking?" he asks with a frown. "What kind of person do you think I am?"

"I'm not sure anymore," I say honestly.

"I think we left off bad for absolutely no reason."

"That's quite an apology," I say, sighing. "Listen, I'm working and need to be on my game. Maybe we can talk another time, but not here. Especially not today."

Something shifts in his eyes. He leans back in the chair, smiling. "So, you won't be taking care of my hair?"

"I don't feel comfortable with that right now, but maybe someone else here can help. . . ."

"That's bad business ethic," he says, standing from the chair and scowling down at me. "Maybe I should leave a review on Yelp. Post it on social media, all that."

This time I'm more prepared for how quick he is to show his true colors.

"Do what you want," I say. "You're clearly seeking attention, but you won't get it from me. Don't come back here ever again."

Just as he fixes his lips to respond, Issac walks over. His brows are dipped, mouth tight, as he glances between me and Darius. "Everything all good, babe?"

"Everything is fine," I say, and give Darius a sharp look. "Right?"

"Yeah. I was just going," he says before trying to shake Issac's hand. My best friend just stares at it, and Darius nods, insulted. "I see what it is."

I hold my breath until he's out of the shop door. And Issac gets my attention by standing right in front of me, looking down at me with serious eyes. "What was that about?"

But there are customers waiting to speak to him. I can hear teenage girls gushing about him from the other side of the room. The interaction must've attracted attention because some older folk are whispering to each other.

"Don't worry about any of them," Issac says, tilting my chin so that I'm focused on only him again. "What was that about?"

"That was Darius coming to *talk*," I whisper.

Issac's eyes widen, but I shake my head, tell him we'll talk about it later. I can tell he wants to fight me on it, but he sighs instead.

"I'm good. I'm just glad you're here," I say. He smiles a little, and I bump him with my shoulder. "And you definitely called me babe when you were talking to Darius. Thought we said that was off the list for terms of endearment."

Issac narrows his eyes. "Some dude is dying for your attention and probably wants his fifteen minutes of fame, and that's what you're worried about right now? You're a piece of work, best friend."

"And you love it," I say.

"Sometimes. But I do wonder how much you keep to yourself so you don't worry me."

"Maybe some stuff," I say. "But I'm working on it."

Issac nods and hugs me. But when he leaves to talk to customers, I release a breath. He's right. It's not the only thing I'm worried about. I can't believe Darius showed up here. I wonder if he'll come back.

If he really will try to do something nasty to tarnish the reputation of Wildly Green.

27

HOW TO TARNISH A TARGET

Promote it on @heaven_of_hair

Please help my daughter with her skin lesions.
Treatment is $3,000 and I . . .

This seems dope. You dusties need to go to RI and seek
help from Ni Ni.

She's so thick it hurts :,)

She's ugly. Bet her hair products don't even work.

Look at my parentsssss. They're so cute together.

Dm to be my sugar baby and I will spoil well and give
weekly allowance

So, is she a maid or not? Why clean toilets if you have a
whole business?

@saratoni1 time for a trip to RI?

Just because she has a Black mom doesn't mean
she should be telling Black girls with 4c curls how
to do their hair.

The last comment makes me wince. Eighty-nine other people
chimed in underneath. The photo they're going on about is one of
Issac in my shop chair and me doing his hair. I anticipated these
kinds of comments but didn't realize how much reading one would
sting. Mom didn't give me much melanin, and my dad was white.
My hair's a 3c, maybe a 3b on wash day, and people have confused
me for Hispanic all my life. Especially because the population in
Providence is so high. It's never bothered me much, but at times I
have felt just a little out of place when it seems like I have one too
many boxes to fit into. But I'm no victim. I understand how nu-
anced and messy the situation is because of the pain Black women
have had to endure due to erasure and colorism.

Issac and Lex just stepped outside to pick up the garbage that lines
of customers left in front of the shop. It's only Mom here with me, and
when I look over, she's smiling down at her own phone. Something
twists in my belly as I recognize it as the kind of smile that springs up
uncontrollably whenever someone special sends a message. For a moment, I consider asking if she's texting Pete because I can't forget
hearing her bubbly laugh across the shop today when she had that
conversation with him. She breathes out, and I can see her smile falter, her hands shake a little. My chest tightens at the thought. Vanessa
Thompson loves hard, often cries over my father still, and I find
myself wondering if she could survive another heartbreak.

And selfishly . . . if I could survive her being in love again.

She catches me staring, says, "Why are you looking at me that
way?"

This is my moment to ask her if something has shifted and she's open to dating again, but my throat is dry, and I decide I don't want to know. "Maybe you should take over the hair-care part of the Experience from now on," I say, which is something I was going to suggest that now feels small in comparison to the thoughts of her circulating in my brain.

After I tell her what the comment said, she sighs and leans against the counter; a stand of gray hair falls over her face. "You're not telling them what to put in their hair, you're helping them find what's right for their hair in *our* product line. That's the point of the Experience, right? Truth is, baby, people are going to have something to say no matter what you do and what you don't do. As long as your heart is in it, be who you are. Be your whole self. Alright?"

The tight coil in my belly begins to loosen hearing the words from Mom's mouth. She's right. My heart is all the way in it. I'm finally fully focused on doing what I love, and I want to share that love with others, if they're open to it.

"Alright," I say. "I will."

"Besides, I thought you were staying off the internet."

"I wanted to see what people thought of our launch."

"Pssh. Let Lex handle that," Mom says, waving her hand and opening the cash register. "You prioritize keeping your mental health in check."

The lady is hardly ever wrong. I'll delete my personal social media accounts. Besides, we have the business page, and that's the one that counts. Issac will understand. Just as I think about him, he walks in the shop and gives me a smile. Yeah. That man will support whatever I choose to . . .

The thought leaves me when a notification comes across my screen.

Darius Palonco tagged you in a post.

That coil in my stomach twists tight again and makes me sick with knowing. Mom's saying something to me, but I can't hear her as my finger hovers over the red button. I force myself to press it, but I'm completely thrown when I find a picture of me with my head flung back in a laugh while sitting across a candle-lit table. Darius took this on our last date. He took this when I thought he was somebody who enjoyed spending time with me. He doesn't have many followers, a little over three hundred, but the caption reads: She's a cheater, he's a homewrecker. She was mine first.

I refresh the picture, and there are several comments already waiting.

Drop the date this photo was taken. knew something was sus

bro, get a life, always gotta be someone coming in with lies

you're the homewrecker

Drop the date!!!!!

@shauna341 See, told you she doesn't deserve Issac. What a hoe.

Show us proof

I start to shake, Mom squeezes my shoulders. "What's wrong, baby?"

Lex and Issac are suddenly at my sides, but I can't even look at them. I pass the phone to Mom. Count my breaths. One. Two. Why would he do this? Why would anyone do this? Then comes the misplaced blame: I should've talked to him when he wanted to talk. I should've . . .

"Where the hell does this boy live?" Mom says, pulling me away from ridiculous thoughts—this is entirely on Darius. "We will go over there right now and—"

"Mom," I say, trying to stop the room from spinning.

But it doesn't help when I look up and Issac is glancing down at my phone, a deep frown on his face.

"And rip off his balls," Lex finishes. "Take his fingers and shove them so far down his dirty throat the doctors will have to extract them through his ass."

"I just . . . everyone stop. Let me think of what to do."

Mom and Lex shut their mouths. Issac silently passes me my phone. The first thing I do when I gather myself is report the post, the second is block Darius from our business page as well as my personal one.

The third is meet Issac's stare.

"You okay?" His voice is unwaveringly gentle. He takes a step closer. "Do you need another minute to sit with this? I just want to make sure your heart is good before we talk about the situation."

Just a couple of hours ago, I was floating from how well the Experience went. Just a few seconds ago, I was filled with fury and hurt over Darius, but now I'm just feeling anxious.

"I want to hear what you think," I say. "What should we do? I hate the attention. Especially for the business, and is this going to affect you? What if he posts something else? What if . . ." I trail off while wondering if Darius has taken other pictures of me. I don't think he has, but clearly he can't be trusted to not have snuck a few. Then I remember the sexy picture I sent him, and my heart ticks in panic. I shift away from Issac, from Mom's worried eyes, from Lex's angry expression, the tips of my ears are burning hot.

Darius wouldn't release *that* picture, would he?

"Everything is going to be fine," Issac says from behind me. "I doubt this will get real traction with all the other stories out there right now, with no real proof that what he's saying is true, and with you mostly a ghost on socials it should die down quick. You saw what happened with the articles about your job. Twelve hours later people already found something else to talk about. Darius is trash for this, but I'm mostly concerned about *you* and how you're feeling."

Lex makes a humming sound at Issac's concern. It's probably furthering Lex's agenda to get the two of us together. But his observing eyes don't stop me from looking into Issac's and asking, "Do you want to go somewhere? Before your flight back to Cali? I could use some air."

He nods, so I hug Lex and Mom.

"Issac's right," I say. "Darius just wanted a little attention; I won't give him any more of mine and let him ruin this day for me. We can't let him ruin this day for us. Promise me you'll both go home and celebrate. The Experience was everything we could've dreamt of."

I see the corners of Mom's lips turn up, some light seep back into her eyes. "And more. It was a dream, baby."

"Shane's waiting in *our apartment* with homemade drinks and his attempt at making my family's recipe for Peking duck. I promise I'll drink a mojito for each of us," Lex says.

28

THE DIFFERENT WAYS
WE MATERIALIZE

THERE IS NOTHING LIKE BEING AT BEAVERTAIL STATE PARK IN Jamestown when the sun is about to set. Issac helps me onto one of the big rocks, and we sit under the transitioning sky, watching waves crash below. I enjoy being silent in his company. So much has happened since yesterday, good and bad, but here, with Issac beside me and the soothing smell of salt around us, I let all of it fade to the background. He unzips his crossbody bag to collect a few pebbles, and I smile, noticing the little things he'd taken from the shop too: a business card, sampling sticks, rose petals. Afterward, he takes his coat off and spreads it over the rock, then pulls me down to lie beside him.

"I miss living here," he says when the sky starts growing pink and purple above us.

"Do you?" I ask, "I thought you loved living in Cali."

"I don't think it's possible to love anywhere as much as I love it here," he says. "I ache for home sometimes."

A smile tugs at my mouth, relief running through me. I turn

on my side. He does the same. We're face-to-face when I ask him to make a list of the things he misses about home.

He starts with "Beaches." California has beautiful ones, he tells me, but there's something comforting about being able to find water within thirty minutes of wherever we are in Rhode Island. Our food. With all the diversity and authentic flavor, the specialties like doughboys and clam cakes and even the red sauce pizza he hated as a kid. He misses the culture of Providence. The way the streets sing with something that feels particular: a mix of hip-hop and fine art and magic.

"And I miss living near you, Ni," he says quietly. "You, randomly dragging me out here when we're both needing to recharge by the ocean." His words settle behind my breastbone, my own get caught in my throat. He pushes my hair from my face to see me better in the darkening daylight. "Do you miss me as much as I miss you?"

The question takes me by surprise. A small laugh escapes my lips. "Of course. Do you even have to ask that?"

He shrugs. "It doesn't ever feel like you're pushing for me to be home. You rarely call me. I'm usually the one looking to hear your voice."

He smiles shyly and averts his eyes. My heart beats furiously in my chest.

Then he says, "I know it was always hard for you to open up when we were younger. You're just built that way, like to keep feelings close to you, but since I moved, it seems like you've had a tougher time. You'll text me for something and wait for me to get the time instead of calling and telling me you need me to find a private jet and *get home right now*."

It hits me that while I was on the other side of the invisible string, wondering why his calls were coming less frequently, he must've been wondering why mine hardly came at all. The thought makes my body warm before even considering how well he knows me. In the past, I'd question why it was hard to share my feelings and thought it's just the way I am, whether good or bad. Now I'm starting to wonder if I've grown quieter the same way my mom did after we lost Dad.

"I know I'm difficult to read sometimes," I say. "But I do miss you, just as much. It's just . . . you've always been such a free spirit. Remember when you moved in with those strangers from Craigslist when we were eighteen? I didn't like it, but it was right for you. I never want to hold you anywhere. You've been flourishing now that you're spreading your wings. And I love that for you. I never want to change you or bother you."

"Lately, I've been thinking . . ." He releases a breath. "That maybe the urge to be a free spirit comes from my parents dying and having no control over what happened to me after I was left behind. At least, it's a thought I've been exploring with my therapist."

My heart swells at his confession. I nod, silently telling him I know.

"But, Laniah Leigh Thompson, you couldn't bother me if you tried. Though . . . I hope you'll consider trying in the future because it might be cute."

A smile breaks across my face. "Oh yeah? That's how you want me?"

"That's how I want you," he says.

So I pull his beard hair, pinch his chin, lean forward, and bite his cheek. He makes a hissing sound when I let go, alerting me to the fact that I haven't done anything that intimate with or to him for some time. Maybe ever. Our eyes lock, mouths inches apart, his fingers tangle in my hair to keep me close. I can almost taste the spearmint on his tongue when his eyes flick to my lips. I'm not imagining it this time. He wants to kiss me. But he must see the apprehension in my eyes, the fear of what a kiss could change between us because he lets me go and shifts to look up at the sky again. I'm breathless when I turn onto my back, thinking my nerves sparked his own fears. As someone who wants a soulmate, why would he waste his time and mine? Confuse our situation, possibly strain our relationship, just for a kiss?

"Ni," he says, and I think he'll mention our boundaries but instead he changes the subject. "I know you don't want to talk about what happened with Darius, but after what he did and the hotel articles about you, I'm nervous you won't tell me that you're stressed. What if it messes with your blood pressure?"

I'm about to tell him about my lisinopril increase to help with that, and that I'm calling Bridget's doctor tomorrow too, but he speaks again.

"I still think we need to make sure the shop is solid—we said until the end of summer, and time is flying by, but I don't want to hurt you, especially if we're not . . ." He trails off, and I let the unspoken reason I imagine sit somewhere in my chest. *Being careful enough*. Is that what he wanted to say?

But would the chemistry between us really disappear just because we call it quits early?

"I'll just go into my hermit shell," I say. "Focus on the business, for at least a couple more weeks. You said the Darius stuff will probably die down. You don't have to worry about me, Issac."

"Yeah," he says, sounding unconvinced. "Alright. And Bernie is already planning damage control with Darius. But people make shit up on the internet all the time." Issac's phone vibrates; he glances down at it and clicks his tongue. "Wow. Can't say the man's name more than once or he'll appear like Bloody Mary. He's probably making sure I'll be on time for my flight back."

My stomach sinks at the thought of Issac leaving so soon. "You could miss the flight back and stay," I joke.

He sits up and looks down at me. "You need me here?"

"Maybe just a little. Possibly so."

"Well." Issac shrugs. "I'll miss a flight when you're sure."

"Jerk."

He laughs and stands, then pulls me to my feet. I pick up his jacket and dust it off. We start to climb back over the rocks, until something below catches my eye. Forty feet down, a man sits near the dark water with a lantern. I walk closer to glean what he's doing. How did he get down there? The rock face is steep in this area.

"Ni? Be careful," Issac says from several feet back. "You're too close to the edge."

I take another step, turn, and wiggle my eyebrows at him. "Am I scaring you?"

"You know you are," he says.

"You'll be less scared standing with me."

"You can be wild by yourself," he says, though he's still watching me closely.

I stick my tongue out. I could safely take two more steps, but Issac's parents were in an accident, so I know he's scared of seeing his best friend this close to a cliff face. Standing right here gives me the rush I need anyway. I close my eyes and lift my arms. Let the night wind race through my hair. Issac is so quiet; I wonder if he started walking to the car. But when I turn back around, he's still there, his white teeth flashing in the dark.

I walk over and he takes my hand.

"Hey, Ni . . ." One beat. Two. "You know, I could handle Darius. Push him off a cliff for the sharks to feast. Bernie will make it look like an accident."

I laugh and let him lead me through the dark. "You are the definition of a gentle giant. You wouldn't hurt anybody."

"Not true," Issac says. "For you, I'd bring down the sun."

29

WHEN HE DREAMS

THE WEEK GOES LIKE THIS: A COUPLE OF CELEBRITIES MAKE APpointments for the Experience; podcasters and journalists reach out for interviews; investors start to call; my UTI test results come out inconclusive, but my doctor sends in a prescription for an antibiotic *in case* I do have one; Bridget's doctor's office makes me a new patient appointment; and Darius keeps his mouth shut. With everything going on, there's not much time to spend stressing *and* fantasizing about the kiss that almost happened with Issac. But every time there's a lull while working, his words echo in my mind. *For you, I'd bring down the sun.*

I'm finally able to breathe about the Darius situation, but the biggest blessing of the week is how special it is that investors are the ones seeking me and Mom out. Most of them wanted us to sign paperwork before even proving what they could do for us, but we got a call from someone who seems promising.

We show up at Henry's office in Warwick for the scheduled appointment, and Lex and Mom are impressed by him right away.

His office is large and organized, there are pictures of his kids on his desk. Unlike some of the other investors, Henry speaks in raw numbers and timelines and is candid about profits and losses and some other things I have to explain to Mom and Lex. But all the while, I can't help looking at the large patches of dandruff sitting on Henry's scalp. Mom asks if he wants to come see the shop and test products, and he says he already sent one of his workers to the grand opening to report back. This catches me off guard. Lex glances at me too. We should've known an investor might do secret-shopper sneakiness, but I take note, wondering why Henry wouldn't want to try our products himself. I think I'd have the perfect remedy to help his dry scalp.

"I'd love to sign some paperwork today," Henry says, eyes set on Mom.

She's all breathy and excited about his offer to provide us the capital we need for the Experience, and we all think it's fair that he'd make 20 percent on a five-year return. But I'm not eager to sign into a partnership with him just yet. I glance down at my phone to read the last text message I got from Shida Anala again. **Patiently waiting for my products to get here. But think I'll need to visit you in person soon <3.** Then I ask Henry if he can give us a minute to discuss. His eyes flick from me back to Mom before he politely excuses himself from the room.

I turn to Lex. "What'd you think of him? Honestly."

"The man seems to really know his stuff," Lex says. "I think the business will do well if you decide to work with him. But I don't know. There's something . . ."

"Missing?" I offer, and he nods his head. "I feel it too. Wildly Green might do well, but will it do the best that it can do?" I turn to Mom, grab her hand. "I think we should consider it for a couple of days. I'm not sure he's invested in our products the way I'd want him to be." Her eyebrows dip, creating frown lines on her face. "And I keep thinking Dad would say to trust myself."

She blinks at the mention of my father. "What if we leave Henry waiting and he changes his mind?"

"I've thought of that too," I admit. "But what if we give it time and someone better comes along? Are you really comfortable signing a ten-year contract with him without making sure we don't have other options?"

"I'm not sure there's going to be anything better," Mom says.

This is her baby, her life's work, her hopes and dreams I'm asking her to put on the line. I hope I'm right. She squeezes my hand.

"But I trust you. I believe in you. If you think we should wait, then we will."

OVER THE PHONE, KATRINA PAINTS HER TOES WHILE I FEED MY plants. When she told her boss she was looking for work elsewhere, it took him two days to pull her into his office and offer the raise she was asking for. She told him she'll give him a decision *after* collecting her other offers. She's already got two interviews and one solid offer from another consulting company. I make a mental note to pick her up some chocolate-covered strawberries to celebrate her bravery right before she hits me with the "Soooooo."

"That doesn't sound like a *so my supervisor is a—*"

She cuts me off. "No, no. Let's talk the juicy stuff. Is the sex better now that you and Issac don't have to hide the relationship y'all clearly had for years? Girl, the way he looked at you on grand reopening day."

"We weren't hiding anything, and you were there for five minutes!"

"And all five of them he was looking at you like you exude sex. Eye-fucking you in front of older folk. It was scandalous. Your momma was there, for God's sake."

My temperature rises. This is very different from the sweet way Bridget said it.

"He was doing no such thing. Why would he?"

Katrina is silent for a second, and I realize I screwed up again. "Why wouldn't he?"

I chew my lip, annoyed over my mistake. "Just . . . we were only about business that day. He was strictly professional. And then you know Darius came in and ruined things."

Katrina hums, and I swear it's suspicious, until she says, "Think what you want, but I saw it and I'm sure everyone else did too. You're the only one who doesn't seem to notice the way he notices you. It's kind of cute, in a silly way because what you should be doing is sneaking to the back room for a quickie when he comes down. The adrenaline of people possibly catching you in the shop will make it ten times more intense. Promise you that. Bet when you go to the art exhibition this weekend, he'll want to rip your dress off right in front of everyone."

I love her. She is unequivocally her. Through and through. It's part of the reason I feel so guilty that I can't tell her that there will never be any sex between me and Issac. Even though my mind and my body have tried to imagine otherwise.

"Since when are you supportive of my relationship with him anyway?"

She runs the sink water on her side, says, "I still think you need to watch your heart because what if the pressure of a long-term commitment starts to get to him? It's been sunshine and flowers now that you're in your honeymoon phase, but what happens when life really gets in the way? What happens when you feel the distance? I'm a little nervous for Issac too. I mean, you've had one serious relationship but you never talk like you were in love with the man. Meanwhile, I've had my heart kissed and broken repeatedly, so I've built a tolerance. And now that I see the way Issac loves you, I'm starting to wonder if you'll be the one to ruin it. But . . . I'd be the worst friend ever if I didn't tell you to enjoy the dick before it's gone either way."

"Now that sounds more like you," I say with a laugh. What I don't say is her evaluation of me was spot-on. I was never *in love* with my ex, so when he cheated on me, it didn't really break my heart.

———————

HOURS LATER, I WAKE WITH THE BACK OF MY NECK DAMP, THE HAIR there sweat slick, and kick the covers off. I sit up and reach for the bottle on my nightstand to ease the burning warmth in my body, but the water is lukewarm and does nothing to settle my heat flash. I need to pee again. It's the third time tonight, and I have to be up in an hour. I've been taking the antibiotic for days and it hasn't alleviated my symptoms. I sigh and start to stand, but then my phone vibrates with a text from Issac.

> You're a heavy sleeper so I hope this doesn't
> wake you, but I dreamt of you tonight.
> Whenever I dream of you, it's usually little
> glimpses. But this one was a story. We were
> making a sculpture together. You had paint on

your face. And I woke up wondering why we've
never done that before.

The burn returns to my body. I cradle the phone to my chest, fighting off a smile. Issac dreams of me. He texted me during dark hours to tell me he dreamt of me making art, something he loves more than anything.

I almost text back to ask him what else happened in the *story* but stop myself because I know where these late-night conversations usually lead. And the last time we were together we both almost did something we might've regretted. Besides, Issac was the one to pull away, probably because he knows that our sexual chemistry is different from romantic love. He's not going to alter his freedom and settle for committing to someone who's not his soulmate. And I'm sure he wouldn't stop himself from kissing her. I'd just get in the way of him finding that person. If he hasn't already.

So I put my phone on the nightstand and promise myself I'll text him something sweet in a few hours. I'd love to create art with him someday . . . after our desires fade.

30

SMALL MIRACLES

A HARD CREASE SITS BETWEEN MOM'S BROWS WHENEVER she's focused. Even with her reading glasses on, I can tell she's trying to make sense of her own handwriting in the shop appointment book. Soon we're going to have to take Lex's advice and have Destiny enter every appointment in the computer too. From where I'm seated to fill out factory order forms, I watch her and Lex hang string lights around the window and decorate the building outside. I was going to do it with them, but they insisted I rest my feet while the shop's quiet. And when I get home, I'll have a couple of hours to lie on the couch, listening to Empty Hour's album *Shades*, eating potato chips and pickles straight from the jar. Maybe I'll have the energy to pack outfits for my trip. I've been sneaking in visions of hugging Issac all day. We may not be able to be romantic, but I miss him more since he left. He's been consumed in a beautiful way with the art exhibition happening this weekend, and he's a little stressed wondering if he's ready to unveil *Secret Sun* that night. So, he's been busy there, and I've been busy here. But in three days, I'll get to go to Cali and hug him as much as I want to.

My last client of the day walks in, and I hope she can't see the sleepiness on my face. Her name is Sherry, and she's a Black woman with beautiful turquoise earrings and the clearest skin I've ever seen. The wig she's wearing is so natural, I can't tell it isn't her own hair until she sits in my chair and tells me herself. She has a straight-to-business tone and doesn't waste any time. She takes off her wig and shows me her tapered haircut. It's an adorable pixie, but she feels self-conscious because of her sparse edges and the few bald spots near her crown.

"It started to fall out after I had my baby last year. I always tease that he stole my hair because that boy has a whole mop on his head," she says with a laugh. "But it seems like I can't get any growth in those areas. I've tried different products, but nothing has worked, so I just wear wigs."

My stomach has been in knots each session after reading the comments about me being mixed race a week ago, but I take a breath and ask if I can touch her hair. She smiles and nods.

"I don't have children," I say, "so I don't know anything about losing hair after having them, but many women come to us for the same thing. I want you to know you're not alone. It's natural. Our bodies are complex."

Something shifts in her eyes, brightens, her shoulders loosen. "Really?"

"Really," I say, "and I'm not going to lie. It's going to take work and consistency, and everybody is different, but I promise you we will do what we can to make you feel your best again. We can make sample-sized products that you can try out over the course of a month, and we'll go from there. See if we need to adjust."

"I really appreciate the honesty that it won't be some miracle treatment."

"It won't be, but if we do the work it might feel like one in the end. Your hair is already beautiful. Your baby boy is winning if he inherited hair like this."

She smiles, and I swirl her chair around until her eyes meet mine in the mirror instead. Then, I touch the crown of her head, play with the coils there. "And this shape fits your face so well."

Sherry touches the back of her neck, unsure. "You think so?"

"I do," I say, and start the work of washing her hair.

Afterward, I give her a stimulating scalp massage with Mom's special growth serum, then show her how she can do the same thing at home. Mom and I both give her tips, which include letting her scalp breathe more and limiting the wigs. I can tell it makes her feel anxious, but I show her tricks to cover up the spots she doesn't want the world to see and remind her that she's gorgeous with or without them. "We're all insecure about something," I tell her. "But I promise you're radiant. And if you feel it on the inside, you're going to notice it on the outside, and so will other people."

I pack her a little goodie bag with sample sizes of free products while she examines herself in the mirror. I try not to watch her, but my soul feels good when dimples deepen her cheeks. Her dimples remind me of Issac's, and suddenly I miss him in an achy, nonplatonic way that makes me a bit uncomfortable.

"Wow," Sherry says, twirling around to face me and glowing like a fluorescent light.

Mom comes up and sticks an extra product in the goodie bag. "Wow is right. You look gorgeous if I should say so myself."

Sherry pops her collar, and we all laugh. "You two really know what you're doing in here. I didn't know if this was a gimmick, honestly. But my hair looks great, it smells good, it's soft . . . and I feel better than I have in months." She winks at Mom, says, "Maybe there's some magic in those hands that you passed down the line."

Mom reaches for me, gives my cheek a sloppy kiss. "That's my baby."

I must be glowing on the outside now too. "I'm so happy you feel good. I hope you'll come back."

"Oh, I plan to." She takes the bag from me before pulling a business card from her purse and handing it to Mom. "I'm sorry to spy like this, but now that I know how you two operate, I'm truly hoping you'll consider working with me."

My mom looks at the card with wide eyes, then: "You're an investor?"

"I am," Sherry says. "And I would be happy to help you get this beautiful shop where it should be. There are so many people who could use the kind of treatment you offer. The affirmations alone. Call me tomorrow if you'd like. I'll give you my credentials, go over numbers and scenarios, different options of what it might be like working with me. No rush, no pressure, but I want you to know I feel confident to say you'll be safe doing business with me. I care about this work you're doing."

Safe.

That's what I've been waiting to feel. How could Henry stand behind Wildly Green's products should he ever have to if he doesn't seem interested to know how we make them? We'd be signing away years with a caveat that says we owe the money in full should the Experience fail the test of time. And his heart wouldn't even be in it the way Sherry's might.

Right as I think it, Sherry says, "It'll be more than just making more money to me."

When she leaves, I turn to Mom and we both begin to dance. She squeals and pulls me close. "You really are my baby," she says. "Waiting was the right decision. You remind me of your dad."

The weight of that admission makes my eyes water. I'm happy she feels like my father left pieces of who *he* was with me, but the thing that my heart latches on to is how much more she's been mentioning him lately.

"*We* did so good, Mom," I finally say. "Sherry's the one. She has to be the one."

Vanessa Thompson shakes out her limbs like she's caught a happy chill. "That woman gave me butterflies," she says. And I can picture it now: everywhere we've been and everywhere we will go.

I'm full of feeling when Issac's face crosses my mind again. I decide I'm going to call him, interrupt his day so that the news can give him butterflies too.

31

THAT'S THE WAY IT BURSTS

THERE'S A PLATE COVERED IN FOIL ON MY PORCH WHEN I GET home. The ceramic is still warm, the food smells good. I turn to see Wilma waving at me from her door. Her idea of a peace offering? I smile hesitantly and wave back before heading inside. My stomach is rumbling, and I have to decide if I'm willing to ingest possible poison at the hands of my neighbor, but when I take off the foil there's a note waiting underneath with her number written on it. *Give this to B*, it says. My heart expands—any more love today and it'll burst. I was ready to convince them to make a connection, but maybe they're two people who are meant to be in each other's orbit without force. And maybe moving to this street was some kind of divine intervention because I'm meant to be a bridge instead.

I stick the note to the fridge so I can text Bridget her sister's number, then hurry to the counter to dig into the shepherd's pie. Wilma made it just the way I like it: with a coating of cheese on top. It's delicious, and I'm working on devouring the plate when

Lex calls. I pray he doesn't tell me something malfunctioned at the shop and I need to head back there.

"Girl. You might want to be seated for this."

Thirty minutes ago, we were so excited about the perfect investor seeking us out, and now the news is so bad Lex must warn me.

"I'm seated, just say it."

But I wasn't prepared for what he'd tell me, and frankly a malfunction at Wildly Green would've been welcome over what he sends me. Darius uploaded a screenshot of our text thread with the picture I sent him. *The* picture. The one of me in lace panties is on the internet. I shouldn't be surprised, but the shock ripples through me. "No. No. He wouldn't . . . this is not. This can't be real."

"I'm sorry, babes. The disgusting creep," Lex says. "Me and your mom are on our way."

Lex hangs up, and blood rushes to my face. White spots blur my vision, I blink back tears and lay my head on the cold marble of the island. Dread coils in my stomach, makes a tight knot there. I take deep breaths, fighting the urge to throw up.

My body. A part of me is for public consumption. How could Darius stoop this low?

My heart races as I wonder if Issac has seen it yet. I cover my mouth and look again. Cringing at the sight. The post has only been up for an hour, and it's already gone viral.

WHILE WE'RE SITTING ON MY LIVING ROOM RUG, MY MOM'S TALKING about calling the cops on Darius or getting one of my uncles to beat his ass. She's livid, but I'm still trying to grasp what happened. How this person who was only in my life for a few weeks would choose to forsake *my* privacy for the power to inflict pain just because things didn't go his way. For a moment, my mind flashes back to that sweet spot between cutting him off and deciding to go through with Issac's plan. Things weren't great but were simpler. I was working at the hotel, sneaking off to talk to Bridget, and no one on the internet even realized I existed. Now they'll be able to better undress me with their eyes.

Issac has been blowing up my phone, but I'm nervous to answer. Sick to my stomach that this furthers Darius's agenda to call me a cheater. Embarrassed, even though I'm a grown woman and Issac already knows about the picture. And I feel exposed and strange. Will this make things more messy between the two of us?

There's the pinching, achy feeling in my flank again. Maybe it really is from stress, maybe because this damn UTI won't clear up, but it's getting harder to ignore.

Lex pats my leg. "Deny it. Other than your name at the top of the conversation, the picture is below the neck. No one can tell it's you. Darius just looks like a loser for that thumbs-down reaction. How dumb of him to post a screenshot like that. Besides, your body is incredible, and people wear a lot less on the internet all the time."

I take my phone from Lex and look at it again. He's right. I'm relieved I didn't show my face. There's nothing here that proves this is really me. And the comments on Darius's post are mostly insulting:

Your face is a thumbs down. Go to hell.

No wonder she left you for Issac.

What the fuck is wrong with you? Perv.

I hope she presses charges.

You're a troll. Reporting you now.

Even a couple of celebrities commented saying they hope Darius gets dragged through the dirt. I only just met Kid Krews at Shida's party, and he makes a video saying he better not see Darius in the streets because he's taking the violation against me personally. I'm glad I can see all of this before Katrina gets the post taken down. I'm sleepy and feeling a little unhinged, laughing while scrolling.

But for all the prayers of protection, the post has double the likes and triple the comments compared to the one from last week. People are screaming for more evidence that it's me, that I'm a cheater. And Darius says he's going to give it to them, despite having nothing else to offer.

32

BEAUTIFUL HEARTS

MIGHT NOT BE MY LUCKY DAY, BUT DESTINY'S FRIENDS THINK it's theirs. Mom hires them to help in the shop while I lay low, and Lex says he'll make sure to record snippets of them working for me. As bad as things are because of Darius, I like to imagine the group of teens goofing around, feeling important, and being able to fill their pockets. My only other distraction from the situation has been spending time on the phone with Bridget, who's happy I'll be seeing her doctor in a couple of months, and refuses to talk about whether she'll call her sister. She does tell me random bits of drama going on at the hotel. I miss her, but don't miss working there.

When Bernie and Issac walk through my door, there are no pleasantries, they're straight to business. The *Year of the Lotus* is in two days and I hate that my problems are cutting into Issac's time to get ready for it, even though he says everything is set. Last night, I called him back and he told me Bernie booked flights as soon as they saw the Instagram post. We kept the conversation brief. And now Bernie's explaining how even without there being any other "evidence" Darius might try to release, the story has caught media attention and damage control needs to be done to ensure Issac's reputation remains intact before the art exhibition.

"No one should know Issac's here right now. I'll take care of it alone," Bernie says, and I can tell the way Issac's gripping my kitchen island, knuckles turning bone-colored, that he's not happy about having to hide instead of dealing with Darius himself.

My head is pounding, and I try to recall if I had my dose of lisinopril this morning. "What's *taking care of it* mean, exactly?"

"I might have to pay the asshole," Bernie says with a shrug, like this kind of thing happens often.

I watch Issac's jaw clench and wonder if he wants to murder Darius instead. But then he looks me in the face for the first time since he's arrived, and says, "What do you want to do about this, Laniah?"

For some reason, his use of my full name in this moment where I'm wondering what's on his mind makes me falter for a few seconds. But Bernie explained earlier that filing charges at the police department would be slow justice and this is the quickest way to immobilize the situation before it gets out of control. I'm not even mad that he's meeting up with Darius alone. I never want to see the man again and will happily pretend he doesn't even exist after all of this. I turn to Bernie and say, "Just make it go away."

"Alright." Bernie shifts on his feet, looking from Issac to me uncomfortably. "I must ask again before I go. Are you positive there's nothing more than sexy conversations between you and Darius? Anything else I should know about that I can make sure to get rid of?"

My stomach twists when I catch Issac's eyes. He wasn't comforting on the phone last night and the way he's staring makes me wonder if I did something wrong. I clear my throat and focus on Bernie's gaze instead. "We didn't even have any *sexy conversations*. Not really. He'd say things, but I'd mostly play it cool, laugh, ignore him. That kind of thing . . . until the picture."

Bernie nods and slides his hand over the tabletop. "That's a good thing. Listen, I'm sorry this is happening to you, but I'll do my best to make sure your name is cleared regarding cheating too. I'll be back as soon as I can." He points at Issac. "Don't go anywhere."

Issac huffs out a breath. "As you wish, boss."

I feel the sharpness of Issac's sarcasm in my bones. Bernie groans and looks like he wants to pull out the little remaining hairs he has left on his head. After Bernie leaves, the room is full of Issac's big feelings.

And he's back to not looking at me, but he does ask, "Are you good?"

"Are you?"

"I'm sorry," he says.

"Stop saying that."

"It's all I have right now." Issac sounds as tired as I feel.

My chest tightens. What if his reputation is already being ruined? What if the people running the exhibit are worried that they let him be a big part of it? Was pretending to be with me a mistake? Will he become a bigger tabloid magnet if Darius doesn't bite and Bernie can't make this go away? The thoughts prick at my skin, seep down into my bones. I want Issac to tell me he's not embarrassed of me. That he's not worried about this being bad for his career. I want him to hug me like he did the first time Darius posted something.

But instead, he grabs my keys off the counter. "Do you think you can bring me somewhere?"

"Bernie just told us not to leave."

"Bernie isn't my boss," he says.

"Where do you want to go?"

He sighs like he's annoyed with the question. "I just have to drop something to Alice and Howard."

"As in . . . the foster parents you've hardly spoken to in years?" He would see the confusion on my face if he bothered looking at it. "What do they want?"

"Will you take me or should I call an Uber?"

I walk over and snatch the keys from him. "Hurry up."

THE SILENCE DURING THE RIDE IS SUFFOCATING, SO WHEN I PULL the car around the corner and park in front of a cute house with a stone step walkway, I'm relieved. But only for a moment. As soon as Issac moves to get out of the car, I reach to touch his shoulder. He might not want affection right now, but I need to give it to him. This house is nothing like the house Issac lived in when we were children. There's a ceramic bird bath at the side and red shutters and a large flower wreath on the door. A lump forms in my throat, bitterness building there wondering how many kids this couple has fostered just for the paychecks, if the money paid for their new house. Issac never speaks ill of them; always says he doesn't know where he'd be if they hadn't kept him all those years. He was already twelve when they took him in and at risk of being stuck at a facility because older children have less of a chance for adoption. I'm happy Issac had a house to live in, but it still breaks my heart thinking about the way they neglected *his* heart. They didn't have to be physically abusive, pretending Issac didn't exist was enough. They didn't care about his good grades, his art, or even his hygiene. They'd sit in front of the television while Issac and the other foster kids had to fend for themselves. Mom felt bad for all the kids, I think. But she took special notice of Issac, *the brown boy who's been wearing the same shirt four days in a row*, and started demanding he bring his dirty clothes over so she could wash them at the laundromat. My dad's the one who bought him his first phone. When he started making YouTube videos and tried to show his foster parents, they brushed him off and called what he was trying to do silly while my parents were proud. Issac never felt love from Alice or Howard, and now the *silly* thing he was doing makes him the money they surely asked him for.

"You don't owe them anything," I tell him. "They seem to be doing just fine, anyway."

Issac breathes out, then puts a hand over mine. The touch makes me sigh. His long lashes press into his cheeks, and he finally meets my eyes.

"Good and bad, they helped make me who I am," he says.

"But they could've loved you better," I insist. "They should've."

A few seconds pass before he smiles just a little. "I didn't need them for that. I had you and Dennis and Vanessa to love me."

When he leaves, his words stay with me, and that thing stirs in my belly as he knocks on their door. I feel a pull to be at his side, holding his hand, but watch from the car as his foster parents come outside. Alice, a bit shorter now, Howard with a gray beard, don't hesitate to hug him. I wasn't expecting to ever see him in their arms, and the protectiveness in me rises to the surface. I wonder how Issac's heart feels hugging them. He doesn't go inside the house, but he smiles and nods and makes conversation. Then he takes an envelope from his pocket and hands it to Alice, who covers her face with her other hand and cries.

I wipe the tears from my own face as Issac gives her one last hug, then waves his goodbye. And I remember all the times I thought he deserved better, and realize that it never turned his heart ugly.

33

DEFINING MESSY

BACK AT HOME, WE SILENTLY WATER THE PLANTS ON MY PORCH while waiting for Bernie. Issac's tall enough to trim the dead leaves off the morning glories without fuss. A monarch butterfly lands in a flower above his head, and I raise my finger at it slowly: a motion for him to be as still as possible until it's gone. After we're done, Issac walks down the stairs and sits in the grass. The weather is perfect for grass sitting, not humid, a warm wind rustling the leaves in the tree to our left, but I don't know if he wants me to sit with him.

I do it anyway. "Do you want to talk about the visit with your foster parents?"

He plucks grass, shakes his head. "Not really."

"Do you want to talk about me? What happened?"

"Do you?"

"I think we need to," I say. "Your silence is painful. I hate walking on *your* eggshells. I know I probably embarrassed you by the picture being leaked. Hurt your reputation but—"

His head snaps up, he looks at me and laughs a little. "That's what you think is bothering me? You really walk *our* world oblivious."

"What's that supposed to mean?"

"I . . . ," he starts, trails off. "Forget it."

"Nope. You haven't been acting like yourself. You're keeping things from me. You—"

"Care about you," he cuts in. Not gently, his tone is sharp. "I care about you, and sometimes I'm not sure if you even know me. Do you really think I'd be embarrassed because of this? Do you really think I give a damn about my reputation because people are sharing a picture of you, without your consent, on the internet? Knowing how private you are, knowing you already struggle with the internet. And that's after already considering that Darius violated your trust. I'm worried about *you*, Laniah. Not me."

"Well, you didn't—"

"It's always what I didn't do. But you don't realize as soon as I heard, I dropped everything to call you, I took the first flight out. I . . ." He exhales. "You're oblivious as hell. You can't even see that I'm hurting because *I'm* hurting you."

His words catch me off guard. I can't fully process what he's saying until he gestures between us.

"This? This isn't good for you. I knew I should've called it quits last week. Maybe if I had, that asshole would've left you alone."

"Or he wouldn't have," I say, raising my voice. "He's pissed, his ego is hurt, and neither of us is responsible for his actions."

"But I came up with this plan. And a shot at fame can make people do reckless things."

"He was already reckless. And I'm a big girl, Issac. I made the decision. If you feel guilty, talk to me like you usually do. Don't shut me out and make me feel . . . insignificant."

His face falls, a small sound escapes his mouth. We stare at each other, the tension thickening the air between us. Finally, he says, "There's no one in the world more significant to me than you."

The heat between us cools to something warmer, and suddenly looking at him hits differently. He's always been beautiful, gorgeous, but right now he's infuriatingly fine. His facial hair and the sharpness of his bone structure, his thick dark lashes and full lips, the way the sunlight gives his skin a godly glow. His round sleepy eyes set solely on me.

My heart races when he lies back on the grass. I want to be closer to him. I ache for it. I lie back without another thought. The sky is cloudless and there's nothing to concentrate on besides consciously working to slow the muscle beating behind my breastbone.

"Ni, look at me." Issac's voice is jazz music and whispering wind. I tilt my head to face him. "I like being like this with you," he says. "I don't think I was clear enough last week at Beavertail that doing this with you is my favorite thing of all. We were sitting quietly under the Jamestown sky, and it just felt right. I'm so busy, things are unpredictable, my work schedule is chaotic, my whole world feels chaotic sometimes. But being with you under a sky, all my stress, my fears fall away. It's just me and you, and a comforting quiet that I don't get anywhere else. From anyone other than you."

If my heart was beating wild before, it's no longer a thing in my body. It gravitates between us. Floats somewhere over our heads. He could reach up and grab it if he wanted to.

My face flushes with warmth while thinking of telling him he does the same thing for me, and wanting to say the words as eloquently as he just did. But then his bare arm grazes mine and the small touch feels like static. He must notice too because he clears his throat and moves away.

"Which is why we're ending this in a week," he says.

I blink, my stomach sinking while fighting the urge to stand up. "What?"

"We'll have to do it carefully," he continues. "I'll put out a statement, say the pressure of our relationship being public knowledge got to both of us and we think it's best to be friends for now. I can talk about how I didn't want you to be hurt by being connected to me anymore. Maybe even make it look like I need to keep testing the waters to find the right person for me and I rushed things with you because I love you as a friend and was confused."

The right person. I flick my tongue over my lips, all I taste is bitterness. "Or maybe you can tell the world you want to be with Melinda and made a mistake. Then you won't have to worry about sneaking around with her anymore." As soon as the words leave my lips, I wish I could take them back. Where did that come from?

I've never seen so many creases on Issac's face. He's confused. Maybe he didn't realize I'd seen her name pop up on his phone. "Melinda? You don't know what you're . . ." He stops, exhales sharply, and looks away. "I just think ending things soon makes the most sense."

Part of me is relieved he ignored what I said, part of me aches to know what he was going to say before stopping himself. Was he going to tell me I'm wrong about him and Melinda? Do I want him to tell me I'm wrong?

"I'm not sure it does," I say. "Why end things early when I've told you I can handle the trouble that comes with it? When Bernie is taking care of the Darius thing? You're going to put your art career in jeopardy; you'll look horrible in the papers. And . . . after everything you just said about being around me, this is what you want?"

The last question feels delicate and heavy all at once. We aren't together, but I made it sound like a real breakup.

"I said all of that so you know why this is the right decision. I don't want to ruin you as a person. And I *can't* lose you as a friend. I can't. Like you said, being with me is *trouble*."

"Neither of those outcomes are even a possibility. And I didn't mean it that way," I say.

But how did I mean it? And haven't I been worried about our chemistry creating a mess and possibly ruining what we already have? That beautiful, comforting thing between us?

Issac sits up, leaves me breathing heavy in the grass below. "I can't promise that."

My throat hurts with threatening tears. I swallow, count to ten. Hating how out of control I feel.

Why would I even cry over this? What's wrong with me?

"You aren't going to ask me what I want?" I whisper.

Suddenly, Issac shifts onto his knees and towers above me. I'm no longer breathing when he braces his hands on either side of the grass at my feet. With the sun pouring down, it's like he's paying a penance, a tribute, as he stares down at me.

"What do you want, Laniah?"

My nipples harden, warmth pools in my panties at how perfectly we're positioned. I open my mouth, start to stutter something unintelligible before he brings his body down between my thighs and brushes his lips against mine. It's barely a kiss, just the softest sweeping touch, a tease that has me arching against him to try to deepen it.

But he pulls back, leaving me at a loss, and says, "Tell me what you want."

It'd be easier for me to lean forward and show him, but he has a hand on my stomach now, and my brain is hazy with the wish that he'd let it travel lower. He's waiting for me to speak, and better words are at the tip of my tongue, but what comes is this: "I . . . I don't know."

He shutters out a breath, his hand leaves my stomach. "I'm sorry," he whispers, and I feel the world around us when he moves away. The wind when he stands. The earth vibrating when he puts distance between us. My heart somewhere beside me on the grass. But then he holds out his hand. Like I'm weightless, he pulls me up, and tilts my chin. I'm shaking at his touch, trembling. Did that really just happen? Could I call it a kiss?

"We promised we'd end it if it got messy. Between Darius and how badly I want you . . ." He trails off, eyes dark, inhaling like it's torture to be this close and not have me. Doesn't he know I'm filled with need for him too?

The questions are at the tip of my tongue. I want to ask how far *wanting* me goes. If what he's feeling is only sexual. But I'm not sure I'm prepared for an answer, I wouldn't know what to say if he asked those questions of me. So I nod in defeat. Issac drops his hand from my face. The rental car pulls up while we're both still breathing heavy. Bernie doesn't get out right away. Probably to give us privacy.

"What about the art exhibition?" I ask, then watch something shift in Issac's eyes. "Do I fly back with you, we put on smiles for the weekend, then that's it? The last time we're seen together as a couple?"

He frowns like he hadn't considered it yet. "I should go to the exhibition alone," he says. "But I promise I'll come visit you as soon as the attention after the breakup dies down."

When he first asked me to go, I was nervous that it would be different than Shida's party, requiring acting abilities I lack, but now I can't imagine not being there with him to see his dreams realized. At his side for this big shift in his career focus, the way he was there for the shop's grand reopening. My heart aches something awful when the worst thought comes: he's okay with unveiling his *Secret Sun*, his *most precious work*, without me?

Bernie clears his throat from behind, and I flinch in surprise. I wonder how long he was standing there and how much he heard. Issac seems eager for the report, but I'm already feeling like the wind has been knocked out of me. What if Bernie has something bad to say too?

What Bernie has to say: Darius accepted an offer. (Bernie does not answer when I ask how much money he's taking from Issac's pockets.) He agreed to factory resetting his phone, even though Bernie couldn't find anything other than what Darius already posted on there. He signed a contract and an NDA. I won't have to worry about Darius anymore. (Are you 1,000 percent positive? Issac asks more than once.) They need to go, or they'll be late for their flight back to Cali.

What Bernie says while Issac uses the bathroom: "Laniah, if you need anything, please don't hesitate to call."

He hands me his business card, and whatever bad thoughts I had about him get buried beneath the appreciation I feel that he cares about how this all affects me too.

34

WHAT'S LIFE WITHOUT SEASONING?

T WAS JUST A JOKE, Y'ALL. MY APOLOGIES TO LANIAH THOMPSON and Issac Jordan. I went on one date with her way back, and I don't even know Issac, Darius posts to his Instagram. Eight hours later, he deletes his account. Just like Bernie said he would.

At the shop, people stare at me curiously, maybe even with some sympathy over the situation, but no one mentions it. In the afternoon, Dr. Rotondo's office releases my records to me and says they're transferring them to my new doctor's office too. When the shop closes hours later, Sherry comes to sign the contract with us and brings a bottle of champagne to celebrate the beginning of our investorship (as Lex calls it). But even with all the good, I've been down throughout the day thinking of how I was supposed to be with Issac. Confusing feelings aside, ignoring the fact that we kissed (if that's what one would call a faint brushing of lips), part of me wonders if the reason why the sky felt like it was falling when he told me he was going to end our fake relationship was because our friendship has felt as strong these past few weeks as it had before he moved to Cali. Chemistry or not, kiss or not, I had a hard time telling him how much I was missing *us*, and now the feeling is setting in again.

My phone dings with his familiar tone—the one only for him—and my stomach flips like he could feel me thinking of him. I stand up from sitting at the bay windowsill. Mom, Lex, and Sherry are laughing and telling jokes, so wrapped up that they don't notice when I slip off to the back room to read the text in private. Issac could be wondering if I'm okay or telling me something about his plans for the breakup, or maybe he's saying he regrets the kiss, asking if I want to talk about it. I brace myself for whatever it is, sit at the table, and take a breath.

> I'm going to say something and it's going to
> sound selfish, but I wish you were here.

I read the text three times, my body vibrating, before he sends another.

> I stand by the decision about ending things but
> regret canceling your flight. I keep envisioning
> you picking one of these dresses a designer
> tailored just for you. Bernie's giving me shit
> because I can't decide on which tux to wear to
> the exhibition tomorrow. But it's because I
> wanted to match your dress, give you the
> choice first. So now that none of it's happening,
> I've been sad as hell. And I really don't want to
> show Secret Sun to the world without you. All of
> this sounds so silly, doesn't it?

No, it doesn't sound silly, I type back, pulse racing, heart feeling a mix of happy and heavy. Then, I'm a little mad at you. I wanted to see your life's work and wear matching outfits and eat fried chicken while talking about your success. Did we really need the distance before you told the media?

</3, he sends. I'm sorry. I made a mistake.

:'(, I send back. It's alright. I wait for him to mention the kiss, but he doesn't.

If it's any consolation, you might find the exhibition stuffy and pretentious. Lots of press, fancy outfits, members of the royal family (kidding, I think), but the food will probably be seasonless, and even though you and I could probably dance to just about anything, the music might be stiff because they didn't take my DJ suggestion. Maybe you wouldn't enjoy yourself at all.

I smile, say, Take Franklin the crab or ask Bernie to be your date. He looks like he knows how to get down on the dance floor.

Oh, Bernie will be there whether I like it or not, and you're right . . . did you know the guy knows how to breakdance? Ask him to do a head spin next time you see him.

I laugh. Not Bernie spinning on that half shiny head.

It is a sight to see, Issac texts, but we won't have to miss each other for long. I'll come down in a few weeks, okay?

Okay <3 . . . but Issac, I would've brought the
seasoning in my purse for us.

That's why I love you, he says. Talk later.

I hold the phone close to me and look up at the ceiling.

Lex startles me when he speaks from the doorway. "I know
that look." His expression is somber when he comes over and sits
near me. "You're pining to be close to him."

"I think . . . maybe I am."

"So, what are you going to do about it, babe?"

35

A FIRST SHOW OF FAITH

THERE ARE ONLY TWO HOURS BEFORE *YEAR OF THE LOTUS* starts, so Bernie has an assistant pick me up from the airport. With no time to waste, we head straight to a boutique. I'm exhausted from the flight, a light headache refusing to leave me. But this is a big day, and I won't let my body, or my mind, ruin it. I allow myself to be excited. I've only ever bought clothing at big department stores and online. I've never shopped for a dress at a *boutique* in my life.

When we arrive, Bernie's assistant tells the workers to let me try on whatever my heart desires, that I should *feel* radiant no matter the cost. I think I'll have to try on ten dresses to feel that way, but I'm wrong. I know as soon as I see it. The dress is romantic. A deep-V neckline with lace flowers and the most intricate beadwork going up the bodice. It flows from the waist in the softest tulle I've ever touched, and it's sage green, down to the smallest embroidered flower. When I slip it on, I feel like a fairy goddess ready to dance in the woods.

"Is this too much?" I ask Bernie's assistant. "Is it the right kind of formal?"

She smiles and pins some pearls in my hair. "Bernie said radiant and that you are."

AS SOON AS WE PULL UP TO THE BOTANICAL GARDEN, BERNIE IS waiting for me outside with dozens of paparazzi surrounding him, red carpet–style. When I called yesterday, he didn't hesitate to tell me he'd help get me here on time, and that he'd keep it a surprise from Issac. I'm happy to see him but shaking at the sight of the press. Praying I don't sweat out of my makeup, hoping that I still smell good, wondering what Issac will feel when he sees me. Luckily, Bernie is like a bulldog as he leads me through the crowd, avoiding everyone in concise movements, not bothering to stop for a single question or picture. I hear my name from everywhere. *Laniah Thompson! Ms. Thompson, you are stunning!* Dozens of cameras click, but the sounds are muffled compared to the erratic beating of my heart.

The entrance to the garden is gorgeous, floor-to-ceiling glass doors that open to a large hall with hundreds of vine plants hanging from the ceiling and leading to the main room.

I begin to panic while wondering if this was a good idea.

But as soon as I walk in, Issac notices. The magnetic force between us pulls from a distance. Even with all the overarching plants and flowers and people surrounding him, I know just how difficult it is for him to hold on to his drink. When the shock settles, his shoulders fall, and the way he smiles tells me I'm the only one in the room right now.

"Come on," Bernie says, and I didn't realize I was planted in the doorway, blocking the way, too stunned to move because of the look on Issac's face. As I glance around, people are admiring me with curious expressions, smiling. I let out a breath and Bernie whispers, "This is what happens when you arrive made for the spotlight."

My cheeks warm, and I'm relieved when he gently pulls me along because my feet are failing to move on their own. Issac meets us halfway, in the center of this room, and gives Bernie an approving nod.

"Remember there are people watching," Bernie says, squeezing Issac's arm before disappearing into the garden.

Issac is wearing black trousers and a cream-colored dinner jacket that has five buttons adorning the sleeves with a crisp white dress shirt underneath to complement the perfectly simple lapels. Something about seeing him in formal wear makes my throat thick with desire, which is made worse by the way his gaze sweeps slowly up my body. From where the dress pools around my feet to the bare skin of collarbone. When he finally makes it to my face, I watch his teeth graze his bottom lip, and I have a tough time swallowing.

"A good surprise?" I ask.

He runs a hand from the bridge of his nose down to his chin, grips the hair there like he's trying to gather himself. "Did you pick that color for me?"

The question is direct, intimate. I'm sure he can see more color in my cheeks. "I did," I admit, smoothing down a soft layer of tulle and hoping he can't see the way my hands are shaking. "It's not from your designer, and we didn't get to match the way we wanted to, but do you like it?"

His eyes flick closed before he pulls me in for a hug. I catalog the scent of his cologne, hoping he chooses to wear this one often. He must enjoy my perfume as well because he breathes in near my neck, hums out a sound I wish I could record and replay whenever I want to ache.

"I'm glad you aren't wearing something from my designer," he murmurs against my hair. "Though I think you might need help getting out of this dress tonight."

My body thrums with unbidden feeling. I tilt my head back to look into his eyes. Thick vines hang above him, and the light of the moon comes through the glass ceiling, giving him an ethereal glow. A thought comes that maybe there's another universe in which we could be in love without ever hurting each other.

"Is that so?" I finally say.

Issac grins. "Yeah, because of all the buttons at the back of the dress. Get your mind out the gutter, best friend." I pinch his stomach, and he says, "Sorry. I'm acting like a fool but I'm so happy you're here. Are you?"

"Maybe a little," I tease.

He steps back and spins me in a circle. We both laugh as my dress rises. "How about now?"

"Possibly a little more. Maybe a whole lot. Ask me again at the end of the night."

"You're as annoying as you are stunning." Then louder to the people staring at us: "Do you see this goddess?"

My face flushes. I swat his chest playfully and drop my gaze. "Stop that."

He touches my chin, says, "No. Let them see you like I see you."

"Alright," I breathe out, aware that every bone in my body is buzzing. When exactly did I become so weak for this man? Of all men? This isn't how it's supposed to be.

But he smiles and takes my hand, laces our fingers like we're meant to be linked. "I only have a few minutes before presenting the other artists and unveiling our work, but I want to show you off."

Issac introduces me to a range of people: celebrities, philanthropists, even ecologists, who keep us talking for longer than we intended. I don't dim my light in the face of their curiosity, and it's not just being on Issac's arm that gives me confidence. It's here, in this space, surrounded by plant life, earth, and glass, air coming through the large overhead open windows. It feels like somewhere I belong. The sounds of four trickling water fountains add to the ambiance of the space. There's a large koi pond lined by stones that sits in the center of tropical trees that nearly touch the ceiling. Red, pink, and yellow flowers thread and climb lattice archways, breathtakingly large mirrors decorated with moss and roses are placed perfectly throughout the room. And I'm impressed by Issac, who chose brown draping to hide the artwork so it doesn't disrupt but adds to the atmosphere, and trays made from recycled wood for the servers to glide through the space with. It's all careful, meticulous detail.

Issac kisses my cheek, and I'm proud watching him command the crowd, talking about the art organizations in each artist's city that *Year of the Lotus* is raising money for. The drapings are dropped, and people gasp at the artwork revealed underneath. There are a total of twelve artists and many pieces, ranging from sculptures to paintings to photographs. We move in small groups to admire each one, and I'm proud of Issac for seeking out artists who are early in their career and are going to benefit massively from this kind of exposure. But as a crowd gathers in awe around Issac's work, which is a large painting of a woman looking off frame with dreamy eyes and flowers made from stained glass coating her skin, I realize I've seen this piece before. It's of his mother, titled after her, and my heart pangs with hurt and happiness. I want to pull him to my chest, tell him how proud I am of him offering the world a deeper glimpse into himself this way, even if it might be painful, and that she would be proud too. Then, realization slowly sets in that this is a different piece. Issac wasn't ready to unveil *Secret Sun* after all. Maybe he decided he wouldn't do it without me.

The thought makes me warm. I'm smiling to myself while admiring a sculpture nearby when I look for Issac in the room. He's always easy to find, but I wasn't expecting who I'd find him with. Melinda is standing with him in front of a photograph of a man lying in the middle of the street. My stomach squeezes. I didn't realize she'd be here. She looks radiant in a tight yellow dress. It's backless, and her slender body makes the simplicity breathtaking. They turn to face each other and laugh. Then I watch as Issac pulls out his phone to show her something. The conversation seems to get serious, Melinda grabs his wrist, gives it a little squeeze. Issac smiles at her and puts his phone away. They're entrenched and unaware of others staring at them, including me. Issac nods, touches her arm, and drifts off into the crowd.

That's the moment Melinda catches me spying. Her lips part, a curious expression on her face before I turn away, accidentally stumbling on my dress and bumping into someone. I apologize profusely and pray the cameras didn't catch that clumsy panic.

The corner I find is secluded, a space behind dense trees and exotic plants. I sit on a wooden bench and take breaths, needing to count to a hundred. Maybe a thousand. Trying not to be embarrassed over what happened, and trying to decide how bad it is that I'm certainly jealous over Issac with another woman when I shouldn't be.

A woman who is suddenly standing above me.

"Can I sit with you?" Melinda asks. The universe is cruel. I slide over, and we watch the fountain water bubble to our left before she speaks again. "I wanted to come to you, woman to woman, even though I don't have to, and explain what you saw happening with me and Issac."

"It's okay," I rush to say, "you don't have to explain anything. It's not my business."

She smiles a little. "I'm going to. Is that alright with you?"

When I nod, she continues.

"The truth is, I wanted to see something with Issac, and I think he wanted to see something with me too. But while dating, we realized we were reaching for something that just wasn't there. He was never going to be everything I wanted. Deep down, I knew that from the beginning, but I couldn't pass up the chance that maybe he could be."

"Why do you think he wasn't? Was it just his tough time with commitment?"

Melinda's eyes narrow, suspicious over my line of questioning. "I think he seems committed to plenty, including being the utmost gentleman while taking me on dates. His decision to hold off on labels and get into a *real* relationship when he finds the right person makes sense to me. I can't even say it's not what attracted me in the first place." Her smile fades, something wistful in her eyes. "I hoped the right person could be me, but it wasn't possible because it was always *you*."

As soon as she says it I raise my brows, wondering if she's being self-deprecating, but she looks at me the way my mother would, as if to tell me without words that I'm being dense.

"I think he's wanted to be with you his whole life, Laniah. It just took him time to accept it for whatever reason. And from the surprised look on your face, I don't think he's told you *exactly* how he feels yet."

For all the faking, I couldn't fake this. "He . . . I . . ."

She shakes her head, laughs, and says, "Don't worry. It hit me late too. At first, I wondered if his team suggested the two of you date for good press or something. Happens more than you know around *this town*. But then I saw the pictures of the two of you at Shida's party and I felt something like relief. His feelings for you are clear as day in them, and everything made more sense. On our dates, I'd ask for stories about his childhood, and you were the star in each one. There was something so endearing about the way I could *hear* the love for you in his chest. It made me want to be loved by him too. But he never looked at me the way he looked simply mentioning your name. I was sad for a bit. Dating for love isn't fun, even for someone like me, who is constantly offered life on a literal silver platter. But Issac wasn't *for me*, and with or without dating me, it was only a matter of time before he realized he already had everything he wanted in *you*."

I bite down on my lip with the urge to taste blood, to ground myself in it while I process what she's saying, wondering who else thought Issac and I were pretending. Wondering if it might make her try to fight for him if she knew that we still are. But . . . what if what she's saying about his feelings is true?

"Has he . . . said any of this to you?" I ask.

"No, and I haven't asked because, frankly, I'm not his therapist," she says. "Though she may have helped him figure *you* out. Either way, I'm just happy he stopped living in denial and isn't in the business of stealing someone else's soulmate. Because neither am I."

The words don't land right away, they're suspended some-where above us, tapping against the glass ceiling, circling the cas-cading lights. When they make it down to me, I'm speechless. I was still reeling over the thought that she believes Issac's always wanted to be with me, but his soulmate? I shut my eyes tight, grip the edge of the bench. When I open them again, Melinda is stand-ing above me, surely aware of how fast my heart is racing.

The words she deserves are tangled in my brain. I open my mouth, close it, clear my throat, and try again.

"Your soulmate is going to be one lucky person," is all I have to offer her in the end.

"Oh, I know that," she says, running her fingers through her waist-length hair. "And just so you know, Issac's doing artwork for a contact of mine who owns a high-end store. Earlier, he was showing me ideas he has for it. We're nothing more than friends, at best, in case any insecurities ever sneak up. Anyway . . . let me get back before my team comes looking for me. But if it's not an overstep, sometimes men are difficult, maybe he's waiting for you to admit you're in love with him first."

A flash of warmth cuts across my chest and stays long after she leaves. My reactions made it obvious to her that Issac and I haven't discussed our feelings; we're lucky she's the picture of grace. And then, there's everything else. I can admit to being a little jealous, but in love? With Issac? Him, in love with me?

What is he projecting to the world that I don't see?

My body moves before my mind can process why entertaining any feelings, heart ones or hormonal, is a bad idea regardless, but I need to see him. Need to prove Melinda wrong somehow. Issac's talking to the press when I walk over. My urges outweigh any fear of their hungry stares.

"Hi, beautiful," he says, wrapping his arm around my waist. Someone asks him a question I'm too transfixed to pick up on, but he sees the serious look on my face and stares into my eyes while responding to them. "I can't imagine another person I'd want to share this journey with. She's constantly inspiring me, pushing me to be brave."

It's those words that cloud my judgment. Suddenly, no one else is here. Just us: two plants that belong to the same botanical garden. And I get up on my tiptoes, wrap a hand around his neck, and press my lips to his. He gasps softly, stiff in surprise for the shortest time before he leans in to deepen the kiss. The chemical reaction is quick, my lips sensitive while soaking in the feel of him moving his mouth against mine. We savor each other with soft, sweet kisses. But when Issac places his hand on my lower back, urging me closer, something bursts and overflows in my body. I open my mouth, wanting for his tongue, but the sounds of cameras clicking pulls us apart.

Shit. No one has seen us kiss yet. This was our first *real* one, in front of hundreds of people, millions with the cameras. Heat works its way up my neck. Issac's pupils are dilated, he's stunned for a few seconds too long, and panic rises in my chest. But then he snaps out of it and kisses my forehead before turning back toward someone with a microphone. He smiles, says a few things about how amazing the night has gone, projects to come, promising to unveil *Secret Sun* soon, and I'm surprised to hear any of it over the rapid beat of my heart. Will his fans see clips and have theories? Someone will surely notice how hard I'm working to breathe and know that kiss wasn't supposed to happen. Incredible as it was.

Finally, Issac puts his hand on the small of my back and leads me through the crowd toward the private entrance of the greenhouse. When we enter a dimly lit hallway, I watch as he starts to pace.

Seconds pass before he asks, "What the hell was that?"

My stomach sinks. I try to play it cool but stumble over my words. "People kiss."

"Laniah, we"—he gestures between us—"don't do that. We had a rule. It was actually *your* rule. We've been pretending enough. We can't pretend with this."

"You kissed me first," I say, trying to be pointed but probably sounding like a child.

There's something in his eyes as he searches mine. I don't know what to make of it. Even with his tone, it's hard to tell if he's upset, stunned, or if I ruined something between us. But then, the corners of his lips twitch a little. "So does this mean kissing is something we do now? Is that what you want?"

I can't tell if he's offering up his heart or body or both, so I tell him I'm not sure.

"Well, I know what I want," he says simply.

The sure and certain look on his face sends a shiver up my spine, a flash of warmth between my legs. "Don't tell me," I demand while trying to tear my eyes away from his lips. "We should talk about this after the exhibition. This is your big night, and I'm ruining it."

After a moment, he smiles and says, "I'd argue you're making it better, but fine. We can talk about our very human feelings later."

"You're so kind, sir," I joke, but I'm thankful for his ability to lighten the mood. Especially when my mind, heart, and body are at war over what human feelings I'm truly having.

"I know," he says. "But I can't promise I'll be nice once I get you home."

36

CORONER REPORTS
DEATH BY CONFUSION

THE JOY BOUNCES BACK AND FORTH BETWEEN US THE WHOLE way to the condo. Issac's already getting an outpouring of love from other artists, designers, and fans. Bernie said he'd received multiple inquiries throughout the night on whether Issac would be interested in doing work for museums, high-end trade shows, other exhibits. As soon as we arrive, Issac tosses his dinner jacket on the couch and throws open the glass doors leading to the pool. He sucks in a breath of warm air, and glances at the stars in the sky.

Standing beside him, I fight the urge to slip my hand into his after the kiss at the gardens. We haven't flirted since our talk in the hall, and I wonder what he thinks of us now. "You were incredible," I say, my voice swelling with unwavering pride. "I remember eighth-grade art class; we had an easy watercolor assignment and you covered yours with gum wrappers and Popsicle sticks. Everyone snickered when you showed the class, but I never saw our teacher more fascinated. She hung your work on the wall, and I'd find myself staring at it all the time."

"You've never told me that before," he says, a twinkle in his eyes, one dimple visible, watching me like I've just amazed him. I shrug one shoulder, smiling. "You know, Ni. I didn't realize that I'd love you surprising me as much as I love surprising you. Thank you for coming tonight. It was such a perfect one."

I bump my shoulder against his, right before he screams happy things into the night. The energy is contagious, and soon I'm screaming happy things too. We celebrate the shop loud and proud, the exhibition, each other.

But then Issac glances at the pool, lit by bright blue lights, and starts to undress.

"What are you doing?" I ask, a hint of laughter in my tone.

"What does it look like?" he teases, turning toward me with a one-sided smile. He keeps his eyes trained on my face while he unclasps his watch, unbuttons his shirt, slides off his belt. As soon as his hands move to his pants, I swallow and pry my gaze away. When I look again, he's already walking toward the water, his black Calvin Klein briefs hugging the muscles in his ass as he goes. Dear God, did Issac really have to be built like this?

He dives in then clings to the side of the pool and looks up at me. "Get in," he says.

"I'm sleepy," I say, half true. But mostly, getting in the pool with him right now feels dangerous, we still need to talk about both kisses, and I haven't decided if I even want us to.

"Just for a little?" he asks, splashing me with water.

"You'll ruin my dress," I say. "Which would require work to get out of if I happened to want to swim. So, by the time I manage to take it off, *you'll* be ready for bed."

After the words leave my mouth, I remember the joke he made

about me needing help to get out of the dress. My face flushes furiously, hoping he doesn't think I said it on purpose.

We're silent for several seconds before he pushes himself out of the pool with ease.

"I'd say I'll throw you in and buy you a new one tomorrow, but you'd say my *new money* is showing."

Nerves bubble in my belly, I almost tell him *Don't you dare*, but then he touches the fabric at my hip and says, "But I wouldn't because the boutique you were brought to only makes one dress of its kind, and I hope you want to keep it forever."

Before I can speak, Issac steals my breath by spinning me around. Goose bumps flick over my skin at the feel of his fingers. He pulls out the pearl clips, and my hair falls around my face. Then he moves to the clasp at the top of the dress, hesitating there, and softly asking, "May I help you out of this?"

A few words that make me swallow a moan. I nod, my body too eager, too willing to see a fantasy through. When Issac lets loose the clasp, I almost come undone too. He moves carefully, his fingers brushing my skin while he works his way through the buttons all the way down to the small of my back.

I prepare to feel his hands at my shoulders, sliding the dress down, but then he clears his throat and backs away. I turn to see him dive back into the water. He starts swimming laps, giving me the privacy to slip out of the dress on my own—until the only things I'm wearing are a strapless bra and panties.

I chew my lip and sink into the water, sliding just underneath the surface and holding my breath while I'm down there. When I rise, Issac splashes me in the face. And that's all we needed for the tense energy to dissipate. We dunk each other, race from one side of the pool to another, see who can stay underwater the longest. I win every time. Then, we float on our backs.

"Remember when we'd walk to the pool and swim all day long? I feel so tired after a few laps now," I say, then try not to think about Dr. Rotondo insinuating that I might be causing my own symptoms. I've been trying not to think about him or my body at all tonight, actually.

"Mm-hmm. At Uni, straight pruny."

I laugh. "Your rhymes are still corny."

"Don't play me. I might be on Shida's next album. Maybe I'll spit on Krews's next track."

"Oh, please."

He sucks his teeth. "You never let me rock."

"Some things can never change," I tell him.

"And maybe some things can," he says, and there's something in his tone that brings me back to my conversation with Melinda. If she's right and Issac does have romantic feelings for me, that doesn't mean he'll be able to commit. And more important, Issac's my person, just like my father was my mother's, and look at how that worked out for them.

But, for just a few seconds, I trace my lips and allow the re-membering to bring me back to the feel of his. We float in silence, and he reaches out for my other hand, laces our fingers. The touch feels good in the way forbidden feelings can, and I can't help humming out loud when he massages my thumb. Issac reacts to the noise with a sharp inhale. But I pull away from him and swim to the edge of the pool to take deep breaths there.

I'm not sure how long it takes for Issac to come up behind me, but he says my name so low it sends shivers through my body.

Without responding, I take a step closer to the edge of the pool, press myself against the concrete.

He moves with me, providing just a sliver of space between our bodies. Then bends low, puts his mouth to the shell of my ear. "Why did you kiss me?"

I can't speak because my body reacts to his proximity by closing the gap separating us. He groans at the feel of my backside against him, but at least *he* still has some control over himself.

"Do you want me? You said we'd talk about it."

"I do want you, but . . ." I trail off, too distracted by the things happening inside of me to find the right words. To tell him that wanting him is dangerous for the both of us.

He grabs the edge of the pool with both hands, locking me in place. "Tell me you can resist this chemistry between us, tell me you want to resist it, and I'll never bring the kiss up again. We can pretend it never happened," he says. "We can act like your body isn't begging for me to take you right in this pool."

His words set me ablaze. I whimper, the feeling of his bare chest against my back stoking the fire, making me arch into him. I'm holding on to sense by a thread, losing logic every second we're connected.

"Tell me, Laniah," he says, lowering himself in the water and pressing his erection against my ass. I throb between my legs, but the direct contact causes other thoughts to come crashing down: our friendship, the deal we made, the fact that, despite fighting it, I'm feeling more than just lust for him, and even if our feelings do align, our lifestyles will never match up. I wouldn't want to do anything to change what he has going on. He's doing good, and I'd be a distraction at the other side of the country. I'm doing good, and he'd be a distraction at the other side of the country.

Relationships are often painful and hard, and even the good ones can end, leaving broken hearts behind.

So I use all the strength in my bones to push myself out of the pool, but my ass slides against him as I go. He winces, and the sweet sound makes me shiver.

It takes everything I have not to turn back and tell him I'm tired of pretending.

———————

IN THE SHOWER, I LET THE WATER BEAT ON MY SKIN, PRESSING MY forehead against the cool tile. I'm swollen between the legs, so filled with need it hurts to touch. After I'm done, I wrap a towel around my body and take a breath before leaving the bathroom, coming face-to-face with Issac. He was waiting at the door, but he can hardly look at me.

"I'm sorry if I pushed, Ni," he says, shakes his head, and passes me to get into the bathroom.

I should've used one of the four other showers instead of the one in his room. I could've made this less awkward for us. He could've done the same. The shower water starts running, and I wonder if he's in there aching worse than I was. The pearl clips from my hair are on his dresser. My body recalls his soft touch when I pull one of his white T-shirts from the drawer and slide into it before throwing myself on the bed to stare at the ceiling. Katrina's voice rings in my head. Her advice to enjoy this before it's gone. And I wonder if Issac and I owe it to ourselves to give in to our feelings just once. Can I really sleep in the same house as him tonight, after what just happened in the pool, and not feel him inside of me?

I clench my thighs and groan, frustrated. If confusion could kill me, it would.

37

WHAT WE PRAYED WOULDN'T BE

SSAC COMES OUT OF THE BATHROOM WITH MORE CLOTHES ON than he usually wears for bed. He looks surprised to see me still here. Probably thought I'd hide out in the guest bedroom. Maybe I should've, but we need to make this work.

He looks even more surprised when notices I'm wearing nothing but his T-shirt.

"Are you okay?" he asks, voice tentative, eyeing me with wonder.

"Don't worry," I say. "I have panties underneath."

He smiles, but that fire in his eyes is gone, replaced with a cool, calm brown that silently begs for me to answer his question with yes. And I realize that it's the same look he's been giving me since the moment he showed up at my door weeks ago. Has he been wondering if I'm okay all of this time?

"Come here," I tell him. "Let me put something in your hair."

He hesitates the way he did when he took the picture of us that changed my life forever. But then he sits between my bare legs on the white carpet and relaxes as I massage his scalp. He's careful not to make a sound. We're both quiet until he tilts his head back a little, his hair grazing the space between my legs and stealing a moan from me. When he stiffens at the sound, I chew my lip, smiling through it.

"Back in the pool, I couldn't say I can resist this feeling between us because it would've been a lie," I admit, and he inhales sharply. "But I am nervous."

"Why is that?" he asks.

"I don't want us to hurt each other," I say.

"I understand," he says. "I don't want that either."

"I wouldn't know what to do with myself if we ruined what we have," I admit. "Especially over sexual tension. I'm wondering if we did already."

He's quiet for so long I'm worried I said the wrong thing. Was it a little much? Not enough? Then, he sighs and says, "We didn't ruin anything. We'll pull through whatever, but this . . ." He huffs out a breath. "Laniah, I don't know if it's just sexual tension for me, and I'll always be respectful of your decisions, but I can't promise it'll go away."

My throat is thick again. For a second, I hope whatever he's feeling *will* go away. I wish it with my whole heart, then unwish it right after. Still, I can't bring myself to ask him to clarify what he means because part of me wants to protect us from whatever might come if we admit to the feelings in our hearts. But . . . I don't think I can live another night without releasing this tension between us.

I steady myself, lean down so I'm close to his ear, say, "If I ask you to sex me, just once. Do you think we'd pull through that?"

He shivers, lets out a low groan. I watch him adjust himself through his pants, and I have to bite back my own moan. "I already told you we can pull through anything."

"I hope that's true," I say.

"I know it," he says. "But I won't promise you it'll be just once."

My heart speeds up. I whisper, "You're not willing to make any promises tonight, are you?"

"I'm not. Because I don't want to hear your mouth when I break them."

Time feels like it stretches into eternity, neither of us moves. All I can hear is his light breathing, the soft wind coming through his balcony window, and the sound of my need.

"Can I touch you?" he finally asks.

I breathe out, then brace my body in anticipation. "Yes."

His fingers brush my ankle first, and even that feels like sex. He walks them up my calf, then cups the space under my knee. The pressure makes me wet. When he lets go, I whimper. What the hell is wrong with me?

He must know that he can touch me anywhere and cause pleasure because he doesn't find my reaction surprising, just walks his magic fingers up my thigh, stops midway, grips as much of it as he can in his large hand, then turns his face to kiss me there. It's gentle and undemanding but drags a winded breath out of me.

I know one thing that will be ruined by this: I'll never be able to do Issac's hair, with him sitting between my thighs, and not think about him kissing them.

I decide right then to release the thoughts in my mind, the heaviness, and let my body lead the way for tonight.

"Again," I beg. "Please."

His eyes are closed when he kisses me again, but this time he opens his mouth and runs his fat tongue over my flesh. While I'm tangling my fingers in his hair and moaning at the feel, his voice sounds hypnotic.

"Dear God," he says. "You don't know how long I've been praying to hear you make that sound for me."

My mind's too hazy with want to focus on his words, but *I know* they're important.

Issac gets on his knees, tall enough that the action puts us face-to-face. We're breathing heavy, but he leans forward and brushes his mouth over mine in the most delicate motion, and I know right then I'll be measuring every kiss of my life to this one.

When he parts my lips with his tongue, I sigh into his mouth; overcome with how perfect he tastes, thinking delirious things like if I could devour and drink him forever, I would. With no need to worry about our surroundings, we're greedier than earlier. Sucking and biting and barely allowing ourselves air. I'm gripping his forearms to pull him closer and his hands are moving to my hips, squeezing the soft flesh beneath the fabric there.

He pulls back for a shaky breath, leans his forehead against mine. We smile, laugh, my heart swells at how swollen his lips are because of me. He kisses my cheek, my chin, my collarbone.

"Are you sure?" he asks. "Tell me you're sure."

The feel of him nibbling my neck makes me shiver. "Issac . . . ," I breathe out.

He stops at the sound of his name, mouth hovering, a breath away from skin, my body aching for him to start again. He grips the bedsheets beside me, says, "Laniah."

Mm . . . That feeling. Something about hearing my name in his mouth while we're in this position sends me wherever it just sent him. I grab his face, kiss his lips one more time.

"I'm sure," I finally say.

He nods, but I see the flicker of nerves in his eyes before he pulls back enough to examine me. "When I came out of the bathroom and noticed you were in *my shirt*, I almost dropped to my knees and begged you to let me touch you right here." I watch him swallow, his hand moves under the shirt until he reaches the crease of my thigh.

My body bucks when he uses the pad of his thumb to brush my soaked panties.

He smiles, and whatever fear he was feeling is replaced by pure hunger, confidence.

"Do you want me to touch you here?"

Another graze, I whimper and throb.

"Do you want that?"

"Yes," I beg. "Yes, I want you to touch me. Please."

"Where? Use your words."

I bite down on my bottom lip, tasting blood. "Touch my pussy."

"Mm," he moans out before rubbing my clit through the cotton. "Like this?"

All of my nerve endings sing. I push close, craving pressure.

"Just. Like. That," I say while he rubs me with slow, torturous circles, intensifying my ache.

He bends low, breathes shallow breaths in the space where his fingers just were, and reaches for the edge of my panties, ready to pull them to the side. I want him to kiss me there but know what'll happen with him devouring me: my mind will race, my heart will too. If we're going to do this, if we're going to pull through, he can't make love to me because I'll need him to do it forever.

I cup his face, force his eyes to meet mine. "I want you to fuck me," I say.

He tilts his head curiously. "Now?"

I lean forward to lick his bottom lip. "Yes."

He takes my tongue into his mouth before pulling out of my

grasp. Then, without warning, he pushes past the fabric keeping us apart and slides his thumb inside of me. My hips rise, I gasp out a shocked breath.

He makes a wincing sound, says, "Fuck. How are you *this* ready for me?"

I'm panting, nipples painfully hard, when he pulls his thumb out of me and pops it into his mouth. *Oh damn.* He examines my face and smiles. "Why are you pouting, baby? You anxious? You need me that much?"

"Cocky asshole," I say, forcing my legs together while wishing he'd call me baby again.

He shakes his head, then pulls my thighs apart. "No one told you to move."

The realization hits me that I'm seeing the sexual side of someone I've known my whole life. I narrow my eyes at the challenge, but don't move a muscle when Issac stands and towers above me because, dear Lord, who would've known I'd like it so much?

His shirt comes off before his pants. Then he hooks a finger under his boxers. Even though I'm eager, I'm happy he goes slow and allows me to enjoy eyeing the outline of his dick, how much thicker it is compared to my dream. I ache to squeeze my thighs together, but he arches an eyebrow, silently reminding me not to move. When I cut my eyes at him, he laughs and finally exposes himself to me.

I thought the outline prepared me, but it didn't. He takes a few steps forward, positioning himself within inches of my face. It's long, dark, beautiful with pronounced veins and a smooth, fat head.

My mouth waters, wanting to taste him, but when I reach for it, he steps back again.

"Sorry, baby. You can't lick me if I can't lick you." I breathe through my teeth, hurt, but he nods his head toward the top of the bed while slowly jerking it and says, "Move up there."

"No," I say. "I want to watch."

"You can watch . . . from up there."

"I don't like you." I frown.

The corners of his mouth twitch. "But you will."

I scowl at him as I move up the bed, but inside my heart is racing.

He holds eye contact, circles me the way a wolf would. "Good girl," he says.

Those words. That look on his face. I reach up to grip the headboard, needing him. "Please," I beg.

"Because you asked nicely," he says, climbing into bed and peeling my panties off. My pussy gushes as he plants both hands on either side of me and stares down at my body. "You're more beautiful than I've tried to imagine." The words are an honest whisper, something he was thinking that slipped right out. He meets my eyes with a serious expression, then dips his head down. When he kisses me, I feel the question on his lips: *Can we really do this without feeling everything?* And I don't know that we can. He pulls back to rest his forehead against mine, and my breaths quicken realizing how close we are to the edge of something different, a territory unknown.

He opens his mouth to say something, but I panic at what it could be and thrust my hips to distract him with my wetness. It works. A sharp flash of need crosses his eyes at our contact. I can't believe how hard he is for me.

He grips the bedsheets, grinding his length against me slowly. "You're so damn wet," he says.

I arch my back, ache, ache, ache with the friction, the pressure he's building. We moan at the same time. "Issac, I need it now," I insist, because any more grinding and I'll climax before he gets to put it in.

He kisses my neck, then sits up to reach into the drawer for a condom, tears the wrapper with his teeth. I watch him roll it on before he pushes my thigh and turns me onto my stomach. I groan into the pillow, ready when he positions himself close, dick resting against my ass. Everything burns, throbs, I'm so ready it hurts.

But Issac says, "Let me take care of you . . ."

A breath. The rapid beating of my heart.

"Until you get on the plane to go back home."

I try to find my voice, try to register what he's saying, but my need for his sex is too big, and I don't want to think. Not now. "We said one time," are the only words that come.

He spreads my ass cheeks and adjusts himself between them. "You said once, but I'm greedy. I want you every way I can get you. For as long as we have."

I smile into the pillow. "You're already looking at it like a loss before you've even had me. Maybe you'll be satisfied enough. Maybe not at all. You might not want me after this."

"Impossible." I can hear him smiling too. "I'll fuck you now, then if you like it I'll fuck you again tomorrow. We don't have to talk about it. I'll read your body language. How's that?"

My mind warns me, but I'm seesawing between coherent and delirious. "Alright," I say. "Fine."

He lets out a soft laugh, then finds my opening with the head of his dick, pushing through before my muscles have time to tense.

A sea of painful pleasure crashes over me. "Oh God," I cry out. We both tremble.

"Fuck . . . ," he says. "Baby."

For a moment, he doesn't move inside of me, just lets himself pulse within my walls. I grip him. Clench, unclench, twitch. I've lost control. My body doesn't belong to me anymore. At this moment, it's rightfully his.

"Issac," I beg, trying to find friction in the sheets below me.

"How do you feel like this?" he says right before he lowers himself flush against my back, bites my earlobe, makes me shiver. "God, Laniah. It wasn't supposed to be this good. I prayed it wouldn't be. How will I ever let you go?"

I agree, I think, maybe murmur something similar. He wasn't supposed to feel like this. We shouldn't be made to fit so perfectly. My eyes roll back when he starts moving inside of me. It's slow at first, finding his way, testing, teasing. But when he reaches for my hands, pushes them above my head and laces our fingers, I tell him to go faster, harder, because with him this close my heart feels like it's reaching for his. And I'm not ready to listen to the voice inside of me that says he doesn't have to let me go at all.

"If that's what you want," he says, and I try to ignore the hesitation in his tone.

He pushes hair out of my face and kisses my cheek before sitting up. I'm still adjusting, still trying to breathe through his thickness, when he pulls out of me. I whine for him, but he tells me to hush and pulls me to my knees by a jerk of my hips. The motion makes me sure I'll drip on the sheets below. I brace myself on my hands, lift my ass in anticipation. He smacks it, shocking me with a sting and stealing a moan. He runs both hands from the backs of my thighs all the way up the small of my back and releases a breath. There's no time to worry about how many bodies he's seen that look better than mine, without cellulite, slimmer, or surgically built to resemble beautiful Coke bottles, because Issac hums and says, "These hips, dear Lord, these hips."

His words make me smile and arch my back with a little more confidence.

"Woof. I was going to tease you and keep you in this position for a while," he says, "ask how much you already miss this dick, but I need . . ." He doesn't finish the sentence, just opens me up from the back and pushes himself in. It takes my breath, how deep it feels from this angle, like he's reaching into my belly. It's pain and pleasure and pain and pleasure as I do my best to meet his strokes. The clapping sound of our bodies connecting makes my nipples ache.

"Dear God," I say. We weren't supposed to love this.

"Grab the headboard," he tells me, and like he can read my mind, anticipate my needs, he cups my breasts and plays with my nipples while he strokes. I'm somewhere up in the clouds while he pinches them, his nails grazing against the small peaks of my areolas.

"Fuck," he says. "Damn, baby. Look at how you're taking it for me. You look so fucking good. You're mine."

My body vibrates at the sound of his pleasure. In this moment, I'm *his* baby. He pulls me back, pushes my head down into the pillow, and fucks me so hard I can't see straight. I cry out his name. He asks me to say it again. I moan over and over again, giving in to him until he groans and drops my hips. My body sinks into the bed, limp, twitching, still needing. He lies flush against me again, and this time, when he reaches for my hands to lace our fingers, I don't resist the sensual act.

"Let me take care of you," he whispers, pushing damp hair from my face, gently kissing the skin of my shoulder. "You're always taking care of me." He starts to move his hips, rhythmically hitting every spot inside of me. Finding places that I didn't know existed. We grip the sheets together as he grinds me into the bed. We're so close, skin to skin, and the pressure of his body against my ass feels too good. He moves like he has magic inside of him, and when he stops to pulse, trying not to cum, I cry for him. He presses his mouth against my ear, licks the lobe, before turning my face and kissing me. We're at an angle, our lips barely touching, both slick with sweat, but it's contact I was craving too.

With this new position of his hips, my clit rubs against the sheets, but it's not enough. He reaches and places his fingers there, realizing I needed the friction. But he doesn't move them, just allows me to grind against his hand while he strokes: already an expert on what I like. I scream his name again, the pleasure building.

"Oh my God. Babe."

He makes a hissing sound through his teeth, then squeezes my other hand, a reassurance I didn't know I needed before asking, "You going to cum for me, Laniah?"

"I'm gonna cum for you, baby," I say, or I think I say.

It might be gibberish because when I release, my body convulses and takes me wherever good things go. Issac slows his speed, allows me whatever I need. When I finally come back down to myself, my body still vibrating, Issac says he has to cum and the thought pricks at the pleasure receptors in my brain, then his moans fill me up again. I can keep going all night just to hear the way he sounds for me. The softness there, the vulnerability, the way he keeps whispering my name, and *fuck*.

"Does it feel good?" I ask, gripping the sheets, arching my back, trying to meet his stroke, help him like he did me, but it's hard with him pressed so close.

It doesn't matter. He's spinning. "It feels so good. Baby, I'm coming."

He finishes, shuddering against my back, biting my shoulder. I receive the soft sting and return a moan. He's tired. Panting and sweating on top of me. My ass twitches, and he whispers ungodly things before pulling out.

"You're dangerous," he says, rolling over and pulling me to his chest.

I wrap my arms around him, welcoming the warmth. "So are you," I say.

Our bodies shake while our brains slow in the work to calm us. He tilts my head, looks into my eyes, and gives me a tender kiss. I'm not sure we were successful at keeping our hearts out of this.

38

AN INTERESTING AFTERMATH

T HE THOUGHTS PILE ON WHILE I LISTEN TO THE RAPID THRUM-ming inside Issac's chest. He breathes; I breathe. He moves; I move. In this moment, we're not just agreeable or adaptable like the call of the moon to the tide, we are two hanging pendulum clocks that start swinging in sync, we are a swarm of fireflies flashing at the same time.

We are best friends who promised boundaries, a no-mess situation. But we just had wild, incredible sex. I should've printed out our rules and notarized the paper. As we lie here, I fight off panic, wondering how the consequences of our actions will unfold, but then Issac puts his hand on my shoulder. It's a gentle reassuring gesture that I receive with a released breath.

"Do you regret it?" he asks, and even though his voice is cool and steady, I can hear the change in his chest, how nervous he is about the way I'll respond.

"Straight to the most important question, huh?" I say, and feel his muscles stiffen. "I don't know what I'm feeling right now, aside from anxiety. But I don't think so. Do you regret it?"

He meets my eyes. "No, and I never will. I meant what I said sitting between those thick thighs on the carpet. I feel more for you than just sexual tension."

Suddenly I'm scared. I want to save him, shake him, say, *We both witnessed what feeling more could hurt like, why would you want that with me?* But instead, I ask, "How do you know? What if the pretending got to your head? Made you think you have feelings for me? Being closer, more intimate, what if this is chemistry trying to imitate something else because we love each other as friends?"

The corners of his lips rise before he flips it on me. "Do *you* have romantic feelings for me? You know, other than the fact that you definitely want mc to sex you silly all weekend."

I slap his chest, laugh, and am again impressed that he can dial down my awkwardness. But then, I try to find the right words to tell him we'd never work. Because when considering the possibility that he has feelings for me, I must remember to consider this: He knows what he wants, but I don't. He won't hold on to someone who's not his *soulmate*. What if we find out down the line that's not me. Do I even want my soul to be bound to another soul? I don't know if deeper discovery is a risk I can take, especially not with Issac. He's crucial to my life.

"I can feel your mind running you ragged," Issac says, lifts my hand, and kisses it. "Before you answer, let's make another deal."

I smile and say, "What are the terms?"

"That we'll do more than have sex this weekend, we'll spend it as a fake couple that's no longer faking it, open-hearted, open-minded, fearless, then you'll fly home and we'll take a week apart to clear our heads. See where to go from there. You can decide what you want after."

It's like he's dipped into my head and given me a free trial on discovery. But he's making it seem like the decision is all mine. That he's good with whatever I can give. "Why a week?"

"Because I already know how I'm going to feel, what I'll want, and I doubt I can last longer than a week waiting to hear from you," he says.

His words find a warm space in my chest, make breathing a little easier. He's not pressing me to decide on anything, he's not forcing me to tell him my feelings now.

"Okay," I agree, and his eyes crinkle at the corners. I'm not sure this deal will change much, but I like to see him happy. I lick one of his dimples and he pinches my bare butt cheek. "I forgot we were naked under the covers."

He shifts so that I feel how hard he is against my leg. "Lucky you," he replies.

"Don't start up again, I'm too tired now. You talking deals has depleted my energy."

He laughs his beautiful laugh. "Pretty sure it was something other than my talking."

"You're full of yourself," I say, and he doesn't deny it. Just eases me off of him so we're lying on our sides, face-to-face. He tangles his legs with mine, our bodies fitting together like tree branches. Then he reaches to brush my bottom lip with his thumb, tugs it down a little.

When our mouths meet, it feels sacred and special. I'm still taken aback by the tingling sensation. The way it spreads from our lips and works its way to my chest. Issac's kisses can still time, stop and restart my heart.

I savor him slowly. But then it sparks a flame, and I can't help but flick my tongue over his. He responds in kind, parting his mouth to let me in. We massage, tease, suck, and moan.

Before it can go any further, he stops and kisses my temple. My forehead, the bridge of my nose.

"As bad as I want you again, you're tired and I'd rather you rest for tomorrow." At my protest, he says, "Don't worry, I'm not going anywhere."

As soon as he says it my eyes start to flutter shut. He pulls the covers up, asks if I'm comfortable while playing with my hair. "I'm happy," I say, and he hums a song until I drift into a dream.

39

IF SETTLING
LOOKED LIKE THIS

WARMTH RISES IN MY CHEST WHEN I WAKE TO A WHITE ROSE beside me, a note in Issac's scroll.

I'd like it if you drooled on my pillows forever. <3

I laugh out loud and lift the rose to my nose. Am I crazy to agree to this? Spending a weekend with no faking might mean smiling with my whole guarded, sometimes hopeful heart. I sigh while dragging myself out of bed, eyes flicking around the room to find my pearl clips gone from the dresser.

After taking my pills, brushing my teeth, and misting Franklin's shell, I slip a shirt and some shorts on to search for Issac. Soft music plays from the room farthest down the hall, making him easy to find, but the door is locked. I knock on it, and he tells me he'll be out in a minute.

"You're always so secretive with your art," I say.

"You're always secretive with what's in your heart," he calls back.

I lean against the wall. Even fake dating turned real for a weekend won't change that.

He shuts off the music, and I hear him shuffling through the room.

"Funny how you said you weren't going anywhere, yet I woke up without you," I tease.

"I'm sorry, Ni. The amazing sex had me feeling inspired," he says.

I'm glad he can't see how hard I'm grinning. "What are you doing in there with my pearl clips? Since they're mine, I think I'm entitled to see whatever you're using them for."

He slips out the door, purposely blocking my view of the room before he shuts it. "You'll see eventually."

"You say that a lot," I complain. "Starting to think you're pacifying me like a child."

He rolls his eyes, then bends to capture my lips. I try not to be embarrassed at the way I sigh into his mouth. It's soft and sensual, and butterflies spread through my stomach. Whatever doubt I had fades away when he curls his arm around my waist and pulls me closer. I made a deal, and I'm going to enjoy this man until I go home.

There's a frustratingly beautiful smile on his face when he breaks the kiss. "Morning, babe."

The casual use of the word makes me want to dance, sing, squeal like a girl. "Morning, big head," I say back.

"That nickname is a double entendre now, huh?" he says, and tugs on a strand of my hair.

"You're so conceited," I snort.

He slaps my ass. "And you should be too."

Heat rushes to my cheeks. I twist his nipple through his shirt, he tickles my armpit until I cry in defeat. When it's over and my pride is wounded, he scoops me from the floor, carries me the way he did in my dream. I protest when he passes the bedroom, but he says, "I'd love to spend all day laid up in your hair, ravishing your pussy, but you should be taken care of in more ways than one. First, food."

"I am more hungry than horny," I admit.

"Of course you are."

"And you love it."

"Of course I do," he says, and I turn to kiss his collarbone.

There's a chef putting finishing touches on beautifully arranged breakfast plates when we make it into the kitchen. When did he get here? He gives us a delighted smile, surely seeing the pink in my cheeks at being held like a newlywed.

"Good morning." I say. "The kitchen smells amazing."

"Thank you, Ms. Thompson. Please let me know if you need anything else," he says, then exits the kitchen.

Issac sets me down in front of the chair, pretending his back is aching from carrying me the whole way, and tries to bite my finger after I shove it into his dimple.

"Cannibal," I accuse.

"Only for you," he says. We sit down and he smiles. "Marco makes the best eggs I've ever tasted. Bougie eggs. I mean, the good kind of bougie that means he doesn't take any full-time clients because he's too busy. I'm lucky he came out here on short notice this morning."

"We could've gone to that breakfast spot we ordered from the last time I was here," I say. Marco's food is plated like a magazine, making the eggs, French toast, and corned beef hash look fancy. But it's breakfast food I can get anywhere. "You didn't have to do this."

Issac sits across from me. "Take a bite before you talk shit."

"Just saying, you know you never have to spend money like this on *me*."

He picks up his fork and fixes me with a look. "Take a damn bite, Ni."

"We aren't in the bed; you don't get to tell me what . . ." He scoops eggs off his plate and shuts me up with them. As soon as the food on his fork enters my mouth, I hum unexpectedly. He nods. That annoying smirk on his face. I try to pretend I'm not savoring the eggs before swallowing them. "You get under my skin."

He wiggles his brows. "How does it feel?"

"Like an unscratchable itch. Ringworm from the sandpit. An ingrown toenail," I tease.

Issac frowns. "Damn. Just a list of things that are opposite of sexy?"

I wink at him and take a bite of the corned beef hash. Issac knows it's my favorite. He also knows I'm a harsh judge, but the hash doesn't disappoint. Not at all.

"Alright, fine. Chef Marco must know magic," I say, and Issac's pleased with my assessment.

While eating, he lets me steal French toast off his plate. Maybe *let* is a strong word. More like he doesn't smack my hand away when I'm reaching, even though he calls me greedy. I eat his strawberries and lick whipped cream off the fork. It feels familiar, like we've been most of our lives, until he reaches under the table and strokes my bare thigh beneath the shorts. He knows what he's doing because as soon as he elicits a shiver from me, he steals his hand back and reaches for my cup of vanilla chai, taking an obnoxious sip.

When he passes the cup back, there's nothing left. "I guess I deserve that after leaving you hungry," I say. "What time do you work later?"

"I do have to stop by the botanical garden to speak with management about something, but I canceled my shoots," he says. "Lied about feeling sick. Bernie wasn't buying it, but I think he's letting me be happy this weekend. Maybe you snuck into his bitter heart."

"I think he snuck into mine too," I say, remembering how he helped me with no hesitation. "But we have time for the shoots and to spend together. I like to watch you work."

He bites his bottom lip. "I like to watch you work too. Those hips swinging when you . . ."

My cheeks flush. "Shhh . . . What if Chef Marco hears you?"

"He's definitely heard a lot worse in celebrity kitchens. I promise I was going to keep it PG," Issac says. "Now tell me what your beautiful heart wants on the agenda today. Maybe we can go get massages or . . . I can book us a private jet; we can go wherever you'd like."

The thought of going anywhere in the world with Issac makes his new life feel large. Once upon a time, we'd try to score bus passes to get to the beach. I appreciate where we've come from and am proud of where we both are now. "I like this real dating thing so far," I say.

The corners of his mouth rise. "Yeah?"

I lean across the table and kiss him in response. His lips taste like cinnamon. I could spend the day just licking them. When I pull back, he goes in for another, then *one more*. "Let's stay in Cali," I say. "I have an idea of what we can do in the evening. It's small and silly. But until then, can we spend what little time we have left together doing simple things?"

As soon as it leaves my mouth, I wonder if I'm being boring. But then Issac says, "Nothing ever feels small or silly or even simple when I'm with you," and there's so much gravity in those words. Images of us grass sitting and watching sunsets and dancing on the porch come to me. I know he means it. "Come on, let's get cleaned up and start the day."

"Will you carry me up the stairs too?"

"Only if you settle for a piggyback ride," he says.

I do. He brings me all the way to the bathroom on his back, keeping us balanced despite me nibbling his ear and pulling his beard on repeat. We're fun and silly, until he turns on the shower and starts to undress. I realize this is the first time we'll be naked together in the daylight. Soft music plays on a speaker while Issac lifts the shirt over my head, slowly tugs off my shorts. We stand in the sun coming through the window and admire each other with sighs and soft touches before Issac pulls me under the hot water. I let him lather every inch of my body, moan out loud when his fingers graze the sensitive skin around my nipples. He turns me around to wash my hair, softly scratching my scalp with his nails until my eyes roll back. He conditions then detangles my hair carefully with a comb. He kneads my shoulders with his knuckles to release some tension there, then moves lower, massaging down my back, pressing me into the tile while he works the muscles in my ass.

Is this really what I've been missing? No one has ever cared for me like this.

I chew my lip as he cups the backs of my thighs, putting pressure there before wrapping an arm around my stomach. I can feel how hard he is against me, but he doesn't try for sex, just stands under the steam with me until the water starts to cool.

40

MIRRORS MIGHT'VE BEEN MADE FOR THIS

SITTING IN THE PASSENGER SIDE OF ISSAC'S CAR MUST BE ONE of my top ten favorite pastimes. Especially now. I unabashedly stare at him as he drives, find everything he does sexy. From the way he spins the wheel to how he tilts his head while concentrating on the lyrics of a song. I know what his tongue tastes like, so when he flicks it over his lips and glances at me with his dark shades on, I can't stop smiling.

"What are you thinking about?"

"Nothing," I say. "You've already got a big enough head from what your followers say about you. You don't need any more compliments."

Articles this morning were looking for different ways to praise him. There wasn't one negative thing in the tabloids about the exhibition. He's gaining more followers by the minute.

"Do you find me handsome, Laniah Thompson? Irresistible? Sexy?"

"Shut up and drive, Issac Jordan." His dimples carve out his face when he smiles. I lean over and lick one. He laughs and puts his hand on my thigh, and I spend the rest of the ride with my face in my phone so he can't tell how good he makes me feel. He's a tease and I won't give him the satisfaction. And I need a distraction from the good feelings myself.

Mom called me an hour ago to give me updates on how we're doing with stocking products and about the discussions she's made with Sherry on ways to get better advertisement for the shop. I e-sign some documents so Sherry can get started. Then answer Katrina's text messages about my dress from last night. Because Holy Shit. Wow. Can I borrow it to wear to my second interview? I'll look like a queen.

She tells how fitting the company felt when she had the first interview with them, but she's nervous she's underqualified, though she won't tell them that.

The job is already yours, I text, then we type it into existence together. We'll go to New York for a weekend to celebrate soon.

Bridget texts about the exhibition too, saying, Way to make a man drool, my dear. Maybe I'll be giving you my grandmother's blue diamond earrings for your wedding, after all.

I blush, imagining me and Issac getting married, then push the wild thought from my head and text, Got the style cues from you. How's reconciling with Wilma going?

Bridget texts, You'll be happy to hear the man in room 1010 got kicked out and I didn't have to get in trouble for harassment.

I'm happy I won't have to worry about him pressing charges on you, I reply. But don't ignore me regarding Wilma. She made the first move. I think it was pretty brave.

Are you calling me a chicken?

I break out the best corny line I've got and know she'll be rolling her eyes for days. **Even the chicken crossed the road, B.**

What if the chicken isn't exactly the best at articulating how she feels? Bridget replies, and I realize we have this in common.

Sometimes all it takes is a Hi, I text, but she doesn't write back.

When Issac pulls up to the botanical garden, he reverses into a spot instead of doing it the simpler way, and even though it's arguably pointless, I find it sexy too. He pulls off his sunglasses. "Do you want to come inside? You can look around the garden if you'd like."

"I'd like to be anywhere with you, please," I say, and the honest admission, a hint of pleading for closeness in my voice, surprises even me.

Issac stares at me with the softest expression. Then he leans to kiss my collarbone. "I want that too."

As we walk up to the garden, I'm astonished by the sun glinting off the floor-to-ceiling windows and creating a slight shimmer above the grass. Memories of the exhibition flash through my mind while we walk hand in hand through the entrance and step into the main greenhouse together. We're here during off hours so it's empty save for one person standing across the room, fiddling with some vines.

"That would be management," Issac says, squeezing my hand before walking toward him.

The garden is just as gorgeous as it was last night but there's something ethereal about seeing this space with the sun touching the flora below. While Issac converses, I walk around the room, dip my fingers into the fountain, smell the gardenias, trace the lines of creeping fig vines.

Sometime later, I see him walking toward me and realize the manager has gone somewhere.

"When you entered the room last night," he says, a few feet away now, touching the grapevine above our heads, "there was no one else."

I imagine a thousand butterflies beating their wings in my belly when Issac looks at me the way he is right now. "Yeah?" I ask, my throat thick with feeling.

"Yeah," he breathes. "Surrounded by a sea of people, by nature and moonlight, and I've still never seen anything more stunning in my life."

Why did I ask for confirmation? If I don't keep control over my heart, those butterflies inside of me will carry it right to him. I clear my throat. "Are we alone here?"

It takes him a second to realize what I'm asking. He nods. "The manager is the only one on the grounds right now, but he said he had to go deal with a water issue in the garden outside."

A thought comes to me, a rush of a feeling. I smile and take a step closer, placing my hand flat on his chest. "Is that all you thought when you first saw me?"

Something hesitant flickers in his eyes, but then he leans forward, mouth brushing the shell of my ear. "I was fantasizing about what it would be like to take your dress off and do ungodly things to you."

I swallow, voice hoarse with want. "Tell me exactly how you would've done it."

He takes a step back and tilts his head. "Laniah Thompson, my sweet, private Ni, are you trying to seduce me here?"

"You said we're alone."

"I can't promise for how long."

"Water problems usually take a while," I say, running my fingers over my collarbone.

He tracks the movement with his eyes, covers his mouth, hides a smile. I think his protectiveness will win; I think my courage will dissolve. But he pulls me to a space filled with dense plant life before pushing on a strap of my dress until it falls off my shoulder.

"I would've started like this," he says, and the raw sound in his throat makes me ache. When he moves on to my other strap, he glances into my eyes for permission, and I place my hand over his to help him push it down.

My slip dress falls to the floor and Issac stands back to see me better. His gaze moves up my body the way it did at the exhibit. This time, the hunger is easier to notice. "After the dress was off, I'd enjoy the sight of you. Your supple breasts, the curve of those hips."

He swallows, and I reach to touch his Adam's apple, needing to feel him again, wishing he'd grab my hips and suck my breasts and stop teasing me. He closes his eyes for a few seconds. When he opens them again, it's easy to tell he's come undone. He begins to circle me, unfastening the buttons on his shirtsleeve before spinning me around. "Then I'd tell you to watch me enjoying you," he says, and I stare at us through a mirror that's still standing after the exhibition. He's behind me, bending his head and pushing my curls to the side to give him better access to my neck. He brushes his lips over my bare skin, sucks there softly, bites down.

"Vampire," I sigh, pushing my body into him.

"Can you blame me? You're beautiful. Look at yourself."

He unhooks my bra, runs his hands up and down my sides, squeezes my hips, plays with my nipples. We both watch my areolas darken. He hardens against my back. I turn in his arms, touch him through his pants, stroking softly while he moans at the feel of my fingers through the fabric.

"I want you," I whisper.

He stills my hand, places his forehead against mine, panting a little. "You don't know how much I want you."

"So show me."

He smiles, kisses my mouth, says, "Alright."

But as Issac leads me through the room, my heart races, suddenly aware of what I've asked for, how risky it is. Even standing on the cliffside might be safer than this. The bench he takes me to is surrounded by an arch of flowers, and I think he'll bend me over it, but he sits me down instead. He's towering above me, stiff in my face, when I ask if he'll let me taste him.

"No," he says. "I'm going to eat your pussy, and you're going to like it."

This time, when he drops to his knees, I don't refuse. When he lifts my legs and plants the first kiss between them, I don't worry about what my heart is doing. When he uses the flat of his tongue for a slow torturous sweep, I don't tell him to stop. I forget where we are.

"Shh." He smiles against my swollen lips. "We should keep quiet."

"I'll try," I tell him.

"Good girl," he says, before burying his face between my thighs.

I rock my hips, wrap my legs around him, and when he starts to make circles with his tongue, I cry out.

"You're not being a good girl," he says, and nips me softly with his teeth.

I pull his hair and he tells me I taste *so damn sweet*, then makes a wounded sound when I push him away.

Our eyes lock, his glossy. I'm panting, he's licking his lips.

"What's wrong?" He glances toward the entryway before focusing on my face. "Scared?"

"I just don't want to cum that way."

His lips twitch. "How do you want it?"

I stand up, he does the same. We're face-to-face when I unbuckle his jeans, push his pants down till they fall to his ankles. His boxers go next. "Sit down," I tell him.

"Whatever you want," he says.

I glance at the sun coming through the open ceiling and then at myself in the mirror behind him. With all the flora and light and greenery around my body, I feel like I can float. Issac kisses my navel, then drags me down into his lap. I grind against him at first, both of us groaning. But when he pushes himself inside of me, I cry out, unprepared for how much bigger it would feel in this position. He clamps a hand over my mouth, allowing me to suck and moan and cry into his fingers while adjusting on top of him with slow movements.

"Watch how good we look," he whispers, and I whimper at his words, knowing he must be watching us in the mirror behind me too.

We are glorious with the sun beating down on our bodies, but when he sucks my breasts and uses my hips to rock me against him, it's hard to watch anything. And in this moment of pleasure and connectedness, here among ever-growing things, I've never felt more alive.

41

DOUBLE QUASARS COLLIDING

W E SPEND THE REST OF THE DAY SHOPPING, FEEDING EACH other ice cream, trying to avoid the paparazzi and failing. They don't know that the flower in my hair is one Issac tucked there after our visit to the botanical garden. They don't know that when he glances at it now, we both blush at a memory made, that there's an increased buzz between us, a secret we share, something brave we did together that we may not ever get to do again. We stop caring when they snap pictures of us. I kiss Issac, he kisses me, we let them see whatever they see.

Night comes fast and Issac's excited about my planetarium idea. Neither of us has ever gone before. When we pull up, we don't get out of the car right away because there's a box of teriyaki fried chicken to finish off. Issac doesn't mention his beautiful white seats or ask me not to stain anything. I lick sauce off his fingers. He tells me I'm being gross, but he likes it.

Inside the planetarium, we find seats under the massive dome-shaped ceiling and watch celestial objects move, twist, and tangle, blink all around us. Issac finds my hand and laces our fingers to show the way we fit under the stars. There's an achy, knowing feeling in the base of my throat about how small we are in a beautiful way, the same as when we're by the water together. Two star-shaped souls who happened to be in the right place at the right time, to find friendship in each other among billions of other souls.

Issac smiles at me in the dark, eyes glinting the way they did when we were kids searching for fireflies in moonlight. I grasp my seat with my free hand, breathe through the overwhelming feeling spreading through my chest. When I stepped onto the plane to surprise him, I couldn't have imagined we would end up like this.

"You alright, Ni?" he asks.

"Yes, I say," and for some reason, I think of my father, what he might've done feeling a million things for my mother in a room like this. Then suddenly, I'm standing in front of Issac and extending my hand. "Will you dance with me, best friend?"

He doesn't glance around the packed observatory to see who's watching when we descend the stairs for a corner of flat space in the room. He laughs when I try to spin him, failing because he's too tall. I pull him close, and we dance under the solar system to imaginary music.

"Sing something for me," I ask.

He chooses Aretha Franklin's "I Say a Little Prayer," and I smile when he scrunches his face and drags the notes. It's funny until his voice softens and the words hit. I lean my forehead against his chest so he can't see all the feelings on my face. My eyes will tell him I never want this dance to end, but it will. With it, my flight home will be closer, the new deal will soon be over. Once it is, what will we have left? If either of us decides friendship is all we can handle, will we ever get to dance like this?

Issac tilts my chin, as if realizing my mind is running. I wonder if he can see the sheen of tears in my eyes under the glowing
lights. I wonder if he can feel the fear in my heart when he bends
to brush his lips over mine.

SINCE ARRIVING BACK AT THE CONDO, THERE'S SOMETHING DIFFER-
ent and unspoken between us, something tender. Raw. A fraying
thread we're careful not to break. Questions we're not ready to
ask. I pack my bag for my early flight, then find Issac out on the
balcony. The sky is dark but he's still searching for stars. I debate
backing out quietly, worried he wants to be alone, but he senses
me behind him and says, "Come be with me, Ni."

Issac's arm grazes mine as we stand on the balcony, looking at
the water in the pool below. When he sighs, my anxious brain
begins creating scenarios. I wonder if I acted too intimately at
the planetarium and it stirred up fear inside of him. Maybe I
won't have to be the one to tell him I'm scared of what it'll mean
if we decide one weekend is too little time to spend dancing together.

"I feel selfish for saying this," Issac says, "but sometimes I find
myself wishing you moved across the country with me. My heart
wants you to stay. But you can't, and I should keep my mouth shut
about things like this because the last time I told you I wanted you
here, you flew out to surprise me. I'm so damn happy you did,
but . . ."

The coil in my stomach starts to unravel. Three years of distance feels like none. I smile and know he'll be able to hear it in
my voice when I say, "You're not selfish. Sometimes I wonder
what it would've been like if I packed my bags and followed you

here." It's the truth but my heart is thrumming when I admit it out loud. Especially since so much has changed since then.

Issac turns, cups my face, and stares down into my eyes. He opens his mouth, and my chest tightens, waiting for him to speak. But then, he exhales and leans in to press his lips to mine. The magnet between us causes a collision. We are two host galaxies merging to form one massive blackhole full of unknown. His hands roam my backside while I catalog every touch, every taste, greedy in the hope that I can collect every feeling, so that reaching for memories in the future will send my body back here too. I search him with hungry want, burning need, finally finding his boxers and pushing them down before my knees join them on the floor.

"Laniah, no . . ." He reaches for me, but I push his hand away.

"Shh . . . let me take care of you too." I move his hand to my hair, silently giving him permission to pull and push and do what he wants with me.

When I brush the veins on his shaft with my thumb, he shudders out a shaky breath. I smile in response, loving the feel of him tangling his fingers in my hair for a better grip. When I move my lips against his sensitive skin, lick the tip of his head, work my way down the pronounced line of his dick, he curses again and again.

His hisses and moans feed a deep desire in my belly, make me soaked between the thighs, wetter realizing I'm causing him such pleasure. He uses one hand to steady himself with the railing, then thrusts his hips to push deeper into my mouth, unable to contain his need. He cries out, calls me baby. His baby. God, baby, God damn, Dear Lord, oh my fucking . . . baby.

When he finishes with a ragged breath, I kiss the inside of his thigh.

He pulls me to my feet, tastes my tongue, murmurs sweet things against my hair, uses his hand to feel how wet I am. At the ready look in my eyes, he turns me around so that I'm gripping the edge of the balcony, then spreads me open and slides inside. My breasts bounce in his hands, and I'm dizzy with the pleasure and pain each time he strokes.

I think he could send me over the edge in this position, but suddenly he pulls out and leads me to the bed. We toss the blanket aside, and I lay him on the sheets, then slide down on his dick, listening as he breathes through his teeth. He reaches for a kiss. Then: "Come here," he says against my lips. "I want you closer. I know you want to be closer too." He helps ease me down so I'm lying flat against him. I didn't have to tell him this is one of the best ways for me to climax. "How are you so perfect?" he says, kissing my neck, moaning through my slow movements.

I become all heartbeat and nerve endings while grinding him. He peppers kisses over my areolas, and wherever his skin touches mine feels like a live wire, small sparks of pleasure and pinpricks. The friction between us, the penetration, the way he grasps my ass and moves his own hips, how he allows me my pleasure without complaint of the way he's curved inside of me. Perfect. Issac is perfect. I'm comfortable, safe in my need for this position, soaring because he likes it too. When I feel my orgasm swell to the surface, Issac starts calling my name, close to coming too. I moan into nothingness. Words are lost to the feeling of him getting harder inside of me. Everything is heightened. Issac touches my arm and gives me goose bumps.

"Talk to me, baby," he begs. "Please."

"It feels so damn good," I manage, but that just makes him wince. I pray for my body to reach its climax, then pray it holds off because I don't want this feeling to end. He stops moving to save himself, just lets me rub my clit against him until the pressure builds. Until it hurts. Until I start to cum with his name on my lips, but as soon as the release hits, Issac starts moving again, faster, pulling me closer. He pushes me past a point, bringing me somewhere higher, and the orgasm I have this time is like nothing I've experienced. My toes curl, my body convulses. He cums with me, then holds me while I tremble, pushing hair from my face and kissing my temple.

We lie there for a few moments, breathing heavily, happy, and when I roll off him, he's quick to complain. "I liked you there."

"I don't want to hurt you longer than I had to," I say, throwing my leg over his.

"You weren't hurting me at all. I loved every second."

I kiss his face, his chin, his eyebrow. "Mm . . . you're the perfect one," I tell him.

He looks like he has something serious to say, that same look out on the balcony before he told me he wished I lived here, but then he kisses me. "You should get some sleep. Your flight is in a few hours."

I want to argue. Tell him we can spend the rest of our time laughing in each other's arms, or watching movies; we could definitely eat. The sex made me hungry again. But I'm exhausted down to the bones too. I lie that I'm not tired before sleep finds me.

42

CAN I GO WHERE YOU GO?

TOM TAKES US TO THE AIRPORT WITH A HUGE SMILE ON HIS FACE like he knows what we spent the night doing. Taylor Swift's "Lover" plays on the Bluetooth and Issac tucks me under his arm. He sighs. I sigh. We meld into each other. I'm thankful we're in the back seat and there's no console between us, but as we get closer, dread coils in my stomach. What if this is the last time we're ever like this? I don't want to leave him or face decisions or address this heavy yearning in my chest. I'm not ready. I close my eyes, cuddle him, smell the scent that is all pheromones and gentle soap after we spent a weekend loving on each other. Just in case.

When we arrive, Issac asks Tom to get the bags and to give us privacy. I think he'll steal some kisses, touch me, but he only lifts my chin, a frown on his face. "Hi, my love."

My heart races, thinking he's going to end things with me right now. Say we don't even need a week to think about how we feel. Say it was fun, but it isn't *right*. It's only lust.

But he opens his mouth, speaks sure and steady. "Laniah. I'm so in love with you."

The words don't float above us, they land with precision, right over my tender heart.

"I've been in love with you since thirteen," he says. "I don't know if you remember the day you found me on the bleachers at Uni park. We never talk about it, but I was so mad you saw me that way. And you, stubborn from the beginning, told me it's okay to cry." He strokes my jaw with his thumb, brushes back the curls from in front of my face with a shaky hand. "You were wearing your hair wild, and I remember thinking it was beautiful in the wind. You had on yellow overalls, and on the way home, you bought us Starbursts with pocket change."

He wipes my wet eyes; his are wet with tears too.

"You let me take all the pink ones, even though they were your favorite. That's when I knew I was a goner," he says. "I fell in love with you that day, and it's been that way ever since."

Words get caught in my throat. I can barely breathe, but Issac exhales like he's been waiting his whole life to say it. And I believe him. He kisses my forehead and, with his mouth against my skin, says, "Spend the week deciding how you feel, just like we said. But I had to tell you because I've had years to process the feeling, recently therapy to come to terms with it. Not because I didn't want to love you, but because I wasn't in the place to do it like you deserved, not when I was needing to find ways to better love myself. And you're my family, Laniah. I couldn't chance losing you, I'm still terrified. But a special man used to tell me to be brave enough to trust my instincts." Issac takes a shaky breath, and at the mention of my father I start to sob. "And my instincts told me not to leave here without you knowing the truth of my heart. This past year, I've wondered if there's a chance you feel the same, but if there's a part of you that's been scared of love for yourself. I'm not going to assume you're ready or even how you feel about me at all, but you should know before you leave this car that you've never *only* felt like my best friend. And I'm ready now. If you do love me too, I'm ready to be right for you."

He pulls back with a sigh, squeezes my hand, then lets me go.

But when I see him reaching for the door handle, ready to give me space, I tug on his sleeve. "Wait."

His deep brown eyes meet mine again, and the memory floods my mind.

WHAT I REMEMBER

Twelve years ago. Pink Starburst. Yellow overalls.

With baggy bottoms and deep pockets, brighter than a banana, Dennis and Vanessa Thompson were at the mercy of a teenager who just *had to have them*. My parents were on a strict budget, but two weeks of begging later and I woke up to the yellow overalls folded at the bottom of the bed. As soon as I slipped them on, I vowed my mom would have to pry them off of my dead body to get me to stop wearing them.

Both of the Thompson adults were at work, but I had to show them off to somebody.

Issac Jordan lived across the street, and we were still finding our friendship, still fighting over silly things when he'd come over on school days for my mother to do his hair, but I knocked on his door, fully aware that he might tease me about how bright the yellow was.

It was a fruitless act anyway. Issac wasn't home and no one knew where he'd gone early that morning. But I didn't give up searching. Eventually I'd find him at Uni park, where my mother would sometimes take the both of us to do our hair in warm weather. He was on the bleachers in a bone-colored crewneck sweater, knees up, arms around them, face buried between. It was clear we were coming out of summer, the wind was rustling the trees, and the air was cool-crisp, but I wondered if he was shivering. Napping? Possibly praying?

He startled at the sound of the bleachers squeaking under my feet, head snapping up.

Issac was crying.

Something twisted in my stomach at the sight. When I asked him what was wrong, he turned away from me, embarrassed. *I'm fine, you can leave, please leave.* But there were tears in his throat, and my body moved quicker than my mind. Reaching and wrapping my arms around him, the way my parents would do with me.

"It's okay to cry. Crying is brave," I said to Issac. They were words my dad often said to me, a kid whose emotions would grow roots on the inside and get stuck there. *It'll take courage, but you must unroot the big feelings*, Dennis Thompson would say.

Not long after, Issac whispered, "I miss my mother so much," and the backs of my eyes burned.

I missed my mother when she was at the hotel, preferred her working in the kitchen. I couldn't imagine missing her because she was gone for good. So I hugged him a little harder and let him cry as long as he had to.

On the way home, I bought a pack of Starburst from the corner store. They were a recent addiction, and I really wanted to eat the pink ones, but Issac looked like he needed them more.

"I like your overalls," he said, and when he smiled, with those big brown tired eyes, something warm glowed in my chest, but I didn't have a name for the feeling.

I didn't know it was love just yet.

43

CAN WE ALWAYS
BE THIS CLOSE?

T'S OKAY, NI. REALLY," ISSAC IS SAYING TO ME. "I'D RATHER YOU take the time to think . . ."

I wrap my arms around him, desperate for the contact, and he holds me just as close, stroking my back in soothing circles, always willing to be the comfort.

But I swallow, pull back, and reach for his face because it's my turn to comfort him.

"I don't need time," I say, and his eyes widen ever so slightly, nervous for my answer. "I'm terrified, Issac. But I can't let you leave me here without telling you that I'm so in love with you too."

His inhale is sharp, his eyes flick closed. Tears slip below his lashes and I want to kiss each one. But he buries his face in my neck, and I can feel his mouth against my skin.

"Are you sure?" he asks quietly, and I think of the boy in the bone-colored sweater wanting to feel love again.

I wish he could hear my heart, the certainty just below the

pulsing fear, but with courage, I unroot the words. "It's annoying that you do whatever you want and even more annoying to admit that I love it sometimes. You're so smug about your music taste, and it's infuriating because there's no place I'd rather be than sitting beside you and listening to your playlist instead of mine. I hate how it feels like you take a piece of me with you when you leave, and I'm missing it until you come home. You make me feel safe in my silence, which is not something just anyone can do. I'm in love with you, Issac. And if none of that is proof enough, I guess I'll admit I can't bring myself to eat chicken parm without you."

He laughs with his heart, shows me his face, the hope in his eyes, and I know what I said was enough before he kisses me. It's tender, soft, and slow. But I feel every single year of longing on our lips.

When we break apart, I realize just how many times we've been in cars, sharing secrets, wishes, and dreams. I'd never let myself imagine I'd be sharing my heart with him like this.

Issac presses his lips to my neck, says, "You'll miss your plane."

"I can stay," I whisper, wanting him to kiss my skin again.

"You can't."

"I know," I say. "Wildly Green needs me."

"I think we need the week too," he admits.

I pull back, look up at him. "Why?"

"You're terrified, and so am I," he says, touching my cheek. "I'm so happy that you love me. I feel like I can float. But I'm trying to stay grounded because the truth is, there's still so much to think about. We have these feelings, but you're my family, my best friend, and that's the most important part. The truth is our dreams take us different places. You're in Rhode Island, I'm out here. I'm high-profile, you're a private person. I want to be with you, Laniah, but your life will be changed forever. Being with me might cause you hurt in the future, we've already experienced it. I already know what I'm willing to give up, but I'm not sure you'd want me to give up certain things. You should take the time to think about what you'd be willing to compromise. To make sure if we try this, a real relationship, we do it right. With clear heads."

I release a breath. Issac just named most of my fears. He doesn't even know about the deepest one. That someone can be *right*, and life can still tear them from you. But I can't help smiling because he said he wants to be with me. Issac Jordan loves me. I love him. And we want to be together.

"I'll take the week," I agree, and reach for another kiss.

Issac speaks against my lips, says, "But don't you dare eat chicken parm without me."

———————

I'M FLOATING WHEN I STEP OUT OF T. F. GREEN AIRPORT AND MY feet touch land in Rhode Island. It's only black pavement, lined with cars and trash cans, but the air smells sweeter, the sun is brighter; I'm not feeling fatigue at all because Issac is in love with me. But Mom's is the first familiar face I see, and I wasn't prepared for the slow comedown I'd feel opening her car door. She offered to pick me up from the airport, and if I was of sound mind to hold on to the high of love for a little longer, I might've texted her and told her I was going to take an Uber. Because seeing her alone here after what just happened with Issac makes my stomach twist with the reminder that my father isn't riding in her passenger side. He never will again.

Before she can ask about my weekend adventure, I bombard her with Wildly Green questions, eager to distract her and hear her gush about the planning she and Lex had to do with Sherry this weekend.

But when she pulls up in front of my house, she turns in her seat. "You've changed," she says, using her knowing mother's stare on me. "You're different somehow. Did something happen between you and Issac?"

I want to sit with what happened by myself for a while, but she'd know I'm lying, and there's no reason to hide. Not anymore. I try to form the words, start over in my head. She puts a hand over mine and I squeeze hers. "He told me he's in love with me, Mom."

Saying it out loud brings sparks of feeling again, and I find myself smiling through old worries.

My mom is quiet for a few seconds. Then: "Finally."

She takes an exaggerated breath, throws her hands up to thank the heavens.

I narrow my eyes at her.

"What, Laniah Leigh? That boy's been in love with you since you were children."

Warmth cuts across my cheeks. "Why didn't you say anything? How come it has always seemed like you didn't want us together? You even warned me a few weeks ago."

"Because you're both dense. I mean, after years of pretending, I figured when the truth finally came out, one or both of you would find a way to ruin things." She cocks an eyebrow at me. "You didn't already ruin it, did you? You told him you love him too?"

"Have a little faith in me," I say. "But, yes. Right before my flight."

She squeals and dances in her seat. "Did you run through the airport like in the romance novels?"

I laugh and lean over to hug her. "No, Mom, but I would've if I had to."

She rubs my back, and asks, "How are you going to get this cross-country relationship to work?"

"We're going to discuss it," I say, leaving out the agreement we made to take a week. She'll think we're being silly. "All I know is that I can't ever lose him."

She makes a small, startled noise over my vulnerable confession, and hugs me tighter. "Baby, that boy is never going anywhere."

"Even if I eventually break his heart? Even if he breaks mine?"

"Even then," she says. "Do you know what I see when you and Issac are together? Two people who get to be their entire selves. When you're with him, you look the most like *you*. I recognized it because I used to have that with your daddy. He was my soulmate."

She doesn't know that comparing me and Issac to her and my dad was the most perfect thing she could've done, and the scariest thing I could've heard. My eyes well, heartbroken for her, nervous for me.

"Mom," I whisper. "I'm so sorry."

"Shh," she says, and pulls back to brush tears from my face, even though her eyes are brimming with them too. "There are other loves, but you only get this kind once in a lifetime."

44

FOREVER AND EVER

ON DAY ONE, MY THROAT IS THICK WHILE TRYING TO CON-
sider what I'd be willing to give up. What I'd be comfortable with Issac sacrificing. He texts me to make sure I'm okay, but
we don't talk about us. And that's good because it feels wonderful
to be back in the shop with countless customers returning to tell
us our custom products are working for them. And it's quite nice
to hear the compliments on my exhibition dress. They call me a
fairy, recite Issac's lines from the magazine, and say I'm a goddess.
Lex jokes I'll have to wear the dress to the shop this week and
grant them three wishes. Then he says someone will surely ask for
a man *just like* Issac. I don't know if there's anyone in the world
quite like him, but I'll wish they find someone that is perfect for
them. At the end of the day, I conclude that maybe sacrifices aren't
necessary. Issac and I can live in a fairy-tale-like bubble where
distance, our careers, and my privacy don't matter. We'll hop on
flights to see each other, maybe settle down and buy homes on

both sides of the country, we'll spend our days smiling and laughing and having incredible sex.

I don't text him this though, because he'd tell me to keep thinking.

On days two and three, I miss him something awful and try to
recall his scent from memory, but it does nothing to stop the
ache in my chest. I should've brought home one of his unwashed
T-shirts. I wonder if he's sitting somewhere missing me too. I almost send him the lyrics of "Lover" so he can remember what it
felt like during the car ride right before we confessed our love to
each other, but he'd say I'm breaking the rules.

Day four comes and I wake with pulsing flank pain. My new
doctor's visit isn't for two months, but this nagging feeling in my
body is hard to ignore. On break in the back room at the shop, I
examine my medical file, reading instances where my doctor made
special notes about my anxiety, my weight, blood pressure readings with mentions of my family history of heart failure. It's all
things I figured I'd find until I get to the printouts of bloodwork.
My stomach clenches as I wade through tests, watching various
labs increase and decrease throughout the years. Some have been
flagged over and over again, and I wonder if it's a mistake. How
many people have looked at my labs throughout the years? Would
the nurses have caught something my doctor might not have?

Between customers, I spend the day on Dr. Google but it's a
scary place with scary answers. I look up the flagged acronyms
and abbreviations, read about creatinine clearance and GFR and
feel sick over what I find. Mom doesn't want to hear any of my
worry and insists I call my former doctor for an explanation before
panicking.

"There's no way something is wrong and he never told you,"
she says.

Lex makes me promise to stay off the internet, then says he's going to ask for Shane's medical opinion. Thinking of speaking to my old doctor again is what fills me with panic, and I hate to bother Shane, but there's no way I won't break my Google promise, which will mean drowning in worry about things without context for eight whole weeks, so I let Lex take my lab work off the counter before he leaves the shop.

And I sleep a little easier when he doesn't call me with bad news.

On the morning of the fifth day, I lie in bed and trace my fingers over my lips, close my eyes at the ache of wanting to kiss Issac again. He texts me as soon as I open them.

He must hear my heart from miles away.

Day five, and I'm still in love with you. Just like I've always been. I'll understand if you have doubts about your own feelings, but I know how your mind runs you ragged sometimes, and I don't want you to have any doubts about mine. I love you. I want to be with you. In a real relationship. I'll give whatever I can to make it work. Have a good day. PS: Don't respond to this. You have 48 more hours.

I smile at his reminder because he's so annoying and I absolutely love him that way. And he doesn't have any doubts. He still wants to be with me. The feeling in my body is too big to contain, I roll over, scream happy things into my pillow. Will two days feel like twenty?

At work, I reread the message every chance I get to feel the high again, then decide that day seven is taking too long to get here. I want to tell Issac how *right* it felt to touch him and hold him and think of him as mine. I'm his. It doesn't matter if he's there, and I'm here, he'll always have a piece of my heart with him. There's nothing we could discuss that'll keep me from wanting to try.

When the shop closes for the day, I'm smiling as I pore over paperwork in the back room, deciding that I might just call him as soon as I get home. Tell him it's my turn to break the rules. But I hear the shop bell go off and inwardly curse. Mom's going to be annoyed that, in my distracted state, I forgot to flip the OPEN sign to CLOSED.

Minutes go by and I hear low voices, and then . . . then I think I hear her cry out. I push away from the table, and hurry to the door just to come face-to-face with Lex. He called out sick this morning, so I'm surprised to see him, but before I can ask him what's wrong with my mom, he shifts to the side, giving me a clear view of who she's talking to. Shane, a tall, fair-skinned man with huge hands gives me a small wave, though he's not smiling like he usually is when I see him.

Lex clears his throat, and my eyes flick to his face. His are red rimmed, his cheeks are drawn. Why is he here if he's sick? Has he been crying? "We should talk. All of us," he says.

I follow him to the front, the whole time a warning wrings my stomach, my heart races. Mom can't even look at me. She shakes her head, tells Shane that *this is all wrong*, and I look at the three of them, demanding answers with my eyes, before, "What is it?"

Lex is the first one to speak, but he's rambling on about the debate he had with Shane over whether they should tell me because Shane isn't my doctor and he's a cardiologist, but he did make sure to check in with a specialist at his hospital and . . .

"Just tell me," I whisper.

Shane steps in front of Lex, pulls a stool for me to sit, uses a soothing tone to say, "I've checked your lab work with a nephrologist friend named Dr. Baldwin at my hospital and the GRF test you were worried about . . . That test does show how well the kidneys are functioning and your results are consistent with a chronic kidney disease diagnosis."

I take a startled breath. Last night, I fought the urge to self-diagnose with a Google search, praying all the articles on the internet were wrong. Praying I was just looking for something that wasn't there. That couldn't be there because . . . "My doctor—"

"Deserves a malpractice suit," Lex injects, anger flashing on his face.

I look at my mother again, hoping she'll shake me awake like she did when I was a child struggling through a bad dream, but she looks like she needs someone to say this isn't real herself. When Lex reaches to hold my shaky hand, I ask Shane if there's more he can tell me, and he hesitates while searching my eyes.

"Please," I beg, desperate to know what this all means for me.

"Alright," he says. "Well, Dr. Baldwin, the kidney specialist, said the numbers are consistent with stage three kidney disease, which means it's advanced enough to begin addressing now in the hopes of helping it from progressing to the stages with more serious complications."

I let go of Lex and hug myself, remembering what I'd read about the five stages yesterday. How three is between a healthy organ and complete kidney failure. Advancing to stage four might mean anemia and heart disease. I didn't allow myself to read any more because my father was diagnosed with heart failure at forty-three. I'm only twenty-five. There's no way something that's supposed to be keeping me alive is failing. But Shane's telling me that it is.

"The way you live your life should change, Laniah, but Dr. Baldwin can explain it better than me. She offered to squeeze you in for an office visit soon, so that you don't have to wait months to meet your new primary care doctor, who will probably refer you to see a kidney specialist like her anyway."

He lets out a small sigh, and I find myself wondering how many times he's had to deliver bad news like this.

"Okay," I say, and they all stare, expecting something else. How can I explain to them that it feels like oxygen is being stripped from the room?

Shane clears his throat. "I'm sorry this is happening to you. I wasn't sure whether it was wise to tell you this way, but Lex thought it might be better for you to be surrounded by people who love you and . . ."

Whatever else he says falls to the background when Issac's face materializes in my mind. He loves me and he's not here and . . . didn't I already know there was something wrong deep down? Didn't I warn myself?

I try to swallow, but air isn't making it to my lungs and the earth is spinning and I get off the stool because if I can just make it outside, where there's sunlight, then maybe . . . maybe . . . But suddenly my mom is right there, steadying me by the door with her strong arms and whatever was holding me together cracks as soon as she hugs me. "Momma," I cry, and she brushes the hair from my face, says, "I'll give you both of my kidneys if I have to."

45

THIS TIMELINE

W HILE MOM AND LEX ARE IN MY KITCHEN COOKING SOME-
thing they're going to make me eat, I'm in bed, doing
exactly what they told me not to do: googling chronic kidney disease. Symptoms, dialysis, transplants. Shane left me with a couple
of pamphlets, but they weren't enough. I read about complications
from toxins building up in the bloodstream when the kidneys
aren't functioning properly enough to remove them, which is what
could cause the heart to work harder to circulate blood and can
lead to heart disease.

I see my dad, his labored breathing, and remember my mom
at his side, her tears falling as she clasped his hands in her own.

I remember the appointments, the canceled plans, the tired-
ness in my mom's eyes—the slope of her shoulders while she cried
by the sink.

I read about the possibility of a shortened life span—that the
average life expectancy for a forty-year-old woman diagnosed

with stage three is only twenty-eight years. I'm not *even* twenty-eight yet, what would it mean for me?

When I get to the part about pregnancy and higher risks and life-threatening complications, the tiny flickers I'd begun to imagine of Issac and a tiny hand in his now ignite panic inside of me. Will that light inside of him dampen with worry for me? Will we make choices out of fear instead of joy?

What did my mom give up, and what would Issac?

All of these years I've been afraid of losing someone I love the way that I love him, but now I'm envisioning the opposite. Can I really give him my love then risk him losing me and feeling alone in the world again?

The pain is sharper as I scroll our text thread, reading his older messages like a masochist, because I already know what needs to be done. I should call him, but I can't handle hearing his voice while breaking his heart. And he'll hear *me* break through the line and try to fix it like he always does.

Except he can't fix *this*.

So I take a breath and type, delete, try again. Call myself a coward for doing it this way. I hope he'll forgive me. God, please let him forgive me. I try to pick the perfect words while listening to Mom and Lex whispering about me from the kitchen. Then I realize there are none. Because the perfect thing would involve asking him to hop on a flight the first chance he can to hold me, make love to me, let me hear his laugh in person. Be with me.

But I love him too much for his future with me to be *this* uncertain.

Issac, I had the best time of my life with you this past weekend, I say. **You were perfect. I'll never forget it. And I know we said a**

week, but I've thought hard about what it would take, and I can't be with you.

I choke on a sob as it sends.

Issac looks at the message right away. Doesn't hesitate to type back, says something I wasn't expecting. What is this? I don't believe you, Ni. I knew what you wanted before you got on that plane. I could feel you like our hearts were in the same body. What has happened since we last spoke that has you running scared?

He knows. He knows he's worthy of love. That he deserves someone to spend forever with. He knows he has my heart. For a moment, I sit in that feeling. Happy for my best friend, proud of the love of my life who grew up unsure. But my fingers are faster than the reassuring words I want to tell him, because I don't know if I'm someone he can spend forever with.

Can we forget the weekend happened and please go back to being friends? Please. I need you in my life, I love you in my life, but not like this. I'm so sorry, I say.

He tries to call right after he reads my message, but I reject it. He leaves a voice mail. My heart hurts as I listen. "Was it something I said on socials? We can fix it. Laniah, I'll adjust whatever for you. You don't even need to come out here anymore. You don't need to show your face at events. I'm so damn in love with you. Whatever it takes because I know you feel it too. Talk to me. Tell me what's wrong. Let's work through it together."

The tears run hot down my face; my chest burns too. What happened since we last spoke is that I was diagnosed with a disease that can kill me, by doctors who weren't mine because the one I had for years didn't care to tell me. And I decided I won't let all of this do damage to Issac, who's already lost so much in his life and is finally in a good place. He deserves to be with someone healthy. And I don't want to feel the weight of not being that for him. But I can't tell him this right now. I need to be in a better place emotionally, mentally prepared to be strong and not allow him to change his whole life for me like I know he would. Especially when I can only offer friendship. Anything else might hurt both of us too much. I'll tell him about my diagnosis soon, but I hope by the time I do he won't connect it to me saying I don't want to be with him.

It takes everything left in me to type what I do, to hit Send, but I know it's the right thing for him. If I can save him a lifetime of possible pain, then I need to. That's the thing, Issac. I really took the time, and I do love you. I always will. You're my family. But a romantic relationship is not worth risking what we already have. I hope we can pull past this. I'm sorry.

I just told the love of my life that being with him isn't worth the risk.

The sharpness in my sternum makes me clutch my chest.

I wait for him to demand a real explanation while trying to catch my breath and fighting the urge to call and tell him it's all a lie, that I need him now more than ever.

But Issac doesn't write back after that.

SOMEHOW, I MANAGE TO GET SOME SLEEP, BUT I DOUBT MOM DID. IN the morning, she has tea ready for me by the bed, and she's sitting at the edge waiting for me to wake up. And I think of making a joke about how grown I am, that she doesn't need to watch me sleep, but I feel comforted that she did. Until I remember all the time that she spent sitting by my father's bed.

"Morning," she says, then gestures to the steaming cup. "Since we can't talk to your new kidney doctor for two weeks, I had to use the internet to find out which tea is still safe for you because the pamphlets Shane left mentioned that some herbs aren't great for the kidneys."

I swallow and reach for her hand, say, "You've been researching for me."

She laces our fingers. "Did you know I saw something online about horsetail root being bad too? We make products with horsetail root; you use them all the time. I can't believe your asshole of a doctor didn't tell you about this. I'm sorry for not listening to you when you—"

"I'm not upset with you. It's still hard for me to wrap my mind around too," I say, and the anger and betrayal swell inside of me again. Dr. Rotondo knew my labs were off for years. He made me believe I couldn't trust myself, I couldn't listen to my body. Why? Why would he do this? How many glasses of herbal tea would I have sipped on without knowing I was unintentionally doing more damage to my kidneys before he thought my disease was serious enough to tell me about it? How many bottles of ibuprofen might I have gone through for my headaches before learning that it's hard on my already weakened kidneys? How many people are afraid to sound stupid or *bother* their doctor with questions and worries, then end up leaving visits feeling inferior because of a power dynamic that shouldn't exist? Doctors are here to help, not to create complexes because of a system that gives them superiority.

I'm so wrapped up in my thoughts, I don't notice when Mom begins to cry. But then she hollers out, a deep sound from her throat that brings me back to my teenage years: her painful shower cries when she thought I wasn't home to hear. "I don't want you to have to give up the things you love," she says.

"Oh, Mom." I sit up in bed, squeeze her hand, rush to reassure her. "We don't even know what will change yet. I'm sure Shane's nephrologist friend will give me all the answers soon, but nothing bad is going to happen to me overnight. Not with one cup of tea. I'm okay. I promise."

"And what about your heart?" she asks, wiping her eyes with her shirtsleeve. "You're telling me we don't know what will change, yet pushing Issac away prematurely. Don't you know about God's timing, baby? You and Issac both realized you are soulmates before you found out about this so that you can be together through it."

I bite back a bitter laugh because of the irony. I was scared of having a love story like my parents had and look at what fate offered me. "Or maybe I found out just in time," I tell her. "Right before I said yes to a relationship that we both might regret for the rest of *my* life."

My mom sighs. "Don't you see that you're spiraling, baby? You're running to the worst-case scenarios in your mind and hurting him for no reason. It's okay for him to be with you when you spiral. That's what partners are for."

Her answer feels too simple for someone who spent years suffering. "I don't want that for Issac," I say. "And I don't want him to make promises now that he might struggle to keep later. What if he resents me for it? What if my body changes and eventually I can't do the things that make him happy? It's better I end things now, set him free. Set myself free from a future of constantly worrying about how my health is affecting him."

Mom looks sad, and so tired from spending the night watching me sleep. "Oh, baby. You don't know the love you're depriving him of, the love you're depriving yourself of," she says. "I think you're doing the opposite of setting him free. I think you're putting his love in a box because you're scared of seeing how big it can be."

My eyes burn. Big love leaves a deeper hole once it's gone. I wipe at angry tears, afraid if she says one more thing, I'll tell her how devastating it was watching *her* spiral after we lost Dad.

She turns away like she doesn't want to broach the topic either.

"Fine. I'm not going to argue with you. I just want you to rest," she says.

I shake my head. "I don't want to rest anymore. Let's get dressed and ready for work."

Her face clouds with confusion. "We're staying closed today."

"What? No, Mom. This news is not going to mess with our dream," I say, and hope she can't hear my voice crack when considering the possibility that my illness might eventually affect my ability to work. I get out of bed and pull her up too. "Nothing is going to make me happier than being in our beautiful shop. Let's create something good today. Okay?"

She nods, but the tears are steadily falling, even after I wipe them away. "We'll make something special," she finally says.

When she leaves for the bathroom, my phone buzzes on the bed.

Laniah, I made a promise, and meant it, Issac texts. I'll love you no matter what. You're the most important person in my life, and I don't want to lose you just because you don't want the things I want. That's life. Just be patient with me while I settle my silly heart. Talk soon.

Relief and sorrow take turns with me. The words are so heavy they hurt. But I let the weight settle somewhere below my breast-bone. Let it take as much space as it needs there. I never thought I'd meet a man as kind as my father. Issac deserves the sun and the stars and the moon and a magnet made just for him.

With tears in my eyes, I send a heart back, wondering if we'll have a chance at *forever* in another timeline.

46

ON THE OTHER SIDE

THE NEPHROLOGIST SHANE SET ME UP WITH IS A WOMAN. DR. Baldwin is gentle, listens quietly, but is blunt with her responses. She worries over my flank pain, she orders an ultrasound to get an idea of what my kidneys look like and see if any arteries to the organs are blocked. Like Google, she's a well of scary information about possible anemia and early bone disease, but she also reassures me in a way that online research couldn't. She tells me she's had patients younger than me diagnosed with the disease, and that stage three is the largest among the five. Even though I'm already feeling symptoms, most of her patients have lived long lives before they dealt with any of the more serious complications in later stages. She's going to try to help me live a long life too. The moment the words leave her mouth, a memory of Issac kissing the bridge of my nose comes to mind and I wonder how many of her patients had long-lasting relationships.

"But the hardest part falls on you, Laniah," she says. "Trying to slow the progression of the disease with lifestyle changes is easier said than done. You'll have to implement more exercise into your routine, change your diet to take care of your heart health, and make sure you're not consuming too much salt so that your kidneys don't have to work as hard. Eating healthy to lose weight is different from eating healthy for the kidneys, so I'd like to refer you to a nutritionist. Do you have any more questions for me?"

Eating pho with Issac, adding extra soy sauce to my dishes, ordering pizza late at night and devouring chicken parm. These are the memories I try to shake away while my new doctor waits patiently. "Actually, yeah . . . Um, I make these natural hair products and they have horsetail root in them, and I was wondering . . . are they still safe for me to use?"

Dr. Baldwin smiles and places the cap on her pen. "I think using them in moderation in a hair product should be fine, but I'd suggest staying away from herbal supplements or high doses of it to keep it from affecting your potassium levels."

I hope she can't see my eyes glistening. "Okay. I'm sorry if it was silly."

"No question is silly. I'm here to answer to the best of my ability. Feel free to message me through the online portal if something comes up and you don't feel comfortable calling."

The sigh comes from my heart. I feel better with a plan in place, and as much as it hurts to officially hear the news from her mouth, there's solace and relief in knowing the past few months of being in pain weren't in my imagination. That there's someone who will listen now.

"Thank you so much," I say. "For all of this. Especially seeing me on short notice."

"I'm sorry for what happened to you," Dr. Baldwin says, and I can tell by the frustrated look on her face that she wishes she could say more about my former doctor. Everyone is furious. Mom and Katrina are insisting I file a medical malpractice against Dr. Rotondo, but Shane said they're hard and taxing to win. I'm not sure why Dr. Rotondo kept this from me, and maybe I'll never know. He deserves a suit against him, and it might be the right move for someone else, but I'm too tired to fight in court. I just want to do everything I can to try to prolong the need for dialysis or a potential transplant for as long as possible. Maybe I'll change my mind down the line.

"It's alright," I say to Dr. Baldwin.

She shakes her head. "No, it's not. But I'm going to do my best to make sure you're getting the care you need. I'll be sure to check in with your new primary care doctor once you're in her system. I've heard great things about her practice. You'll have a team now. Okay?"

I cry right there in her office. And she lets me without a word.

———

FOR TOO MANY DAYS AT THE SHOP, EVERYONE WAS WALKING ON eggshells around me, including little Destiny, who hardly had a clue what was happening. Lex was ruder than ever to paparazzi. I had to remind him to be careful about what he said to them because they'd be out for blood with any hint that something is off between me and Issac. If Mom wasn't hiding her tears, she was distracted between customers, squinting at her phone to look up kidney-friendly recipes she could make me. This was all before I put the BE BACK IN 20 sign on the window last week and played Whitney Houston's "I Wanna Dance with Somebody," pulling my family around me and telling them to *shake their blues away*. Destiny called me corny, but she smiled when I spun her around.

It took a while, but soon we were all letting our limbs move like wildflowers.

Since then, the deadweight has lifted from around the shop, and, each day, I've made it a point to remind myself that I'm still alive. To live like it.

But after Dr. Baldwin sends me for more blood work, I let myself have a bad day. She ordered me a twenty-four-hour urine sample, and with each collection, I allow myself room to feel fear and sadness over what the results might show. I cry into my pillow, on my porch, in the shower. I let myself wish Issac was here telling me bad jokes, hogging the covers, offering a chest to lie on with a steady heartbeat to soothe me.

When the doorbell rings, I want to ignore it, but the person is insistent. I drag myself off the couch, make sure my face isn't wet, and answer the door. It's Katrina with a bag in her hand and a smile on her face. "I might not be who you need right now, but, honey, I'm gonna try my best," she says.

I choke on my tears and throw myself into her arms.

Last week, I told her everything. About my kidneys and about Issac too. She was offended that I didn't trust her enough to tell her about faking a relationship with Issac before then. She told me how mad she was that she couldn't hold her hurt feelings for long because of my other life-changing news. I told her I was counting on it, and then we hugged it out.

She lies on the opposite side of the couch while we rewatch feel-good movies like *Never Been Kissed* and *She's All That*. She tells me about gossip in her new office, how respected she feels there, about the cuties without rings on their fingers, and how her old boss sent her an email begging her to come back. We play card games till she's sick of me beating her at spades. And each time I have to get up to pee, she stands outside the bathroom door to tell me a joke because *it's what Issac would've done*. I realize how much of a difference it makes having someone to laugh with when the sad things are trying to keep me under.

At the end of the night, Issac texts me for the first time in weeks. Maybe he could sense me smiling, or maybe he knew how much I needed to hear from him.

"Or maybe I'm good luck," Katrina says while getting her stuff ready to head home.

I throw a pillow at her, but say, "Yeah, probably."

Hi, you, Issac says. I'm sorry it's taken me so long. I don't really want to talk about it, what happened with us, unless we really have to . . . I'm sure we might have to in the future, but for now, I'm hoping we can ease back into some normalcy starting with these messages, and maybe we can FaceTime in a few days? I miss my best friend. And we should talk about the fake breakup too. Bernie's kept the media from wondering if something is wrong, but if they don't see us together soon ridiculous rumors will ensue. And I want to stir the narrative before they start. I know I should've done it already. But . . . silly heart stuff.

My chest grows heavy. Issac spent these weeks hoping I'd change my mind. And I've spent these weeks wishing I could. Your heart is far from silly, I reply.

He starts to type, stops, then starts again. Finally, Talk to you soon, Ni.

Katrina sits on my coffee table. "From the look on your face, I can't tell if you're feeling happy or sad."

"Both. One more than the other, but I don't want to talk about it right now."

She nods. "Thank you for letting me be here with you tonight."

"Thank you for being hard to ignore," I tease with a smile. "You showed up and shined your bright light in my face, and now I have no choice but to glow too."

Her laugh is loud and obnoxious, but then she says, "You should let Issac be here. Promise me you'll fix this with him soon?"

I blow out a big breath. The anxiety of knowing how heartbroken Issac will be if he finds out how long I've been keeping this from him makes me want to postpone the hurt feelings by keeping it from him even longer. But that's not fair for him, and I'm ready for him to be here for me too. So I promise: "I'll tell him about the kidney disease when we talk in a few days."

"That's a start," Katrina says.

While I watch her walk to her car from my front door, I notice Bridget's small red Mercedes-Benz parked across the street. For a second, I wonder if she came to demand a visit from me too, but then I glance up at Wilma's house and see the kitchen light on. Two estranged sisters sitting at a table, sharing a meal with the window open.

A warm feeling passes over my heart.

I smile and shut my door, feeling hopeful about telling Issac for the first time in a while.

47

THINGS THAT
HAVE GONE UNSAID

THE NEXT DAY MY MOM HAS AN EMERGENCY, BUT SHE'S QUIETLY pacing her living room, biting the polish off her red nails with curlers in her hair. When I ask her what's wrong for the third time since I rushed over here, she turns to me and says, "Pete just asked me on a date."

For a second, the confusion on my face makes hers fall, but then I recount the details of time before my diagnosis and my stomach squeezes, something blooming there. "I knew that was the reason you've been smiling at your phone," I say.

"I have not been smiling at all," she responds, hand on her hip.

I can't laugh like I probably should. "Are you sure you're ready to date?" The question is unfair, and I know I sound like a child as soon as it leaves my lips, but I can't take it back now.

Mom's arm drops to her side. She tilts her head at me, a frown on her face. "I think . . . maybe I am. But is that okay with you?"

Suddenly, I am sixteen-year-old Laniah Leigh Thompson and my world is crashing down because the man who always helped me be brave cannot breathe and I will not ask my mother to keep the sky from falling on me because she's already buried beneath it.

But when I sit on the arm of the couch and look up at her, I realize I've grown and so has she. I can't even imagine what these weeks have done to her with the memories of my father being sick fresh in her mind because of my disease, and yet she has continuously stirred me from darkness with a light in her eyes. It would be selfish of me to express my fears that opening her heart again gives it room to break, and that if it breaks she might pull away from me like she did during the darkest hour of her life. I have to trust and love her and let her love and be loved however she decides to.

So I say, "I want you to seek joy in this world wherever you can. You don't need my permission to date. But if he fails to keep you smiling, I can't promise I won't short him on rent."

She snorts. And then, "What about your dad? Do you think it'd be okay with him?"

This is a question that feels easier to answer because if I know anything about Dennis Thompson, it's that whatever brought Vanessa Thompson joy brought him even more of it.

So I stand, wrap her in a hug, say, "Grief is hard, and you did it for so long. And you'll probably do it forever, but Daddy would want you to experience all that you have left to experience while you're here. Because the love you had with him might be once in a lifetime, but there are other loves. And you're allowed to care about something other than me and the shop."

She nods against me, cries while she does. When she pulls back to catch her breath, I ask, "Are you going to tell him to bring you to fancy fine dining or mini golf?"

"I'm going to suggest church," she jokes.

"See if grump is open to being your version of godly." I laugh. "Smart move."

"Or I was thinking we could try the movies," she says, and I feel a pinch of pain remembering her and my father going to the drive-in theater on warm summer nights.

"Are you sure mini golf wouldn't be fun? When it's daylight and there are lots of children mucking up the grass nearby, and absolutely no kissing?"

She rolls her eyes. "Anyway, now that this is out in the open, are we going to keep ignoring your own happiness? I've been giving you space, Laniah. Listening to your orders, but enough is enough." She claps her hands together, so I know she's serious. "What's really keeping you from Issac? I need more details because it's not making much sense to me. You've finally stopped being certain that the worst-case scenarios are going to happen to you. Now you should be letting him love on you. Lord knows you need it."

She's waiting for an answer when I walk off into her kitchen to grab an apple. I don't even like apples, but what else am I going to eat that's low in sodium, has less potassium than a banana, and isn't too many calories? Mom snatches the apple from me and starts to cut it.

I lean against the counter and sigh. "It's simple. I don't want to make his life complicated. It's finally *not* complicated. After all he's been through, he deserves easy. He deserves so much more than I might be able to give him in the future, or anyone for that matter. I still feel that, even if I'm trying to avoid thinking of the worst scenarios for my own future now."

She inhales sharply, her shoulders fall. Seconds later, she puts down the knife and turns to me with tears in her eyes. "Oh, baby," she says. "I hear it now."

"Hear what?"

"Do you think *you* don't deserve love anymore? Just because you're sick?" She swallows, and my stomach twists before she says, "Do you think your dad didn't deserve love anymore after he got sick?"

I take a startled breath, the urge to argue with her rising in my throat. "Of course he did. But you were already with him and . . ." The words die in my mouth while watching my mom's bottom lip tremble. What am I saying? My dad deserved the world and many more years of love.

She tilts her head, stares at me awhile. "Laniah, have you been feeling sorry for me?"

When the question comes, it peels away the layer of protection I've padded over my heart. I've never had to answer the raw, deep, and painful questions because she's never asked them. And because before loving and losing Issac, I never had to face the feelings full on myself.

"You don't know how hard it was watching you struggling to provide for our family and take care of him too," I admit. "We had help from palliative care, but you were so tired. He got sicker and sicker, and I watched you suffer with sadness each day. Then . . ." I close my eyes, tears slipping from them and running hot down my cheeks. "Then when he died, you dropped into the depths of despair. For months, you wouldn't eat, hardly spoke. Sometimes I wondered if I lost both of my parents. You to a broken heart. I remember thinking I never wanted to love the way you loved Dad. Not if it had the power to kill parts of me. I don't even know when you started smiling again or why . . . I just know how horrible it felt when you weren't."

My mom doesn't say a word, she just envelopes me in her warmth. We cry together in her kitchen until there's nothing left but silent sobs between us. Finally, she pulls back and cups my face.

"I'm so sorry for not handling my grief better. For making you feel alone."

"You handled it the best you could," I say. "And I wasn't alone. I had Issac."

She nods. "You still do."

"I know," I tell her. "He really loves me."

"He does. And you shouldn't think spending the rest of your life alone is a solution."

"Mom . . ."

"No," she says, holding my face a little tighter. "Do you want to know when I started smiling again? It wasn't because of another man or even because of how much I love the shop. It was when I realized your dad's love was all around me still. Each time I heard a guitar strumming a song, or when tulips would rebloom in the spring, or any time I looked at you. You're right, the grief doesn't go away because it's really just the extension of our love, and he loved me until the end of his life. I'll love him until the end of mine. I don't regret a second. And I'd do it all over again to feel an ounce of our happiness, even knowing we'd have a hard road ahead." She kisses my forehead then lets me go. "Issac won't regret it, no matter what your life might look like in ten or twenty years."

I turn away from her, push around the apples on the plate. "We don't know that."

"You're right. Loving someone, regardless of illness, requires taking chances."

"I'm not sure I can. Not with his heart. Not with mine."

"Then I'm afraid you'll be the one living with regret."

I'M BARELY THROUGH MY FRONT DOOR WHEN MY PHONE RINGS. IT'S a FaceTime from Issac, two days earlier than we scheduled. I slide out of my shoes, slam my door, stare at the phone while it's still ringing. I'm sweating. He was supposed to give me time to gather myself. I should be sipping on lemon water and sitting on my front porch, ready for him with random questions that aren't about us to pass the time before drawing up the courage to tell him my news. But when I answer the call, my throat is sandpaper dry, my hair is in a sloppy ponytail, I'm wearing days-old sweats and a graphic tee with a stain from who knows what. Issac looks perfect as per usual.

Except he isn't smiling. In fact, he doesn't seem happy to see me at all.

"Hi," I say, nervous that he's changed his mind and *normalcy* feels far away, but he couldn't wait forty-eight hours to tell me.

"You have . . ." He takes a shallow breath, and every organ in my body alerts me to what's coming. "You've been diagnosed with kidney disease, and you didn't tell me? I had to hear it from Vanessa. How could you keep something like this from me? Why?"

Did my mom even send Pete a text after I left or did she call Issac straightaway?

"Listen . . . ," I start to say, but trail off in search of words.

"I'm listening." He stands from where he's seated. I can see the pool in the background. The light from the moon casting shadows across his skin. And even in this tense, screwed-up moment, I think about how much I've missed his face. I remember our desire for each other being too big to contain in that pool. I ache for him to touch my fingertips while we float.

"I wasn't ready. I didn't want you to pity me. I—"

"Pity you?" His laugh is sharp, laced with pain. "Are you serious? I love you. No matter what is going on between us. And it'd be different if you decided you needed time to yourself after finding out, but your mom told me you were purposely keeping it from *me* because—"

"The reasons don't matter," I rush to say.

"They do." He runs a hand down his mouth, then steadies the camera so he's looking directly at me. "Oh, Laniah Thompson, I think they do." His big brown eyes lock me in place, even though I want to look away. "Tell me that you ended things with me because you didn't think I could handle loving you with this. Be honest."

I open my mouth, close it, but I can't stop looking at him.

"Please answer me. I want to hear it from your mouth. I need to hear it from you."

One breath. Two. "I kept it from you because I can't be responsible for how much your life might change if you decided to be with me," I say.

And even though he'd already heard it from my mom, he looks stunned. "Wow. Just . . . wow."

We fall into a silence so dense, it's hard to breathe. Some nights I wake up short of breath just like this.

Why does love have to hurt?

"I'm sorry for keeping it from you," I say.

"A couple of weeks ago I asked you not to hide your health issues from me and you said you'd try not to. We were in my kitchen, and you said—"

"I'm sorry," I cut in, frustrated, sad, ill prepared. "What else do you want from me?"

"Laniah, will you look at me?" He sighs. I meet his gaze and watch his features soften, his voice does too. "Before the news, were you going to tell me you want to be with me?"

"I was," I whisper, the confession feeling necessary but unsafe for his ears.

He closes his eyes, says, "My silly heart."

"I told you it wasn't silly," I say. "But, Issac . . . I can't be with you. And not just for your sake. For mine too. How do you think I'll feel if . . . no, when I start getting sicker . . . what if I need a transplant down the line or dialysis three days a week? What if I don't want kids because of this but you do? What if we find out that I'll die young? How do you think I'll feel knowing I could've saved you from a life with me?"

I watch him sit back down; he covers his face with his hand. Is he crying? "God, Laniah. How could you say that? You're hurting me right now. Did you want me to stop loving you because of this? Hearts don't work like that. And regardless, it's my decision to make."

"But I need to take the decision out of your hands," I say desperately, needing to hold on to my logical decision no matter the reassurances Dr. Baldwin has given me, no matter what my mom said about love, because the alternative is too scary. There's too much unknown in my future. It feels like being alone is the bravest thing I can do for both of us. "I love you, Issac. But I need you to be okay with us being friends."

"What if . . ." Issac's voice cracks and cuts into my defense. "I can't only be your friend?"

"You promised," I say.

"That's not fair," he replies.

I breathe out. Then with whatever sense I have left, "So be it, but you should announce our breakup to the media tomorrow and take as much time as you need from me. I'll be waiting, as your friend."

"The media? Really? We're going to do this now?"

"That's what our planned FaceTime was supposed to be for."

He's annoyed. Pissed. If there weren't so many miles between us, his pain would suffocate me. My chest is already tight enough. "What do you want me to tell them?"

"Anything," I say, softer now. I'm hurting him and I hate myself for it, but it's hard to make things better if I can't figure out what's wrong and what's right. "I trust you, Issac. Please trust me. When we hang up, maybe you'll realize I'm right."

"And maybe you'll realize how happy we could be," Issac says. "That your sickness doesn't define you. And it shouldn't define our relationship. Your mom told me some of the things you said. And all I could think about is how, while you were only witnessing the hurt and pain between your parents over the years, I was getting to watch two people with a love so strong even the doctors couldn't predict how long they'd get to have it." The admission makes memories flicker at the back of my mind, but I'm not ready to reach for any of them. And before I can respond, Issac ends the call.

The silence in the room gives way to hearing my mom's words in my head again.

I'd do it all over again to feel an ounce of our happiness.

And the flickering ignites into a full glow.

WHAT I'D FORGOTTEN

A span of time.

THUNDERSTORMS

My father running outside to help my mother carry in grocery bags. My mother shaking her head, telling him to go back inside. He'd just gotten his diagnosis and she was already worried for his safety. Rain beating against the glass window in my bedroom while Issac and I watched Dennis Thompson take the bags from the trunk and place them on the porch anyway. Vanessa Thompson refusing at first, then throwing her head back to laugh, pulling off the hood hiding her recently blown-out hair to go dance with him in the thunderstorm. Them, calling up for me and Issac to *come play*. Letting us splash in muddy puddles even after the lightning began to break the sky open.

My mother sitting by the window at the shop, smiling to herself whenever it rains now.

MOVIE TICKETS

Summer coming again. My father saying he felt good enough to go to the drive-in theater and the twinkle of hope in my mother's eyes. Me, letting Issac eat all the popcorn because I was too busy paying attention to the sounds of my father breathing while we watched the movie. Not taking my eyes off him until my mother reached for his hand, laced their fingers, smiled when he kissed hers. Sinking back in the seat beside Issac and stealing his candy while we struggled to see the screen from behind my parents, who still had inside jokes and still acted out parts of the movie in the most annoying way, and never weren't touching somehow. Even still.

THE GUITAR

My father growing weaker during his last days. Some fluid retention, an IV drip to manage his symptoms. Still communicating with us through a foggy brain, but completely bedbound. Barely able to play his guitar. Me coming home from school one day, shocked to hear the sounds of his strings, no matter how badly they were being played. Creeping to my parents' bedroom, seeing my mother sitting beside my father, trying her best to play his favorite song. They laughed together when she hit the wrong note, and my heart fluttered at that sound.

Later, I'd realize it was the last time I heard my father laugh, but until now I'd forget how happy my mother was to be the one he was laughing with.

48

TAKE ME HOME

SUMMER MORNINGS AFTER PHONE CALLS WITH ISSAC AREN'T supposed to look like this: stepping into a darkened ultrasound room that matches the thick overcast outside, being surprised by the pain when the tech pushes the probe down against my skin like she's digging to get glimpses of the organs hiding inside of me. Telling her not to worry when she apologizes for applying pressure but squeezing my eyes together to keep from crying. How often will I have to do this? Will I always walk back out into the waiting room to find Issac isn't in the seats ready to sing me a song, make jokes until the worry of the future falls to the background?

After the appointment, I drive to the shop, still upset with my mom for telling Issac, but when I arrive, she's giggling while showing Lex text messages from Pete and suddenly I'm not in the mood to ruin her day. She gives me a curious look, squinting with a small smile on her face, as if to ask me if we're okay. I roll my eyes, but begin counting the cash register drawer for her and she takes this to mean we are.

While most of us are quietly working to open the shop, Lex is laughing while scrolling his socials. When he shrieks at something he sees, I pay no attention, just stare longingly at the high-sodium Slim Jim hanging out of Destiny's back pocket as she stocks some shelves across the room. But Lex gasps again, louder this time, and "Oh my God. Girl! Issac posted a video."

As we gather around Lex's phone, I realize I didn't brace myself for Issac telling the media about our breakup and now I'm reluctant to see what he said. He could've had Bernie release the news in an article, but instead I get to see his face again. Last night, it was dark, but today in the sunlight it's clear he's exhausted, unshaven, hair unkempt. He doesn't care what people might think and doesn't say what I expect him to either.

"I can come on here and pretend for the world like Laniah Thompson and I aren't having some deeply personal bumps in the road, and maybe we won't be able to overcome them, but I just want everyone to know that when I said she was my person all those weeks ago, I meant it. She's the best human I know. She's been my person since we were kids, back when we'd use food stamps to go buy sandwiches at the corner store up the street. You all know I always talk about soulmates, finding the right person, but it took me too long to accept that my soulmate was already in my life." He pauses to take a breath, and I hold mine as I wait for him to speak again. "I had my reasons, and one of them was worrying that she wasn't ready to be that for me. So I waited, you all know how much I dated, but nothing came close to the feeling I get when I'm with her. Whether we're in a relationship or choose to be just friends, I want to spend my life working through problems *with* her, healing with her, going through the good, bad, and ugly with her. So, for anyone who needs to hear it, when you find your person, do everything you can to keep them close. Because I know I will." He pauses for a few seconds. Then: "With that being said, I'm ready to unveil what you all have been waiting years for, a lifetime's worth of work."

My heart races as Issac exhales, a small smile on his face before he stands and walks to the wall. He tugs on a drop cloth and says, "This is *A Love Like the Sun*. A dedication for *her*."

The work is intricate, covered in Polaroids and prints of *us* as kids, my parents playing in the rain, my face painted beautifully in front of a warm orange background, an old movie flyer for the drive-in theater, cutouts of stars to symbolize our visit to the planetarium, me on the cliff face at Beavertail, arms spread, the wind moving through my hair, unaware he was taking a picture. When the camera zooms in, gliding over Issac's careful work, I notice other things: old records we loved, rocks and seashells, notes we passed in class, a guitar pick, the pearl clips that were in my hair at the botanical garden, a senior prom ticket, dried flowers from the pots on my porch right below a single tulip, one faded green Vanessa Thompson business card, a menu from our favorite restaurant for chicken parm, song lyrics on sheets of paper, the title "Lover" above a drawing of us playing video games in a room turned upside down, shoestrings, and a preserved pink Starburst wrapper. A drawing of me in yellow overalls. A fraying eagle sticker.

I'm stunned seeing our story like this, but my eyes don't burn until the camera pans on a pen, my father's. Taped right above a bracelet made of worn string, the letters of my name weaved together in gold beads.

Upon seeing it, my hand rises to clutch Issac's mother's ring on my neck, and something breaks free below my breastbone. Issac is my soulmate, and he's called me home.

I glance up to see the tears in my mother's eyes as she recognizes a part of her love story laid out too.

When Lex takes his phone from my hand, he asks if I'm okay. I walk into his waiting arms, hugging him while remembering Issac's words from last night about the strongest love we've ever known.

"No, but I think I will be," I whisper.

I'M DRIVING HOME ON THE HIGHWAY IN THE POURING RAIN AND have to remember to go slow, avoid the slickness of the road because my mind is somewhere else. It's in the botanical garden under sunlight, staring up into Issac's eyes. It's at the planetarium while we dance and he spins me under the stars. It's in Jamestown, lying on the rocks beside him while the sky changes colors above us. It's in each kiss and caress, every single time he looks at me with *feeling* in his eyes. As soon as I walk through my front door, I'll search for flights to Cali. I'll show up at his condo to surprise him, and then he'll get to see the feeling in mine.

But when I pull up at home, he's already there. Waiting on my porch. And I can't move, even though he's watching me, because my heart is a thing outside of my body. I lay my head against the steering wheel and count my breaths. By the tenth one, I look up and he's still there.

When I get out of the car, I hold eye contact with him the whole way up the stairs until I'm standing in front of him. My hair is drenched in rainwater, his clothes are damp. Droplets fall from the morning glories above his head and land on his shirt, but he doesn't seem to notice. I'm shivering from the shock of seeing him only eight hours after he posted the video. He reaches to touch my arm, but the contact never comes.

Instead, he pulls his hand back and frowns. "Let's go inside, get you dry."

"Issac . . . what are you doing here?"

He's quiet for a moment, then glances down at the brown grocery bags at his feet. "I bought some food," he says, rubbing a thumb under his right eye, swallowing hard enough for me to see. "Some things to make a low-sodium meal. I'm going to cook us dinner."

It takes a few seconds for his words to register, but then my stomach flutters. My eyes burn. I blink back tears. "Why tonight? Why already?"

He takes a step closer, then another. Soon, he's almost pressed against me, another inch and we can share the same breath. He can probably hear how loud my heart is pounding even over the falling rain. "You said you love when I don't listen."

The corners of my lips twitch. "That's not exactly what I said."

"I know, but I chartered a flight because I don't need any more time to realize that it is going to be *me* for *you* regardless," he says. "Even if you don't want to be with me, I'll hire a private chef if you get bored of my cooking, or if you want one for tired days. I'll move back home and work out of New York. We'll go to the gym together. I'll take you to appointments, hold your hand when it hurts." Tears slip from his eyes, and I start to cry remembering the ultrasound. "I'll give you pieces of me if I'm a match, Laniah, because I know they'll be *home* inside of you. I don't care if you meet someone else and fall in love, it will be *me* here, regardless.

Whether you like it or not. Because you are my best friend, and I don't know what your future looks like, but mine won't be right without you in it. So, let's go inside. Get you dry. I need . . ." He breathes out, voice breaking. "I need to cook you dinner. Make me happy by letting me cook for you."

I reach up to dry his wet face, and he leans into my touch. "I have a confession," I say, and he waits for it with sad eyes. "Before I saw you standing here, I was going to book a flight to tell you in person that I'm sorry. I made a huge mistake because I was scared. But, Issac, you tilt my world sideways and somehow that's when everything makes sense. I've loved you since yellow overalls and pink Starbursts, and I'll love you till my last breath. You already know that, but what you don't know is I want to be with you, good, bad, and ugly. Because I know if the situation was reversed, it would be me for you, regardless. So please forgive me. Cook dinner, move back home if you want to, but know that if you don't, I'll be asking you to miss flights to Cali for me."

He laughs, and I know we're both remembering our talk on the rocks. For a moment we're back there, and when I reach for his hand to kiss each of his knuckles, I can smell ocean on his skin.

Issac came here and brought me the sun.

I breathe out, then say, "I want to spend my days with you like they're the best-case scenario. I just need you to do something else for me."

A happy sob escapes him before he bends to lean his forehead against mine. While we're touching, melding, and blending, I ache to be closer, to be wrapped up in him so completely it'll be hard to tell us apart.

"Anything," he whispers. "Anything at all."

"Tell me that you can be brave when I'm not."

He pulls back to wipe the tears from my face. "That's easy," he says. "I'll be brave for the both of us."

The soft, sweet kiss he presses to my lips feels like it's already patching up parts of me, and I realize the sun is somewhere inside of me to help us too.

I ask for one more kiss. Issac smiles and gives me three, then two against my collarbone, trails several down my neck. His fingers climb my spine, and his mouth moves back to mine, teasing with some tongue. The heat sparks fast and he presses flush against me. The moment I hear him moan, I can't wait until we're inside, out of these clothes, alone to touch and taste each other. I crave the sounds of him coming undone while I do that thing he likes, and the feel of his beautiful brown eyes drinking me in when I climb on top of him.

But first, I drag him out into the rain because we can't waste a chance to dance in it.

WHAT WE ADD TO
A LOVE LIKE THE SUN

- Tickets to comedy shows.
- Our favorite low-sodium recipes for chicken parm.
- Backstage passes to Shida's concerts.
- A Polaroid of us doing cartwheels in front of our new home.
- Cutouts of Issac walking in fashion shows with flowers in his hair.
- An article noting Wildly Green's the Experience as a Best Beauty Start-Up, another naming my mother's scalp serum as an *Allure* Best of Beauty award winner.
- Invitations for Issac's art to be on display in *the world's most admired* art museums.
- Freeze-dried blueberries from the overgrown garden in our backyard.
- A flyer from when Issac curated a local art exhibition at the WaterFire Arts Center in Providence.
- Unchanged blood work results, slightly changed results, improved ones.

- A room card we said we "lost" on a sexy getaway in Maldives, where we could be as wild in the sun as we wanted to be.
- Sheet music of the first songs I learned to play on the guitar.
- A 2 of diamonds from the time we were demolished playing spades during our first cookout as a couple.
- Photos of our friends and family with sun-kissed skin and happy smiles while sitting on beautiful wooden benches inside the Roger Williams botanical garden to listen to soulmates say their vows.
- One of me in a white gown with something blue from Bridget glistening in my ears as I walked toward my husband down the aisle.
- And another canvas added to the first so that we have plenty of space to document the rest of our lives together.

AUTHOR'S NOTE

Dearest reader,

A Love Like the Sun came to me in a rush. I feverishly wrote the first draft during November's NaNoWriMo (National Novel Writing Month) when I was supposed to be writing another book. But Laniah and Issac's love story was weighing on my heart, begging for release, and it poured out of me.

Here's what I remember in the months before it came to be:

Listening to my doctor joke that I was a hypochondriac, him prescribing me anxiety medication with weight loss advice to alleviate my symptoms. But feeling fatigue down to my bones, new deep aches in my body that weren't there before, other things that made me begin googling flagged blood work results I had obtained. And then realizing there could be something serious going on with me.

That was two years ago, I was only thirty-three at the time, and I no longer trusted my primary care doctor with my health. I booked an appointment with a kidney doctor myself, who upon meeting me looked at my compiled lab results throughout the years and confirmed my suspicions by diagnosing me with stage-three chronic kidney disease. As soon as I heard that my vital organs weren't functioning properly, I felt both a sense of relief to have found out and devastated that my primary care doctor neglected to tell me.

I was a single mom of two daughters, months shy of becoming a published author and my dreams coming true, and in love with a great man whose life timing unfortunately didn't match with mine. As my new reality came crashing in, I stressed for a long time about what it meant for my future, the future of my children, and what it meant for me regarding a future in love. My day-to-day would change drastically, people would go on to perceive me differently, and I'd find myself wondering what life could have been like if I had been diagnosed sooner.

Both solace and deep sadness came when I looked into this type of medical negligence and learned I wasn't alone. So many women aren't taken seriously, often told our symptoms are only anxiety, and statistics prove we are much more likely to be misdiagnosed. Women of color experience delayed diagnoses at an even higher rate. This isn't just my story or Laniah's; it might be your story as well.

Because of this, it was important to me to write about a chronically ill main character finding love and being loved. Laniah has a soul-soothing connection with Issac, who finds her sexy and loves her deeply and wholly as she is. Writing their love story has helped heal me internally, and I think I'm able to better devote attention to the beautiful things happening all around me now, and even to me. Knowing this book is going to be in the hands of readers who might find joy in its pages is one of them. No matter your story or why you've read this one, I wish beautiful things for you too.

I hope you've enjoyed *Sun*.

With all my love,
Riss M. Neilson

ACKNOWLEDGMENTS

This book came to be with the collaboration and love of many special humans.

Starting with my agent, Jess Regel, who has unwavering faith in me and my work. You're my hero, Jess! Thank you for being there for me, for being gracious with my million questions, and for believing in me years ago. Thank you for believing in me still. I love our partnership!

Thank you to my dream editor, Amanda Bergeron, who was in the thick of it with me, poring over these pages, pulling on important threads, pushing my writing to a potential I wasn't sure of myself. Laniah and Issac's love story wouldn't be the same without you. The vignettes wouldn't be what they are without your deep questions and the passion you have shown our book baby. I'm eternally grateful. <3

To Sareer Khader. My favorite thing is when Amanda sends you a chapter and asks for your eyes because I know something special from you is coming. I'm especially thankful for your help with my epilogue vision. :') It's perfect.

To Jessica Mangicaro, Dache' Rogers, Yazmine Hassan, Hillary Tacuri. Thank you all for being on team *Sun*, for the thoughtful work and care and passion it must take to get books into the hands of readers the way you do. I'm so happy you're here! And to Craig Burke, Jeanne-Marie Hudson, Bridget O'Toole, Lindsey Tulloch, and everyone else at Berkley who helped this book become everything it is. I hope I fit right in with the Berkley family. It's a nice home here. ;)

To our incredible art director, Anthony Ramondo; Rita Batour and team; and incredibly talented Vivi Campos, who gave *A Love Like the Sun* a stunning cover. Every time I see it, I'm overcome with warmth. A happy beating heart. I'm in love with it. Thank you.

To my amazing UK editor, Rhea Kurien, and the lovely Orion family. Thank you so much for giving me and my books a home and ushering them into the hands of readers across the pond!

To my children, My'ah and Jada Abreu, my girls. The light and loves of my life. You can't read this book now—maybe don't read it ever, LOL—but I hope you know how much being loved by you, wanting love in its many forms for both of you (in the future), meant to me while writing this story. I love you both. Thanks for eating low sodium at home with me—most of the time, anyway.

Thank you to my parents, Angelique and Antonio Gagnon, for being my support system, my constants, for caring for me and your grandbabies and everything in between. I love you both.

To Shirlene Obuobi, one of my best friends and a platonic

soulmate, who had eyes on this book early—as she does with everything I write. Thank you for loving me thoroughly, for workshop sessions, morning voice notes, and a well of shared passion. We're nerds together. Or like you'd say, "Hot Girls." And you're a cardiologist, so I must thank you for being an advocate when it comes to my health. Love you!

Thank you to the father of my children, Nilson Abreu, for checking me at times when I can't bother to check myself. For feeding me when I'm deep in edits and forget.

To my nana Constance Neilson for making me watch *Days of Our Lives* and Hallmark movies as a kid. You showed me just how passionate people can be, haha. Love you, Nana!

To my papa, Jose Rivera, who was the first one to teach me to be brave, and has always felt like a kindred spirit, even before we were both unfortunately diagnosed with CKD. Let's continue to be brave together.

Thank you to my brothers, Jadin Gagnon and Carlos Cruz, for being brother besties, brainstorming sessions, and listening to all of my book woes.

To Ashley Baldwin, Yoli Rodrigo, Carmelita Bisignani, Lolita Villueneva, Emily M. Danforth, Em North, Uncle Jose Rivera Jr., Charlie Hinsch, Troy Perry, Kathy Reyes, Shylene Lopez, Jennifer Nieves, Jenna Cavalieri, Bobby Savage, Gibran Borbon, Marlisse Payamps, Isha Abreu, Made Rodriguez, Tyler Palmer, Beryl Fisher, and Zü Serpas for support, love, encouragement. For being humans who make my life better.

Huge thanks and many hugs to my lovely author friends, and the romance writers who welcomed me into the adult space from YA with open arms (a special shoutout to Jessica Joyce).

To Phil M. Johnston. One summer morning, you titled *A Love Like the Sun* with me, but more importantly, this book wouldn't exist without you. In this case, you know it to be true. Thank you for that first crossroads after Julian's, ocean water and window views, healing sunlight, shared lyrics, and for being my best friend. I love you. Forever.

To God, I'm grateful each time I open my eyes. Thank you for filling me with stories too.

A
Love
Like
The
Sun

RISS M. NEILSON

READERS GUIDE

DISCUSSION QUESTIONS

1. Laniah has a hard time expressing herself, but throughout the book, she starts sharing her hopes, fears, and matters of the heart with family and friends and even Issac. Do you have a hard time opening up to people? What helps? What makes it harder?

2. Laniah and Issac share music as a love language. Is there someone in your life you share playlists and songs with? Who is your favorite person to sit in the car and listen to music with?

3. Have you ever felt afraid to ask your doctor a question?

4. Issac and Laniah have a close platonic relationship for most of their lives until they give in to romance. What are the differences between romantic and platonic love for you?

5. Laniah and Vanessa's small business is based on a shared passion and connection. Could you ever imagine yourself going into business with a family member? A friend? Do you have any shared passions with anyone you love?

6. Laniah eventually finds a health care team with whom she feels safe. What qualities do you find reassuring in a doctor?

7. Have you ever had symptoms dismissed as anxiety? Do you know anyone that has happened to? How do you think Laniah's identity as a woman influenced her interactions with Dr. Rotondo?

8. One of Laniah's goals is getting Wilma and Bridget to reconnect. Are there any relationships in your life that you'd like to rekindle? Are there any you'd like to make stronger?

9. Have you ever had a dream about someone who you probably shouldn't have had a dream about?

10. Laniah and Issac both had experiences that helped shape their views on love and relationships. Do you feel like anything from your childhood, good or bad, has affected your view on love?

SOME BOOKS RISS ADORES
THAT SHE'D SUGGEST READING

- *Malibu Rising* by Taylor Jenkins Reid
- *Divine Rivals* by Rebecca Ross
- *Every Summer After* by Carley Fortune
- *Excuse Me While I Ugly Cry* by Joya Goffney
- *The Hazel Wood* by Melissa Albert
- *Pachinko* by Min Jin Lee
- *People We Meet on Vacation* by Emily Henry
- *Tomorrow and Tomorrow and Tomorrow* by Gabrielle Zevin
- *You, with a View* by Jessica Joyce
- *Fourth Wing* by Rebecca Yarros
- *Between Friends and Lovers* by Shirlene Obuobi
- *The Dead Romantics* by Ashley Poston
- *Before I Let Go* by Kennedy Ryan

All of these authors have truly inspired me. <3

Author photo by Jadin Gagnon

RISS M. NEILSON is a magna cum laude graduate of Rhode Island College, where she won the English department's Jean Garrigue Award, which was judged by novelist Nick White. Her debut young adult novel, *Deep in Providence*, was a 2022 finalist for the New England Book Awards, and her novel *I'm Not Supposed to Be in the Dark* was published in 2023. She is from Providence and lives for the city's art and culture scene. When she's not writing, she's watching anime or playing video games with her two children. *A Love Like the Sun* is her adult debut.

Ready to find
your next great read?

Let us help.

Visit prh.com/nextread

Penguin
Random
House